I CONFESS
DIARY OF AN
AUSTRALIAN POPE

Melvyn Morrow

Publisher's Cataloguing-in-Publication Data
Names: Morrow, Melvyn, 1942-.
Title: I confess : diary of an Australian pope / Melvyn Morrow.
Description: Granada Hills, CA : Henry Gray Publishing, 2023.
Identifiers: LCCN 2023911861 | ISBN 9781960415097 (pbk.) |
ISBN 9781960415103 (ebook)
Subjects: LCSH: Catholic Church. Curia Romana - Fiction. | Catholic Church
- Corrupt practices - Fiction. | Catholic Church - History - Fiction. | Papacy -
History - Fiction. | Popes - Election - Fiction. | Vatican Palace (Vatican City)
- Fiction: | BISAC: FICTION / Religious. | FICTION / Alternative History. |
FICTION / Christian / Contemporary.
Classification: LCC PR9619.4 M67 2023 | DDC 823 M—dc23
LC record available at https://lccn.loc.gov/2023911861

Made in the United States of America.

Published by Henry Gray Publishing, P.O. Box 33832,
Granada Hills, California 91394.

For more information or to join our mailing list, visit
HenryGrayPublishing.com

I CONFESS

Diary of an Australian Pope

Melvyn Morrow

Granada Hills, CA
"Select books for selective readers"

For definitions of words and phrases
in Australian English, French, Italian, and Latin
please refer to the Glossary at the
end of the book.

Monday, December 1

Feast of St Edmund Campion (1540–1581) and St Charles de Foucauld (1858–1916).

Campion is surely the greatest of the English Jesuit martyrs. Towering intellect. Magnificent preacher. A priestly Scarlet Pimpernel. Hideously tortured then hanged, drawn and quartered. The hero I could never be.

Charles de Foucauld, Jesuit educated aristocrat—a long way from Christian Brothers Wollongong. Dismissed from the army for misconduct. I can relate to that. Became a priest in mid-life. Worked in Morocco. Translated the gospels in local language. Shot in the head by a 15-year-old bandit. Such is saintly life.

Not mine, I hope.

And so to something I've never before done in my life: keep a diary.

Wrong.

It's not at all like that—a sudden whim, a bright idea.

Oh, no. Far from it.

I've been knowingly avoiding this all my life because deep in what's left of my heart, I know what a volcano of fear, confusion, hatred, love, hypocrisy, struggle and jagged truth will explode over my carefully disguised persona.

Once I start, I know precisely what this will become: my cv of shame and confusion; a map of my soul; the hollow resounding echo of my shallowness; the catalogue of my failures; the unpacking of my emptiness… and the relief of the saying, the naming, the acceptance.

And, crazy as it sounds, the gratitude.

Even crazier, this morning in my chaotic mind, I had the original thought that in this world, not too many people get to become the pope, and from a few months' brief experience, I have an inkling of what it's like to be one—and to date, I don't recommend it—so it might be quite revelatory to myself to explore what it feels like.

Well, at least what this pope feels like.

Who knows what I might find out?

I do.

Note to self: always remember this isn't your day book, your checklist of what you imagine you've done—even achieved, ho! ho!—over the papal working day.

That's a mere calendar, and Dario looks after that with his amazing efficiency.

No, Mario, this totally private monologue is the conversation of your secret self, your spirit, your essence, your journey with God.

So, what do all these ingredients say?

The first step is the hardest, in which case, best take that first step before the last one pops up unannounced.

I've been put in a creative mood by tonight's reassuring dinner cooked by my housekeeper, friend and bizarrely angular commentator on my life as a mere pope, Sister Angelica.

She's the chief papal cook and bottle washer, and tonight's farfalle pasta with asparagus, chilli and garlic (yes, there is a God, and garlic is God's blessing on most crises) was in every way satisfying and was appropriately accompanied by a glass or two of a modest barbaresco… well, maybe three, but who's counting?

Deep in what's left of my heart…

My heart.

Where did that go?

If it ever existed.

And to whom?

God help me.

Already, I know I'll regret this commitment to truth.

Truth.

Firm as rock, which is what the church and popes are supposed to be all about.

And slippery as life.

Aye, there's the rub.

When sinners become popes…

The Jamesons, I'm thinking.

Deo gratias.

Which is why I know I'll regret this... confession to myself.

Can a pope forgive himself?

God only knows.

Cheers!

And go, God!

Yes, a top-up, Mario. Why not?

So, Mum, guess who?

How much do I love you and thank you and pray for you—to you, indeed—for being what's left of my possible salvation!

You spent your whole life embracing me, protecting me, encouraging me, hiding me from myself which you somehow always understood and you just loved me for all the Wollongong fucked-up mess I was—and still am—and that disastrous whatever-it-was which resulted in this disastrous whatever-it-is... yes, as both of us still refuse to believe in real life… that confused little Illawarra wog—that irritatingly clever little photographic memory wog—is now pope!

Yes, beyond madness, Mum, but never beyond your love.

I'm glad you're in heaven, Mum, because on earth, this ongoing craziness beyond belief continues.

I mean, the ultimate insanity of a world and a church not even God could come up with after half a divine eternal lifetime of angels singing endless praise.

You couldn't make this nonsense up.

Fucked-up confused Wollongong son, lost adolescent, let's skip over the after-mess of that, but somehow or other this accidental priest becomes accidental bishop becomes accidental archbishop becomes accidental cardinal becomes accidental Pope.

OK, yes, my fault. Absolutely. If only you knew the half of it.

Well, maybe not.

Yes, of course I know mothers know, but mothers also know what not to know.

Well, now—and a shorter top-up prayer of thanks to Saint Jameson of Bow Street Dublin.

Don't worry, Mum. You can take the boy out of Wollongong but they'll never take the Wollongong out of Mario Gino Pietro Francis Xavier Castaldi.

Or the pope!

Mum, let's both laugh as we share the mysterious bond that's the proof of both mystery and love. I weep in gratitude, laugh in disbelief, pray in hope... and start each day wishing that your always accepting love will guide each moment of what will most surely be my beyond unbelievable next twenty-four hours.

It's like that now. An hour is crisis, and a day can be World War Whatever in the surrounding holy madness I surreally inhabit.

Fortunately, Wollongong's North Beach surf remains my cleansing grace. There is a God, and how grateful can an accidental pope be for Wollongong's North Beach surf?

Totally.

And so, Dad, are you there? Listening?

Good. Then listen up.

From one infallible household male legislator to another, hello again and welcome back to the well-intentioned universal cluster-fuck which was...is our mutually painful worlds since birth or whenever before.

No, Dad, for once in your life, shut up and let your eldest son explain...not to mention all those gazillions of other—what shall we call ourselves?—tragically eldest sons of even more tragically fucked-up Catholic fathers...the whole damn lot of us all lined up and still volcanically waiting to explode.

No, for once in your controlling life, listen to me, Dad.

I love you, right?

There, I've said it. So now for the rest.

Another tiny Saint Jameson, I'm thinking.

Dad, yes, you meant well, but as a father, you were an Aussie-Italian disaster, and now half a world away from Wollongong, here I am, still the pathetic absurdity that despite Mum's gentleness, you helped produce.

So my beloved elder sister, Maria, was killed in a road accident when she was six. God loved her so much, God somehow was so clumsy up there that God needed her in heaven.

I'm still coming to terms with that justification.

And Mum died in agony of cancer.

And you and bloody Father O'Buggery praised the Lord for her heroic endurance (that blasphemy still stings beyond faith) and to top it all off, little Tonio, your favourite because he was such an

Aussie sporting legend and spoke better Italian than I did, my little brother, Tonio, hit adolescence head-on and just about wiped himself off the map by the time he was 17.

And I haven't heard from him since.

For all I know, he was swallowed by a crocodile in north Queensland or maybe died of AIDS.

It'd be nice to find out.

And just to top it all off, muggins here is now the Pope. Pope John the Twenty-Fourth, better known in these parts as Pope Vegemite the First and Last, an Italian-Australian-Irish Catholic fiasco.

Sorry, Dad, but that's where your son is now.

In my heart, I know you meant well, but I guess that's how an Australian De La Salle Brothers' education prepared you for fatherhood, and why you might have hoped that the Wollongong Christian Brothers would do a better job on me and Tonio.

Bad luck.

What we got dumped on us was a lifetime load of God-bothering torture and eternally hell-bent sexual guilt.

I couldn't even enjoy my first jack-off without fear of the eternal fires of hell, and I reckon it was the same for all our class. Probably the whole school until we left. And God knows, wanking was the home industry.

And looking back, how did Brother Edmund know so much about those everlasting flames?

But let's leave all that for the moment—the fact is that this diary, this act of clearing and cleansing is to myself and for myself.

Still, in the best of my good faith, each day before making my entry, I'll read through the brief lives of the saints of the day—our church has many saints, so they all have to cosy up and share each feast day—and I'll choose one, try to relate to them in some way and also ask all the other saints of that day to pray for me because God knows, I desperately need their prayers.

I'm exalted by saints.

I'm also driven nuts by them.

I think I see through all this saint stuff and I see through all this contemporary saint denial stuff, yet with every heroic and saintly life I reflect on, even as pope—especially as the first and almost certainly last Wollongong pope—I have to ask questions that deep in my mind and deep in my soul lacerate my faith.

You see, Dad, I'm the questioning pope.

It's like this.

Whenever I read the oh-so-pious lives of the saints, my mind flashes danger. I simply can't help myself. I chuck out all the holiness stuff and try to imagine that particular saint as someone I've just bumped into and whom I would like a bit of a frank and fearless chat with, leaving aside all the treacly hagiography.

I mean, I'm the pope, so why can't I give myself permission to explore the truth?

Let's call it spiritual therapy—the unintended pope's necessary adventure under the confessional seal of this diary.

And just for the record, at some future time I look forward to frank and fearless discussions with the Third Person of the Blessed Trinity about the integrity of the papal conclave voting procedure.

OMG!

Anyway, in the blessed event of my death, should this ongoing confession to myself not have been destroyed by this penitent on-screen diarist, I have left a personal letter with my dear and faithful friend, Cardinal Dario Silvestrini, now appointed by me Secretary of State, instructing him to destroy this testament without reading any further.

And dearest of dear friends, Dario, I know you will, so now read no more, loyal confidant, and please delete forever, this, my sad soul's searching.

And God bless you, friend of my heart.

And so to the unburdening.

Dad, you always told me that January 1st was the Feast of the Circumcision.

At a certain moment—maybe in Year 7—I understood the words, but not why that bizarre feast was celebrated. Why was I, a ringbark, to be praised and my uncut mate, a roundhead, unworthy of the divine blessing of a feast day?

I mean, since Jesus and I were ringbarks—and apparently that snipping was some kind of weird feast—would all the roundheads go to hell?—in which case it could be crowded and with some pretty innocent victims but bloody good blokes and probably more confident lovers.

I wish.

Perhaps my first theological question. Plato's Republic in the Wollongong swimming pool showers; the unspoken concerns Catholic pubescent boys wrestled with while masturbating on the highway to hell.

Well, this one sure did.

And so to today.

The first Sunday of Advent.

A new church year begins with an Australian pope in the Vatican and the guarantee of all-out civil war with our uncivil service: the comfortable, conservative, controlling and diabolically crafty curia (I prefer to deny them that capital C they use to describe themselves) versus the pontifex minimus whom they dismissively mock as Pope Vegemite the First and Last.

Still, all petty squabbles aside, I must believe that we're a civilised convocation adjudicating on this life and in all humility, faithfully projecting to the next.

Dangerous territory, as history has shown and death will eventually adjudicate on.

OK, Dad, all my school reports observed that I was a worthy student—just remind me what student is unworthy?—and, Dad, you may remember that you always told me that second-class honours in the New South Wales Leaving Certificate meant second-rate in life. In retrospect, not the most encouraging spur to an immature seventeen-year-old, but, yes, God knows you had your reasons, and they made you who you were. While helping make me the mess I became. And still am.

Over time, I've come to understand and eventually forgive how religiously messed-up I became because, I mean, just how screwed-up at the time was the Australian Irish Church? Not to mention those well-intentioned, football-mad and spookily—no, disastrously—celibate Christian brothers who belted the fear of God into us.

As you sow, so shall you reap. The sins of the fathers shall be visited on the sons. Doesn't seem all that fair to me, but them's the rules according to...

Don't get me going. 'Visited on the sons.' Dear God, where does your bewildered but faithful servant start? I mean, leaving aside the daughters who now are the blessed cohesion holding together what's left of the rapidly disappearing western church... where was I?

Where I've been for so long.

Dad, I managed a second class result in Honours Latin, and to my shame and stupidity, I believed I was therefore second class. So how right was your prediction?

In my clerical career, I fulfilled your prophecy.

To cite the corridor gossip in these parts, 'forgettable Bishop of Wollongong. Charmingly ineffective Archbishop of Adelaide. Compromise cardinal of Sydney, then out of the blue, whisked off to Rome as Cardinal Protector of Pilgrims and Patriarch of Relics— even by Vatican standards, a laughably useless job awarded as a consolation prize in the red hat stakes. A comfortable retirement for an ecclesiastical nonentity.'

Learn the ropes, do as you're told and don't rock the boat—as if you could—and most of all, ensure that you serve good wine to your brother cardinals. Which just goes to show where second-class honours in the 1959 New South Wales Leaving Certificate Latin can get a conflicted lad from Wollongong.

Pope.

Your triumph, Dad.

My bewilderment. Until recently, Dad—the papal conclave six months ago—and I kept asking myself what went right?

Or wrong?

And, Dad, now I don't need to ask—and it's no vote of faith in me, because from the moment my frankly ridiculous vote in the papal conclave suddenly began to surge—from idiot nothing burger to odds-on favourite—from that moment, I knew why.

After the papacy of Francis, a pope of vision and an administrator with a purposeful agenda, the church needed to pause and breathe. The conservative faction—the majority of Vatican civil servants known as the curia—had two strong candidates. One was my former friend from seminary days, Cameroon-born Olivier Gabriel Foncha, who brought most of the African cardinals' votes with him. Face it, Olivier is the pope from central casting: handsome, black, eloquent, ambitious and in all too robust health—though the latter isn't always a plus for a pope as it augurs a long papacy.

From the same right-wing faction but quite the opposite in his austere personality was the second candidate: Ernesto Mendoza, old, Spanish in name though Italian by birth, white and reportedly in dicey health.

Mendoza is brilliant, literate, forensic and a workaholic. Problem is, he sees his role as Prefect of the Congregation for the Defence of the Faith as that of The Grand Inquisitor. Worse: Gestapo *Obergruppenführer*. Nothing escapes his investigations, and he's 'exposed' dozens of progressive contemporary theologians for heresy and then brutally silenced them into the bargain.

That should have made him an ideal stop-gap curia candidate since discipline and obedience are the clerical markers of God's church triumphant, but two strong candidates of the same side can, ironically, cancel each other out, hence the eventual election of the warm, human and holy Italian Archbishop of Florence, Renato Carosella, who took the name of Leo XIV.

To the curia, 'holy' is important in a pope: it means he's malleable and with clever advice from his heads of dicasteries, he will enact the 'right' decisions—'right' in every sense—to reinforce the Vatican status quo.

Why we have to call departments here 'dicasteries' I forget, but I guess it sounds important and may even suggest divine overtones, though such association has to date eluded me.

After 13 ballots—proof that it sure is the devil's number—the two implacably opposed conservative candidates stalled, neither team of backers willing to shift their vote, and so our lovable Pope Leo was eventually elected.

There was just one unforeseen problem in Leo's election.

Curia strategy envisioned a relatively brief papacy—three or four years—during which time either Olivier or Mendoza would emerge as the next strong pontiff—the Vatican is always about the politics of the next papacy—but what they didn't take into consideration was COVID. And in God's wisdom, the God of equality of all creation permitted the passing of gentle Pope Leo in under a year.

Back to square one.

Another provisional pontiff required: beige, inoffensive, low profile and controllable. What's the term?

Second-rate.

And here I am, Pope John XXIV.

On the positive front, I must confess that though my Wollongong Latin has improved out of sight, I still need a Roman classicist to brush it up to papal *motu proprio* standard, and my chosen Secretary of State, Cardinal Dario Silvestrini, is just the man.

Oh, and Dad, a papal *motu proprio* is a document about some special subject the pope's interested in. Not definitive church teaching or infallible or anything razzle-dazzle like that, but His Holiness sounding off and expecting the troops to smarten up and take his opinion on board. Which, of course, plenty do and plenty don't, these days the latter being increasingly vocal and issuing their own individual *motu proprio's* to anyone who'll read or listen to them.

But back to Dario. He's an outstanding scholar; a conventional but progressive-leaning theologian; a diplomatic yet exceptionally efficient administrator; loyal—not a virtue much practiced in these parts—and a colleague I'd trust with my life. And the icing on the cake: a bon viveur with an excellent wine cellar yet enjoying all things in disciplined moderation. Well, friends have to differ over some issues.

Yes, Dario is my best appointment and my greatest supporter. And I'm sure I'm the only person in the Vatican who knows his best kept secret—his amazing double life of priesthood and fatherhood. No wonder he's so sane. Puts me to shame. I'm blessed in his friendship and allegiance.

And so, Dad, here we both are: you, dead, and hopefully in whatever heaven is, and your second-rate son, alive and desperately treading water in the Vatican.

And for the record, after six months of oleaginous Vatican obsequiousness, I have to say their chilling and elegant diplomatic obstruction of every initiative I've tried to introduce leaves me wondering whether there's a difference between purgatory and hell.

Dad, what do I have to do for you to be finally proud of me?

Hopefully, this December to December diary of your Australian pope son, sentence by painfully truthful sentence is the answer.

Somewhere, somehow, you'll read it as I write. There's always hope. There has to be.

So, today's positive.

Ennio told me in beautiful simplicity of his love for his partner, Mirella.

It wasn't confession. No. Sadly, Ennio's generation isn't into that. Rather, it was a spontaneous and glorious outpouring... an acclamation of passion, trust and faith by a twenty-year-old Swiss Guard from Lugano, talking about his twenty-year-old lover of three years.

Three years!

O oriens. O morning star, splendour of light eternal: come and enlighten those who dwell in darkness.

O Ennio, my secular confessor, how I envy you your youth and your liberated love life!

Grace sometimes descents from where we least expect that gift.

Yesterday. Solemn High Mass. Full house, of course, and concelebrated with Cardinal Gino Luciano from Sardinia, arguably the campest of curia cardinals—quite an achievement—and Cardinal Marcel Brulé from Paris: smooth, sharp, academic though, I suspect, capable of Gallic ambivalence. One, I think, who watches whichever way the papal wind blows, but that said, a mind admired by many waverers for its informed balance.

What's the French for *Vichy?*

Stop it, Mario!

Oh, and also, the even more anodyne and affable Cardinal Archbishop of Luxembourg, His Eminence Jean-Franz Hoffmann.

If anyone can determine what this convivial man of God does or doesn't believe in, I'd be fascinated to read the dossier. Better still, the abstract. Which indeed it would be. That said, we chatted briefly after Mass, and I have to say I like Jean-Franz enormously. A man to have on side—if ever he'd declare his hand.

Anyway, my sermon seemed to hit the mark. The shock of the brief. If you can't say it in under two minutes, you don't know what you're talking about—and conciseness especially annoys the old guard... a consummation devoutly to be wished.

Choir energised. O Rex Gentium moving as always, though 'the king of nations' royalty rubbish stings.

Mind you, Christ the President sounds even sillier.

Superficiality, Mario. For your penance, Mario, three Hail Mary's.

Next, Christmas present to self: remove that Maltese Dinosaur, Cardinal Paulo Di Giorgio, Prefect of the Dicastery for Divine Worship and the Discipline of the Sacraments and install someone remotely connected to the twenty-first century. Di Giorgio's part of Benedict's fifth column to subvert the Second Vatican Council and restore the Latin Mass.

St Pope John XXIII, pray for your Aussie successor.

This 24th Pope John won't go down without a ding dong Aussie barney, and to replace Di Giorgio, Cardinal Thierry Etcheverry of Reims is just the man.

He lays down the law and doesn't take any prisoners. But isn't that more than half of the problem? 'The man'?

Can I appoint a woman—after all, I am the bloody pope?

Steady on, Mario.

No!

By now you surely know that 'steady as she goes' means nothing changes, even if the change is decreed by the pope. Despite his secretarial efficiency, not even Dario seems able to turn my commands into eventual action. The bloody curia know how to stall till doomsday with questions and draftings and committees and the rest of their age-old delaying road blocks.

So, from now on, it has to be action stations. Summon my good generals to the front, fixed bayonets, go over the top, storm the enemy trenches and occupy their territory.

Oh, and while you're at it, Mario, canonise General Haig. Now there's a worthy papal thought for the first Sunday in Advent.

'My good generals'. Indeed. Who and how few?

Dear God in heaven, how on earth did I land this shithouse gig?

The triple tiara's a bloody crown of fucking thorns.

Thanks heaps, God.

Sorry, Sister Angelica.

Yes, five decades of the Rosary.

And so to bed.

Tuesday, December 2

Feast of Pope St Silverio (480–536), son of Pope Hormisdas who became a priest after raising a family.

My kind of pope. Humble, not all that bright. My kind of guy. Caught in a papal political plot. My kind of mess. Convicted of treason on trumped-up charge and exiled. My kind of fate. Died of starvation. Won't happen to me while Sister Angelica is around. Quite the opposite, thank the Lord.

A heavenly crisp and sunny winter's Tuesday in Rome.

Winter mornings on my board in the Wollongong surf were my teenage lauds, my liturgy of the hours, my fleeting yet thrilling sensation of the numinous. Little did I think that sixty years later I'd be dodging the dumpers on the Costa del Vaticano.

Calm down, Mario, and remember: gratitude for one grace every day.

Praise the Lord, my soul. And especially praise the Lord for Sister Angelica's heart-starting morning *doppio* coffee blast-off.

Sister Angelica is grace personified. Discretion, too. Without her, I'd be totally lost in this maze instead of just three-quarters lost.

The bracing Italian cold charges me with optimism—well, at least until my Secretary of State, Dario, brings me the day's agenda and I see the name Cardinal Ernesto Mendoza as a recurring penance for my sins.

I've begged Dario to keep Mendoza as far from me as he diplomatically can, but the wretched man somehow manages to appear on my appointment list at least twice and sometimes three times a week. Not even my worst transgressions deserve more that fifteen minutes with our very own Taliban mullah. I should have fired him on the first day of my papacy, but I foolishly thought it papal to move gently.

More fool me.

Mendoza doesn't look well, but I doubt whether illness or even death could stop his fanatical jihad.

'Love your enemies', commands our Saviour. All very well, but that doesn't mean you have to like them.

Maybe, in fraternal affection, I should promote Mendoza into prestigiously irrelevant retirement.

What role can I invent? Perhaps Cardinal Prefect of the Dicastery for Vestment Design, Material and Colours. No, he'd smother every mass celebrant in acres of pleats and lace, then discipline them severely for incorrect seasonal shades. When will our clergy cease being policemen and take on the role of good shepherds?

Good shepherds. Doesn't that cast our 'flock' as 'sheep'? Hardly a compliment to the millions of worldwide intelligent laity, women and men, most of whom could run the Vatican ten times more efficiently than this present mob I'm landed with.

And after being pope for six months, my deepest wound is that my once African seminary friend, now Cardinal Olivier Gabriel Foncha and promoted from Yaoundé to Rome, is now my sworn enemy. Or should I say my sworn enemy in Christ? I'm the stop gap pope treading water while Olivier redeploys his red-hatted cavalry for the next charge.

How has this happened? This supposed holy state is a battlefield for civil war and a playground of clerical espionage.

But to the day's achievements!

Refugees: I've set up a congregation to insist on our mission to them and managed to get Florence-based Muslim scholar, Izzedin Abdul Torsello, as consultant to the congregation. He's Sunni, sensible and about as close to ecumenical as a mullah can get without receiving death threats from the demented Islamic faithful.

Did I write that?

Yes.

Just between you and me, Dad, OK?

Liturgy. New committee for approved English bible translation for use at mass. This whole storm in a chalice should have been sorted out years ago. British Nicholas King SJ to chair it: Jesuit, scholar, translator and a catalyst for consensus; and he'll elegantly steer the outliers to the right choice.

Discussion with Cardinal Guido Montano—young for a cardinal, progressive in his thinking and one of few cardinals I'm sure are loyal to Pope Vegemite the Last. Subject: to revise canon law and delete as much of the wretched stuff as possible.

I'm with Francis: we're meant to be pastors, not lawyers. Talk about the thickets of regulation! As it stands, you'd think this canon law catechism of infractions was dreamt up by some maniacal dictator to ensure that any accusation results in an immediate guilty verdict against the transgressor.

It reminds me of an absurd non-crisis I read about back in 2022. Some careless or less-than-well-educated priest in Arizona (one of the many, I fear) had baptised thousands of babies using the words, 'We baptise you' instead of 'I baptise you'. Then years later, according to some very well-educated Vatican canon lawyer, this meant that every one of those baptisms was invalid and as a result, all subsequent sacraments received by those 'unbaptised' infants, including confirmation, marriage and holy orders were necessarily invalidated.

As Gilbert and Sullivan might have merrily sung, 'Here's a how-de-do!'

Gotcha, God!

You're not getting away with this one!

OK, a mistake's a mistake and, arguably, it wasn't your fault, but like it or not, God, the law's the law, and we administer your law.

So it's canon law 1, God 0, and bad luck for all those innocent but, let's face it, invalid victims.

P.S.: and a suggestion to God: get your act together.

Laugh, weep or celebrate?

Meanwhile, back at the ranch, I'm trying to imagine what Jesus would make of this inescapable maze.

God would probably find God is self-excommunicated for breaking ninety-nine percent of the nit-picking ordinances. And what can I say other than 'Serves you right, Lord.' Time to lift your game.

In the end, life sucks, and it's only the lawyers who win—especially the canon lawyers.

And we wonder why good people are leaving the church in droves.

Anyway, my feeling is that Montano is in favour of reform, though I wouldn't exclude clerical advancement from his motivation. Time will tell.

Back to sanity and God's gifts.

The last grace of my day and best of all: my offertory prayer at mass—no, my plea—answered in the diamond understanding of a sacred, cold, crystal *vademecum*: 'Where you must go, there you must. And there must I. And there must we. In faith and strength and humility.'

Wow!

'But have you that strength, that vision, that humility, my son?'

Yes, Lord, but I might need legions of angels by my side.

'They surround you, so boldly fight with their support.'

Oh, angels of God, be at my side.

And so to the sleep of the reassured.

Wednesday, December 3

Feast of St Francis Xavier (1506–1552) patron saint of Australia.

Jesuit mate of St Ignatius, intrepidly adventuring evangelist. Preached the gospel to India and Japan (failed, so to date we have something in common). Died aged 46 (that young!!) with China in sight. Just beats Wollongong, Adelaide, Sydney and Qantas business class to Rome.

So this week, it's Wednesday that's Bounty Day.

'Which of thy bounty we are about to receive.'

Once or very occasionally twice a week on a day of her choosing, Sister Angelica prepares a dish she has never before cooked. It's her day of experimentation, thanksgiving and hope, and no correspondence will be entered into, from anybody, His Holiness included, forever and ever, Amen.

'Watch therefore, for ye know neither the day nor the hour.'

From the parable of the ten virgins. Five of them kept oil for their lamps and were rewarded, five didn't and missed out on the wedding reception.

Sister Angelica is one of those wise and gifted virgins.

Actually, better to say 'women'.

And what ignoramus or idiot would challenge her choice? The result is, almost inevitably, yet another gastronomic proof of the existence of God, and for her culinary theology, we—not infrequently, just me—at table of an evening joyously say grace before and even more fervently, after.

I quickly understood that while words are not Sister Angelica's language, cooking is, and it's a language she has total command of.

Tonight's bounty was simple but superb tuna and rocket penne. She informs me that rocket is cleansing, which I have no reason to disbelieve. Or believe. But uncomplicated faith is a gift to be grateful for.

If only clerical life could be that easy and grace-giving!

Overheard in the further grouping as I paused before entering my first meeting today: 'He was elected to be a do-nothing pope, warming the throne for <u>our</u> contender next time. He's deluded himself into thinking God put him there to run riot over centuries of tradition and truth.'

Good to know the lay of the curia land.

If I've learnt one thing as a cleric, it's that petitionary prayer is little more than desperate noise ascending to oblivion.

True prayer is the stillness of listening, and that confidence in divine counsel gives me strength.

Something tells me the time is right for a re-examination of the validity of Anglican holy orders. It's an historical scandal that we're not one family in Christ. I must invite the Archbishop of Canterbury to the Vatican. She'll give the curia a run for their money and the Prefect of the Dicastery for Divine Worship some enlightening historical homework.

What if the Archbishop and I concelebrated mass in St Peter's?

Or even better, in true humility, ought I to ask her to invite me to Canterbury? I'd have no difficulty with the King James Bible.

Though I suppose canonising Cranmer might be a step too far.

How, then, to find the right go-between? Given that the slow-motion marathon of ecumenism seems to push the finishing line ever further away, maybe running riot over centuries of tradition and truth is best done sprinting.

And Zwingli on the Eucharist was surely ahead of his time theologically: 'Eating the flesh of Christ is not a physical act, but a spiritual one.'

Then, of course, there's the question of the Greek and Russian Orthodox churches.

Might need a day or two for that.

Or another couple of centuries.

All I've learnt in six months is that each day offers a brief papal lifetime of guaranteed failure.

Certainly, some so-called miracles must be believed... for those of us who believe in miracles.

But is it God or the faithful who work those miracles? I mean, why should God have to rock up and 'prove Himself' when the going down here gets tough?

'Down here'. Nonsense. Whoops! There I go again. 'Himself'. No, God's genderless self. Or genderful self? God's self, if we can ever have even a glimpse of that mystery.

And surely that everyday grace is God's greatest miracle? The rest of it strikes me as pious delusion or well-intentioned—though souvenir marketable—show biz.

As that duplicitous American Cardinal Marcinkus said, 'You can't run the Vatican on Hail Mary's.'

The Jesus I know and love and live for, the Jesus whose message I try to bring to the world... he was no desert showbiz illusionist.

No way.

Before the Resurrection, his dumb and despairing apostles didn't have anywhere near the smarts between them to stage manage a continuing miracle roadshow. Amateurs and pessimists all.

No, surely every real miracle is that sudden grace from nowhere... that baptismal gift to look beyond the evil of worldly despair.

To dare to hope.

Baptism's water is the sign of radical reorientation.

Bit of a problem here with infant baptism—a problem those infant baptised-now-adult searchers repeatedly present me with.

And being one of them, I'm with them.

Surely, then, adult baptism should be the go. Babies are innocent, and the pious nonsense preached for centuries that the unbaptised can never enter heaven is, frankly, a cartload of bullshit invented to ensure that priests run the show.

No wonder we're now watching those honest baby baptised questors leaving the church daily in their millions.

Something's radically wrong here. Either God's thrown a spanner in the works, or <u>we</u> have.

We, the church.

Yes, folks, we, the infallible church, have got it infallibly wrong.

Now <u>there's</u> a sales pitch. Might need to give it a little more space before releasing a *motu proprio* or even an encyclical, but, hey, what the hell?

I'm the pope.

Yes, indeed. What the hell!

And that concept of hell's been gnawing at me since... well, looking back—and that's a long way—since my second teenage wank. But fortunately, popes don't and have never wanked, any more than Jesus did.

Dangerous territory.

Discuss.

That second glass of Inigo shiraz from my Jesuit friends at Sevenhill in the South Australia has a lot to answer for.

Those vignerons do St Ignatius proud.

And let's face it: if there can be integrated schools in Northern Ireland, accepting Anglican holy orders ought to be a walk in the park.

I mean, throw in solving the Israeli-Palestinian problem on the way.

And on the subject of running the Vatican on Hail Mary's, I believe that Francis was absolutely on the money when he stopped all the Holy See offices and dozens of Vatican institutions from being, in effect, their own banks and made them move all their secret piggy banks to his newly created Institute for the Works of Religion.

Suddenly, their dodgy investment and expense accounts were totally out of dangerous reach.

Francis did, however, go what I thought was one step too far in giving up the Holy Father's personal discretionary account, so I instructed Dario for that to be discreetly returned—which it has been—and knowing how Vatican clerical ambition and plotting can give the mafia a run for their money, I decided that my Secretary of State also needed a discretionary account to ensure that when I want something to happen, it's not impeded by endless committees.

The deal is that he privately clears things with me, then on the nod, it's a swift transfer on his part.

And Dario's is financially shrewd *as*.

Unlike his boss.

I know that Francis intended there to be no exceptions to the Institute for the Works of Religion, but in my experience, I've come to learn that in this life there are exceptions to everything, and as pope, in this matter I trust my own judgment. Though to date—and, yes, it's early days yet—my little plan hasn't produced any significant results.

In vino veritas?
I'm tired.
And so to the prayer of sleep.

Thursday, December 4th

Feast of St Ada of Lemoins, French nun. (7th century. Dates unknown. Fancy that. She must have been a woman).

Thank God, she was the niece of St Engelbert, who at least is remembered (like remembered <u>not</u>, except for his memorable name and for being the patron saint of all Humperdincks. And, of course, he was a man). Unlike poor old St Ada. It would appear that after her lifetime of piety, for which she was apparently acclaimed, details of her piety were, sadly, not recorded. Well, I never! She must have been a woman to have been so totally forgotten. Apparently, she died. Good heavens! Ada, I'm with you. I only hope that long after today, your eternal reward will be ultimate recognition by the conspiracy of centuries of celibate males who seem to have forgotten you. St Ada, pray for me. And as for those gazillions of other forgotten women the church has relegated to dusty history, I can only apologise. Profusely.

But then, late in the day, who says God doesn't answer prayers?

News just in this afternoon is that the Ernesto Mendoza has been rushed to hospital and been diagnosed with terminal pancreatic cancer.

And to think that he might only have been pope for a few months.

Clearly, heaven is in urgent need of a ruthless grand inquisitor.

In all charity, I must visit him.

Friday, December 5th

Feast of St Pelinus. Birth date unknown but was beaten to death by pagan priests in the reign of Roman Emperor Julian the Apostate.

Pelinus must have been quite a bloke because when he prayed before the temple of the pagan god, Mars, it came crashing down. Some people around here seem to think I'm doing the same for the Vatican—and without praying. Perhaps I'll be martyred by curia cardinals bashing me to death with volumes of canon law.

In my days as a young priest, I learnt that marriages end long before there is a parting of the ways by the couple.

In their hearts—and their bed—they know that after the first fine careless rapture comes the settling in, followed by the routine, then the responsibilities, then the knowing of the other all too well, then the annoyance of the other's faults (especially those little ones), then the sense of burden that comes with the cancer of measuring who does and doesn't do what home duties, and then the treading-on-eggshells type politeness which is usually the last stop before the terminus.

I haven't been married, but in a mere six months as pope, I've been through almost every stage of that anti-pilgrimage of estrangement.

A sure sign is the increasingly careful yet slightly chilled politeness of those curia cardinals who've done their sums, believe they've now got their man to the top of the exit queue and are frankly marking time impatiently until the present incumbent departs.

With the politeness goes the faux friendly assurance of efficiency in all dicasteries and the guarantee of maximum refined opposition and delay to any reform that means change.

The basic rule of the road is that all change is bad and that any change ordered by Pope Vegemite is an infringement—no, an invasion—of the territory of a much more experienced, wiser (and conservative) pontiff.

And in any case, as it will be rescinded by the next proper pope, there's really no point in expediting it, so the strategy is to play the game of going through the slow and slower motions. And to give them their due, they're skilled players. If we fielded a Vatican cardinals soccer team—the Red Hats—we'd be undefeated world champions from here to eternity.

There are two layers to the curia: the exploratively theological movers and shakers, a small but powerful elite, and the steady-as-she-goes prophylactic and bureaucratic conservatives. And in the latter, a good half or even more of them are crusading obstructionists, usually Italians, despite all that Francis did to reform the system.

What's the medical term?

Metastasis?

Not a medical or theological concept familiar to those whose world vision remains in the middle ages.

But we… Well, I. No, <u>we</u>. We, the confident and always questing faithful, <u>we</u> must support our theological pioneers. These scholars dare to search and dream and sift and then offer insightful explanations of texts of former times.

Surely by now we've come to understand that all learning is inevitably in the context of available knowledge at the time of writing, which is why we must examine and interpret those believers' contemporary understanding of the universe in the light of our current understanding.

Furthermore, we need to have the humility to protect that insight however many years ahead so that those believers on our shared faith journey will summon up the same intellectual rigour and historical humility to contextualise our current understanding.

And, no, this isn't being slippery.

Rather, it's digging deeper.

Back to the cardinals, and believe me, Dad, in this part of the world they're consummate politicians.

They network like there's no tomorrow and are experts at the numbers game: who's papabile (likely to be a contender to be pope—we speak Italian here!) and where they currently sit on the next conclave hit parade.

And they take no prisoners.

As I explained, Dad, I'm here because the backers of Olivier Gabriel Foncha and Ernesto Mendoza reached stalemate.

Both cardinals are arch-conservatives but with radically contrasting personalities.

Olivier is the embodiment of French-African charm and unsurpassed efficiency, while Mendoza, who's older and Italian, is as rigid and shuttered in his theology as he's experienced and expert in his field.

He would have made a brilliant Grand Inquisitor.

Correction: <u>is</u> one: judge, jury and executioner.

So as that's the state of play, it's now time for me to draw up a list of the two teams and main players: the Vatican Two Liberators loyal to the not necessarily holy Father from Down Under, and the Foncha Traditionalistas demanding a return to authority, obedience and sin, all in bold capitals.

In the home team corner I have my Secretary of State, Dario Silvestrini. Dario's 64, which is young for a cardinal. He's discreet—very. He has to be. He closely follows the numbers game, walks in the middle of the road though inclines to the left, is hard-working and most of all, loyal.

My anchor.

Prefect of the Dicastery for the Causes of Saints, Cardinal Adrian Jellicoe is a kiwi. He was briefly Cardinal of Auckland before being promoted to the Vatican. A moderate progressive, he's scrupulously balanced (to the point of slight annoyance... 'on the one hand... on the other') and before entering the seminary, he was a medical doctor trained in Dunedin. This background allows him sane and expert insight into potential miracles. He's diplomatic, charitable and moderate in all things including food and wine.

That said, no matter the church season, dining with him is a somewhat Lenten experience.

Though it might also be noted from these heights that, well... nobody's perfect.

To sum up, a friendly and safe pair of hands.

Despite his Italian name, Cardinal Gino Amato, Prefect of the Dicastery Promoting Christian Unity is an English-speaking Canadian (equally ironic is that he was based in Montreal) and passionately devoted to the cause of bringing all Christians together under a widely based agreed set of beliefs.

After Dario, Gino was my second appointment on becoming pope. He's a cleric of inspirational integrity and generosity, and I count him as a close friend, which is why I also appointed him *camerlengo*, the cardinal who acts as administrator on the passing of a pope and the election of his successor. It's a role requiring efficiency and diplomacy, not least in organising the conclave in which he counts the ballots after each vote. Needless to say, the Traditionalistas dismiss Gino as soft-headed heretic who'd trade truth for the delusion of unity. In British terms, he's *The Guardian* to the Tradionalistas' *Daily Telegraph*. If a man can be judged by the quality of his enemies, Gino is a living saint.

Prefect of the Dicastery which is the Economy Secretariat and also one of my appointments, Filipino Cardinal Carlos Caringal is a class act. He comes from a rich, established Filipino family, was educated in England at Stonyhurst and graduated in Law from Georgetown in Washington DC. His brilliant mind is like a calculator or computer. His amazing mathematical gift is to look at a spreadsheet and immediately see what doesn't add up. Needless to say, he's one of the most unpopular members of the curia—think the drive and determination of the late George Pell though without Pell's theologically dogmatic fundamentalism. Because of Carlos's detective work in only six months, he probably knows more about financial corruption than even the Italians here, not to mention his insight into the odd Vatican banker's murder. I trust Carlos in everything.

And finally, my major triumph (historical outrage according to the Traditionalistas) to date, Prefect of the vital Dicastery of Doctrine of the Faith is British Professor Alison Broderick, formerly Professor of Catholic Theology at Durham University and the most controversial appointment to the curia since... well, whenever.

And then some.

And then some more.

Lots.

Francis did God's work—after however many centuries—in opening the way for the laity to be included in the leadership of the church. And the laity means the entire backbone of what's left in the pews of the church: women. I mean, there's not much use for all the Vatican administrators furiously administrating all over the place if there's only a few doddering or deludedly camp clergy each sharing half a dozen parishes and no faithful within cooee to be administered to death by the rule makers.

And unless or until Africa sooner or later takes over the Vatican—which it almost certainly will (and what an abandoned orgy that will be)—then over to God, and good luck, God, with that one.

And as with the crucifixion, it's the women who remain faithful in the crisis, and in Africa, that means strong women.

Where was I?

Oh, yes, the redemptive Alison Broderick.

A class act if ever there was one!

A Master's degree in Church History from Cambridge and Doctorates in Sacred Theology from the Gregorian University in the Vatican and Canon Law from the Angelicum, The Vatican's Pontifical University of St Thomas Aquinas. No Cardinal has superior qualifications, and most of the time, she nails her outraged opponents on chapter, verse and meticulous logic. What's especially rewarding is the speechless fury of some of the dreamtime cardinals that a woman is not only their superior but also that she not infrequently has to correct them on points of canon law and theology.

Francis increased the number of women in senior Vatican roles to about 25%, and I intend to double that, God and the curia willing.

I'm sure God's backing me, but as for the curia…

So that makes six Vatican Two Liberators, and if I include me, that's about six and a half.

Now to potential Pope Olivier Whatever-Name-He-Takes and his co-Traditionalistas. Olivier's a formidable foe never to be underestimated.

Prefect of The Dicastery of Communication: Cardinal Desmond Wilenski from Colorado. American arch-conservative. Takes no prisoners. Rules the English-speaking neo-cons. Was a close friend of George Pell. Say no more.

Prefect of The Dicastery of Laity Family and Life: a layman, Franciszek Kamiński. Lawyer. Polish. Enough said.

Prefect of The Dicastery of Divine Worship & the Discipline of the Sacraments: Chilean Cardinal Carlos Silva Gonzales. Clever, prissy, evasive, predictable. Pretends to be a centrist—runs with the hares, hunts with the hounds. Everything old is true again.

Prefect of The Dicastery of Promoting Integral Human Development: Honduras Cardinal Miguel de Hernandez, formerly Archbishop of Tegucigalpa. Any human development in his case would be appreciated by the church and would almost certainly be a miracle.

Prefect of the Dicastery of the Evangelisation of Peoples: Cardinal Francois Nzapayeké from the Central African Republic, formerly Archbishop of Bangui. Civilised, shrewd, has major influence in French Africa, fence sitter, not without ambition (I wonder whether

Olivier takes this into consideration) and about the only cleric who understands the corrupt machinations of northern African politics—that's if anyone does, which I strongly doubt. Interesting but not to be trusted.

Prefect of the Dicastery of the Doctrine of the Faith: Cardinal Ernesto Mendoza. Despite Spanish name, Italian from the north. Arch conservative previously described in detail. Knows where all the bodies are buried. He buried them. Aged 78 and the other main conservative candidate for the next pope.

Prefect of the Dicastery of Catholic Education and Culture: Sister Monique Agard. French, Member of the *Religieuses du Sacré-Cœur de Jésus*, that rarest of contemporary female religious, a highly intelligent but conservative nun. Warm, multi-lingual, outstanding educational leader and one of the most widely read scholars you're likely to meet. What Alison Broderick is to Theology, Monique Agard is to world literature. Her company is a delight, and in conversation, she always elegantly outsmarts me. We'd be friends were it not for the fact that she quite charitably but correctly has me summed up as the second-rate mind I am. No token female she.

Prefect of the Council of Cardinal Advisors, Cardinal Bruno Westphalen, German. Formerly Archbishop of Hanover, financial wizard, approachable yet oddly oblique—has no small talk—runs a tight ship, highly respected by his clergy, one of the few German cardinals who emerged from the child abuse nightmare (not that it's anywhere near over) with clean hands, but Teutonic in his respect for discipline and hierarchy. A great pity. He should be one of us. Unfortunately, like Monique Agard, he's an excellent judge of character—an even greater pity.

Finally, Prefect of the Dicastery of the Institutes of Consecrated Life and Societies of Apostolic Life, Cardinal Olivier Gabriel Foncha. Once my friend.

Nine to six and a half, and that ain't shoe sizes.

Both teams will be running out of the sacristy onto the field any moment now.

Saturday, December 6th

Feast of St Santa Claus (Nicholas of Myra 270–343).

Two fascinating stories about him. Hearing that a local man had lost all his money and planned to sell his daughters into prostitution, Nicholas went by night to the man's house and threw three bags of gold in through the window, thus saving the girls from a vile life. These three bags of gold became the three golden balls that indicate a pawn broker's shop. Nice one. According to another legend, Nicholas raised to life three young boys who had been murdered and then pickled in a barrel of brine to hide the crime. Sadly, I do not possess such powers. Are we really expected to believe this kind of stuff? I can see why adolescents and atheists—probably synonyms—chuck out the baby with the bathwater... or the boys with the brine.

Dreamt last night of silent music. Contradiction. Categorical mistake. Life experience. Take note. Give thanks, Mario. Religion is founded on paradox. An excellent reason to embrace its mystery.

The blessed trinity: one in three and three in one. If bewildered, think triangles.

Born of the Holy Ghost. What on earth does that mean?

Immaculate conception. Virgin birth. Magical thinking.

My kingdom is not of this world. The last shall be first. Blessed are the poor.

Really? Then let us consult them more frequently.

The whole absurd concept of royalty and kingship is another unknowable realm and fake gravity.

Bread and wine are body and blood. Death is life. This whole imaginary world sure beats the prosaic banality of our earthly drudgery. It's the glorious contradiction which justifies the major moments of our days. Of our minds. Of our hopes.

Contradiction and paradox are the slippery springboards our lives bounce off, and in that exhilarating elation of rebounding, mystical insight sure beats the barbed wire sterility of logic.

On my good days, I believe that only in such poetry can we find the warmth and reassurance of our conflicted selves.

Yes, those contradictions infuse me with faith. Even more: with hope.

As I say… sometimes.

Calm down, Mario. Are you losing it? Who do you think you are? Some kind of freak, weirdo pope?

Fair question.

If anyone in this God firing Hadron Collider madhouse gets to read this… do not complete this sentence. No, do. Yet that's who we are. Each one of us, God's precious particles.

What do you reckon, Dad? Magnificent contradictions? Momentary ascension above the mere laws of nature?

Not wrong, Dad.

But wrong, Dad.

Maybe I'm the only pope since Peter who dares to doubt; both of us, for a magic moment, walking on water then doubting and… Splash! Sink! Human.

And what kind of sacrament is 2018 Sevenhill Inigo Shiraz?

Discuss… with gratitude.

To be continued.

Sunday, December 7th

Feast of St Ambrose.

Ambrose was the highly educated son of a noble family. He was acclaimed bishop of Milan by an overwhelming majority of the faithful, declined the invitation but was eventually persuaded to accept. He was a highly respected scholar and theologian and received St Augustine into the church. He introduced antiphonal chant in which each side of a church or choir takes turns in singing a text. Lovely. A holy conversation. Altogether, he was a magnificent and successful cleric. All the qualities this Bishop of Rome lacks.

Faced the morning cautiously with my 'to do' list.

Question: how to find beautiful and dignified contemporary church music.

Most of what's sung in parishes today is either banal jingles or grating country and western clichés: McHymns. Tasteless on every front.

And at the present moment, I'm one glass of Clare Valley Inigo shiraz too many. Not a good look for a pope.

Pressures from wherever—all over, actually—within the curia. Most of them mouth loyalty, but such loyalty I should fear. 'I know not the man.' A bit early, surely?

I'm tired. Not sleeping. Not exactly Gethsemane. Come on, Mario, get it together. You're supposed to be the pope.

I know. Supposed to be. Pope Wollongong the Second-Rate Dickhead. God knows, I know.

But, God, why?

Ask the pope.

But I <u>am</u> the pope. I should know.

Yes.

But I don't.

Inigo, Ignatius, guide me.

I mean, for Christ's sake, you were a bloody Basque. Teach me to be Jesuitical. And now your Jesuit Clare Valley shiraz brings me to...

Should I be thinking this, let alone writing this?

The wine must speak. The wine betrays my unworthiness. My unworthiness from deep inside my deepest... unworthiness.

Rewind.

I wonder whether the sacred music search should start with lyrics—horse before the cart. James McAuley and Richard Connolly managed it brilliantly in Australia with their Living Parish hymns. Can't understand why they didn't catch on worldwide.

Where is today's literate liturgical poet?

All the American stuff I find beyond embarrassing—greeting card lyrics and maple syrup music. Walt Disney's cartoon take on the divine. Must consult our Director of Music.

Next on the endless agenda I'm victim to: here's today's barrel of laughs: 1 The German Church; 2 The African Church; 3 Synods; 4 LGBTQI matters.

Well, that menu covers more than a good many of the Vatican employees, and that's the bloody short list. Sufficient to the day are the contradictions thereof. When, O Lord, will we be granted the grace of walking together?

I keep trying to imagine Peter the Fisherman drawing up international issues in order of urgency and attributing strict time frames for their discussion. Then I remember that in The Acts of the Apostles he's described as 'uneducated and ordinary'. Nice way of saying 'illiterate', though no doubt he could discern the names of his catch at the fish market.

Yes, Peter is *my* pope—not very bright and a thrice denier. Too many issues, not enough faith. Plenty of doubt, though. But almost always, enough and then—finally—more than enough love.

And the greatest of these is love.

And so to prayer.

St Peter, pray that your poor literate successor may learn the price of fish.

With 2018 Sevenhill Inigo Shiraz.

Amen.

Cheers!

Monday, December 8th

Feast of the Immaculate Conception.

The church teaches that Mary, mother of Jesus, was the only human conceived free from original sin. This was because the human mother of God had to be the perfect human to give birth to Jesus, the son of God. This is a most beautiful and spirit-heartening belief. Or myth. It compliments the human race with the tantalising hope of eventual perfectibility and in our most agonising hours, it should reassure our faith in eventual happiness when we are restored with the Father. And as I see it, like so many of our sacred mysteries, it's not physical or medical; rather, its metaphysical and poetic. Yes, it short circuits the larger question of Adam and Eve and so-called original sin, our metaphor for the imperfection of humanity and the mysterious and frightening power of evil. Of its very nature, like the virgin birth, the concept of the immaculate conception is obviously undisprovable, and in all intellectual fairness, like the virgin birth of Jesus, it certainly suggests overtones of recoiling from what some prophets, evangelists and celibate theologians might consider the messiness of human sexuality. Still, as with music and poetry (and lower down the list, gastronomy, but don't tell Sister Angelica whose cooking is musical poetry and poetic music) it's best to embrace the gift with gratitude and rejoice in the exaltation of the mystery. Openness is everything. With certain dimensions of religion, too much logic is restricting and strangles the glory and hope of the deeper, more important message. And, yes, I speak this logic as a pope. Religion sanctifies contradictions. Discuss. But much more importantly, live! And enjoy.

The church in Africa, Europe, America, South America, Middle East, Australasia.

The problem is surely imagining that those nations are united entities rather than bundles of feuding bailiwicks and kingdoms. What can a mere pope do? This one can't even begin to rein in a totally out of control Vatican.

Properly observed, this place is a mad metaphor for the whole world; the lunatics running the asylum. I mean, if <u>we</u> can't function in the way we're supposed to, what hope has the poor planet?

If only the Swiss Guards were an army, we could simply invade, restructure, appoint the right leaders, then move to the next war zone.

Francis understood. 'Time is greater than space, and reality more important than ideas.' By doing we learn. Let us do, therefore, in good faith.

Now, about cardinals—hats for chaps. And yet canon law permits that cardinals needn't be clerics. As I've always said, 'Good old canon law!' Just imagine a papal conclave of women; or, say, fifty-fifty: men and women.

No, that way madness lies.

Or does it?

Dreamer or dunce?

Prophet or fruitcake?

Lord, inspire your humble servant to dare.

Oh my god! Of course. Of course! How long does it take for a pope to understand who this pope really is? How could I have been so naïve these past five months? Exactly. Totally. The age-old trap: they dictate the agenda. <u>They</u> call the shots.

Simply brilliant and brilliantly simple: the devil is in their endless and eternally extended detail.

Commissions, investigations, results offered to concerned dicasteries, recommendations to further committees, opinions from all relevant congregations, submissions to canon lawyers and so it goes on. Like, how dumb can an acclaimed mediocre Australian cardinal be?

Don't answer that.

And shut up, Dad.

Henceforth, the pope and only the pope sets the agenda.

Per omnia saecula saeculorum.

But hang on, Mario. Your Secretary of State draws up the daily agenda, and he's your most loyal supporter.

How come?

Is he, too, victim of the Traditionalistas brigade?

Or...?

No. Impossible. Not Dario.

And so to my bed of nails.

Tuesday, December 9th

Feast of St Peter Fourier (1565–1640), a French monk and teacher who was so extraordinarily bright that he could recite the Summa Theologica of St Thomas Aquinas by heart.

This splendid publication comprising 38 tracts, 631 questions, almost 3000 articles, 10,000 objections and their answers. Well, at least I have a photographic memory, though not to St Peter Fourier's excessive extent. Mind you, that said, I still have trouble remembering why I wander into rooms. Peter also founded the order of The Daughters of Our Lady for the education of girls, so he was more than just bright; he was good and wise. I should like to have met him. Something tells me he must have enjoyed French cuisine, though this is not mentioned in his biography. I must ask him.

Heard that Mendoza has put his affairs in order. Together with Sister Angelica, I visited him. I wanted her to understand that our brother theologians holding different views may be adversaries but they're not enemies.

Not quite true in this case, but a counsel of perfection nonetheless.

He looked ghastly and was in considerable pain. I said I would pray for him as he undertook his final journey and I complimented him on his great faith. I even said how much I envied his secure beliefs, which wasn't altogether true—in fact, it was altogether almost a lie, but in the circumstances...

Mendoza smiled, perhaps for the first time in his life. He said, 'Holiness, the truth is, I've got a thimbleful of faith, a bucketful of doubt but an ocean full of hope.'

I'm surprised it wasn't me who dropped dead.

It was as if he'd been released from a lifetime of hiding behind the fortification of rules… of suppressing his emotions… of denying his deepest, most honest self; his soul, indeed: the very ground of his being.

Extraordinary.

It was a God moment to invite me to reassess my own judgment and my own prejudices—some luminous angel suggesting that I might have the humility to...

I found myself suspended between disbelief and forgiveness.

And envy.

Best to leave it there.

I administered the last sacraments to him. He thanked me, closed his eyes, and Sister Angelica and I left him.

He will be missed by some in the church, though not by me. We must put those surviving aspects of the Inquisition behind us. I shall have the Dicastery for the Doctrine of the Faith reformed.

But as he was dying, against every instinct in my attempt to understand what we're all about, I felt envious of his final courageous confession.

Requiescat in pacem.

Wednesday, December 10

Feast of Our Lady of Loreto, the alleged name of the alleged house where Mary was allegedly born and where the Annunciation of the Angel Gabriel allegedly occurred.

Tradition tells us that the house was lifted up by angels and carried first to Dalmatia and then to Italy, presumably by the same angels. A slightly more credible justification for the house's relocation is that a chap named Angeli was involved in the removal. Either way, Our Lady of Loreto is the patron saint of builders and construction workers and, appropriately, of people in the aviation industry. Our church provides patronal assurance for everyone from removalists to flight attendants. Much more importantly, Loreto nuns are highly educated, formidably independent, superb teachers and marvellous women of God. On this day, I give thanks for an inspiring Australian Loreto nun, Sister Veronica Brady (1929–2015). She was one of the first Australian nuns to teach in a university (Western Australia, where she became an Associate Professor of English), to broadcast on radio (she was a champion of public broadcasting) and to vigorously join in socio-political debate. She spoke out fearlessly against the Vatican stance on abortion, homosexuality and contraception, and was involved in the Aboriginal rights movement and the anti-uranium mining lobby. She also supported the ordination of female priests. This glorious larrikin nun was supposedly the only literary critic whom the cantankerous Australian novelist, Patrick White, trusted and admired. He was right. To me, she was and is the kind of saint I insist must be in heaven, and something tells me that St Veronica Brady will put in a good word to God about this misplaced larrikin. And more and more, something tells me I'll need it.

Can't put it off and won't.

One item only on today's agendum—note the Latin singular, Brother Edmund—and on this week's agendum, if necessary.

And this month's.

And this year's.

And I've set it in stone: the wretched, filthy, agonizing, deadly ongoing cancer of our church: sexual abuse. Dear God, give me strength. And discernment.

OK, the question is complicated, and the answers are doubtless complex. Or not, as the case may be.

And as the case will and must be. In which case, keep it simple, stupid.

Question: Who are the perpetrators of sexual abuse?

Answer: mostly clerics—professed celibate priests and brothers. There are lay criminals too, though statistically far, far fewer than there are religious.

Question: Who are the victims?

Answer: Mostly young males. Yes, there is a number of female victims, but far, far fewer than there are males.

Question: How many female religious perpetrators are there?

Answer: A few, but proportionately they're very small—as far as we know.

Question: So does this look like a problem of homosexual orientation in supposedly celibate religious males?

Answer: You bet. I mean, bloody hell, how long has it taken the church to come to terms with what the whole world understood from the get-go? If a second-rate Aussie mind like mine can jump to the extraordinary conclusion that one and one make two, how come the apparently greatest Catholic intellectuals, holy men and non-movers and non-shakers in the Vatican can still be pondering the fucking obvious?

And any fool can see the answer staring them in the face. It's an ongoing cover-up by the prissy and precious rainbow resistors within these walls.

God knows I've got no problem with their sexual orientation. That's God's problem if God has a problem with it, or no problem whatsoever if God is loving and all gracious in God's gifts.

But I have every problem with the guilt gay clerics are happy to impose on so many of the faithful worldwide while these same frocked-up old mins in the Vatican are partying away nightly with their rent boys. Or who knows? Their true, for the moment, lovers.

Too much information and too much truth.

Still, in faith and trust in the Lord, it offers endlessly exciting new areas of theology and canon law which could occupy the Vatican bureaucracy for a further good few decades or, with their luck, centuries. So...

Question: Dare we ask whether it's celibacy that is 'intrinsically disordered'?

Answer: Is the Pope a catholic? On second thoughts, change that to 'Surely it's screamingly bloody obvious.' Sexual needs must surely be God given gifts. As normal as... well, normal. And the theological perversion of demanding in God's name that everyone on earth observe total sexual restraint except in marriage (same sex?) must surely be against all the non-confessed experience of every released human being.

It's clear to me that the ban is psychologically crippling. Ask any human from the age of their first glorious discovery of God's gift of pleasure.

Question: Would married priests contribute to a reduction in these crimes?

Reply: You'd have to think so. A considerable reduction, surely.

Question: But what of the gay clergy who want to be protected from women and don't want to be married?

Answer: Problem here. Since I'm assuming that sexual orientation is a gift from God, then it's a contradiction to ban gay men from being ordained because they might possibly become predators. So what's the answer?

Answer: Don't know

Question: Could it be that the church has just been plain wrong for a couple of centuries, and that we should now admit the truth?

Answer: Yes. Whoops! Not sure popes should think like this, let alone say it. But that still begs the question of ordaining gay candidates for the priesthood. This is where it does get complicated.

Question: Well, surely allowing women to be ordained would more than likely at least reduce the problem?

Answer: Yes, but that's no justification for ordaining women. Quite the opposite, in fact. It's insulting. Either women have a right to be ordained or they don't, in which case, what kind of insane God made the possession of a penis the basic qualification for the priesthood?

Question: It's that simple?

Answer: Ask the faithful. And stand back. And then ask for absolution for the masculine arrogance of the church's history. I mean if Christ is with us, then let's put aside the ludicrous nonsense of penis priority. It's time to embrace all of the questing human race and invite them to celebrate the gift of Christ's eucharistic blessing. Seems bloody obvious to me. And I'd bet a few bob on some women being in attendance at the Last Supper. Can't see those apostles cooking and serving. Indeed, some of these working women may well have been in the room when Jesus said, 'Do this in memory of me.'

Fanciful, yes, but not totally impossible.

More of this later.

Much more.

Question: Time to go to bed?

Answer: Thank God.

Thursday, December 11th

Feast of St Damasus 1 (305–384) who was perhaps the first pope to rule with swagger.

Damasus was of Spanish origins, and his father was likely a married priest. I like that. He was elected Bishop of Rome in 366 but not without some controversy. A rival was aggressively supported by a violent minority who defamed Damasus. As if. Not. He was shrewd enough to employ a talented young priest-scholar, Jerome, much cleverer than himself, as his personal secretary. The result? Jerome's lifelong compiling of a new and literate Latin version of the Old and New Testaments. Damasus also insisted that bishops lived a less extravagant life than most of them had done for some time. He also preserved the catacombs. In his humble and lived faith, Damasus was, as papal history notes, a Christian first and a pope second. I need to think of him daily. That said...

I'm not being paranoid, but somewhere in this palace of mirrors there's a mole undermining my papacy, and yes, admitting such belief is the first sign of persecution syndrome and mental illness, not to mention unchristian and distinctly unpapal suspicion.

But there is.

And, no, I'm not in need of psychological help—yet—because I've been around these parts long enough to know that so many of our over-promoted clerics working in this pantomime of vestal virgins (and more than a few non-vestals) wouldn't survive half an hour in a parish where our religiously wounded parishioners desperately need spiritual triage.

This place is about power, influence, whispers and plots; the Kremlin politburo, or whatever they now call it, could learn a lot from our centuries-old professional slitherers. They slide with the elegant ease of Winter Olympic ice skaters or eels and snakes avoiding capture. Sanctimonious slither: gracefully lethal.

The simple fact is that from the moment of the announcement of this current pope's election, the whistle's been blown for the sacredly vicious manoeuvres for possible future papal candidates in the next conclave, and as they exit from the Sistine Chapel chanting praises to the Holy Spirit, the short list is lining up and preparing their next election campaigns.

I can feel it in the smarmy smiles and the always slightly over-acted condescension of everyone around me.

They're all reporting to their future patrons on the campaign trail.

The more I think about it—and I think about it every day—this war is both personal and political, and that's simultaneously absurd and insulting.

Here we are claiming to be the one true church of the God of love, and at mission control, the generals are behaving like squalidly ambitious parliamentarians and unworthy, immature clerics, myself absolutely included in the latter category. It really is a disgrace, and arguing that the church is human as well as divine strikes me as a cheap and uncheerful get-out argument of devious over-simplicity.

That said, the only three current exceptions to this endless war of succession seem to be Sister Angelica, my rock and head of papal intelligence, Dario, my loyal Secretary of State and valued adviser, and Ennio, whose young, liberated indifference to everything going on around us both bewilders but reassures me in its unmanipulative innocence.

Oh, and, yes, all my Second Vatican Council Liberators support me and help keep me afloat.

And of course I realise that in defending these particular three, I'm as much a participant in this nonsense as my opposition is.

Here we go round the moot, miserable and maddening moral mulberry bush.

Sadly, John Le Carré's dead, so he's not much use in sniffing out the mole, and I doubt Ronald Knox, even though he was an Etonian, would have had the necessary cynicism to detect the Judas. And in the *dénouement*, Father Brown would first have to find his umbrella and then take far too long explaining his brilliant reasoning. So no help there, alas.

Nonetheless I feel... no, I know I'm being watched.

Or heard.

It's creepy. And disconcerting.

Tomorrow, I'll have the place swept by outside IT people. Our own IT mob probably planted the listening devices. Paranoid but in no way unlikely. In every way likely, actually.

I might ask Ennio for advice.

I've come to suspect (not without envy) that after hours, this intriguing young man might well move in colourful bohemian circles—of which this independent state and the wider country of Italy offer a menu of enticements. And as I've come to learn—not without amusement and satisfaction—that lad knows more than his prayers.

Much more.

Friday, December 12th

Feast of Blessed Ludwik Bartosik (1909–1941), Polish Franciscan friar (ordained 1935) and buddy of my hero, St Maximilian Kolbe.

Captured in Poland in 1939 by invading German troops and after being sent to various prisons, Ludwik ended up in that unspeakable (yet must be spoken of) hellhole of Auschwitz, where he ministered to other slave labourers. He was tortured to death on the night of

I CONFESS

December 12, 1941. What a man of God! He inspires me. I am humbled by the memory of him.

Today was Sister Angelica's Bounty Day. Grilled freshwater trout with garlic, rosemary and anchovy butter. Angelica says trout brings good fortune, a superstition I suspect she has made up, but then what am I to make of today's news?

Mendoza, who should have died two days ago, seems to have been transformed into miraculous remission.

The doctors can't explain it, and he certainly wouldn't have been given trout with garlic, rosemary and anchovy butter in hospital. Angelica has medieval cookbooks she consults in the Vatican archives and, I suspect, a few she secretes away, but often she admits to just brilliantly inventing recipes on the spot.

The ways of the Lord are strange—in this case, bloody questionable—but this Mendoza turn-around is the last thing the church needs at the moment.

WTF!

Technically, as he's still alive, he remains in charge of The Dicastery for the Doctrine of the Faith, and if he really is in remission, it won't be a good look for me to fire him straight away.

What to do?

Grant him extended leave to recuperate and let his deputy take over for a few months? His Number Two is only about half as bloodthirsty as Mendoza—and half as bright—which still makes him a monster.

I've been thinking that to limit the powers of the dicastery, I'll make the worst they can do to punish exploratory theologians will be to invite them to Rome for conversations, not just with the head honcho of the Dicastery for the Doctrine of the Faith, but also with the Holy Father.

Still, I'll do it after Mendoza has had a couple of months of R&R.

Saturday, December 13

Feast of St John of the Cross (1542–1591).

Hard to believe that I admire this great saint, but then opposites and contradictions are part and parcel of trying to live the faith. When his young father died, John was brought up by a single mother. He was an ascetic (not me) and believed that his beloved Carmelite order had slipped into far too comfortable and un-Christlike ways of living (me and food. And wine. And spirits of the non-immortal kind). John was hailed as a purifier (hardly me) and many discontented Carmelites in the order worked against him. (I know how he must have felt.) Thus according to the pious lives of the saints, John suffered exile, hunger, public lashings, imprisonment, and defamation (I can relate to the last). He loved solitude and contemplation (I've made some effort here, though come to think of it, not much really) and exhorted Carmelite monks and nuns to spend much more time chanting their prayers together (good, though I wouldn't necessarily go overboard on this) and recommended much more rigorous fasting (can't see Sister Angelica buying into this) and to refrain from eating meat (all unmartyred saints are probably a bit nutty. I certainly am, though as yet unmartyred). And if proof of dottiness were needed, St John of the Cross branched out with a new Order of Discalced Carmelites—no shoes. Taking penance too far. Bonkers, in fact. (I'm suddenly feeling sane.) He worked as chaplain to universities and recommended falling in love with God: the soul seeks God, John says, as the bride seeks her bridegroom (Human. Nice. On a good day, my kind of theology). He also recognised The Dark Night of the Soul (genius. Insightful psychology long before that science even existed. Bravissimo, John. You really understood religious life). Furthermore, he insisted that central to religious belief was the acceptance of mystery (Yes!). Every soul has a mystical craving for and union with God, and that can only be experienced through contemplation. (Nailed it. An absolute winner.) All this before he died at 49. OK, overall, a few loose screws—in the metaphorical sense— but some quite wonderful truths. Inspirational. Gives me hope.

It's now a regular custom for me to invite my late morning Monday Swiss Guard, Ennio, in for a sandwich and a glass of wine. He's forbidden to drink on duty, but as I explained to him, I'm his commander-in-chief, so in the circumstances, he's only obeying orders, and I'm unlikely to prosecute myself, though as he grinningly replied, 'In this place, anything can happen.'

True.

Anyhow, no one else in the Vatican talks to me like that. It's unbelievably liberating.

Ennio is one of the happiest people I've ever met. He's one of life's free spirits and merry talkers. Whatever the subject, Ennio is happy to express an opinion, informed or otherwise—usually charmingly otherwise.

He enjoys his job, doesn't seem to have any guilt about anything including nattering away with the pope when he freely admits to having no particular religious beliefs except that God is love, an approach to life his lively company reaffirms in me.

Today, for some reason or other, we got to talking once more about the joys of sex—as you do—though not too loudly in these corridors. We moved to my bedroom which I doubt is bugged, though you never know.

20-year-old Ennio bubbles with adventure and laughter and affection for his partner, Mirella, and I think he secretly tries to embarrass me with his frankness about what they get up to.

I have to admit I've never met anyone quite like him. He seems to have no fear about anything whatsoever in life, and he certainly now has no fear of drinking on duty and he has faultless manners, always insisting on washing up and taking out the empty bottle. Discreetly.

I also found out he's a computer whiz whereas I'm a computer klutz.

At home in Lugano in Switzerland, he has all sorts of recording equipment which he plays with and apparently makes a few bob from recording local bands in his garage. He loves anything electronic just as I loathe the very sight of any instruction manual, and he tells me that at school, he once planted a recording device in the deputy principal's office.

Apparently in his final year at school, the strict lady had given him a week's detention for after-school misbehaviour with his girlfriend in a music department practice booth. What they were practising apparently wasn't on the syllabus, so in revenge, while she was teaching, he bugged her office phone. I thought only covert government espionage departments had that capability, but Ennio assures me that via the internet, I'd be surprised what can be done.

This at the age of 18!

Do teachers realise that their students are probably twice as tech savvy as their IT departments?

Anyway, he learnt some interesting details about the lady's romantic life.

I expressed friendly but firm disapproval, and Ennio agreed, saying that he realised he'd overstepped the mark—I suggested 'done wrong', but he just smiled and said that it was even easier removing the device and, right or wrong, it proved what a hypocrite she was for punishing him for behaviour she, too, indulged in.

And his ongoing revenge was to always smile when he passed her. He liked the way it made her uncomfortable.

Talk about tangled webs.

This winning young man is completely guileless. Innocent he's not—understatement of the century—but frank and fresh he most engagingly is.

All this being intriguing conversation leading to him saying he could easily help me with my online diary and could install what he calls an 'airport', which would guarantee that everything I wrote would be instantly saved somewhere between the Vatican and heaven, and that he could absolutely set things up to ensure that no one here could access my diary.

Normally, I abhor airports, but Ennio's virtual 'airport' is surely a godsend.

To my delight, I've arranged that our weekly encounters have now become daily.

Sunday, December 14th

Feast of St Margaret of Fontana (1440–1513).

Orphaned early. Became a lay Dominican. Devoted to the sick and the poor, Margaret would spend whole nights praying with suffering patients, and given how dreadfully patients suffered in the 15th century, she really was a spiritual—and probably a medical—wonder woman. Hardly a surprise that there were reports of miraculous healings as a result of her care. Those are the kinds of miracles I thank God for. And also, apparently, she drove demons out of tortured and possessed souls by making the sign of the cross. That woman predated psychiatry by blending faith and prayer. Perhaps there should be more of it. Indeed, much more. I'd like a present-day saintly woman to accompany me on my death bed.

A nun friend of Sister Angelica's from Formia, on the coast halfway to Naples—I've forgotten her name, but they're both in some kind of nun-like herbal conspiracy—anyway, Sister Whatever-Her-Name-Is visited Angelica yesterday bringing a gift of kilos of parsnips, celeriac and herbs from the Formia convent garden. And, of course, all gifts must be graciously received, even humble parsnips.

We didn't eat them in Wollongong, and I must say I've politely avoided them as much as possible since moving from the Illawarra area south of Sydney (that is, throughout my entire adult life) but Angelica expressed delight.

I expressed slightly fumbled thanks and optimistic expectations. Popes are good at that, while knowing that the outcome is more than likely to disappoint. Even annoy. Sometimes infuriate.

Still, Angelica's friend knows of Angelica's culinary genius, and I pondered that Advent is also a time of self-denial in preparation for the celebration of Christmas. A kind of light Lenten truce: a parsnip penance for the week's rare second bounty.

Oh dear! Dinner tonight turned out to be verging on the celeriac sinful. Talk about Bounty! Roasted celeriac, parsnips and fennel rejoicing in a sauce of parmesan and cream. Luxury. These root vegetables deserve their own patron saint. A useful challenge for a gastronomically precious pontiff. I shall work on it in my spare time. Meantime, I've requested the left-overs for lunch tomorrow.

Nuns and good works and gardens. A reason for faith.

From Cardinal Mendoza, Prefect of the Congregation for the Defence of the Faith:

'Your Holiness,

The abstract noun 'Holiness' requiring deep reflection and, in my case, with humility confronting Christ's Vicar on earth.

I write this letter not only in all humility but also in equal alarm, on behalf of your loyal Curia confreres who wait in hope yet look with despair at the way God's church has been drifting since your elevation to the papacy.

To the matter.

By cheap grabs to the secular press, and even worse, by flippant interviews with what seems calculated indifference to centuries of church teaching and more than the suggestion of defective theology in your embrace of repetitive doubt to the international Catholic press, you have cut the church adrift from its historical moorings and given the world to believe that more than two thousand years of doctrinal tradition and revealed truth are now open to the slings and arrows of atheistic journalists, undisciplined clergy and the ragtag multitude of hedonistic sinners.

God's church cries out for affirmation and discipline, not shallow appeals to the popularity of those who long ago abandoned all belief in the only channel to salvation.

In the Holy Name of Our Divine Saviour together with the urgent pleas of your despairing Curia brothers, I implore you to henceforth desist from your....'

And on and on it goes.

OK, I get the point, though it sounds even more pompous and even funnier in Mendoza's elegantly classical Latin...

In other words, 'Listen, idiot face, you're a yokel from nowheresville, you're out of your depth, you're a dickhead to boot, you're totally ignorant of all Vatican protocols and just in case you don't know, you're an embarrassment to all of us who understand and appreciate how this place runs. So to put it in more licentious and direct medieval Latin, shut the fuck up, stop expressing doubt and leave all commentary to the canon lawyers who from time immemorial have pronounced all the answers.'

Am I hearing the faintest shriek of the desperate—the terror of the bureaucratic gestapo as the faithful see its condemnatory lunacies as the self-serving, clerical nonsense they've been for centuries?

The truth is that the bureaucracy is alarmed at the rumblings of a faithful, formerly frightened but now literate laity, who, after however many centuries of eternal damnation for minor parking restrictions, have finally woken up and told God's Salvation Parking Police to go shove it where the sun don't shine.

And the sad irony is that Mendoza could translate my wild Wollongong-ese into elegant Ciceronian Latin which would keep his prissy cardinal coterie giggling for... but best that I preclude any predicate to this sentence.

Let me get my head together.

At the last conclave, KGB candidate Mendoza was too old and traditional to land the numbers.

To do this legendary prince of the church justice, he's a fine historian, a dyed-in-the-wool conservative, a forceful communicator and as *Obergruppenführer* of God's Gestapo, has silenced dozens of contemporary theologians for heresy.

As I've said before, he takes no prisoners.

Though both candidates are implacable conservatives, they differ greatly.

Mendoza is a theological and biblical scholar, chapter and verse at his fingertips. He believes in tradition and continuity over change—to him, all change is diminution—and has a terror of modern creative theologians causing havoc among the faithful, especially the young. His lifelong work has been to seek out the offenders and silence them.

Olivier, on the other hand, is no scholar; rather, he's a born administrator and policeman. He believes the path to salvation lies in strict obedience to the law. It's all about the shepherd and the flock. The faithful must be disciplined in the same way that the clergy must, and the task of the clergy is to ensure strict adherence to the letter of the law. Infringement—with which I know for a fact he's not unfamiliar—is part of human nature, but once admitted and the penalty paid, life returns to normal, and the faith remains fortified.

I can't imagine our Saviour buying either distasteful approach to what strikes me as crowd control rather than faith, but what would I know?

With the conservative vote split between the old Grand Inquisitor and the younger, ambitious African Olivier, the exhausted conclave decided on this Australian seat-warming compromise candidate, the last one being John Paul I of late unhappy memory—well, loving memory of his gentle and smiling personality but unhappy memory of his almost immediate and curious death.

And now it seems that the current antipodean seat warmer is hotting things up by his questioning and questing honesty.

I'm the pope.

Mendoza and Olivier are not.

Then fasten your scarlet seatbelts; a touch of triple tiara turbulence is needed to set this joint jumping.

And so to happier correspondence.

A postcard from my little brother, Tonio, who always thought he discovered sex, drugs and rock-n-roll before his big brother.

Well, he certainly scored big on the last two and managed to wipe himself off the map of Wollongong and out of the mess of our family.

For a brief time—less than a year—Tonio was a junior reporter at the Illawarra Mercury. The most junior, if I remember correctly, which I do.

He absolutely hated it.

Little wonder, as he covered 'community', which was anything that didn't fit into sport, real estate or classifieds. Trivia, to be precise.

Eventually, either the Gong or Tonio ran out of pointless stories, and Tonio disappeared into wherever, and we never heard from him again except for when I chucked in my work experience at the Gong's worst advertising agency—and back then, that's saying something—and entered the seminary.

Via home, Tonio sent me a postcard of North Beach—postmarked Cooktown Qld, saying 'God is dead but make the most of the funeral. So many fucks, so little time. Must rush, love, T.'

Today's postcard was the same photo of North Beach.

That's the Gong for you, Dad.

Some things don't change, even across the globe.

It read, 'Hi, Guess who? Your little brother. Like Jesus, I'm back from the dead. Someone told me you were pope. I must have been drunk. Been a while.'

Thirty-eight years, but who's counting?

'Anyway, praying for you. T.'

Miracles really do happen.

No address, but he's alive somewhere and praying for me.

I weep with joy as I pray for Tonio.

Today's previous correspondence now gloriously irrelevant.

Deo gratias.

Monday, December 15th

Feast of St Mary di Rosa (1813–1855).

Mary came from a not-uncomfortable family in Brescia. She worked generously for victims of the cholera epidemic of 1836. Think COVID. She could have married a number of eligible suitors but aged 23, she took religious vows and became a sister of the Handmaids of Charity, working with deaf children and the sick in hospital. She led that order until her death at the age of 42. A dedicated and a remarkably unremarkable woman—like so many nuns. She saw Christ in the disabled and the suffering. Perhaps not all that hard, but Mary did something about it. I must try to emulate her daily.

Dear God in heaven! Urgent change of agenda—and not by me.

A lesson for me there.

ISIS attack on a Paris lycée. Over a hundred students killed and many more wounded. Anti-Muslim flash mobs trying to burn down mosques. Terror on the streets of Muslim *arrondissements.* Media going berserk with 'What kind of God allows such evil to flourish?'

Where is God, indeed?

The pope and the Grand Mufti of Saudi Arabia must surely meet and issue a joint plea for restraint.

But hang on. What kind of delusion is it that either or both of us can have the slightest influence on crazed or terrified people obsessed by the shallow certainty of their prejudiced fear?

The weary answer must be that though almost exhausted by unspeakable violence, we must pray for the strength to speak out, the courage to rethink who we are and the wisdom to act with energy and confidence.

Easy to say, harder and harder to do.

God give me strength.

The plain fact screaming at us is that religious certainty is destructive of religious faith and generates evil, and that surely applies to Christianity as well as Islam.

Did I just write that?

Yes.

I remember Francis daring to say that our church must no longer be barricaded in our certainties, an outlook which causes our minds and hearts to be closed. In his words: 'God is not found in neat, orderly places distant from reality; rather, we encounter God where we are on the often-rocky road of life.'

The comfort and theatre of the Vatican seem to me far from the shores of Galilee and the path to Golgotha.

Why must Christ be re-crucified daily?

'Your adversary the devil prowls around like a roaring lion, seeking someone to devour.'

Atheists don't believe in God. OK. Fine. Well, not so fine, though God knows, we all have our moments, but I wish non-believers would consider the devil as more than just an outdated metaphor.

I sometimes think that the certainty of disbelief is really just the same limitation of imagination that causes our lot to insist we're the only mob with the whole truth.

The painful fact is that my belief in the power of evil reinforces my need to believe in a God of the good.

In my moments of desolation, I ask myself whether... no, why there's some objective... some gloatingly destructive form of evil.

Answer: because there is.

The universe is held together in dreadful tension. That's where we start from. God may be all loving but is God all powerful?

Cats and pigeons.

So... how to convince the frightened Parisians that a soft answer turneth away wrath?

I must speak to the Grand Mufti.

And also to God only knows whom.

If God knows.

Tuesday, December 16th

Feast of Blessed Filip Siphong Onphithakt (1907–1940).

Bit of a mouthful for us, but then English must be a bit of a mouthful for the Thai's. He was a catechist father of five children, and when his parish priest was expelled by the Thai government hostile to Christianity, he simply took over the parish and ministered to his parishioners. For protesting against police harassment of Catholics, he was made to report to police headquarters in Mukdahan. On the way, he was ambushed, tortured and murdered. A saint. And halfwits around here blather on about the impossibility of married priests. To my way of thinking, Filip Siphong Onphithakt was a much more inspiring priest than some of the clerical fusspots, time servers and refugees from reality I've bumped into over the years. Possibly including me, but that's another story. Actually not. Actually this bundle of contradictions, actually. Where was I? Of course, Blessed Filip Siphong Onphithakt. My hero. He was ordained not by the institution of the church but by his parishioners and by God. I will pray to him to open the hearts of desiccated canon lawyers and reactionary theologians.

The Grand Mufti is busy.

And no sooner had I made a personal call than a sharp rebuke from Cardinal Mendoza graces my in-box.

'The one true Holy Catholic Faith may invite defective faiths to listen to the church, but we must never allow them to stand beside us as equals. Truth is the truth our martyrs died for. Our task is to keep the faith. Keep it and treasure it.'

Time to face the facts. My suspicion was right. I'm being bugged. Every word I say is being scrutinised by my opponents. Is it just me, or has this been going on... forever? Did the apostles exercise mutual surveillance? Can this current so-called heart of Christianity really be a nest of vipers?

To whom do I turn? And having turned, then have to whisper to...?

This isn't happening... except it's taken me a fortnight to understand that it is. The pope is starring in some tacky Hollywood spy movie set in the Vatican—a travesty of everything we've stood for, evangelised, lived and died for.

Or is it just the technological update of what has always happened over two centuries

God help me. Is anything wholly sacrosanct? The Bishop of Rome is a prisoner in his own bastion of the one true faith.

Do _not_ discuss!

Wednesday, December 17th

Feast of St Olympias of Constantinople.

Birth date unknown, but Olympias died on July 25th 408, which is why we celebrate her in December. Best not to ask too many questions of the legislators in these parts. Like St Mary di Rosa though much, much wealthier, Olympias knocked back marriage proposals and became a deacon, though deacons can marry, but too many questions can lead to etc. Anyway, Olympias brought a group of pious women into her home beautiful and instead of gossiping, holding parties and being generally fashionable and useless to society, they spent their days helping the poor. They built a hospital and an orphanage, worked in both and sheltered expelled monks from nearby nasty Nitria. It's as simple and noble as that. Except not. Olympias gave away so much of her wealth that her friend, Saint John Chrysostom (not that he was a saint at the time but he had his wits about him) told her to steady on and put a break on the philanthropy, which she did, though continuing to underwrite his good works. For her trouble and generosity, she was persecuted, her community was given the heave-ho, her house was seized and sold (I'd like to know the details. Someone, I'd say a bishop, made a motza) and she spent the rest of her days as a refugee in nearby, probably very nasty Nicomedia. All I can say is that I know how she felt. When the time comes, I have one or two questions to ask my Maker. In the meantime, St Olympias of Constantinople, I feel your pain and wish there were many more deacons like you in the church. Personally, I would have ordained you.

'My dear companion in Christ,

I have come to the awful realization that my apartment in the Vatican has listening devices installed, and for all I know, other areas may also be under surveillance. This is scandalous. No, criminal. No, worse. Surely sinful. And these days, that's not a judgment I pass lightly. Let's face it, this supposedly Roman central heart of our almighty and, in extremis, loving God (let's bloody well hope God is all-loving) now is simultaneously and devilishly self-destructive.

What this Vatican double agent state of affairs shamefully proclaims is that our one true church of God has no trust in its divine legitimacy.

Like the brilliant East German Stasi, we're reduced to spying on each other. I wonder what on high even the ever-differing apostles might think of that.

But the fact must be faced that within these walls there is a powerful faction opposed to my papacy and determined to destroy it.

Without being over-dramatic, I recall the sudden demise of my potentially liberal predecessor, John Paul I, and the more than normally swift election of the saintly but staunchly conservative Saint John Paul II.

It would now appear that in our day-to-day lives, privacy may not be assumed.

Accordingly, while our informal exchanges need not be over-edited, our more personal conversations will need to be *sotto voce*. My delight in sacred music is well known, so henceforth, I shall have it played loudly during all encounters which I deem to be delicate. The raising of my right hand will indicate our need to lower our voices on whatever confidential subject we're discussing or whatever personal exchanges we deem needful.

I can hardly believe I have to write this, but then, as you know, I can hardly believe that I am the Bishop of Rome. Nonetheless, sensible caution is vital. It goes without saying that your special friendship is a gift I hold precious, and your loyalty is a support I desperately rely on.

Let all four of us give thanks for the blessing of our happy association while always being alert to such danger as would violate our affinity.

In confidence,

Mario.'
Signed copy to Dario, Sister Angelica and Ennio.

The walls may have ears, but the heart has its needs. And on reflection, flying to Paris or Riyadh might be seen—or be projected—as a stunt. And, of course, accidents can happen. I'll speak from the balcony. I must conserve my strength to fight the external force of evil and the internal force of... ambition?

But it would be helpful to know the listening leader. It can't be Mendoza; I'd be surprised if he believed in the existence of electricity. It surely couldn't be Olivier. He's embraced traditionalism but he'd surely never stoop to bugging the pope's private quarters. What do we call it in Australia? A rat in the ranks.

But who?

Boldness may not always be my friend, but now vigilance must be.

And so to the pathetic reduction of papal conspiracy theories.

The start of madness or the realisation of... this unreal reality the faithful for centuries have believed was God's revelation when all the time it's been little less than grubby power politics doused in pretty putrid holy water.

Thursday, December 18th

Feast of St Mawnan of Cornwall.

Mawnan's dates of birth and death are unknown. In Cornwall—a Celtic country I love, especially when the Cornish say, slightly too loudly, 'I'm going up to England for the day.' I'm with them. Apparently, whenever it was that he lived, Mawnan was considered to be a saint by the locals, and they should know. The official biogs of saints note that no reliable information about Mawnan has survived. If I had a son—which I don't—I wouldn't call him Mawnan, even if I intended retiring to Cornwall, but given all we know about him—practically nothing—Mawnan is my kind of saint. He offers hope to us all.

Three boatloads of African refugees drown. Children's bodies washed up on Italian beach. One baby girl less than a week old. Someone's beloved daughter. My own little daughter. I weep at the thought. My body, blood, soul and divinity. Can a pope understand such love?

This one can.

Is that God's grace or my sin?

My pain and anger explode. I am every father of every daughter. I am the father of <u>my</u> daughter. I flame into outrage. This pope doesn't just feel the pain. He lives every moment of it.

Politicians call for measures to turn back all boats and deny all so-called—nay, defamed—illegal refugees entry to Europe.

We Australians discovered the cruel answer, and Europe trumpets that they must follow our wretched example. I mean, how much shame must an Australian bear for this celebratory denial of humanity?

'It is expedient that one man should die for the people. Even more expedient, one child. The only way to stop the boats is to make it clear to every illegal maritime traveller that they will never <u>ever</u> be permitted to settle in our country. It's harsh but in the end, it's humane and will save thousands of lives, not least those of infants and children. Suffer the little children to stay where they are and fucking well suffer.'

Come to think of it, King Herod probably had the right idea slaughtering babies just in case one of them might grow up to threaten his throne.

Harsh, but in the end, humane.

'Give way to lefty woolly-minded liberals, and before you know it, our streets and suburbs won't be safe from marauding hordes of drug-addled black or brown teenagers robbing, looting and murdering, not to mention radical Islamic mullahs shrieking for sanctions on Israel. It's already happening in Melbourne. People are terrified to leave their houses at night.'

And so it goes on. I read it every day in the Australian Murdoch press.

I gather Rupert Murdoch is a papal Knight Commander of St. Gregory.

With, I'm sure, Saint Gregory, I vomit in the face of such self-serving, wilful blindness, and worse, out and out racism perversely disguised as concern for the lives of refugees.

Every human being has a moral obligation to help those in need.

For God's sake, that's what it means to be human.

But Australia has lifted racism, injustice and torture to a new level of smugness and a deceitful refinement of evil. We have perfected the blasphemy of hiding our victims away from the population and leaving them to rot for years in detention either in hotel prisons or off-shore islands.

These days, the Good Samaritan would report his victim and have him/her and the kids packed off to Nauru, Manus Island or Rwanda, and post-Christian governments would applaud and probably be enthusiastically re-elected for their compassionate stand against 'illegal entries'.

Talk about Pilate washing his hands! Maybe we need a few more sentimental Christmas carols about away mangers and little refugee babies asleep in their haybeds and likely to be stranded off-shore until…

Oh, yes, we outsource our sins and pay the torturers at an astronomic cost—no sin too expensive for the willingly blindfolded voters—and then to put icing on the turd, we specialize in demonising our victims as monsters who throw their children overboard…

another justification for making conditions increasingly painful and hopeless in the name of benevolent deterrence.

'We are a generous and open-hearted people who will decide who comes into this country and the circumstances under which they will suffer for trying to escape tyranny and seek a better life for their families.'

Talk about legalized xenophobia. And most breathtakingly of all, we sanctimoniously describe our victims as queue jumpers in the same way that those Jews who escaped the Nazis were presumably concentration camp queue jumpers.

Jesus wept.

And Australian politicians of both major parties remain complicit in hypocritical persecution.

Like Francis, I must go to the shore of welcoming Lampedusa and speak God's truth to the unwelcoming racist hypocrites of Europe.

'Woe unto you…for ye are like unto whited sepulchres, which indeed appear beautiful outward, but are within full of dead men's bones, and of all uncleanness'.

Friday, December 19th

Feast of Blessed Kazimiera Wolowska (1879–1942).

Polish nun who became prioress of a Sisters of the Immaculate Conception of the Blessed Virgin convent in Slonim Belarus. Together with her fellow nuns, she sheltered, hid and taught Jews during the Nazi persecutions, for which heroic courage she was imprisoned and executed. Indeed, there must be a heaven.

FROM THE ISLAND OF LAMPEDUSA

The Grand Mufti of Saudi Arabia has suddenly arrived at Lampedusa without gracious consultation, but together we have embraced and expressed our mutual concern for all of God's creatures fleeing from persecution.

The compassionate people of Lampedusa have reached exhaustion in their Christ-like welcoming of the persecuted, but in their inspiring faith, they will gallantly soldier on, and yet urgent advice from my Secretary of State tells me that again, every European country except Germany fears an overwhelming invasion of 'the infidel' as a result of my visit.

They claim that Europe's second—and finally—successful Islamic invasion advances in the name of our suicidal invitation for them to pour in and eventually overrun all our democratic and Christian values, and ultimately our very way of life.

The agument goes that in two to three generations, Europe will move from being Christian (which, by the way, it no longer is) to being Islamic.

Best I remain silent for the moment as my prediction is that now in two generations or fewer, the majority of Islamic youth will behave as Christian youth did and do.

Under the influence of our western mixture of materialism and enlightenment—more on that once my anger settles a little—they'll be seduced by the globalization of superficiality and they'll put religion behind them, leaving it to the diminishing number of clergy, the old and the dying.

And given the ever-expanding equality of women—a grace I applaud—I can't envisage new generations of educated young Islamic women (where permitted) continuing to be brainwashed by their revoltingly oppressive religion and its primitive imams into rejoicing in the chains of their scriptural inferiority.

Yes, no pope should ever say this, but it's fucking well true as most Christian women will attest because to our shame and ignorance, we committed the same sins.

Ask any remaining nun.

Will Islam never learn from our Christian historical mistakes and shame?

Yes, I just wrote that.

It's late but not too late to speak the truth which must not be spoken.

Calm down, Mario. You've been sounding off.

A Jamesons, I think.

OK, not the most optimistic of outlooks, but one which seems to me by no means unlikely; the larger and more important message being how on earth our church can re-evangelise two plugged-in, Tik-

Tok and computer game crazy generations. The Stations of the Cross as God of War, and the Resurrection as Diablo 2 Resurrected?

God will indeed have to move in a mysterious way his wonders to perform.

And load up on the royalties.

Needless to say, certain cardinals are quick off the mark to question joint statements from the pope and the mullah. And via informed Vatican sources—in this case the likeable and always well-informed American Vatican correspondent for *America*, a Jesuit monthly magazine—I learn that three nights ago in a private room at the disgustingly expensive Imàgo Restaurant in Hotel Hassler Roma (not too many of God's poor make the pilgrimage to that gastronomic shrine) Sardinia's Cardinal Gino Luciano and Malta's Cardinal Paulo Di Giorgio were hosted by Honduras Cardinal Miguel de Hernandez and, surprise surprise, Cardinal Olivier Gabriel Foncha, the latter picking up the tab.

I wonder what principal subject their conversation touched on.

But back to Lampedusa: may those poor victims of evil whom we prayed for and buried today rest in peace.

'Weep not for me but for yourselves and for your children.'

Let us pray for guidance and reflect on the nature of the pilgrimage of faith before our church trumpets too triumphantly our supposed answers to life's mysteries.

How to combine humility with hope?

Amen.

PS: Dear Lord, I think I'm losing it. Not a good look for a pope. Please help me to effing well go to sleep.

I know, Angelica. My penance: the rosary. The Sorrowful Mysteries.

Saturday, December 20th

Feast of Pope St Zephyrnus about whose life before becoming pope apparently little to nothing is known.

He was probably born after 150, and because of what he did that we don't know much about—or, indeed, anything—he was elected as our 15th pope. What's not to like? Rumour has it that he wasn't much of a theologian—fine by me—though he was a competent manager. He had it easy. There wasn't a Vatican then. Zephyrnus decreed that all ordinations should take place in front of the faithful—not what I'd call wildly controversial—and it would appear that he had some difficulty in convincing all the faithful that Christ was God—what I'd call pre-post-modern with sanctus bells on. Oh, and he got on well with the future Pope St Callistus I, which is always a nice thing for a pope, though believe me, bloody hard to set up. Zephyrnus died of natural causes, which endears him to me, and for which grace I pray, though something increasingly niggling in me would like to know what those natural causes might be. Intimations of mortality. Probably healthy. Anyway, I doubt that there's a movie in the life of St Zephyrnus—as I'm sure there won't be in mine.

Today, for some reason, Ennio seemed on edge. Almost upset. It's absolutely not like his carefree confident self. I decided not to mention it during our usual snack time, but later this evening when he called by and still seemed disturbed, I felt the need to try and get him to talk about it.

You don't seem yourself today. Is something bothering you?

'I'm fine.'

You don't give that impression.

'It's nothing.'

Would you like to talk about it?

'No, thanks.'

I'm not just the pope, you know. I'm also an ordinary priest used to helping people.

'I'm fine.'

Have you been... seeing someone?

'Perhaps.

You're missing Mirella. When's your next leave?
'Not until next month.'
I could arrange for it to be brought forward.
'I'm fine.'
I wish I believed you.
'Cose accadono.' (Stuff happens.)
Que cosa di cose? (What kind of stuff?)
'I'm fine. Just a bad day.'
If I can help in any way. You know you can always trust me.
'Yes. Thank you.'
We trust each other.
'Yes.'
Did my letter cause you concern?
'All good.'
You're sure?
'Like I said, all good.'
I've had one of those days, too. I don't suppose you feel up to...
'Of course. The pleasure's mine.'
Likewise. *Piacere.*
'I'm glad.'
Ennio's both a man and a lad. I must try to find what's worrying him.

Sunday, December 21st

Feast of St Peter Canisius (1521–1597).

Jesuit theologian, major force in the counter revolution, basically very conservative though always polite and patient in argument. Knew himself well and had no delusions of intellectual brilliance. Seemed to believe that while he was a second-rate mind, he was a clear writer who adapted his style for the audience he was writing for: children, adolescents or adults. His catechisms became the teaching books of the reforming Catholic world. He was also fearless in his Fr James Bond way. Instead of guns and martini mixes, he travelled with boxes packed with huge tomes of the decisions of the Council of Trent. We have one or two things in common, though for all his fame and achievements, I don't think I'd like him much. Nor he me. But I admire him.

Expected, yet always more heart-breaking news from Afghanistan.

Girls' education even further limited—if that were possible with these demented, prehistoric barbarian imams.

Inevitably.

It makes we want to scream out to the heavens against these primitive pagan hijackers of God. These mental defectives are as contemptible as they're blasphemous. And all this criminality and sin is carried out in the name of the Prophet.

What is it about male-invented religion which causes this evil prejudice?

Mind you, we Catholics are almost as primitive with our views on women priests.

Time for a third whiskey.

Monday, December 22nd

Feast of St Zeno, martyred in 303.

This intelligent, though arguably foolhardy soldier was seized and condemned to death for laughing while that deluded, feral, blood-thirsty, preposterous and deeply evil Emperor Diocletian offered a sacrifice to the Roman God, Ceres. Whenever I see a photo of the Emperor Putin, I think of the vomit-inducing Diocletian. Zeno had his jaws shattered and was then beheaded. A sceptic after my own heart but a hero who, shamefully, I fear I'd never have the courage to emulate. The Romans really were a disgustingly sadistic mob. And here I am, Bishop of Rome.

The struggling on-going story of making synods central to our faith is testament to the power of its eventual success. And that struggle remains both on and going. And proof of the synods' power of revival and renewal is the calculating opposition to the movement by conservative bishops and preciously lace vestment liturgical traditionalists who are the increasingly concerning graduates of frightened, die-hard seminaries.

The proof of the wisdom of synodal conversation is the terror hidebound, clerical conservatives have of being replaced by the faithful—or what's left of them in parts of Europe and Australia. Mind you, I have to congratulate the sharp insight of Chilean Cardinal Carlos Silva Gonzales who slyly and not inaccurately remarked that synods spend time listening to the Church that no longer goes to church.

He certainly has a point, though on reflection, when the one-time faithful hordes who reject the institutional church in their millions are willing to continue their conversation from the outside, something tells me that the Holy Spirit is surely sending us a message.

Not that it's all that simple or clear. No way. And I wish I had a clear answer. But then we've always had a clear and unquestionable answer. The only one, according to us.

We're totally right and the rest of the world is wrong.

And look where it's getting us now.

No questions, thank you. Father knows best, and His Grace knows even better. Jesus wasn't the divine prophet of democracy. He was the Son of God who preached the truth as delivered to the world by two centuries and more of infallible certitude.

It's called revelation.

Full stop.

Since when did the divinely unfranchised faithful decide that they could challenge the informed and ordained clergy? Who are the baying flock to advise the caring shepherd? So now, on any number of issues, the so-called sheep presume to out-argue the shepherds.

With what result?

The out-argued shepherds fall back on the good old Roman Empire rule of total obedience of the slaves to their masters.

And to make matters worse, as you'd expect, so many of those pesky questioners are women. Like, WTF would they know?

Answer: since they began to do so, and when told to hold their tongue, they simply used their qualifications to out-argue the increasingly wrong-footed male clerical experts.

And then to add insult to injury, so many of those women were and are nuns—women who are infinitely more academically and theologically literate than the gavel-banging priests and bishops who are threatened by what they see as the insurrection of the peasants.

And I'm now in the middle of this unholy shit fight—as St Peter might say. I mean, is it so very hard to face up to the historical truth of our many mistakes?

OK, God may not make mistakes, but his creatures sure have and still do.

Can't we just admit all the pathetic nonsense of our wrongs—our sins—of the past and listen to the voices of our dearest sons and daughters—especially of our dearest daughters.

In my heart, I know that those who have so angrily rejected the church—and God knows, on a bad day I'm probably one… almost definitely one—in their heart of hearts, these honest deniers yearn for the solace of the sacraments which, in their anger, they've deprived themselves of.

I believe in the divinity of everyone. Yes, everyone: believers, half believers, non-believers… even, after a few drinks, the fruitcake fringe of Pentecostal mania. And after a chaser, maybe even the Mormons.

Though on brief reflection, no to both those last two madnesses.

Sorry about that, Holy Spirit, but if your wisdom and blessing somehow move even the theological train wreck of that apple pie, self-congratulatory American fantasy, then I guess…

I don't know what I guess.

It's all getting too much.

All I ask for, God, is please, please just let me get to sleep.

I'm going mad.

Amen.

A-bloody-men

Tuesday, December 23

Feast of St John of Kanty (1390–1473).

John came from the back of beyond (I'm with him) and went on to shine—nay, dazzle—at Krakow University in Poland. (I'm miles behind him.) He was ordained (yes) and became professor of theology (not exactly Yours Truly). He created enemies (I'm with him) and, as a result, was booted out of his flash job. (In anticipation, I feel his pain.) He was shunted off to Olkusk, aka Nowheresville, where what do you think happened? Wait for it! Yes, he proved to be a total flop, the locals greatly disliking him (pain feeling again). But John persevered (I suppose that in my way, so do I. Or at least I try to) and eventually the oiks came to like him. (Still waiting). He looked after the poor who—spoiler alert—took advantage of him and his money. (It happens, though not to me I fervently hope). According to tradition, 'he slept little (ditto) ate sparingly (non ditto) and took no meat (like most saints, a bit weird, and wouldn't have pleased Sister Angelica). He went on a pilgrimage to Jerusalem, hoping to be martyred by the Turks but wasn't. (I don't feel his pain, but then neither did he). He ignored his health (not exactly a capital offence, though something tells me I should act on that front even though I know I won't) but went on to live for quite while (as I fervently hope to, though that niggling continues to niggle). He remained a good man (as I must try to be) and died of natural causes (as I prayerfully hope I will). A meandering and all-over-the-place kind of life, yet somehow John of Kanty became a saint. There may be a message in this curious biography.

A largely unspoken form of child abuse: the children of priests and religious who are virtually abandoned by the church.

Paul VI called clerical incontinence 'lamentable defection' even though, as we know, like it or not, the professed celibate, being normal, may elect or even need—yes, need—to 'sin' (and, yes, the quotation marks are aggressively mine) and the result of that failing may be conception of a child.

Surely such a child must never be aborted, and for that same reason, that the child's life is sacred because it is God infused, then the church must recognize its responsibility for the raising of that child.

Thus it must surely follow by the natural law that this special child has the right to know both their parents.

And the child surely also has the right never to be taught or allowed to think of themselves as tainted, unnatural or somehow cursed and apart from other children.

All these challenges, I must confess, have not infrequently demanded my painful consideration, and the plea for action by the founder of an adult group of such offspring must be retrieved from the dark recess in which the church has swept it.

Definitely a task for Dario.

Wednesday, December 24th

Feast of St Emilia, aunt of Pope St Gregory the Great.

She lived a holy life in her comfortable surroundings and advanced in piety, peace and love. When, after years, she and her sisters approached death, Emilia had a dream with a message from her great grandfather, Pope St Felix II, assuring her that she had a place in heaven. Divine networking. When friends and doctors tried to prolong her life, she told them to get lost and then died and went to heaven. It's a lovely story. Come to think of it, I'm a pope. I could reserve a place in heaven for my daughter, and if I knew how, I would. Who knows? I might. Never give up hope, Mario. This surely pious and apocryphal biography should not be lightly dismissed. Hope springs eternal, and for all we know, St Emilia may have had an out-of-body experience way ahead of her time. In this case, I choose to believe the truth within the myth. And all fathers, including popes for that matter, if the tiara fits, should pray for their daughters' eternal salvation. Amen.

It's a weird feeling waking up and then remembering I'm the pope. Not a natural Aussie reflex. And the sensation's even weirder when I say to myself, 'Good morning, Your Holiness. So what does it feel like being pope?'

Pretty uncomfortable to say the least, Your Holiness.

'I'd like to think that popes ought not to undergo some of the mad ravings I find my mind involuntarily entertaining.'

Did you entertain sinful thoughts, my son?

'No, father, they entertained me.'

Is this how a pope should be starting the day?

And that nutty dialogue aside but while we're on the subject, why does God's vicar on earth harbour what he knows are crazy prejudices? Against Pentecostalists, for example, babbling and yelling in their pathetically incomprehensible ravings.

'The Holy Spirit as K-pop. Our Top 40 Salvation Sensations this week see a shock with *Jesus, No Need for Visas* dropping out of our Top Ten Choral Christian Commandments, while *Jesus, You Are My Gracebook Friend* is rocketing up the charts from Number 12 in the Choral Commandments to Number 7. And this week's Beatitude Bullet is *The Seven Gifts of The Holy Ghostest with the Mostest*, and believe me, they ain't the seven deadly hymns. And remember, for a mere ten bucks a week—all credit cards accepted—at home you can download every new Raise the Praise Classic and sing along to choral accompaniment by the Band of Angels and the sweet beat backing of our all-girl Faith Hope and Charity combo. Delaying would be a sin. Donate now, and salvation sensation will be yours.'

My second-rate Wollongong teenage disc jockey phase has never left me.

Indeed, for all I know, I'm the first teenage pope.

This madness keeps erupting.

Too little holy water with the Jamesons.

Which brings me again to the Mormons. I mean, let's face it, The Book of Mormon is the great American novel.

I know we Catholics subscribe to some pretty wacko beliefs—The Apostles' Creed to name but twenty—but Joseph Smith and the golden plates in reformed Egyptian translated by him—clever dick—and afterwards returned to the angel who whisked them safely back up to heaven, though this was well after Christ popped over to the USA post-resurrection with the good news—not all that good, though, for any black men wanting to be ordained, well, until 1978…

I mean, it's Donald Trump meets *Finnegan's Wake*.

And they all lived Americanly ever after.

So now to ecumenism; and I'm just the pope for it.

Item on today's agenda: Catholics For Coal: Climate Change Sanity in a Woke World.

Is the International Latin Mass Anti-Vaccination Gregorian Choir thrown in for comic relief? Is this some kind of April Fools' Day joke?

I'm sorry, but no. I'm still the bloody pope. Or supposed to be.

Why the fuck is this on the pope's agenda for today? It's really beyond endurance. I mean, what's happening in this madhouse, and why am I being railroaded by my most loyal ally? He's my Secretary of State and yes, of course he has my confidence, and I know I have his, but...

He knows my stance. The earth goes round the sun, and gravity's gravity. The science is in. The world isn't flat, and <u>their</u> world is round the bend.

Laudato Si, full stop.

From now on, I'm calling the shots and... but...

No, it's surely not possible.

He never would.

Not Dario.

I'm <u>not</u> going mad and I will decide which particular bunch of raving loonies I have to meet on an hourly basis.

Anyway, they're all bloody bonkers.

Except the ones who aren't.

And I'm the pope.

And I'm <u>not</u> going mad.

And this is happening.

Unless it isn't.

And I need another a drink.

Thursday, December 25th

Feast of a baby boy about whom much is known, much is myth and much more is inspirational.

When I think about a boy from the wrong side of the tracks growing up and ending up in the God game, all my boyish and adolescent experiences and tin triumphs and messes and discoveries and disasters and bewilderment and accidental progress... all these and all the rest of the joy and confusion that is growing up... when they cascade into my memory, I have to ask myself whether gentle Jesus meek and mild went through all the madness and the mayhem and the muck that I swam through. And, of course, did He know He was God (as we believe) as He ducked and weaved and denied and delighted? His first... everything. What was it like? First sitting on the pot applause. First catch of a ball. First birthday party. First day at whatever school was. First sleep-over. First failure at anything. First kiss (He's fully man as well as fully God, remember). First wet dream. First wank. Any guilt, or was it super and natural and great fun? First yearning to embrace another human being. And when He was naughty (surely he must have been... just a teeny-weeny bit) did He ever get caught? And did He try whatever it was lots more times? And with His mates? Or did He spend the day reading the psalms and helping old Jewish ladies cross whatever the road was? I guess only God knows the answer, which, of course, isn't an answer but a lifetime lingering question. I can somehow hear his twenty-something-year-old carpenter father saying, 'Joshua's a bright lad, but he's too enthusiastic to do everything in a single day. Measure twice, cut once; It's the only way to make a table.' And Mary replies, 'Leave the boy alone. He does things his way. He'll be alright. Anyway, he mightn't want to become a carpenter. 'Fine by me. He can become anything he likes as long as it's not a fisherman. Rum lot, that mob. Not too bright and smelly with it.' As usual, I can't just embrace the nothingness and everythingness of this great big mystery. I always have to spoil the party by being me. But it's not my feast; it's His, so I lose myself in ritual in St Peter's and that way wish Him a happy birthday and a holy Christmas. Still, that other part of me always wonders whether He ever dared to have a blast of a birthday and a merry Christmas, or are those concepts too unGodly? But... and this is seriously shit: also sharing this baby's birthday are the Blessed Michael Nakashima (1583–1628) and four women of the early church, St Adalsindis, St Aburga, St Anastasia III and St Eugenia. All religious. Ever heard of any of them? Well, neither had I until I started out on this rocky pilgrimage. Don't know about you, Dad, but I reckon that having your feast day lumped in with the Son of God's has to be a bummer. Oh, yes, always on the side of the authorities, you'll rabbit on about them sharing their elevation. Bullshit. Hard for a star, however luminous, to shine when the Son of God is centre stage and in a follow spot. A bloody hard act to follow I'd dare to suggest. But they did. Michael Nakashima was a native Japanese Jesuit martyr with belief and balls. He hid missionaries and priests on the run. When the authorities caught him, they hauled him off to some place called Shimabara where they scalded him to death in the hot springs at Mount Ungen, wherever that may be. Interesting festive trivia. So every Christmas, let's also wish all five a happy feast day and a holy and a happy Christmas.

Christmas Day mass in St Peter's is one of my favourite celebrations. With the singing and the incense, you can smell joy, good will, happiness and hope. And now I'm the celebrant.

All the responses to the liturgy seem to be offered with a smile. It's a bit like being father of a family of 1.5 billion. You hope they'll all behave themselves for the day and not get too out of hand in the evening.

And as a good father has to do sometimes, it's best not to see some of the things they get up to. A father isn't chief of police together with judge and jury. Well, yes, he is, but a good father knows what not to see and then when to have a little chat.

One-and-a-half billion little chats.

Thinking about that, I decided that today would indeed be a holiday/holyday and I wouldn't spend any time at the office.

Sister Angelica hasn't pronounced on whether today is bounty or normal for the feast, so as with so many abstruse theological projections, I think it prudent to observe Wittgenstein's commandment: 'Whereof one cannot speak, thereof one must be silent.'

Christmas lunch was traditional: plate of mixed seafood, linguine with lobster, roasted salmon with potatoes, roasted vegetables seasoned with olive oil, rosemary, garlic and balsamic vinegar, then chestnut meringue. Small portions and large satisfaction.

Feast days should indeed be feasts, especially this one. And if all this wasn't bounty, I don't know what would be.

After lunch we exchanged gifts. I gave Sister Angelica a Japanese kitchen knife set with Damascus blue handles bought by Ennio half-price on the net. This Wollongong pope isn't one to miss a bargain.

She was delighted and said that she might now even try a Japanese recipe once she had mastered the surgery on some willing vegetables.

For Ennio, I got Dario to buy online a bottle of Giorgio Armani Acqua Di Gio fragrance, something Mirella will doubtless find alluring and, as a plus, will also grace my quarters during his visits.

Christmas present to self: a siesta and then listened to a cd of Bach's Christmas Oratorio by the *Weihnachtsoratorium* with Christa Ludwig and Fritz Wunderlich. Glorious and soul enriching.

Greatly enjoying, by now, my own company, I then read three Henry Lawson stories: *The Drover's Wife, The Bush Undertaker* and *The Union Buries Its Dead.* I thought back to a time when for me, Christmas meant searing heat and a cold beer, and then with self-indulgence verging on the sinful, I went early to bed.

Christus natus est.

Friday, December 26

Feast of Stephen when Good King Wensceslas looked out.

Stephen was one of the first deacons and he was ordained (if that's what they called it then) by one of the apostles. He was a fine preacher and argued that Jesus was the fulfilment of God's plan for the Jews. Not exactly good news for the temple high priests, and I expect you could chuck in the low priests with them. I mean, if today some zealot rocked up here at the Vatican and announced that we were all yesterday's religion and that he—or she. If only—had the new truth, I'm not sure that we wouldn't, in our own way, get rid of him/her quick smart. Another loony, probably a west coast American on the make. A crazy who preached salvation and accepted all credit cards. Anyway, the Sanhedrin recognised a disrupter when they saw one, condemned him legally (so clean and Godly) and had Stephen dragged out of Jerusalem and stoned to death. That awful murder was witnessed by Paul of Tarsus. And we know the rest. Oddly enough—superstition, perhaps—I've never met a Stephen I didn't like, even when their name was spelt with a 'v'. Well, not one I disliked so much that I remember disliking him. Which snobbery just goes to show that even Wollongong boys can be totally up themselves. Or true to themselves.

Awoke at 5 a.m. after a glorious night's deep sleep and feeling ready to take on the world.

Some prayers, however impudent, are clearly answered.

And by now I should have learnt that doubt is the flip side of faith. So, taking on the world... I shall summon to Rome the leaders of all male religious orders of priests for a debate on the theology of admitting women to the priesthood.

There will be an adjudication committee of three cardinals, three lay theologians and three nuns who lead their religious orders. Their adjudication will be advisory but not binding.

Next, every member of every religious order will vote as to their acceptance or rejection of the adjudication. This vote will also be advisory—the conservatives will at least love that. Finally, the synod of every parish will send one vote—yea or nay—to the Vatican, and parishes without synods will have forfeited their right to vote.

The pope will then decide on what action to take.

Even the Vatican Taliban who specialize in trumpeting the centrality of the church's unchanging laws and the unchallengeable authority of the pope will then have to obey.

Nothing like good old-fashioned authoritarianism to stymie authoritarianism.

I shall ask Dario to organize that this vital conversation takes place within the next twelve months and that no curia committee is to have the power of review. Sure, the church isn't a democracy, but the consensus of the faithful has long been regarded as the Holy Spirit's guide, and wisdom lies in listening. Then after listening: prayer, decision and authoritative action.

A first-rate decision, eh, Dad?

And while on the subject of listening, that particular faculty, together with the equally important capacity of watching, the simple fact is that they're the home industry of the curia. And, for that matter, the whole of the Vatican. ASIO, MI5 and the CIA combined aren't half so vigilant as the keen-eyed clerics who glide through the corridors of this place.

The political subtext of any papacy is the lobbying—nay, call it by its name: crusading—for the likely next pontifex maximus, Bishop of Rome.

Power is its purpose, and gossip is its currency.

No one drops in on, eats with, reviews a book by, delivers a sermon about, travels abroad on 'business' to meet... this litany could go on for pages and ages, the point being that in the subtlest of ways, this is a surveillance state. The Stasi were rank amateurs compared to our venerable intelligence network. And it's all conducted in the most brilliantly casual manner. 'I saw Cardinal X going into Cardinal Y's office this morning. Struck me a little odd.' 'My nephew who's now the sommelier at Santo Palato tells me that the other night, Cardinals A, B and C were entertaining Cardinal J who's just flown in from Wherever in Asia. He has a lot of sway in those parts. Our ever-vacillating friend Cardinal B picked up the tab. Interesting.' 'Cardinal Q's sermon on extending the third rite of confession appeared as an article in both *The Tablet* and *America*. Rallying the troops? An authoritative response is needed quick smart, wouldn't you say?' 'Not altogether sure about Cardinal J's interview on *Che Tempo Che Fa*. He was heavily pushing that it's time to re-examine Anglican orders. Do I detect the odour of Vegemite?'

And so it goes on daily. By all factions. Not least, the pope's, thank God. And most informative and useful it is, not least when gathering support for an initiative which might suggest that the church is capable of thinking and acting as if we weren't still living in the middle ages.

I call it INW. Information Never Wasted.

Dario is Mission Control and ensures that all INW intelligence is passed on to him by the Vatican Two Liberators and our allies, and once a week over a cup of coffee (or, with luck and after 4.49 p.m., something stronger) he gives me a summary of the state of Vatican play.

The play's the thing.

Saturday, December 27th

Feast of St John the Apostle.

He was a late teenage fisherman, probably of the handsome variety preferred by Oscar Wilde in Italian exile. And when this amazingly charismatic Jesus rocked up and said to John and his brother, James, 'Follow me,' they rolled up their nets and followed him, taking their nets with them I've always assumed. Tradition has it that John was the most faithful apostle of Jesus—good times and bad. The others tended to shine more during the good times. No wonder I wasn't christened John. He saw Jesus transfigured—easier said than explained, but that doesn't mean it didn't happen. He was at the Last Supper and he stayed at the foot of the cross with Jesus until the end. The others there were women, the gender we still refuse to ordain. John also saw the resurrected Jesus. It's not for nothing that he's known as the beloved disciple. In his old age, he wrote his gospel, and his message was and remains simple and resonant: God is love. John was the first genius to announce this about a god. And he either did or didn't write The Book of Revelation, the first modern book of religious science fiction, and as we all know, science fiction is narrative prophecy. Sceptics should remember that Dick Tracy's fantastically absurd and impossible (but oh, so longed for by us young readers) visual wrist watch is now the phone in everyone's pocket. St John was way, way ahead of us. I would have liked him, but then, who wouldn't? And he's the patron saint of authors, so I guess that however distantly, we both have writing in common. In my case on the computer. And pretty boy young John became a wise bearded codger who lived to a ripe old age, being the only apostle to die naturally rather than being martyred, and I hope to follow, however humbly, in his footsteps.

Met briefly this morning with an engaging canon lawyer—never thought I would write that oxymoron—from the UK. He tells me he's disturbed by the highly conservative views of English seminarians over the last ten years. He sees too many of them as wanting to flounce about in vestments and say the Latin Mass in what he calls nostalgic clerical romanticism and he blames the teaching of JP2 that somehow on ordination, priests are ontologically changed. Don't worry, Dad. It's just a fancy word meaning 'enhanced' or 'something transcendental'. The point being that after ordination, these new priests see themselves—and are taught to see themselves—as some kind of clerical aristocracy.

This strikes me as disturbing.

Speaking as an accidental pope, I feel quite the opposite of such social elevation. I thought I was meant to be the servant of the servants of God and I see myself more on a treadmill than a pedestal but then what would I know?

I questioned the engaging canon lawyer as to whether this dressing up outlook—religious drag—resulted from repressed homosexual inclinations. He smiled and suggested that I might not be wrong.

I've asked him to write me a detailed analysis of his observations with recommendations for reforming this dangerously unChristlike delusion. I also mentioned that such misapprehension was not unknown in the exalted ranks of the curia and that deference in these parts not infrequently combines theatricality with hypocrisy.

His smile broadened.

If he were fifteen years younger, I'd have made him a bishop on the spot.

And for some reason, I'm worried about Dario. Well, perhaps not so much worried as uncomfortable. Concerned even. Over Christmas he seems to have been... I don't know... distant. Something in his personal life, no doubt, unless he's party to some knowledge he fears will distress me should I find out. Which, of course, I will, though whether I'll be distressed remains to be seen. Nothing shocks me now. Everything is par for the Vatican course, and papal politicking doesn't slow down for the sacred season; rather, the celebrations lubricate the conspiracies.

I'll find the right time to have a friendly chat with Dario.

Sunday, December 28th

Feast of the Holy Innocents Martyrs.

And just in case we want to delude ourselves that humanity has made strides in putting such barbarism behind us, we only have to look at the holy innocents blasted off the face of the earth today in wars and terror attacks. Sometimes, I near despair when I consider the power of evil in the world. I suppose it would be impossible for believers, agnostics and atheists to band together for the sake of civilisation. And yet, why should it be impossible? As I'm clearly part of the question, what further can I do to be part of the answer?

Seeing is disbelieving. In tomorrow's *L'Osservatore Romano*, an interview with Ernesto Mendoza.

Either he or the interviewer were drunk or stoned.

Or both were both.

The Grand Inquisitor says that there are 'divine Holy Ghost moments' in the life of a person and the life of the church. Suffering cleanses the soul and clarifies vision. He thanks God for this blessing and now feels empowered to reform the Congregation for the Doctrine of the Faith. He will consider that rather than ending the careers of 'over enthusiastic' theologians, 'it might be more fruitful to engage them in respectful conversation with the Prefect of the Dicastery to discern points of agreement and focus on propositions deserving of ongoing study and clarification.'

Mendoza's fan club will be having heart attacks before they reach the end of the article.

As well they might, since it concludes: 'The church of Christ must have the confidence to welcome ongoing revelation through the prayer and the scholarship of theologians, clerical and lay.'

'And lay'!

Next, he'll be campaigning for optional celibacy of the clergy and compulsory yearly synods chaired by women.

And if these revolutionary insights continue, papal power play has suddenly swerved dangerously left, and Olivier will be having the holy heebie jeebies.

If he sends me gifts of chocolates, fruit or wine, I must insist he tries them first in my presence.

Saint Pope John Paul the First, pray for me.

Fervently.

Monday, December 29th

Feast of St Thomas a Becket (1119–1170).

He was a bright student, then a brilliant administrator and soldier. When his father went broke, Thomas had to set to work and he quickly proved to be a shrewd businessman. He became Archdeacon of Canterbury and immediately caught the eye of King Henry II, who made him chancellor. The two of them—Thomas 15 years older than the monarch—became the closest of friends. In today's terms, Thomas in office behaved in an extravagant and vulgar manner, somewhere between Mr Nouveau Out to Prove, and Mr Flash with

Panache, but either way, he was very much the King's man. Little wonder that Henry made him Archbishop of Canterbury. And the rest, as they say, is why we celebrate him today. To cut a painful story short, Thomas refused to follow the king's instructions (money, of course) and stood up for the church in England. Neither would give way. 'Who will rid me of this troublesome priest?' followed by murder in the cathedral. In a moment, Thomas made a choice and paid for it with his life. I've never experienced that pivotal moment, not even when elected pope. I knew it wasn't the Holy Spirit who had me elected; it was the unholy mess of the divided conclave. My life has been one of unworthy advancement, always for the wrong reasons. At least I can admit it, but it still... I don't know... at midnight, it leaves me... reassured how second-rate I really am. I wish I had Thomas a Becket's fire in the soul. But I don't.

Revolutionary insights.

Just when my despair at the clerically eunuch trumpeting of truth, tradition and unquestioning obedience reaches its nightmarish depths—no wonder so many of my priestly contemporaries fled the church in search of sanity over guilt—the invigorating wind of the Holy Spirit enters my soul in the witness of America's true prophet, Sister Joan Chittister.

Her life awakens my nightmares to fanfares of faith, hope, charity and—God help us—tradition rediscovered.

In her bluntly eloquent but theologically liberating way, Sister Joan talked more sense than however many busloads of bishops or charabangs of cardinals... well, frankly, since the Second Vatican Council.

She speaks experience, hope and Eucharistic consolation to just about every Catholic who has left the church in despair at the tsunami of sin, guilt and salvation which depends on strict obedience to the clergy's road rules—an insistence which the statute-following subjects were swamped with—no, submerged under—in their Catholic education.

America's own Sister Joan Chittister speaks to all denominations and all faiths in inviting them to join hands rather than push each other aside in the name of terrifying truth.

Her simple message is that God, who is love, has faith in us all, so with faith in that love, we can be confident that even our stumbles can become steps to eternal love.

And heroic disciple that she was, she accompanied condemned criminals to death on their last walk to life everlasting.

This holy woman must surely have distant roots in Wollongong.

She was and is of the surf, a wild and confident rider.

She should have been pope.

Tuesday, December 30th

Feast of St Hermes of Moesia in Bulgaria.

It appears that he was an exorcist and died about 300. We know nothing else about him, but somehow he landed sainthood. What would he be today: a psychiatrist, a shonky American TV evangelist or… an exorcist? Possession by the devil interests me.

If the exorcism ritual works, do we explain it away? Is the devil unable to conquer ancient religious ritual (wouldn't that be nice?) or can faith move psychological mountains? Would have been interesting to watch St Hermes of Moesia work. Ah, the supernatural!

I believe in angels because I believe in the need for them. They're surely the most glorious metaphors ever created by the human poetic mind.

They fight, they sing, they fly, they announce, they're beautiful (ask any artist), they guard, they go psycho in dreams, and as messengers, they put all the world's postal services to shame, especially Australia's dreadful excuse for one.

And William Blake's angels' perfectly sculpted non-bodies are obviously the result of punishing work-outs between hymns.

Angels deliver.

They also have the most exotic names ever imagined: Seraphim, Raziel, Uriel, Sandalphon, Yesod, Malkuth… check them out, Dad. If I had a son, I'd certainly consider calling him Netzach or Hashmallin, though obviously I'd have to discuss this with his mother. And for the record, I bet cherubs don't pee or poo.

Angelic shit is unimaginable—a further proof of their existence.

And when it comes to special pleading before God, Mary aside, they're by far the best lawyers in the heavenly court, every one a KC.

If only they could cook, they'd be perfect, but I guess God has to reserve a few special gifts for the deity, and only God knows how to cook up a whole universe with a deliciously heavenly icing of angels.

Mind you, those fallen ones are absolute buggers: envious, rebellious, ugly (yuk!) and devilish workaholics who deserve to have their wings clipped.

Interesting, too, how other Christian religions—even the wacko fruitcake brands—feel the need for angels.

And while on that subject, a big reach out to Islam for keeping these heavenly creatures busy. If they didn't exist, we'd have to invent them.

Where would God be without angels? Praising himself to the point of boredom, you'd have to think.

My own guardian angel combines admonition (frequent) with tolerance (always), and back in the day when I was a parish priest and later a bishop, my guardian angel was an almost infallible finder of parking spaces.

I suppose today's more out-there theologians would call angels 'energy', but in that anti-poetic abstraction, what a loss of form and beauty!

Let us follow the reassuring message angels always deliver: Do not be afraid.

My advice, *urbi et orbi*, is: don't leave home without one.

Wednesday, December 31st

Feast of Pope Saint Sylvester I (died 335).

Steady as she goes for the church in the time of that spiritual shape-changer, the Emperor Constantine. Can't see my obit as simple or as comprehensive as Sylvester's. He'd better set about praying for me—after all, we're in the same game.

Bounty. Wild garlic risotto, and as the bible says—somewhere... I forget... or perhaps it doesn't—but much more authoritatively, Sister Angelica insists that garlic is good for absolutely everything, so that's that, and I may well live forever. And so another eternal question is answered. But seriously, is there any dish on earth to trump risotto?

Glory and praise to you, oh Lord Jesus Christ and to your servant and cook, Sister Angelica.

Confession gets a bum rap these days.

Big mistake, especially when you can't avoid millions of uncertified crazies and raving ratbags on talkback radio and on social media shrieking out loud their agonised souls to rapt audiences worldwide.

In those hyperbolic circumstances, the simple duo of wounded but honest penitent using the function of a hidden and anonymous confessor to unburden themselves surely looks like the miracle cure from heaven the world has been waiting for.

Let's face it: The church discovered mental health two thousand years before psychologists got round to understanding it. And to top it off, our process is accessible, simple and free.

Yes, free.

And yes, Dad, I know everything's complex, not least institutional apology for ignorance and prejudice—which, by the way, has always been the curia's excuse to prevent all progress and keep the church comfortably in the middle ages—but basically, when we do things which in our hearts we feel or know aren't the expression of our better and true selves, then it's healthy that we face up to these limitations and express a desire to become our truer, better or even best selves.

You'll note, Mario, that I've carefully avoided the concept of sin.

Deliberately, because until recently, our theology hasn't dared to distinguish weaknesses and failings from sin.

Sin is huge and because of that, it's mortal: criminally deadly to the spirit.

Failings are different and are as weak as they're frequent.

God knows I should know.

On a bad day, my tally can be an endless explosion of my human imperfections, and let's face it, you'd have to reckon that papal weaknesses are quite rightly punished by gazillions of extra years in purgatory, though given life everlasting, God and God's gloriously unimaginable eternity as a beyond beautiful concept, I'm more than willing to place an each-way bet on God's mercy rather than my shortcomings.

And to hell with canon law's eternal hell verdicts!

I've always felt sad for George Pell's imprisonment: I refer to his lifetime languishing in medieval superstitious theology.

He was a historian first and then one of God's parking police forever after. A man trapped in authority and fear of human reality. God knows, I believe in the liberation of confession, but a cleric without doubt is unsuitable to hear confessions. He—disgracefully, always 'he'—becomes a bureaucrat in the ecclesiastical public service of eternal spiritual revenue-raising and authoritarian power.

Think of all those centuries of the wretchedly guilt-haunted penitents condemned to a lifetime of soul-destroying sins and their fiery consequences because of eating meat on Fridays, missing Sunday Mass, using contraceptives (it's called responsibility), expressing their God-given sexual inclinations (apparently God's curiously 'unnatural' gifts. Like, hello!) and, much more importantly… well just about every pleasure life offers.

That Australian Green Catechism the good nuns drilled into us (not without more than few ruler slaps on the knuckles) has a lot of twisted lives, rejecting faithful, despairing souls and millions of heartbroken mothers to answer for.

Certainty, almost everything it offers as truth is relative.

Of that, I'm now certain.

And as a lifetime wounded and fragile mistake maker, I speak for the lifetimes of wounded victims of that tradition because being wounded is something I sure know a lot about, and being pope doesn't in any way diminish the truth of my experience.

Believe this pope.

It's humility which will lead to the acceptance and redemption our faith freely offers humanity.

Over centuries, with the best of intentions and the worst of political power, we haven't actually encouraged the development of mature, adult consciences. But one thing I know is that it's never too late to start.

I believe that goodness is inherent in all humans—though in my experience, pretty latent in a good many of the curia, but let's not go any further down that track at the moment—and I fervently believe that something divine inside us speaks to us when we do wrong.

Of course, we can shout it down, and my theory certainly needs to come to terms with the sheer industrial scale evil of Stalin and

Hitler and Putin, but I must believe that deep down, we're all unsatisfied and unhappy when we go against our conscience.

That's why I fervently believe that the confessor—merely another vulnerable and frail human channel to God—should avoid giving amateur psychological advice and instead, encourage the penitent not to argue with God but rather to listen to God.

That way, we can all be instruments of our own healing and so gradually grow in faith and love.

And I'm a long way from liking certain contemporary American styles of confession as in the 'Go and buy two coffees, come back, and let's have a chat about this.'

It seems to me that the listening but invisible confessor offers greater freedom to the penitent than, with the best of intentions, the well-intentioned psychoanalyst getting in the way of God's unique highway of communication to each individual.

Trust in the Lord.

Which is why twice a week, anonymously, I secretly slip into the confessional boxes in St Peter's for an hour and do the work of an unknown good pastor: encourage the penitent to open themselves to their loving God and then listen.

That experience nourishes my faith and reinforces my hope.

And, I firmly believe, in the secret seal of the confessional.

The idea of mandatory reporting seems to me as misguided as it's impractical.

I mean, what am I supposed to do? Whip out my mobile phone, pop out from behind the screen, take a photo of the penitent, ask them for their mobile number and shoot the information off to the nearest police station?

It just doesn't work like that.

Yes, there are lacunae in my overview, but to support it, I'd reinstate the brilliantly conceived third rite of confession. It's in every way benevolent and complimentary to all us fragile humans and occasional sinners.

At the beginning of mass, we invite the congregation to silently consider how and where they've done wrong—for Christ's sake, we all bloody know—then we exhort them to open themselves to forgiveness for their failings. Then we invite them to receive communion.

As a result of that amazing grace, we can confidently leave the next stage of the process to God.

Confession has been, is and surely will always be the miracle drug the big pharmas can never isolate, manufacture nor patent.

Why?

Because as I've tried to outline (yes, to myself) our weakness becomes our strength when in our heart of hearts we swallow (great word in this case) not a pill, but an act of deep acceptance of our bewildering and bewildered humanity.

That gift of acceptance I try to live by.

Yes, like the rest of frail humanity, I often fail. Frequently. Often over and over again. But in my deepest and most truthful being, I know I want to become a better person, and that gives me strength.

Beat that, big pharmas!

And I say to all you agnostics and atheists and psychologists and the rest of us screwed-up ordinary mortals... when confession works, it works big.

And without expensive prescription drugs.

Bad luck, big pharmas.

Praise be to our loving and credit card-free God.

So, unbelievers, put aside your prejudices and dare to consider the sheer mental health genius of this spiritual gift of psychological soul-searching and cleansing.

Of course, you're probably scared to admit to the efficacity of this sacrament of genius because your whole professional and financial lives are at stake.

OK, ours too, but we live in a more dangerously glorious and poetically projected world.

You lot measure statistics. Nice. Clean. Reassuring on graphs.

I simply can't believe that an all-loving God files records of the human frailty our mysterious God has apparently graced us with.

Sin, yes.

Serious stuff, and we bloody well know when we commit it.

But mistakes… God invites us to a better way of life, especially in serving others less fortunate than ourselves.

Sounds good to me.

And after confession, God brilliantly looks after our next few battling days of the week because God's confessional church brings grace and peace to each and every confessional statistic.

Like me.

To sum up—and with a lifetime's experience of the confessional, painful as it may be for all you infallible doubters—the poetry of faith and its healing grace will always work in harmony with medical advancement.

Science and the sacraments.

The ongoing new miraculous partnership.

Thursday, January 1st

Feast of the Solemnity of Mary, Mother of God.

In the beginning was the Word and via Mary, the Word was made flesh. Let's face it, poetry. And Christianity's hugest and most glorious claim. All the rest of our faith which evolves from that is built on and predicated on this life-enhancing mystery. Thinking big. God clearly did. And yes, belief takes courage and daring… and, alas, not infrequently, willing suspension of disbelief in what less generous logicians might describe as fiction. But religion is imagination sieved through traumatic experience and more. So much more. And, frankly, so much more daring than the mathematics and gymnastics of logic. In the end, logic reaches its limits. Experience tells us that love conquers all, and in the realm of love, theology aspires—though not, God knows, without its historical stumbles!—to celebrate the inherent truths of poetry and music. And I'm also disposed to include dance in that yearning for and exploration of meaning. So, yes, dance and poetry and music and love… our grasping glimpses of God. And for most of us, all our faith and hope struggle with the painful reality of an increasingly ghastly world of injustice. Throw in the deaths of millions of innocents, and where does that leave us? Lifting our desperate hopes to on high.

If there's even the remotest arithmetic in theology, Dad, you do the maths.

And how many of us popes and cardinals and bishops in our comfort can remember the pain, let alone the deadening reality of the rest of that condemned but totally innocent world?

Discuss.

And in that daring department, my New Year's resolution is to confront a huge problem facing the church.

Well, the western church.

The pews are not full but they're peopled with the old; 70% female I'd put it at a conservative guess.

Two demographics have dropped out: 30- to 50-year-old parents and the 18- to 24-year-old post-school demographic.

I need to get my mind around both, but it's the latter that gnaws at me.

To get into a Catholic school, certain basics of belief and practice are meant to apply, and principals I meet assure me that references for entry would suggest the adolescent world is brimming with young potential saints-to-be, eager to say the rosary, attend the sacraments, join in parish life and who come from a home positively glowing with faith, good works and nightly family prayer.

These referenced exemplars go through ten or so years of informed, moderated and positive faith instruction.

They attend school masses, do amazing community work, especially with the marginalised, with handicapped children and with the poor in third world countries where they not infrequently put in the hard slog of building houses.

That astonishes me, especially when I remember that when I was educated by the brothers back in Wollongong, our only corporal work of mercy was helping out for one afternoon at the annual bazaar.

But after being rightly celebrated as they leave our schools, by the first weekend of 'freedom', the vast majority of our Catholic students don't find any need for the sacraments or the mass.

I've had this conversation with Ennio.

He comes from a comfortable Swiss family. As a schoolboy, his family took him to mass, and he received basic instruction in scripture and Catholic doctrine, but once he left school, with no axe to grind, he ceased being a practising Catholic.

Sadly, so what's new?

Ennio believes in God and being good and kind (especially to this pope) but the whole beauty and imaginative structure of Catholicism, the big questions of life, death and the universe... they simply don't register with him.

So what went wrong?

So much for contemporary Catholic education, and I think it's the same story the world over—well, for the western world.

One reason I've considered is the contemporary irrelevance of sin and hell.

The young simply don't believe—and certainly don't care—about eternal punishment. And once guilt and hell cease to figure in their outlook and their moral behaviour, not least their sexual lives, there's no speed limit on life's freeway.

And again, Ennio's experience seems to get to the nub of the issue: mass is boring, especially sermons, and sex is much better.

Out of the mouths of babes… well, let's say spunky and sexually athletic and adventurous young adults.

As a pope, I'm trying to come to terms with this freedom of experience.

No, freedom plus.

Liberation.

Wish I'd been born in that generation.

Ennio listens to pop music (if music it be) but doesn't seem to read.

Is this relevant or was it ever thus?

In my more wicked moments, I feel like suggesting to Ennio that as he's open to trying all kinds of mind-altering experiences, why doesn't he experiment with holy communion? Too scared? But I refrain lest I stop sounding like a good friend and bang on like some missionary pope.

Deep down, though, I have a hunch that this might well be a way to challenge—even dare—the young, but on second and third thoughts, I tread softly in that dimension.

Am I blasphemous, immature or mad?

All of the above I hear me say.

Anyway, there must be more to this huge question than sex being more fun (must there?) so this year, I'm going to put my mind to the issue.

Not a million mortal sins away from that question and years too late, I've just finished two of Richard Holloway's confessional books, *Stories We Tell Ourselves* and *The Heart of Things*.

Holloway's always interested me because of his dangerous honesty and his daring—some might say barmy—behaviour.

The fact that he's a no-nonsense Scot probably explains much of his theological and vocational to-ing and fro-ing. The primate (it might be primus—the Scots are such bloody contrarians on every front) of the Scottish Episcopalian Church (its very existence is proof of Scottish stubbornness), Holloway's always been outspoken on theological issues, not least the existence of God, about whom the bishop became so sceptical that he announced he'd become an agnostic and resigned from his comfortable position in his church.

Mitres off for that, says I.

Holloway certainly has more humility than many bishops and cardinals I've come across, and he regards the earth as merely 'a fragment of stardust'.

After a long, questioning, and I have to say fascinating and (dare I say) entertaining, and (yes, I'll say it out loud—quietly) challenging dark night of the soul, the agnostic bishop has returned to his/the church.

Though his church 'without God'.

In place of God, Holloway rediscovers belief in Jesus because of Christ's message of peace and love.

I wonder whether, when courageous bishops, after they've chucked the whole thing in… when, over time, they rethink, can they go back to being bishops?

Well, I suppose a Scot can, and getting back into the episcopal swing of things would surely help make the world a better place.

Yes, Richard Holloway is the kind of cleric a pope would want to have dinner with.

No, <u>ought</u> to have dinner with.

And will.

I hear that he's coming to Rome, so I've invited him to a special Sister Angelica dinner and offered to put him up at the Vatican.

Might ask a few cardinals to join us for post-prandial drinks, including Olivier.

Qui audet adipiscitur, which I assume is Latin for 'nothing venture nothing win'.

Or Wollongong-ese for 'Give it a go, mate.'

At worst, you can only lose.

Well, I can.

But by now, that's pretty much a given.

Friday, January 2nd

Feast of that great double act, Saints Basil the Great (329–379) and St Gregory of Nazianzus (329–390), Bishops and Doctors of the church.

They were formidable theologians three hundred years after Christ, and to cut a three-hundred-year long story short, they worked out and delivered as gospel that God the Son is consubstantial with the Father while the Holy Spirit proceeds from them both. Simple, really—once someone… or some two have worked it out. The words are clear but… this time of year is a theologians' picnic, though one that's a bit overcrowded as the day also celebrates 37 other nominated saints and God alone knows how many martyrs gathered into different categories. I'd call it a holy bloody traffic jam—too much for this ageing pope to come to terms with. How the average punter in the pews copes is beyond me. An each-way bet, I guess, though it must be the most wall-to-wall photo finish heaven's had to cope with for a bit… well, excluding All Saints' Day and even more crowded, All Souls' Day. Don't think so much, Mario. You know it only confuses you.

Last night, I had this mad dream of synodal conclaves to elect a new pope with female and male cardinal voters, and of the rules having been changed so that popes had to be between the age of 60 and 80 and have a papacy of 7 (deadly sins?) years, but with the option of a further seven years if a second conclave agrees.

Already in my dream, there are complaints that males now seem to be second-rate papal candidates and that our previous five female popes have changed the church beyond the recognition and for the better.

If wishes were horses, beggars would ride... with popes out in front.

Dream on, Mario.

Saturday, January 3rd

Feast of The Most Holy Name of Jesus (0–33).

Why not? God knows, these days it's taken in vain ignorantly and unpleasantly. I wonder what the deep complication is when people who couldn't care less about religion exclaim, 'Jesus!'

Double bounty to celebrate—if that's the word—the new year.

Strozzapreti with fennel, tomato and olive vinaigrette.

Pasta for the gods.

Even better, for the angels.

Angelica certainly took the right name at her religious profession.

In our groping for the eternal and our understandable desperation to embrace the numinous—and what blinded, unadventurous pilgrim would settle for less? Someone terrified of exploration and discovery?... where was I?

Oh, yes.

I find my always sceptical but ever-questing self clinging to... how to describe it?... pulses of spiritual yearning: viz, candles and bells.

What universal sound is more aspirational than a lit candle, and what light is more resonating than a consecration bell?

And vice-versa.

That's the beauty of letting our imagination run riot.

'There are more things in heaven and earth, Horatio, than...'

Funny how those lines from Brother Edmund's bashings come back.

He certainly ensured via his thrash-it-into-them process that I remembered my poetry learning homework, though because of this sadistic educational philosophy, he didn't teach me to love what I learnt.

But now, a million years later, I think that, yes, in his twisted way, he did.

And, yes, Brother Edmund was victim of his guilt-drenched theological education in the same way that I was.

OK. Credit where grudging credit is due, I guess.

But what of the church and that church's screwed-up theology that screwed up Brother Edmund?

And those generations before him?

I mean, how far back must we go?

Christ, where was I?

Oh, yes, the humble and ever-wavering candle.

Desperate. Valiant. Vulnerable. Burning but not singeing.

Like my faith, flickering.

Beautiful.

Words don't always do it, but a single candle does.

My fragile prayer.

And the bell… that brief thrill… that dying echo of eternal possibility resonating in our souls.

The music of the spheres sanctifying a moment.

Holy. Holy. Holy.

Ring out wild flames and burn softly sweet bells that in our mystical questing, we may be worthy of your enlightening contradictions.

So may it be.

Sunday, January 4th

Feast of Saint Elizabeth Ann Seton (1774–1821) a devout American Episcopalian who, after her husband's death in Italy, became a Catholic, so impressed was she by Italian Catholicism at the time.

Things have changed since then, but brava Elizabeth Ann, not least when as a widow, you further lost two of your five children. No pope (or probably even priest, but you never know) has had to come to terms with that burden. The tests of my faith are nothing compared to such losses. I can only genuflect in admiration for this fine Maryland saint who founded the order of nuns called The Daughters of Charity of St. Vincent de Paul to educate girls, particularly the poor ones. I don't doubt that today, Trumpist Republicans would call her a communist—even, heaven forbid, a socialist, such is their ignorance. I call her a gift from God, and God knows, America could do with a few more. And then many more. Just imagine if she had been ordained and the resultant boost in... well, everything, for the women in America! We've missed the boat, the tide, the zeitgeist and the message of Jesus, all because of bloody old men made cler-

icalism. I find it hard to control my anger and my contempt for the theologically terrified. Hardly a very papal disposition. Well, the way I currently feel, too fucking bad. When will someone tell the curia that the world isn't flat and that if Mary can give birth to the Son of God (how many priests, bishops, cardinals and popes have undergone the agony of labour?) then maybe the requirements for the candidature for priesthood should be reversed? No males unless... But I rave on. St Elizabeth Ann Seton, get to work up there!

Diplomacy or challenge? The individual's divine right of conscience and the equally divine right of every individual being entitled to be treated with justice and respect. Speak softly or speak out?

China and Russia—to name but two gross offenders—place the state's safety as deemed by the government and understood by their corrupt judiciary above an individual's right to their beliefs, especially when those beliefs challenge the political status quo.

Result? Thousands upon thousands are found guilty of the crime of standing up for freedom of thought and expression. To make matters worse, these victims are generally kept in appalling conditions of deliberately cruel punishment and torture, and the sufferers haven't the slightest chance of appeal.

Who will vigorously defend human dignity if the church whispers rather than shouts?

Sometimes, I think that non-believers have more courage and moral fibre than this institution which safeguards its own interests above the rights of the afflicted.

I mean, who would wish to belong to a church claiming to be the people of God but double shuffling when dealing with autocratic governments in order to protect our spiritual (and real estate) territory?

And I speak with the authority of an autocratic governor trying my best to limit or at least share that power wherever possible.

We must be the world's paschal candle, that fragile but inspirational flame symbolising life, freedom, hope and salvation.

And so this pope will call out the tyranny of China and of Russia and for that matter, of every other autocratic state, tin pot or nuclear, while at the same time inviting their leaders to dare to visit the Vatican and take part in a public conversation.

Shame the bastards!

I can hear the entire Vatican diplomatic corps shrieking for me to shut up and leave my thought bubbles to the professionals.

And with all their silent to-ing and fro-ing and banqueting, what have they achieved in China or Russia? I can't just sit here any longer dressing up in period costume and waffling platitudes.

Call the autocratic buggers out!

Did Jesus ask the moneylenders in the temple to thoughtfully and humbly reconsider the morality of their blasphemy?

No. In righteous anger, he overturned their tables (in every sense!) and chucked the fuckers out.

So one autocrat to another, let's thrash it out it public, and may the worst man lose.

And one thing's for sure: the offenders are always men.

Well, mostly.

We boast that we embody God's truth. Well, let's go into battle with truth as our shield. Surely our strength lies in our belief in the integrity and power of our conviction.

I'll get my Secretary of State to find an appropriate feast day to offer the monsters a microphone.

It's time for a fine Old Testament warrior.

The Prophet Amos: 'I despise your religious festivals. Your assemblies are a stench to me. Away with your songs, but let justice roll on like a river and righteousness like a never-failing stream.'

Do-nothing pope, indeed!

And Information Never Wasted: Cardinal Nzapayeké and Sister Monique Agard apparently had a ninety-minute meeting last Friday. By some whim of fate, Sister Angelica happened to be passing Agard's office and saw Nzapayeké going in, and by a similar coincidence—she's always busy—noted his time of exit. And if I remember correctly, there are 28 or 29 Francophone countries in Africa. Quite a nice bundle of conclave votes you'd have to think.

I CONFESS

Monday, January 5th

Feast of Pope St Telesphorus, martyred in 139-ish.

He started the tradition of midnight mass and the Gloria in the mass being sung. Arguably radical, though hardly grounds for martyrdom, but being pope isn't for the faint-hearted.

A truly blessed day of joy and satisfaction.

Listening to the Lord in my meditation, I came to realise that for pessimists and paranoids, life turns out to be exactly as they predict because their negativity is a self-fulfilling prophecy.

In my mass, I prayed for the grace of optimism and perseverance.

Went to breakfast in a peaceful state, and orange juice has never tasted sweeter, bacon and eggs more deliciously strengthening or coffee more energizing.

First interview of the day was with the new Archbishop of Perth I recently appointed.

Michael Boland was Bishop of Port Pirie when I was Archbishop of Adelaide and did an outstanding job—miles better than second-rate me.

He's a people person par excellence, a man of intuitive pastoral warmth, and was, as Francis used to say, a shepherd with the smell of sheep.

He was also very popular with young Catholics and invited groups of them into his home to talk with him about whatever issues they were concerned about, and if those topics were sex, drugs (though not rock-n-roll, which he's absolutely not a fan of. A man of taste) or whatever (all of which they inevitably were) he listened, asked questions and in a Socratic fashion, got the young people to articulate their values and consider all sides and repercussions of each of their stances.

He always began with, 'So, tell me your story' and very occasionally he would ask a question but never hit the storyteller with a sermon.

Eventually, some of the narrators would ask him a question, in which case, he'd reply, but always conclude with, 'What do you think about that?'

Should be taught in all seminaries.

He majored in philosophy at Melbourne University and specializes in two-minute sermons. No wonder people flock to his masses.

Well, those people who still go to mass.

I've appointed Michael Perth's new archbishop because he's just the tonic Western Australia and, indeed, the whole nation needs after a sad episcopal succession of... but in holy charity, best I leave that sentence unfinished.

Certainly, Michael will be a first-rate media performer, and I think such young clergy as there are will find him open, approachable and inspiring.

He's in Rome for a week, so I've invited him to dinner on Thursday with Dario, Kiwi Cardinal Adrian Jellicoe and Alison Broderick who runs the Doctrinal Dicastery.

Michael's faith is calm, carefully thought out and charitable. He speaks of respect, integrity and the need to walk in the shoes of another in order to understand and love them. Mind you, he'll be tested by some of the new conservative curates who seem to like dressing up and who bang on all the time about commandments and sin.

He'd make a magnificent cardinal, and I'll see to it that it won't be too long before that red hat arrives.

He'd certainly be a force for sanity and reform in the next conclave.

I was in such a positive mood after our hour's conversation that my next meeting—with Mendoza—proved to be almost friendly.

I can't believe he's mellowing in what's left of his old age, but on the subject of inclusive language in biblical translation, when I expected him to insist on strict literal translation from the original, he seemed open to a touch of contemporary interpretation. Or was I in such a state of consolation that I misheard him and just presumed he said what I wanted to hear?

And even more congenial was the fact that he apologized for only being able to have twenty minutes with me because of a doctor's appointment. I told him I totally understood, wished him well and after he left, I thanked the Lord for large as well as small mercies.

After lunch, I heard confessions incognito in St Peter's and reassured my penitents that the very fact of their asking for God's help is proof of their faith and a reason why they should be proud of themselves.

Confession isn't a court; it's an open conversation with the Lord, a conversation we must always leave from with relief, gratitude and confidence.

Late in the afternoon, it was a delight to meet a group of Papua New Guinea university students who had spent their holidays tutoring students in Timor Leste. Their PNG spirits were high, and they were rightly proud of their efforts, saying how friendly and grateful the students were and how rewarding they (the PNG uni students) found the month. They intend to invite more of their student body to donate their services to Timor Leste once a year.

One lively female in the group said to me that they'd also like to help their brothers and sisters in Indonesian-occupied West Irian.

Throwing diplomacy to the winds (hopefully of the Holy Spirit) I replied that in my opinion, the inhabitants of West Papua are no more Indonesian than I am and that I wished the population well in their struggle to liberate their nation from Indonesian occupation and violence. And economic greed.

Cheers all round.

I expect to receive an outraged complaint any day now from the Indonesian government.

I might just reply and remind them of the tens of thousands of years difference between Melanesian and Indonesian civilisations, of the truth that Indonesia is there against the ruling of the United Nations and—as is screamingly and shamefully obvious—is only there for the oil, and that the brutality of the Indonesian troops is similar to Russia's war crimes in Ukraine.

And for good measure, I'll add that I'm utterly ashamed of Australia's betrayal of the Melanesian Papuans of PNG. I might also attach some photos of Indonesian murders and massacres.

I felt totally reinvigorated by these wonderful PNG students and told them I'd love to visit their country and speak out for its reunification.

How about that, Dad, for a first-rate papal rebuke to the invaders?

Such was my good mood at the end of the day that I decided to watch *The Two Popes* for the third time and invited Ennio to join me.

He'd heard of the film but never seen it.

What struck me even more than last time I saw it was the subtle politics of the sub-text about football. Both popes seemed to recognize their differences—conservative ascetic Benedict and liberal pastoral Francis, simultaneously Jesuit and intuitively Jesuitical.

Ennio seemed more interested in the football than the ecclesiastical overtones but he though the idea of two popes nattering away like a couple of pensioners was weird but funny and reckoned they should have watched the game with a few beers.

A soothing neck massage before bed.

Tuesday, January 6th

Feast of Twelfth Night, not the play but the event of the Visit of the Magi.

The three wise men somehow received the divine message that this lowly boy was someone exceptionally special. There's a lot to be said about wise people who transform their thought into action. If the Visit of the Magi happened, it's beautiful. If it's myth, it's beautiful. It would have been nice were three wise women accompanying the Magi, but as all these stories were written by men…

Predictable mudslides in Brazil. Not unexpected volcanoes in Indonesia. The usual devastating floods in Bangladesh. The eternal earthquakes in northeastern Italy causing ancient cathedrals and churches to crumble while killing the faithful worshiping within. Hardly surprising famine continuing in the Middle East. The inevitable hurricanes and tornadoes in Louisiana and Florida. Lethal hailstones the size of cricket balls in London causing more havoc than Australian bowlers at Lord's, and to top it all off, what few koalas are left north of Newcastle are apparently dying by the minute in New South Wales. Oh, yes, and whatever disasters continue happening in Africa.

And apparently I'm supposed to have the answer for all this.

God knows.

And I joke not.

If the bloody faithless world expects me to explain the mystery of the universe, the prevalence of suffering and our old friend, the problem of evil, then they've come to the wrong address.

This pope doesn't do quiz shows.

Despite rumours to the contrary, I'm not God, and, indeed, given the current state of international atheistic despair and excited theological exploration, a second-rate Australian God is the last thing the world currently needs.

Mind you, the world could do with a good dose of 'Listen, mate, shit happens. Always has. Almost certainly always will. We bloody well didn't make the world, so stop bloody whingeing, grab a shovel and make yourself useful. Help the poor bugger trapped underneath that pile of rubble in front of you and thank God for the sacramental beer you scull when you've saved that one grateful person.

'One bloody miracle, mate, beats a doctoral thesis on divine intention. And as for the bloody reason for all this endless shite, try prayer, mate. It has its moments and arguably beats dope.

'And if all else fails, stand as an independent, withdraw your wealth and move to a safer place, then ask the same questions all over again cos, honky tonk, the disasters will sure keep coming, and if you haven't worked it out by now, whatever answer you arrive at will be a mystery in one form or another, at which point you crash into a brick wall.

'And I crash into the humility of faith and the desperation of hope.

'Or is it vice-versa?

'Anyway, believe me, it works.

'On and off.

'Mate, I'll come to your side, if you'll come to mine. I mean, for Christ's sake, surely we can consider this over a drink. And if we can't, I fear the abomination of desolation may be following on from the koalas.

'Taking the boy out of Wollongong and all that. And, mate, take it from me: the universal Wollongong is what it's all about. Except for the spiritual gap, and I still don't know whether that gap is Wollongong or me. I mean, in some weird kind of way, most of the world is or aspires to be Wollongong—except should Wollongong become the rest of the world's Las Vegas... at which point, we should all give up.

'Sun and surf and sex and... or is that just me?

'Or survival? And values? And justice? And vision? And faith. And the glimpse of whatever salvation is.

'Cheers, mate!'

Anyway, after that cleansing rant I feel much better now, Dad, so I'll compensate with the nearest I get to sanity: dreaming.

I think one of the most beautiful words in the English language is 'bread'.

This morning, I meditated on the poetry and power of that word and its function.

Breaking my fast with communion bread and the sacred silence with which it fills the soul has never tasted better.

As an unmolested altar boy in Wollongong (insufficiently pretty?) I was brought up on the Tridentine Mass and quickly learnt to love its soothingly mysterious Latin. It somehow united the global church in universal unintelligibility yet had us sharing pride in our membership of this exclusive channel of salvation.

I was attracted to its disciplined ritual; its reassuring hierarchy of priest, altar boy and congregation (God forbid girls should ever pollute the sanctuary with their wombs and menstrual blood—though Our Lady was surely an exception because... and I never quite got to the end of that justification); and the platoon on parade structure of the celebration with the ordained and commanding officer, the young NCO's and the foot soldiers arranged in hierarchical order. Well, that's what we were taught, though I'm not all that sure about the well-meaning but wobbly theology of physical proximity to the luminous figure of the celebrant being particularly helpful.

Actually, he seemed to hide what he was doing at the altar, and I found that strange, though definitely mysterious. I was also taken in by what I now consider to be its frankly obsequious and sickening respectfulness to the assumed royalty of God.

Royalty has well and truly had its blasphemous day of being associated with divine appointment.

But even after all these years, with gratitude and satisfaction in nostalgia, that adolescent religious experience lingers warmly in my memory, in my religious education and in my soul.

It provided the strange intimation of the numinous, and those bells sure worked as a focus for sanctifying moments.

When it comes to ritual as theatre and interior drama, the Latin Mass delivered to its three-tiered congregation in spades—and a big cheerio call to all those nuns who polished the sacred vessels, hoovered the sacristy, ironed the albs, laid out the vestments, arranged the flowers on the altar and trained the altar boys to reply in Australian Latin they never really understood but felt enormous pride in rattling off—and, I might add, gave them the rich experience of somehow responding to the reassuring bells and glorious smells rising up to the heavens.

In our pious innocence, we were sipping the religious alcohol of the transcendental, and let's face it, not a few of the few remaining faithful still get high on that fast lane to God, so why should their Church deny them the solace which their fidelity to mystery graces them with?

This view, of course, confuses my traditionalist opponents, but all I can say is bad luck in the overall scheme of things.

I mean, who are we here at Mission Control to tell the faithful that what makes them faithful is somehow defective?

No, give that small band of the faithful their beautiful mode of worship and prayer, and have confidence in the Lord's beneficence.

And in all truth, I can celebrate a Tridentine Mass and with grateful nostalgia be exalted by its beauty, its majesty, (Whoops!) and its striving to access the divine. And while my Italian remains stubbornly Aussie in pronunciation, at least I understand the Latin and appreciate why this sacred experience is cherished by those for whom it's a channel to God.

That said, I mean, God only knows what Jesus and the apostles would have made of the Latin Mass.

Not quite the Last Supper, but strange though it perhaps sounds, in the scheme of things, what works works.

I have no doubt that the Second Vatican Council was absolutely right in restoring the vernacular together with the sacred banquet concept and the inclusion of the congregation by the celebrant facing them as host of the feast.

And the council was especially on the second collection in making visible the moving rubrics of the offertory, the consecration, the sign of peace and communion in the hand and under both species.

I remember writing down the wisdom of Pope Francis on the subject of the celebration of the Mass.

He argues that today, most of the world has lost the capacity to engage with symbolic action. We've become incapable of experiencing symbols. He argues—to my mind, brilliantly—that we can discover the divine 'through created things that are the opposite of spiritual abstractions. 'Bread, wine, oil, water, fragrances, fire, ashes, rock, fabrics, colours, body, words, sounds, silences, gestures, space, movement, action, order, time, light.'

He states that as such things are, in their purpose, fundamental and essential, then we must arrange ourselves in their presence with 'a fresh, non-superficial regard, respectful and grateful.'

Francis says in a paragraph what would take me two pages to try to explain.

Yes, Dad, I know.

That said, for me the unintended consequence of the changes has been the appalling pop-ification and devaluation of the sacred mystery.

At a civilised feast, one does not serve fairy bread, popcorn or jelly beans.

Clichéd and banal songs lower the tone, reverence and atmosphere of so sacred an event, and greatly as I admire aspects of Pope St John Paul II's contribution to the church, I can only hope that the heavenly music of the angels has absolved his execrable taste in popularising the country and western dreadfulness of that so-called hymn, *Here I Am Lord.*

It's an embarrassment which should only be sung in a crass faux-Texan accent with violent vibrato while semi-intoxicated and facing Nashville or its New South Wales vile musical equivalent, Tamworth.

If ever I scrape into heaven and hear the choirs of angels crooning that rubbish, I'm off.

And I seem to be on some kind of high because I'm feeling up for a fight.

Wednesday, January 7th

Feast of St Raymond of Penyafort, patron saint of canon lawyers (1175–1275).

A canon lawyer who lived to 100. No comment.

Today I received a sharp, written rebuke from my, alas, former friend, Cardinal Olivier Gabriel Foncha.

He castigates me for inviting Richard Holloway to dinner and goes off the deep end regarding my using the Vatican as a bed-and-breakfast for heretics.

Oh, well, I guess that's one fewer for after-dinner drinks.

While reading his sound-off with a painful heart, I remembered with a gentle and amused heart the first encounter which led to our robust friendship over years and, sadly, to our current state of war.

We met however many years ago when we were seminary students here in Rome, albeit in different seminaries. A pilgrimage to the sacred mountains of Mount Como was part of our spiritual formation. These mountains are believed in these parts to symbolize the nine mysteries of our faith (over the years I've come to enumerate quite a few more) and each of us was to be paired with an unknown fellow ordinand less than a month or so away from ordination.

Et in arcadia ego.

As he told me, Olivier was intrigued to find his older pilgrim companion an Australian with an Italian name and studying at the English College.

In the euphoric spirit of the sacramental gift that was approaching, I told Olivier how I more or less bribed my way into my seminary of the English College. I claimed British association on my maternal uncle's side. The English College enjoyed a reputation for traditional theology, and because of my then conservative leaning, they accepted me.

The irony resonates.

My new pilgrim friend explained to me that at least as a Cameroonian, he didn't have to lie to be accepted as a candidate for the priesthood at the French Seminary of Santa Chiara. We laughed, and in Ghiffa, at the Restaurant of the Holy Trinity, we bonded over a meal of merry fellowship.

The indifferent food seemed to be also dedicated to some kind of gastronomic mystery, but over that second, or was it the third bottle of Barbaresco or Barolo—Olivier was the wine expert even back then—he confessed to me how he was on the verge of expulsion from his seminary for his radical theological views, especially about the church's teaching on sex and contraception when considered from male African perspective.

The subject had more than a general interest for me, and I remember saying that in our young lives, it was surely understandable that we might have not infrequently been... shall we say... more passionate than obedient to church teaching on that subject.

My clear memory was that Olivier replied, 'Enthusiastically so.'

One doesn't forget such a wild pre-ordination admission. Well, not this one—albeit under the influence of Olivier the connoisseur's wine choice—and ever since, I've held the view that Africa has a lot to offer Australia in radical theological conversation, especially on the subject of sexuality.

The irony of course being that at the time, this faux conservative, immature Australian candidate for the priesthood was attracted by Archbishop Lefèbre and what I now regard as that desiccated prelate's blind, reactionary, medieval logic.

The church's laws come from God thus they never change. Full stop, no new paragraph. Don't argue. Do as you're told and give generously to the second collection. That way salvation lies.

And there I was, subscribing to Lefèbre's endless pontifical judgments and sympathising with his deluded followers.

Bizarre how, over the years, our theology and politics have been completely reversed.

Have we both finally grown up or are we both just as juvenilely perverse?

It seems that only in wine do we still share the same taste.

Thursday, January 8th

Feast of Severinus of Noricum who died around 410 in North Africa.

He was a wealthy Roman who became a hermit but then became a powerful preacher. He prophesied the invasion of Austria by Atilla the Hun and founded centres for refugees while also establishing funds to ransom and rescue captives—noble works of charity we need more of today. During Lent, he went barefooted and slept on sackcloth on the ground. Interestingly, he predicted the date of his

*own death and died singing Psalm 150, Praise the Lord. Indeed.
I wonder how I'll die and whether and what I'll sing. An unusual
thought to be explored. But that niggle...*

OMG! Depressive reverse of yesterday.

Another Australian, this time that insufferable Jesuit, Claudio
Gaspari, flattering me to death with his endless volleys of hyperbolic
insincerities.

He's a smarmy and gross snob and enjoys (well, <u>he</u> enjoys) the
reputation of using his family's wealth (Gaspari Constructions,
builders of dodgy tower blocks) to entertain handsome and athletic
young males at expensive restaurants, all the while deluding himself
that this is some form of evangelization.

How do I know this?

Try being bishop of three cities the private schools of which have
more than a surfeit of handsome and athletic young males. Gaspari
travels the nation giving retreats to final year students.

Informed chaplains describe them as advances more than retreats, but this dodgy outlier who seems to have immunity above all
suspicion, somehow projects himself with religious glitter into the
tempting mosh pit of muscular male adolescents.

Talk about Frequent Flirting Points.

He natters endlessly about important businessmen he knows and
talks about their wealth. He even seems deluded that there is some
kind of Australian aristocracy and that he knows who has married
whom and how they're all related and where they went to school
and how large their houses are... as if I were somehow meant to be
interested and even impressed by this banal banter.

How on earth did this absurd Jesuit wangle a papal interview?

I must let Dario know that this self-important humbug must never again to be granted an audience. I find him deeply shallow—all
performance and effusive through obvious disguise.

Mind you, he's certainly well-informed about Vatican gossip—
hardly a virtue—and he tried hard to find out more titillating news
from me.

And failed.

I think he's a tiresome, terminally immature fraud who should
be returned to some Evelyn Waugh or Tom Sharpe satirical novel

where he belongs. How his brother Jesuits put up with him I can't fathom. I suppose they just have to write him off as 'a character'.

Needless to say, he insisted on being photographed with me, though I managed the most insincere semi-smile I could.

As the unpleasant Gaspari was leaving, Ennio arrived on duty, and when Gaspari saw him, he just about had a heart attack, praising the lad for being 'so explosively handsome' and he most inappropriately suggesting that Ennio's 'sex life must be a twenty-four seven festival of orgasm.'

Enough said.

Ennio just smiled, which, of course, sent Gaspari into further raptures, and I had to order him to stop touching—I should have said 'molesting'—a Swiss guard who was simply turning up for duty.

It was all most uncomfortable and very concerning.

The most charitable thing I can say about Gaspari is that at best, he's a superficial pest.

At worst, I fear to imagine how and where he'll finish up.

Later, Ennio asked me whether this crazy *finocchio* was some kind of Australian comedian.

In charity, I avoided answering.

Charity to whom?

And here's me casting the first stone.

Melius esse honestus quam auto-fallax.

I must pray for charity in judgment, except that I think that instinct in judgment needs to...

OK, mea maxima culpa, but still...

Thank God for dinner tonight with the sane.

But to INW.

Slippery Chilean Cardinal Carlos Silva Gonzales apparently spent last weekend with two other visiting Chilean cardinals, Jorge Fuentes of Santiago and Fernando Ventura of Concepcion at the lavish Anzio villa of Contessa Chiara di Moretti, a very rich widow known for her extremely conservative political and theological views as well as for her generous donations to the Latin Mass Society who regularly celebrate mass in her chapel.

Gonzales' guests are both sensible, middle of the road prelates, faithful to tradition but open to the new. This out-of-town get-together suggests lobbying for Olivier, both cardinals having considerable networks in Chile and beyond, thus being able to influence a large number of centrist South American conclave voters of the same balanced disposition.

Ventura is a friend of Guido Montano's and mentioned the séjour in passing before the event—a mistake Gonzales would certainly not be happy with should Ventura let the cat out of the bag.

Which he now has.

To me, this signals a hotting-up of Olivier's campaign.

Information definitely not to be wasted but rather acted upon.

To keep them on the conclave straight and narrow, I'll get Dario to invite both cardinals for a friendly cup of coffee while they're in Rome.

Friday, January 9th

Feast of Saint Marciana who, as a young Christian girl, was beaten and tortured then handed over to gladiators as a sex toy during the persecutions of that monster, the Emperor Diocletian.

Accused of vandalising an idol of the goddess Diana, she was thrown to wild animals in the amphitheatre of Caesarea in Mauritania around 303. She was gored by a bull and mauled to death by a leopard. The cruelty of humanity should surely cause atheists to question the potential nobility of humanity—just as it causes the same dilemma with theists—well, this one certainly—to not infrequently question the dubious gift of free will. I almost despair of the problem of evil and often dream of the hideous death of martyrs in Rome and of latter-day Jews in extermination camps. It's the horror and power of evil which desperately drives me to prayer. I know that somebody once said that Bach's music offered 'a ladder of tears on which our longings for God ascend.' On some days, though, I feel as if I need to listen to Bach all day to retain even a glimmer of my faith.

Last night's dinner with Dario, NZ's Cardinal Adrian Jellicoe, Alison Broderick, Boss of the Doctrinal Dicastery and our special guest, Perth's new archbishop, Michael Boland, was spirit-raising.

It was joy not to have to be cautious in bringing up controversial subjects and then having to be even more cautious in expressing an opinion.

Well, almost.

But first, Sister Angelica's invigorating menu.

Three small courses, all the more tempting for them being entrée sized: mushroom risotto with lemon and capers, cacio e pepe topped with truffle shavings (how on earth did truffles get smuggled into the Vatican)? and veal scaloppini with sautéed broccolini, then a cheese plate of fontina, gorgonzola, montasio and Sardinia's fiore sardo.

And let's just say that the dessert of tiramisu was less than Lenten.

I decided to serve wines which had been given to me as gifts from visiting cardinals but I only revealed their labels once we'd tasted them and given our opinions: 2016 Gunderloch Rothenberg Riesling Grosses Gewachs from Germany; Catena Zapata Malbec Argentino 2015 from Argentina; as a surprise conversational catalyst, Lyme Bay Pinot Noir 2020 from Devon in England (the evening's surprise, though Dario thought it ordinary, but of late, like the wine, he's seems to have been a little off-colour); and finally, *Rioja Gran Reserva 2010*, two bottles of—though I hesitate to concede, I'm afraid even superior to Australia's Clare Valley Inigo Shiraz. Oh, and with the tiramisu, we shared—well… anyway, over conversation we consumed a bottle of Italian Sangue di Giuda sparkling red. And I have to admit to refilling my glass more frequently than my guests', but as somebody somewhere once observed, too much moderation can become something of a fetish. I forget who the somebody somewhere was, but that proposition surely merits a little reflection.

In gratitude, I pray for my connoisseur cardinal benefactors, and I certainly felt at home with my questing self.

No wonder our conversation was inspiriting.

As we agreed that on the usual topics of papal parley among close friends, none of us needed too much reinforcement, so, around the table, we decided to talk about new issues or ideas which each of us felt ought to be considered on our church's agenda.

And what a synod of five it turned out to be!

Michael Boland challenged us first with an original proposal: all seminary training should have one year in a seminary a world apart—in every sense—from the candidate's home one. Thus an Australian should spend twelve months in Africa or Europe or America—even including those prehistoric American conservative dioceses, if necessary. Michael's justification was that with all our differences, our church is our family of believers, thus we must learn to fully understand and respect opposing theological viewpoints otherwise we exclude our own dissent from the conversation of God's pilgrims, all of whom have a place at the Last Supper's table. 'Inclusive' must mean just that: including all. And then he added that just as today we look back on certain theological interpretations—Inquisitional torture, the burning of heretics, limbo and so on—and regard them, however well intentioned, as plain stupid, wrong or frankly evil, so we need to consider how our contemporary confidence in certain of our stances may be similarly judged in a century or two.

Generous listening and respectful silence all round until when Adrian Jellicoe smilingly asked whether that meant that the foundation of all our beliefs might therefore be relative.

Michael replied that included in faith is always the tremor of 'might'.

That's when Lyme Bay Pinot Noir was opened.

Alison Broderick suggested that the Vatican should subsidise the Latin lyrics of the greatest Gregorian chants and hymns being translated into the vernacular by poetic masters in their respective languages. While mysterious incomprehensibility has a certain mystical uplift, fully understanding noble thoughts sung to gloriously powerful music must surely be a superior worship experience. As she said, 'Language exists to clarify and advance awareness and discernment, and in any case, great poetry encourages imaginative exploration which is invigoratingly dangerous. And should that mental journey into the unknown lead to doubt, such hesitation can be as much an imaginative advance as a stumbling block.'

An intriguing contradiction and an insight which certainly reassured me. I only hope it's true.

Dario's contribution struck me as curious. He claimed that because of the exponential decline in church congregations and therefore in the faithful's financial contributions, within a relatively short time the economic security of the church will become precarious and hundreds of buildings would have to be sold to prop up our vast administrative structure. He therefore proposed the immediate bringing together of a committee of the most successful Catholic bankers and estate agents to invest internationally in properties guaranteed to increase in value with a view to later selling them for large profits and then investing the windfall in even larger investments.

The general view was that this wasn't God's work and would quickly end in scandal—or rather, even more financial scandal of which we've had even more than enough—though I did remind the room of Archbishop Marcinkus's dictum that the Vatican can't be run on Hail Mary's. Dario argued that we had to live in the real world and that despite the reality deficit of the curia, wisdom wasn't confined to theology.

Despite our warm friendship and openness, this proved to be… shall we say an awkward subject, and I was glad when at just the right moment, Adrian Jellicoe moved discussion on.

His issue was the alarming rise of Pentecostalism and its impact for Catholicism, especially in Brazil and Asia-Pacific.

I regard this whole Ponzi-Jesus prosperity gospel as the equivalent of theological punk rock. It's the calculating perversion of all gospel values: good old Jesus applauds the rich, and his message to all you paupers and invalids is to get on your bike, go earn more, donate it to Hillsong of whatever rip-off religion you've wandered into, and in return, Jesus will ensure even greater profits.

Vomit-inducing blasphemy.

Which is why, for once I shut up and let the others offer their suggestions.

And the extraordinary thing was that none of us could come up with even the beginning of an explanation or of a practical way to confront this Jesus Christ Superannuation Star faux biblical bubble-gum bullshit.

Even now, looking back on it, it's beyond me why such fatuous flim flam, such mendacious *merde*, triumphs among the religiously illiterate and vulnerable.

If the answer is education, then God help us! I mean, how many generations do we have to make grammatically, syntactically and most importantly of all, religiously literate before they stop buying—and that's the word—before they stop buying cloying country music and high-octane rock-n-roll fuelled tabloid theological trash?

And swallowing this garbage as the pilgrimage of faith and not the credit card to tax-avoiding eternal comfort?

I never said this, but religion can drive people to believe the craziest and most destructive nonsense.

Whoops! Did I just write that?

Oh, dear!

Anyway, it was perhaps no surprise after this last topic that our frank and fearless and friendly and gloriously stimulating dinner and after-dinner conversation eventually led to the subject of abortion. Proof, surely, of genuine friendship and the confidences it guarantees.

And on this issue, I didn't hold my tongue. Rather, I held forth.

I've nailed my freedom-and-dignity-of-every-human-being colours to the mast, and now must face up to and declare my stance on abortion and a Catholic's right to receive communion if they support the right of non-Catholics to undergo abortions.

It's somewhat complicated but not complex… well, until…

OK, Dad, I know what you're thinking, but, please, let me explain. As I did.

First of all, it seems to me obvious that there must be a holy moment when the dynamic mucus of potential life in the womb suddenly becomes what we regard as human life: a person.

What a glorious gift of salvation when God so gracefully enters into the complex processes of the human condition and blesses potential with identity!

In our traditional teaching, this begins when a foetus receives a human soul—a mystical moment—but the soul is a theological concept, an unprovable belief and not a medical fact, so when, precisely, does this divine blessing happen, and when is such temporal precision of entry possible?

I've always been uncomfortable with the abstract noun, *ensoulment.*

Yes, it's mellifluous, but at the same time less than graspable. It blurs. It's elusive. It's ambivalent: somehow trying to be precise yet simultaneously being unable to isolate what it claims. And God knows, I've spent agonizing hours trying to come to terms with those consequences. More so than many might understand, but that's' a story for another day.

My story.

And surely the pope needs to open his heart to God's creatures whose surprise and bewilderment at the mistake of conception—a sudden moment and not an intended state—when these lovers ask the same question: passion, yes, but unintended consequence, no.

Our pleasure was just that—gloriously fulfilled—and both of us never at any moment desired offspring, so if, by our human negligence yet also by our human medical knowledge, we find ourselves faced with the potential for a life which we had no intention to issue, no commitment to foster… then why the bloody hell shouldn't we cancel your crazy weird and totally unprovable concept of *ensoulment* and get on with the glorious gift of our continuing sexual ecstasy?

Like, for God's sake, do the fucking maths.

Is God or fumbling and irresponsible/responsible us responsible for this… yes, we all know the word: fuck-up?

Literally.

That's a huge question both parties have to answer.

And this admittedly selfish and self-justifying thought process continues.

It seems to me that mathematically—mathemagically—sex is meant majorly for delight, then for love, and then by division sums for the propagation of humanity, but certainly not the unintended propagation of the species.

And, God knows, this pope totally understands that desperate cry while equally understanding a degree of selfishness in the claim.

Totally, in fact.

Am I even thinking, let alone writing this?

Yes, because somehow I respond to the historic revulsion of abortion—the very word is revolting, at least to me.

I understand that the masculine attitude to it has changed, and the concept of all women having full right to control their bodies is now trumpeted as secular holy writ. And while I'm sympathetic to the emotion of those pleas, I can't bring myself to be convinced by volume over logic.

Surely whether they like it or not, male and female are both equally responsible for what happens to a foetus they have engendered. I mean, after all, the insemination requires the consent of both agents, both of whom are old enough—or should be—to know the risks and take appropriately responsible precautions.

Imagine the outcry if, admitting that the woman should have total control over her body, the man announced that in that case, the woman can just get on with guarding, protecting and nurturing her possession throughout both their lives and not expect assistance of any kind, financial or emotional, from the mere momentary sperm supplier.

Women can't have it both ways. 'You own the child. Right, well, you look after the child. You argue that it's your body, your choice.

OK, it's got nothing to do with me. Goodbye and good luck with your body. And with the child you're responsible for because of your negligence.'

The resultant outrage would surely be universal in its condemnation of such inhuman, selfish avoidance of what most would regard as equal male responsibility.

The natural law, if you like.

Actions have consequences, and both parties in creating a foetus must surely be equally responsible.

Now of course I see the diabolical problem of a woman's predicament as, say, becoming pregnant as the result of rape, and for the life of me, I wouldn't dare to presume that I had any experiential understanding of that person's heart-breaking and soul-questioning dilemma.

Yet another argument for having women priests.

So it seems to me that from a theological point of view, since we're unable to discern when a foetus is *ensouled*, then we should admit to having to live with this unclear concept and err on the side of caution in protecting the foetus.

For non-believers who dismiss the concept of the soul, I wonder whether they regard a woman's first or early experience of life within the womb as a special moment after which that potential life deserves protection.

As for the aborting of deformed or mentally defective children in the womb, the question I would ask the parents is whether they agree that they are accomplices in killing a human being.

The conversation that then follows must surely be how to give that human being the best life possible, and I accept how difficult and tense and painful that conversation must be for all concerned.

And celibate men who have never brought up children should be humble and listening in their pastoral assistance.

Our hearts must go out to couples not wanting the child they have conceived. And if the church demands that such children of God must be allowed life, then the church must surely set up loving institutions to protect and nurture them.

And here I realise that the church simply screaming, 'Life! Life! Life', while understandable, is surely not the way to the heart and soul of the pregnant woman, and she's the one we must surely be bringing God's consolation to.

We must develop all possible positive measures to assist that woman, and if that means spending vast amounts in the process, then that's just one of the ways we can show how much we value life.

And if in the end, the mother still doesn't want to love her child, we must understand and then deploy our resources to find loving adoptive parents for that child.

So we must stop shouting and must start helping even more than we currently do. And, yes, I concede we currently do our best, but we must… well, do much more.

Much.

That said, I do find myself assenting to the morning after pill and also, in the case of rape, having to tolerate the similarly horrific possibility of allowing abortion for a very limited time—until, say, the woman feels life in the child she is carrying.

All this from a man who will never understand in the slightest way the mystery of life which the woman is experiencing.

In other words, I find many of my arguments unsatisfactory in their assumptions and contradictions.

Tell me I'm not losing it to honesty.

And this man is the pope, for God's sake.

If I were chairman of the board, I'd fire him.

What do you reckon, God?

And, Dad, please steer clear of this one, OK?

Your opinion is macho Italian irrelevant.

And by now—I hope—you probably know why.

Oh, and just for the record, as she was leaving last night, Alison Broderick slipped me a note saying that earlier yesterday, there was a long meeting in Olivier's office, and those present were Cardinal Desmond Wilenski, the Colorado cowboy, Malta's staunch conservative Paolo Di Giorgio, Hanover's highly intelligent and influential Bruno Westphalen—his integrity will get quite a few waverers voting for whatever candidate he favours—and that in the middle of the meeting, Luxembourg's Jean-Franz Hoffman joined the cabal. I thought he'd returned to his Grand Duchy. Actually, I'm sure he had. Strange that he'd return to Rome so quickly. Two hours must have seen them traverse every mystery of the rosary five times at least. And I'm sure they offered a prayer for the long life of the Holy Father. Well, his eternal life.

Saturday, January 10th

Is it because it's Saturday? Is it because I've been forever uncomfortable with certain aspects and dimensions of the faith I vowed to follow all my life and now have been promoted and simultaneously dumped as an all-powerful yet apparently powerless CEO?

Is my terminal immaturity reinforced by my having a middle-aged crisis in my 80s?

Well, whatever it is, I'm having it today.

I'm sick to bloody death of all this 24/7 God stuff.

It's unnatural. How did I end up in this gilded solitary confinement cell?

Normal people have lives to lead. They're doctors or lawyers or butchers or bankers or actors or prison warders or whatever. They wake up, go to work, use their skills to do their job, come home to their families and every now and then think about God.

Millions of them go to mass and communion every week and are much the better for it. They're strengthened to get on with their lives and relationships.

But this bloody lifetime of endless God bothering with billions apparently hanging on your every parenthesis, let alone sentence… it's crazy.

I don't have personal relationships. Well, yes, in a funny, nice kind of way, one with Ennio. And in a funnier kind of way, yes, I share thoughts with Sister Angelica, but those are almost all gastronomic, not really personal. Well, yes, they are, but no they're not. Except they are. But that's for another day.

And in our formal professional exchanges, Dario and I share a good friendship, but as for an on-going, deep, long-term relationship to come home to each night with all its ups and downs… that's what I've given up for the Lord, and pretty late in the day, I'm questioning it big.

Yes of course, we all need God room, but yes, just as importantly, every human being needs 'me' room, not least when you're living over the shop. I mean like coming home to someone every night and putting the business of the day behind you. Kicking off your shoes (or in my case, slippers), maybe making a meal, talking about the news, asking how your partner's day was and then just watching television.

At school in Wollongong, there was a lay master who taught music—piano and choir, actually: that's all music comprised back then. His name was Mr Jenkins. He was a slightly pudgy, middle-aged, friendly bloke, always smiling and forever saying 'God bless' to us boys, which I felt a bit uncomfortable about, but I guess that was just me. Or maybe not.

Mr Jenkins used to write hymns which we then had to learn and sing in chapel. They were OK, sort of, inasmuch as horny male teenagers find hymns helpful in dealing with serial surprise erections, though he seemed to think they were some dramatic religious breakthrough for those of us singing what we called his Jesus jingles.

Basically, they were full of 'Lord, make me, help me, grant me, lead me, show me, embrace me, consume me…' lines which got a bit boring, and I can remember wondering whether bachelor Mr Jenkins was really happy or just kidding himself with all this piety and using it for an excuse for never having any deep emotional relationships or even an accidentally fumbled teenage fuck.

I always presumed Mr Jenkins went home to a flat full of loneliness.

Some of the boys used to mock his lyrics with pretty disgusting sexual predicates after, 'Lord, make me… help me… grant me… lead me… show me… embrace me… consume me… specially this Saturday night.'

They were gross though funny, and for a lot of us, vaguely religious wish fulfilment fantasies.

Not, however, for our Captain of Swimming, a drop-dead handsome, muscle bound, devil-may-care teenage god we all secretly envied. Let's call him Xavier, since that was his name, and while on the subject, why the bloody hell are all Xaviers body beautiful teenage gods?

Anyway, Xavier's alternative lyrics to Mr Jenkins's God-pleading hymns, while lacking prosody, were glorious, graphic, athletic, almost step-by-step descriptions of his weekend romantic activities. Come to think of it, they were my detailed (arousingly detailed) sex education—that's apart from the deadly litany of 'don't's' the brothers and the Green Catechism piled on us.

Girls flocked to Xavier—and quite few other verbs starting with 'f'—and I remember in Fourth Year being jealous of his conquests.

We got on well enough once he'd had his daily laugh-in with the jocks, and when I once shouted him a salad roll and coke at the tuck shop, he told me that one of the secrets of scoring girlfriends at swimming carnivals and water polo games was wearing swimming costumes one or two sizes too small.

I tried it. I borrowed my still pre-pubescent little brother Tonio's' speedos.

Nil interest.

Actually, come to think of it, in many ways, Ennio and Xavier at their age understood a whole lifetime more than I did at the same age.

Funny, that.

Why am I raving on like this?

I guess because I realised that Xavier had exciting relationships, and up until the beginning of Fifth Year (our Leaving year) I didn't have any, and I saw myself growing up to be like Mr Jenkins—having some kind of love for God but channelling my explosive emotions into prayers rather than passion, and spending my life saying 'God bless' to everyone, trying to convince them I was fulfilled and happy instead of really being randy as a 16-year-old Italian-Australian male virgin—a dying race as I increasingly gathered in the smoking circle behind the grandstand at lunchtime down at the oval.

The Mr Jenkenses of this world may go home to their dog or their cat or their piano, but frankly, having been an inconsistent, mucked-up kind of celibate for most of my life and also having lived with many other priests in presbyteries and now with princelings and princes of the church in this sexually simmering mega-presbytery, I think the whole set-up is bonkers.

And more and more I wonder why we've never heard of how the apostles' wives and kids fared once the husbands and fathers jumped ship and set out evangelising.

It goes against everything we endlessly carry on about: the centrality of family to God's message… and to spread that screamingly bloody obvious truth, we've set up a structure where the salesmen—yes, still almost all men here at mission control—where all these celibate men have allegedly never tried the product and, indeed, taken a solemn oath never to.

What a way to run a business!

Whoops! An institution!

Whoops again! A Church.

And another whoops! <u>The</u> church.

Whichever one it is, the whole shebang is crazy beyond belief! Yet belief seemingly set in theological concrete—mind you, long before they found that there was such an alarming defect as concrete cancer.

Impossible and absolutely totally sexually fucked-up contrarian though he was, Luther at least understood the centrality of male sexuality to any kind of sanity.

God knows and God must laugh out loud at my lifetime festival of sexual fumbles, but it took me a long time to realise that maybe the all-weekend conquering Xavier was exaggerating a bit about his triumphs, and maybe the others, too, were relating con-cock-ions not conquests.

Still, the whole lonely isolation left me scarred… for life… which is why this Pope Jenkins the First sometimes screams out silently because of nightly coming home to what I've spent all day doing and then talking to myself about how satisfying it's been.

Soft pedal on the 'Thank you, Lord, for the joyful grace.'

Though probably, if I'd ever got married or had a long-term partner, I'd have been divorced or ditched within the year.

Anyway, I'm a total fucking mess and I've had enough.

Oh, my God! I think I've just been to confession to myself.

In which case, I'll rattle off the prayer of absolution and hope that God will forgive God's absolutely unworthy servant.

Come on, God. Only kidding.

Not.

Amen.

And by the way and just for the record, today is the feast of Pope Blessed Gregory X (1210–1276).

Interesting bloke. He was preacher to the last Crusade and while in Palestine, was elected pope after the longest conclave in the church's history and—how about this?—before he was ordained a priest! Now there's a precedent to remind some of these locals of. Who'll be the next elected non-ordained pope I wonder? Indeed, I wonder wonderfully. Seems Gregory was competent enough, which

I'd also rather like to be, but an unordained pope elected by conclave? Hope springs eternal.

This evening's bounty was a Sicilian sweet and sour dish called caponata. It's made of chopped fried aubergine and other vegetables, seasoned with olive oil, tomato sauce, celery, olives and capers, to all of which deliciousness Sister Angelica adds poached eggs. The agrodolce sauce is apparently Arabic in origin. Aubergines, our cook decrees, contribute to weight loss. Given that I enjoyed a second helping, I'll have to accept this as another article of Angelica's culinary faith.

Anyway, all that aside, call me old-fashioned, but I think popes should spend a very great deal of their time praying.

Prayer is health-giving to the inner life as well as to the outer. A person of prayer is calm, far-seeing and generous. A mere administrator is busy, efficient (well, at least they can't call me that) crisp and prone to delusions of infallibility. Another defect I've yet to demonstrate.

The trouble is what British Prime Minister Harold Macmillan called 'Events, dear boy. Events'. So often we don't have control over them, and invariably they erupt at the wrong time and cause even more trouble bouncing against one another in chaotic indifference.

Welcome to my life.

Yes, I pray for an hour every morning and for a shorter time before sleep. Such openness to the Lord bookends my day, but in-between, papal business as usual is an over-stuffed salmagundi of issues, each seen by those involved as terminally urgent and demanding immediate priority.

How I long for an agenda item reading 'something to plant, let grow, learn from, project, discuss, reflect on, then, perhaps, initiate.'

Still waiting for that one.

Today's highly confidential, exceptionally serious, incredibly urgent and potentially explosive event concerns the alleged conduct of an eastern European cardinal archbishop—very bright chap, though a bit too smooth for my liking—and a high-powered, extremely attractive female CEO of a major Catholic charity—the temptress from heaven or hell, depending on your point of view.

Apparently, emails between them have been leaked by an unknown source—almost invariably an ambitious cleric anxious to replace his boss.

The emails are affectionate, indiscreet and inconclusive.

Nothing to worry about there in the general scheme of things, but catnip to the tabloids and dynamite for the local church on bad news days.

The confected outrage of the secular press when a professed cleric breaks his vow of celibacy is marvellous to behold and even more spectacular when the cleric concerned is a bishop or a cardinal.

With popes, on the other hand, it tends to be expected—or at least was in times past. Given that we're all sexual beings and all prone to the needs arising from same, the rush to judgment by journalists has always struck me as more than a little hypocritical.

My younger brother who's been everywhere, done everything and by all reports (well, both of them over the years) is still alive... my younger brother... you remember him, Dad, Gino... well, now I remember, Gino was, for a very brief time (all his timelines are very brief) editor (and just about every other job) of a not-really-popular weekly news magazine in Australia. It went broke in a very brief time, but Gino's tales of journalists' and politicians' hi-jinx and low-jinx when they're onto a story—and especially a story on a boat— make *The Song of Solomon* sound like *Noddy and Big Ears*. Though on second thoughts I've always had a suspicion about what those two got up to after bedtime.

Anyway, even though the alleged indiscretion or liaison might make both parties repent and grow as a result—and certainly ensure in the long run that the cardinal is a more sympathetic pastor—we'll have to choreograph the usual gavotte.

He'll strenuously deny and offer his resignation. I'll wait, then when the dust settles, I'll not accept his resignation. Then six months or so later, I'll promote him to head some pointless Vatican dicastery and appoint a new archbishop in his place and suggest the cardinal thank, apologise to, but refrain from all further association with the good lady.

Amen to that.

And let he who is without sin cast the first editorial.

Sunday, January 11th

Feast of Pope Saint Hyginus (died 138).

Seems that during a time of relative peace in Rome, this Greek—and presumably hygienic—pope had a busy enough life dealing with the usual odd heretical nut cases (par for the course) and either was or wasn't martyred. I can relate to his uneventful or possibly eventful life. Perhaps of me they'll say, 'He either was or wasn't pope.'

Of course, it had to happen on my watch. Here we go again. A severe earthquake occurred in the Calabrian city of Gagliano causing the local church to collapse. The tragedy happened during Sunday mass. Almost always does. Can't fathom why. And dozens of people, including the priest, were killed, with many more missing. A search in the rubble continues, though with little hope.

So once again the cynics ask, 'Where was God?' and once again I reply, 'I don't know. I'm not party to understanding the indifference of nature, the problem of suffering and the apparent injustice in the universe.'

Of course, I can trot out the usual clichés about the victims going straight to heaven—sudden death arguably beats slow cancer—but that just kicks the can of the problem of suffering down the theological road.

My only honest reply is that frankly, while I can't make sense of a loving God inflicting suffering on the world God loves, I… well, accept it as a mystery of life.

Yes, Jesus suffered appallingly, and if I were God, I'm sure I could have come up with a universe less challenging.

But the disappointing fact is that I'm not God, and in moments like these, all I can do is hang on to my faith by my fingernails.

Wiser minds than this pope's will have to provide a more credible and convincing answer.

Sometimes, humility and acceptance are all we have left.

The alternative is treading water mid-ocean, in despair and at midnight with the waves crashing over us.

Together with all the faithful, I pray for all the dead. 'Your eyes saw my unformed substance; in your book were written, every one of them, the days that were formed for me, when as yet there was none of them.'

There's a certain beauty in that psalm. And an uncertain feeling while praying it.

God and the universe are a mystery to be lived, not an equation to be solved.

A certain avoidance in the platitude.

An uncertain resignation in the hope.

God sure is a mystery, but then which of us would argue that <u>we're not</u>?

Today is also the feast of Blessed Franciszek Rogaczewski (1892–1940), a patriotic Pole hunted by the Nazis for being a priest.

He was imprisoned and tortured for months before being shot. I weep for the power of evil and give thanks for the fortitude of Franciszek's faith—courage I know I could never summon. Such martyrs should have been popes rather than mediocre Antipodean seat warmers like me. How I pray for the assurance of faith.

Uncharacteristically, I had a first-rate idea after meditating this morning.

To be sure that I'm being bugged, I'll have a conversation with Ennio in which I propose to offer one young man and one young woman a week's work experience as pope.

Yes, Dad, you heard me right.

Indeed, I might suggest that as his commander-in-chief, I'll order Ennio to be that young man.

It would certainly make the week rewarding on all fronts for us both, and the fact that a female is even considered for such a post will, in all likelihood, be seen as the end of clerical civilization as we know—and hate—it.

Such will be the disbelief and outrage that an exquisite storm will erupt, almighty offence will be taken by the entire phalanx of the ultra-conservative Neanderthals, and I'll have proof positive of my suspicion.

And anyway, why shouldn't a pope and his young bodyguard enjoy a little innocent, if mischievous fun for a change?

Monday, January 12th

Feast of St Peter of Abessala martyr, burnt to death in 309—a hideous death so many thousands of martyrs have endured.

Otherwise, we apparently know nothing else about him... other than praying that the inspiration of this heroic unknown saint's agony will fortify this unworthy successor of St Peter in the time of my final anguish. If only he knew... and may he now know in whatever heaven might be in reality, or in a greater reality, or in a reality beyond all realities... and that projection is just the beginning of where mere human knowledge may stumble, so go dare to dream you sad, mechanical atheists... What on earth am I rambling on about? Where was I? Oh, yes, may the tortured and faithful and un-known St Peter of Abessala come to my aid in extremis and advance me to the hopefully unknown known. Or known unknown. And may Sister Angelica be at my side as well, recipe books as cabin bag-gage. I'm as yet not quite sure of Ennio's potential ascension; if you experience heaven on earth, I'm unsure how the Vatican Scribes and the Pharisees have theologically nutted out the appropriate-ly uncomfortable, barren, dangerous, pot-holed, diversionary and singeingly penitential B-road to on-going eternal ecstasy for the carnally happy. Not that I envy them. Heaven forfend. Except at my advanced age I still do. I somehow believe, however, that on the day of judgment, Ennio will still be upgraded to business class. Lucky bugger. Et dans l'esprit d'escalier, I owe an apology to those sad, mechanical atheists: we Catholics burnt people, too, for not hold-ing <u>our</u> beliefs. Blast!

Skimming back through these diary entries, I think I'd be right in describing myself as a terminal whinger. I mean, for God's sake—and in my case, that's the gig: God's sake.

So get your act together, Mario, and try to look on the bright side.

Dad, I see you nodding.

Well, one of the bright sides to any day is meeting with the head honcho of one the church's however many religious orders.

I say 'however many' because to date, I haven't yet found anyone in this city state who can give me an accurate answer. Even the experts tell me that it all depends on what is meant by the term 'religious order'. At a rough guess, something upwards of 120, and meeting one a day each year takes at least four months.

And I find every one of the leaders—well, almost every one... there's always the odd nut case, which makes you wonder whether they were elected as the least or the most crazy in that particular menagerie—but I have to say I find almost all of them impressive and inspiring.

And I'm fascinated by the individual charisms each order of men or women professes. For the aspiring cleric, there's a menu to suit every pious taste no matter how particular or precious. It amazes me how Catholic men and women with a vocation to religious life find themselves attracted to the curated spirit of a particular congregation of believers.

Of course, in these bad new days, there are thousands and thousands fewer priests, brothers and nuns than back in the good old days, which, alas, have now, to our shame, been to a shocking extent revealed as the very bad old days, but I can vouch for the fact that heads of just about every order have now finally taken responsibility for their predecessors' appalling sins.

The slate can never be wiped clean—must not—but admitting to the evil which was allowed to fester and poison the otherwise noble work of the many disciplined, dedicated and virtuous men and women who tried to follow the charism of their order has been a vital penance and a necessary moment of growth for the church.

In the last half century, every religious order has seen a diminution of its members, not least the Jesuits, the largest and, arguably, the brightest and most dynamic labourers in the vineyard.

The current general of the Jesuits is a formidable man. 'General' is *le mot juste*. He strikes me as shrewd, competent, intellectually honest and most of all, holy, and I should know because I share little or none of those character traits. He combines grasp of detail with clarity of vision and he exudes confidence in the face of rapidly dwindling numbers.

He is proud that for five hundred years in which the order has been following the inspiration and discipline of St Ignatius of Loyola in the fields of education, scholarship and social justice, 'they have more reason for satisfaction than for shame'.

Nice understatement.

Their current work with refugees is magnificent, and he tells me he is totally behind my insistence that were Jesus alive today, he'd adapt his parable of the Good Samaritan to a refugee story.

This calm warrior also tells me that there is no reason why the order should despair of falling numbers.

Those remaining should continue their energetic commitment, and should it come to pass that one day the order has no new members, the surviving labourers in the vineyard should consider this outcome to be the will of God.

Everything on this earth is subject to the reality of time, he says, and it is ignorant and arrogant to delude oneself that there should be any exceptions to this.

I asked him whether this applied to the whole church.

He replied that should such a state of affairs come about, it will either be the last day or perhaps the first day the church could claim with any conviction to have finally achieved humility.

I count him as an ally.

How refreshing to be able to trust someone in these parts.

And as for the leaders of the nuns' orders, I think the best of them make the general of the Jesuits look like a rookie.

These women of God surpass in their faith, hope, charity and sheer leadership panache so many of our priests and bishops. And cardinals. And certainly, this pope.

They combine strength with independence, daring, compassion and humility. And what I can only describe as divine common sense.

They strike me as understanding the good women in their order and looking to enable the most and least gifted of their charges to offer the world their skills so that to the best of their ability, they combine commitment and creativity to the satisfaction of themselves, their ideals and their God.

One in particular inspires me: Sister Amahle Zwane, South African Superior of Sisters of St. Joseph of Cluny.

Sister Amahle is the dazzling successor to the nun who should have been the first female pope and prophet: no, not Pope Joan, but American Sister Joan Chittister who was and remains the real thing.

And Sister Amahle is that second prophet.

Her parents were black farm labourers, but she went to a mission school run by her order.

She topped every class, turned down a university scholarship in Cape Town and entered her convent's order at the age of twenty.

She was professed at twenty-three, and her superior appointed her to teach at a Cape Town secondary school, but she appealed against that placement, requesting to study physics at Cape Town University. Her superior vetoed this proposal, arguing that basic religious education for the masses was much more important to the nation than the esoteric irrelevance of advanced physics, so Sister Amahle left the order and went onto be awarded an MSc and then PhD in Physics and, unsurprisingly, was asked to join that university's faculty.

Instead, she re-entered her order, was required in holy obedience to spend six months in the novitiate (yes, women can be just as dumb and vicious as men) which she undertook and then quickly became principal of her order's largest Cape Town girls' school.

After her first three years there, during which she was popular with staff and students, she broke every rule of feminist political correctness and proposed that for the potential faith, academic advancement and social welfare of her female students, her school should become co-educational as should all her order's convent schools in the diocese, and she intended to lead the way. She argued that the single sex ship had sailed a couple of centuries ago, and that only by recognizing that the world is largely heterosexual and thus educating girls with boys, would the church have the remotest chance of adjusting to the current reality in South Africa and, well, the world.

She insisted on a male deputy, and that henceforth, the running of the school must alternate between male and female principals and deputies.

When he heard of this proposal, her bishop—the inevitable conservative African male—rang her school and left a message with her secretary that she was to meet him at his residence at the end of that week at a specific time.

Sister Amahle told her secretary to reply that unfortunately, the principal was very busy until the end of the month but that she had two windows of opportunity to meet with the bishop and would look forward to talking with him at either, and that she would happily arrange parking for him at her school.

No meeting eventuated.

And to cut a long story short, she convinced her order's superior to trial co-education.

It proved to be success on most fronts, and moves are now underway for more brother-sister schools to follow suit.

But Sister Amahle's an educational realist and understands that traditional African attitudes don't change overnight.

Her school has a crèche, and student parents are guided in the care of their offspring, teenage fathers being required to do equal duties with the child's mother.

She also ensures that contraception is taught as central to African adolescent development, and her next hurdle is trying to create respect for the school's gay and lesbian students. I felt like saying, 'Good luck with that one in Africa,' but she's determined, and someone has to stand up for all of God's children.

Hardly surprisingly, she was appointed superior of her order.

I laughingly suggested to her that the church might consider such a sharing concept for the papacy: male pope and female vice-pope, then alternating the genders with each new papacy. She replied that given her leadership experience and my relative lack of it, she was ready to take over now if I'd agree to accept the secondary role.

I'm not entirely sure she was joking.

This magnificent woman could run the United Nations Mondays and Tuesdays, the papacy Wednesdays and Thursdays, America of a Friday and then take the weekend off.

There must be many more like her, and here _we_ are bumbling around in the Vatican with a leadership structure deep frozen in the middle ages.

The crazy irony is that women keep the church going, and the male clergy do their best to keep them in second-rate servitude.

In this vital matter of survival, the Anglicans are showing us the way, thanks be to God.

Tuesday, January 13th

Feast of Saint Remi of Reims (438–533).

Remi was of noble birth from a pious family. He must have gone to a good school because by 22, he was famed for his eloquence, and even though a layman, he was made Bishop of Reims by acclamation. Aged 22!! Vatican and synods take note. He served in that diocese for 74 years (the longest episcopate on record) during which time he converted Clovis, King of the Franks, thus making France Catholic: a reasonable line on any cv of the time. Perhaps we need to take note of bright, religiously committed 22-year-old lay men and women. How blind and dumb and imprisoned by tradition do we have to be not to realise that our future is with them? Let me answer my own question: totally fucking dumb. And then some. Think twice before you mock Nazareth. Or Wollongong. And just for the record, this boy wonder Remi is now patron saint of epidemics (hello?) fever, plague, snakes, throat pain and religious indifference (considerable work on that still to be done in the Illawarra area south of Sydney). He would most certainly have been bullied in the Wollongong playground for being a pansy, let alone speaking French, and bullied and belted by Brother Edmund for being a jumped-up, non-footy playing, arrogant little know-all... which, history tells us, he most assuredly was—knowing much more than the bogan ignoremuses (OK, 'ignoremi' for the precious) who persecuted him. There's a lot about St Remi today's church needs to take on board. Before it's too late.

I've come to the conclusion that in her own way, like Sister Joan Chittister, Sister Angelica is a prophet—a prophet who speaks, not in devastatingly delicious prose, but rather in devastatingly delicious poetic plates. Heaven has surely given us so many prophetic registers.

When Sister Angelica wants me to stay on course, the daily menu remains the same, but when she feels that I need to know or investigate something, she delivers an amazing new dish which speaks to my... I don't know... which speaks to my... I still don't know, but boy, it works.

Meanwhile, for the moment, it's stay on course time.

Two invitations in one day to visit shrines of Marian appearances: Medjugorje in Bosnia and Knock in Ireland.

Oh, dear!

Far be it from me to be diplomatic—let alone heretical—but while I completely understand devotion to Our Lady and see that for millions it helps them to glimpse the numinous, I find all the Mary Queen of Heaven routine—Our Lady as a shortcut to a very busy and possibly exhausted or partially-deaf Second Person of the Blessed Trinity... someone at court to put in a good word or do a special favour for us in return for a bit more prayer and praise—I find this approach medieval to say the least, not to mention devaluing of the Supreme Being to say—well, whisper—the most.

But such devotion is so widespread and probably causes little harm to the faithful that my reservations are best kept to myself.

And then, of course, there'd be those hundreds of religious congregations founded on devotion to Mary, and if I expressed my papal view, they'd have to find a new patron.

And I'd have to find a new job, though fortunately a pope can't be fired; he—or she. Stop it, Mario!—can only resign or die, and I don't fancy being locked up until I pop off the perch in some Vatican convent and being ordered by my successor to shut the fuck up under pain of excommunication or to meet a sudden, mysterious death like you know who.

That said, call me a Protestant, but I simply can't get my mind around the theology of apparitions.

They seem to me to take place in precisely the countries where there's little or no need for such affirmations of the divine and never in states where proof of celestial intervention in world affairs might well cause a nation's political or spiritual direction to change radically and, in extreme cases, cause Catholicism to replace Protestantism, Islam, atheism or even consumerism.

If only—especially replacing the false god of consumerism.

I mean, surely Our Holy Mother would set in motion even greater triumphs if such miraculous apparitions happened to the Archbishop of Canterbury or The Grand Mufti of Somewhere-or-Other or the presidents of Russia or China. And beatific visions to audiences of hundreds in Norway, Iceland, Tibet, Afghanistan and, arguably, North Korea, I'd certainly be interested to seriously investigate.

I don't deny the spiritual and/or psychological power of an imagined heavenly appearance offering healing to the afflicted and the hopeless. Surely the so-called medical miracles of Lourdes support that explanation.

The most generous lens through which I can observe this phenomenon is that visions are internal to the faithful and not granted to the faithless in need of just such an experience, otherwise, it seems to me, a couple of shrewdly considered visitations to assembled thousands of sceptics and rejecters would make a miraculous contribution to world peace.

And don't get me on Little Pebble, a con man who had repeated visions of Jesus, Mary, St Joseph and other saints—not to mention troops of angels—in Nowra, south of Wollongong.

This religious fraud founded the Order of St Charbel and attracted a couple of hundred doubtless good people of limited intelligence to his so-called order.

They dressed up in a range of clerical attire from either op shops or some third rate costume hire company, gave all their savings to Little Pebble, and on the command of Mary (making monthly appearances as conveyed, of course, by the Le Petit Caillou himself but never seen by the dim-witted faithful) they rejoiced not only in their prophet's right to 'mystical marriages' with selected females—all younger than his wife—but also in their pebblecrete saviour being selected by heaven to be Pope Peter the Second, an adornment to the see of Peter even less likely than myself.

Though not (yet) pope, he's finally out of jail, has married for a third time and according to the Gospel according to Wikipedia, has fathered more than 20 children during his glory days as a cult leader.

I'm suddenly feeling saintly.

I know I've said this before, but sadly, religion can do strange things to people.

Healthy scepticism may well be the eighth gift of the Holy Spirit.

I CONFESS

Wednesday, January 14th

Feast of St Successus of Africa, dates unknown, martyr about whom nothing is known.

Amazing. His parents sure got the name right.

Asparagus with chopped egg vinaigrette—simple and thought-provoking: don't overcomplicate things.

And Sister Angelica reassures me that asparagus will keep my blood pressure low, a command I'm sure each asparagus spear will obey.

Not that I'm much of a theologian—truth to tell, not that I'm much of an anything as I've spent a lifetime being told by my religious colleagues—but last night when the rain from nowhere suddenly cascaded on Rome—unprepared as Rome and Italy always are, the Vatican being no exception... don't even ask me—I had this old testament question.

That Noah and the flood story.

True or not, it must surely contain a message.

The current interpretation is that humanity—'mankind' as it was arrogantly known until recently—had, to coin a phrase, made a total stuff-up of life. God gave them free will, and what did they do with it?

Rather than praise and serve Him—as God was gendered at the time—they opted for sex, drugs and the old testament version of rock-n-roll.

Result: God decides to send a subtle message that the 'free' in free will has its consequences when exercised too freely—viz, a universal catastrophe such as wiping out almost the whole of humanity with the exception of 300-year-old Noah who 'found favour in the eyes of the Lord.'

So following supernatural advice, Noah packs his family and half of Taronga Park Zoo into his ark, down comes the rain, Noah and the menagerie set sail, and God makes His point.

'Here's My gift. Use it wisely.'

I've always had a problem with an all-knowing God gifting free will but necessarily knowing in His omnipotence that stupid mankind—especially the males who run the show—would bugger things up.

In the seminary, our wise theology professor had a clever explanation for what still seems to me a contradiction, but like so much from those days, I've forgotten it. Second-rate mind and all that.

But as the rain pelted on my window, I wondered whether all this disastrous climate change business might be God's updated flood to wake up and shake up an increasingly irreligious world to the selfish way we've just about ruined a wonderful gift.

It doesn't make much sense to me, and were I God, I'd probably try to get the message across in a gentler way, but then, as has been noticed in these parts, I'm not God.

Just a thought.

Thy kingdom come.

But to information wasted!

To celebrate his birthday, Prefect of The Dicastery of Laity Family and Life, Polish Lawyer Frinciszek Kaminski, a close associate of Olivier's and known for his efficiency, has invited thirty cardinals to cocktails and hors d'oeuvres at La Zanzara, an excellent restaurant just outside the walls of Vatican City.

Needless to say, a predictable few of these princes of the church are on our list of conclave waverers, but a good many are, happily, new to us.

How do I know?

Hilarious!

While Kaminski is famous for his organisation, his secretary's standards are, happily, less thorough. Emailing the general invitation, he cc'd the entire thirty, one of whom is Irish Cardinal Liam O'Rourke, Prefect of the Dicastery for the Eastern Churches. Liam's a delightful fellow, academic by intuition, impressively multi-lingual and trusting to the point of naivety. A cardinal of the extreme centre. He's also a buddy of my good kiwi friend, Cardinal Adrian Jellicoe, and with the innocence which makes Liam so congenial, he forwarded the email invitation to Adrian, asking him whether, given Kaminski's extreme traditionalist leaning, it would be advisable to accept.

I had to look up the Italian for 'cock-up'.

Un casino totale.

Anyway, Adrian immediately copied all the addresses and forwarded them to Dario suggesting that he might use them as a litany and repeat 'Pray for us' after each name.

Talk about a gift from above!

I wonder whether national intelligence agencies ever enjoy such accidental good fortune.

Dario says he'll update our files labelled *sparse ed esitanti!*

We now know for sure the wider who's who of waverers.

Adrian replied to Liam that he should accept and afterwards, when he has a moment, pop by and let him know the campaign mood of the celebration together with any little whispers or tittle-tattle that might be useful.

Manna from heaven!

You couldn't make this stuff up!

Thursday, January 15th

Feast of St Cosmas the Melodist (706–760) a monk who became a bishop in the Holy Lands and wrote beautiful hymns.

Lovely.

Still on miracles, I keep trying to clarify my stance.

As with apparitions, I remain sceptical though able to live with the faith of those who feel the need for apparitions, especially as at some future date, medical and scientific knowledge may well be able to offer an explanation other than a sign from heaven.

That said, as with angels, I'm in favour of miracles as they cause us to wonder, and wonder is the beginning of wisdom.

Certainly, the current church process for canonization is rigorous regarding miracles—three now being required—and since most contemporary miracles are the medical variety, qualified doctors have to declare that there is no current natural explanation for a sudden cure.

To me, there's a certain theological ambiguity as to why, for example, some petitioning believers at Lourdes are cured of their affliction while most aren't.

The traditional theory is that either those unfavoured have deficient faith or that God's all-knowing love is such as to allow the continuing sick further time to explore the mystery of pain and its relationship to eternal salvation.

I wish I were convinced of the satisfaction of both these options. Like, why does God always have a Get-Out-Of-Jail Card? Because God's God, I guess. And we're certainly not. But I do believe that in the end, no matter what, we must entrust ourselves to God's wisdom, care and mercy.

At its foundations, our Christian understanding of the world requires faith, hope, charity and acceptance, and at the present stage of my strange vocation, acceptance is the virtue I'm in most need of.

But in what is, I suppose, my characteristically elliptical way of looking at things, I'm more interested in the grace which those alleged miracles bring to the fortunate.

But I'm still challenged and troubled by miracles. Like those not graced with sudden cure, I almost certainly need to pray harder.

Mind you, if an absent arm or a leg were to be suddenly restored, even my unworthy scepticism would be banished in astonished gratitude and faith.

Definitely a miracle!

So, miracles?

Here's to many more of them!

Friday, January 16th

Feast of Saint Priscilla, dates unknown, but she had a villa near the catacombs in Rome ('Saint Priscilla owned a villa.' Stop it, Mario!) and she supported St Peter. Good on her.

From the start, strong women worked closely with some of the apostles. I wonder what St Peter's wife thought. For that matter, I wonder what St Peter thought.

Yesterday afternoon, I overhead one of my *soi-disant* loyal French cardinal supporters suggesting to another Vatican-Vichy *collaborateur* that the time has come in my papacy for there to be *un instantané*—a snapshot.

Thank you, Brother Edmund, back in Wollongong for your belting into me those daily vocabulary lists to be learnt by heart in fear of a cut of the strap for each mistake.

And the entire class knew you were longing for every slip-up so you could belt the victim *avec plaisir pervers*. And thanks to you, my French accent now hovers somewhere between sophisticated ocker and third wave immigrant Marseille *patois*, though Ennio tells me it's even worse, so many of the bloody Swiss being annoyingly tri-lingual.

But my understanding is sharper than those Gallic cardinals *à deux visages* give me credit for, and I'm more than happy to act the primitive Australian ignoramus while understanding three quarters or more of their asides.

And yes, why not a snapshot, not so much of my papacy, but of the church as I see it?

Truth's supposed to be the name of the game.

So as I see it, the church in its hierarchy remains pretty much like the Roman empire, which, if I remember correctly, eventually collapsed.

But the problem should the church become a democratic institution would be that it would lose all cohesion and turn into an ocean of wandering islands all believing whatever they liked and probably crashing into each other.

Or have both things happened or are they happening as we look on?

OK, we believe we're the church of God, so that's a pretty good insurance policy against total wipe-out, though my general impression is that we're way behind in keeping up with the payment instalments—i.e., keeping the spirit of the commandments rather than redefining them out of existence in miniscule detail and proscribing punishing retribution for all infringements. And faithfulness to the mass and the sacraments could increase by a few million percent without our being in danger of overpaying those instalments.

Are we at the stage of having many more lapsed Catholics than practicing ones?

I think the ayes have it. So, I ask myself, who is the CEO of this failing endeavour? And what is the board doing about it?

That second question, my papal friend, is indeed the question.

And the answer is plotting like there's no tomorrow—or rather for when the right today signals the strategic tomorrow when the vote for the next pope has been tied up and the Holy Spirit only has to waft by blessing the result *en passant*.

Coup de conclave.

Chile's Cardinal Carlos Silva Gonzales has asked for an urgent private interview tomorrow morning.

I've told him I'll happily make myself available but that my Secretary of State will be there to record the conversation—and, probably foolishly—I added, 'should further recording be deemed necessary', emphasising 'recording'.

No response.

In retrospect foolish. In the moment, uncharitably satisfying. In the end, a failure.

Nonetheless, Carlos is no fool. Actually, he can be the most charming of informed company because no one in the Vatican is more informed, including the holy father. Carlos is whisper central. And he's sharp and measured to the last theological and papal putsch millimetre. I think he's a genuine man of faith—let's hope good faith, though I wouldn't bet the ceiling of the Sistine Chapel on it. And he may well have missed his vocation as an utterly reliable weather forecaster, especially when it comes to which way the wind will be blowing.

I suspect an elegant trap, but that may well be my exponential persecution complex.

We'll see.

Saturday, January 17th

Feast of St Anthony of the Desert (251–356).

He was a rich young man who read Christ's exhortation to the young man to '...go, sell all that you have and give to the poor, and you will have treasures in heaven.' Anthony did—literally—and spent the rest of his life living alone in the desert with God. Amazing. Today people would probably call him bonkers. I think he may well have got closer to God than those of us living in the Vatican. He's the patron saint of butchers, skin diseases, gravediggers, and swine. Sounds about right. Butchers and grave diggers. Saint Anthony of the Desert, smile down upon this increasingly lonely pope.

I was right. An extravagantly elegant trap, though so over the top as to be… what's the French phrase Brother Edmund would say? *De trop.*

Carlos arrived on the dot with Cardinal Francois Nzapayeké from the Central African Republic as his unannounced recorder.

I should have told both of them to brush up their clerical good manners and fuck off as their uninvited extra visitor was obviously party to a tactical movement in Olivier's conclave strategy, but my natural refined Wollongong upbringing—read fear, though, more truthfully, a hundred to one Melbourne Cup bet that I might outsmart the conspirators—caused me to welcome both with cold charity.

Nzapayeké means African votes. He has the dirt on every African cardinal, bishop, priest, and for all I know, President and Chief of Police. His extended family of millionaire African entrepreneurs ensures that for whomever he might contact in that tangled knot, obedience is the best survival strategy.

'The children of this world are in their generation wiser than the children of light.'

In Nzapayeké's case, doubly so.

And, yes, they surprised me, but no, even I recognised Olivier's subtle hand in their wily temptations.

And even Dario undiplomatically winked once or twice while they looked to each other for reassurance.

Their oleaginous suggestion was that from all my sermons, conversations and comments, it would seem that I was highly uncomfortable defending our Catholic tradition and beliefs.

My reply was that my aim has never been to make the faithful feel safe and contented in their dogmatic chains; rather it's to liberate them into the invigorating and rewarding pilgrimage of a spiritual life.

That said, François Nzapayeké observed that it was clear to my many admirers among the Curia (Ho! Ho! Ho! Pull the other one!) that I was a vigorous advocate for world peace and that were I to resign from the papacy, I would be immediately appointed to the exalted post of Emeritus Pope Pastor for World Peace with all the necessary bureaucracy and finance to carry out my mission.

Carlos then drew my attention to the magnificently selfless work of former President Jimmy Carter in his retirement and suggested that an original thinker and dedicated apostle like myself would almost certainly find such work as satisfying as it would be challenging.

I lied and told both of them that my current role as God's Vicar on Earth, my election inspired by the Holy Spirit as is traditional church teaching, is in every way challenging and satisfying and that I intend to fulfil this role to the best of my ability until such time as it was evident to me that I could no longer cope with my graceful burden.

I'm surprised that I wasn't immediately struck by lightning, but as neither that nor thunder happened, I thanked them for their presence and suggested that the vital role of Emeritus Pope Pastor for World Peace seemed to me the ideal post for Cardinal Olivier Gabriel Foncha, and that they had my blessing to offer him that fulfilling apostolate.

Game, set and match—well, for the moment, at least—and for the rest of the day I was on a papal high.

Sister Angelica's simple bounty dinner this evening was manna from heaven: a fluffy Spanish omelette of lightly curried cauliflower with a subtle hint (what's the word? 'undertaste'?) of cheese.

Cauliflower, of course, being absolutely vital to the memory.

I must try to remember that.

And talking of memory, I have a confession to make. To myself—my schizophrenic self.

I've been a bit too hard on poor old Brother Edmund.

Well, only a bit.

He was the brutal basher I described, and his French accent was, as I've noted, nothing more than broad Australian phonetically pronouncing French spelling.

As for his ludicrous insistence on the importance of sport for manly character building (code for avoiding masturbation) playground and shower jesting and boasting suggested it failed 100% to achieve its goal.

Still, to do him justice, he was the product of his training (Irish penitential discipline adapted to Australian conditions) some of which actually did introduce its juniorate and seminary students to literature.

In his contradictory way, he had a love and a sound knowledge of traditional English literature—Shakespeare especially, poetry in general and grammar to the last, lonely gerund.

Weird how it all floods back. Only now do I think I understand the problematic complexity of Brother Edmund's focus on me throughout secondary school.

I was a good reader out loud and, for that matter, always found it easy to learn stuff off by heart and remember great swathes of whatever I read that interested me. I could perform poetry well (for Wollongong) and in class, when we were studying Shakespeare, Brother Edmund would read the heroic male roles and he always got me to read the female heroines.

I guess as a result of my delayed puberty (unnatural given my racial background) my woggishness eventually transformed me to some extent into being something of an Italian-Australian pretty boy, even though I was skinny—no washing board abs like all the swimmers and water polo gods—and my voice didn't break till Term 1 in Intermediate, and I certainly didn't find it at all spooky that in Second Year, I was Juliet to Brother Edmund's passionately read Romeo.

I assumed that I landed the role because I was by far the best reader in the class.

Actually, the only reader.

All the others thought acting was poufy, and in retrospect, this memory is increasingly uncomfortable, but when manhood finally descended on me in Intermediate, we were studying *Macbeth*, and I was Lady Macbeth to Brother Edmund's tortured Scottish monarch.

There was one dreadful legendary lesson when I was reading (powerfully, so I thought) and delivered the line, 'I have given suck…'

Suddenly the whole class erupted into chaos.

Kids were jumping up and down and yelling, 'We all know that!' and 'Tell us who!' and quite a few more graphically detailed interpretations of my supposed sexual activities.

And suddenly, Brother Edmund went totally psycho.

In a split second, the classroom changed from titillation to terror.

This man of God screamed and ranted and shrieked and foamed at the mouth about what pagan animals we all were, then he took out his strap and went round the whole class giving six of the best to every boy.

Clearly, what pubescent boys found funny, Brother Edmund found nightmarish and apparently took personally.

It was a terrifying public breakdown, in retrospect as revealing as it was traumatic for all concerned.

And when he finally came to me, he said, 'And you, Castaldi, you smart-arsed little squirt, just because your balls have finally dropped, you think you're some kind of comedian so you deliberately paused on that line to play to this pimply, foul-mouthed gallery.'

I protested, but he was totally out of control and dragged me out the front of the class and bashed the be-Jesus out of me.

The man was feral.

Possessed.

And after the sixth viciously cutting slice, in a millionth of a second he calmed down as if nothing had happened, said softly, 'Back to your place, Castaldi. Read on.'

And that was that.

You've never heard such petrified silence in a class of forty fifteen- and sixteen-year-olds.

The matter was never referred to again.

Only much later in life did I glimpse the twisted truth that 'You always hurt the one you love.'

Maybe poetry and role-playing were this tortured man's way of coping with the anguish of celibacy: Brother Jekyll <u>and</u> Brother Hyde.

That said, the Brother Jekyll in him surprised us all by encouraging us to dare to dream.

For Brother Edmund, the dare was to choose a poem or a line from the Bard or the life of a saint, and while going to sleep, hope to dream about it and in so doing, explore our souls.

Truth to tell, as adolescent males, the subjects we selected tended to be less pious, though I once had a wonderful dream about Prospero's farewell, *Our revels now are ended*, which Brother Edmund made us learn by heart.

I'm writing this because the power and exploration and release of dreaming stayed with me in the priesthood, and throughout my life, I've frequently had bizarre dreams combining and confusing theology and history, about saints and sinners (lots of popes therefore) and about characters I seem to have invented and who came from nowhere but somehow embodied problems or hopes I suppressed.

I've always felt a bit guilty about these experiences, Dad. Well, no, not so much guilty as embarrassed.

I sometimes wonder whether I'm just plain crazy or whether I should have been an actor or a playwright. And I have to admit that this weirdness is also due to Brother Edmund.

And now I recall another occasion when he gave me four cuts of the strap for getting four words wrong in *Our revels now are ended.*

One way to teach you to love poetry.

Looking back to the 50s, religious training, religious teaching and religious teachers really were like something out of Dickens: a mixture of *Oliver Twist, Bleak House, Great Expectations* and *Hard Times.*

I've often thought of writing down these dreams as a form of therapy to cope with the complexity (distortion?) of being me, but I've never dared to.

Now that I'm writing this diary, though, I might just try. I might learn a few things about myself. Who knows?

Thank you, Brother Edmund.

You bastard.

And having said that, slowly coming to terms with myself, maybe I'm finally forgiving you.

Sunday, January 18th

Feast of Blessed Christina Ciccarelli (1481–1543) prophet, healer and visionary, noted for her piety, humility and generosity to the poor.

She also experienced ecstasies. On the feast of Corpus Christi, The Body of Christ, Christina was seen to levitate, and the image of a host in a golden pyx (I love that cute little word for 'container') appeared on her breast. A vision she had on Good Friday caused invisible stigmata (how did they know?) and the pains of crucifixion until the next day. Sitting next to her at dinner must have made for interesting table conversation. 'So, how was Holy Week?' I really don't know what to make of all this. Some things I guess I just don't understand. I'd love to meet her, though. Who knows? One day, I just might. BYO Pyx.

Surprise early bounty. I'm beginning to think it's all about control!

Asparagus, aubergine and red pepper soup with black bread croutons. Must be time for me to confront some impending crisis or think outside whatever geometrical figure I'm treading thought in.

Vegetarianism. St Francis of Assisi. The environment. Italian Australian painter Salvatore Zofrea whose Francis of Assisi paintings and plates bring this holy man to antipodean life.

Health. *Mens sana in corpore sano.*

Balance.

I'm increasingly intrigued and strangely satisfied by my diary discipline.

It seems to me to be long-form gradual confession to myself as well as vague clarification of my second-rate intellectual and theological fog.

And, I'd like to think, of my struggling honesty.

Indeed, I think I'm talking to myself with what psychiatrists might venture to call self-diagnosis and, I suppose, the odd dose of self-medication.

Oddly frequently.

God knows what my closest brothers in Christ might call it, but I'll put my trust in God and God's good time.

While always keeping it to myself.

So... I'm increasingly interested in my own interest in nature and the environment.

A nun colleague of Sister Angelica is a strict vegetarian. She won't even eat eggs. Not surprisingly in her convent, she cooks for herself.

Certainly, Sister Angelica's miracles of celestial cuisine—definitely miracles I believe in—such gifts of God are not for this good nun, whom I nonetheless greatly admire.

St Francis of Assisi and Pope St Francis (as he soon will be if I have any say in the matter. Mind you, I'm only the bloody pope) will surely be leading her cheer squad in heaven where, I assume, the angels are also committed vegetarians.

But on reflection, my high regard for this nun and for all vegetarians is tempered by questions.

I know, Dad. When will I grow up?

Answer: when I discern convincing and comforting answers to my quest for spiritual security.

Do you a deal, God: convincing or comforting. Like most of the church, I'll run with one and be bloody grateful for that. If only my spiritual bewilderment would...

Yes, Lord, I hear you. 'Shut up and believe.'

OK. Help me out with a few clues on this one.

Of course I accept as given that the natural environment is entrusted to us for the continuation of itself and for the welfare of humanity.

William Blake beautifully proclaimed that 'everything that lives is holy', and centuries before, St Francis of Assisi regarded the natural world—rocks, plants, animals, air and water—as sacred and demanding of respect and care.

But as I gather from conversations and reading—not least, to my slight surprise, in the *L'Osservatore Romano* of which I'm the boss but very definitely not the editor—the current direction of scientific thought is that perhaps plants might have some kind of feelings.

What, then, are we to make of eating a salad or of cooking vegetables? And should I consider the feeling of an oyster or a scallop or a squid? And is caviar some hideous form of marine abortion?

Jesus's apostles were fishermen so they would have watched hundreds of thousands of fish struggling for life after being caught and then being chopped up for dinner, and presumably Jesus dined with these fish killers and never lectured them on their indifference to the suffering of sea creatures.

So after such a bad example (did I say that?) where does that leave this vacillating vegetarian? And if we all refrained from eating dead animals, would there be enough vegetables and flowers to feed the world? And if it's eventually established that stones, too, have some basic sensitivity—not unlike some of the curia cardinals—will we all have to tread gently like St Francis of Assisi? And come to think of it, why then have humans been given incisors? Or are they just a purposeless divine oversight?

Reductio ad absurdum, I know, but...

Perhaps in this coming Lent I should clear my mind by abstaining from all forms of meat.

And fish.

Though not, perhaps, from Sister Angelica's crostata cantarella, surely the sixth proof of the existence of God—the one St Augustine left out.

Monday, January 19th

Feast of so many saints whose brief biographies for some reason fail to inspire me. The failure is mine. My own biography will also fail to inspire, and should, by some ludicrous Vatican bureaucratic error, I finish up a saint, all I can say is God help all those who aren't.

Bounty in quick succession, and what liquid Spanish bounty tonight! Ajo Pelusa. Salt cod, garlic (naturally) and nora pepper soup with bitter orange juice and chopped flat leafed parsley. That last ingredient leaves me almost speechless. What if the leaf isn't flat? Time to call in the gastronomic canon lawyers. Apparently, this delight takes over a day to prepare. That said, the extra virgin olive oil sends positive vibes, and in these challenging days, anything extra virgin must be regarded as… well, helpful to salvation.

What's that old Spanish pious ejaculation? 'Cry cod for Harry, England and Saint George!'

And, 'leaders must lead.'

Now there's a thought.

I sometimes think the bits and pieces I overhear have the volume deliberately increased for my less than accidental edification.

But not this afternoon's eavesdrop.

'Leaders lead. Fortunately for us, Vegemite is one of life's followers, which we must make sure remains the case—that's if the dimwit can actually find anything to follow. Keeping him busy must be our strategy.'

Mmm. We might just see about that.

An idea to inspire and renew. A major advance. With minimum lead time to cut them off at the pass.

Come, holy ghost creator, come,
Inspire the mind they scorn as numb.

Meanwhile, back at the ranch and on which subject, a reality check tells me that it seems like forever that popes have spoken out against aggression and war, and I'm trying to remember when it has made the slightest difference to either side's military actions.

But I absolutely believe that by speaking out, the pope has a chance—and an obligation—of touching the hearts of the wider gathering of humanity in reassuring all people of good will that somehow, in the end, good will triumph over evil.

And despite the exhortation of two concerned (and heavily politicking) curia cardinals, I shouldn't have to resign to make my point.

Pause for settling of muddled thought above.

Yes, the cost is great—no, heartbreaking almost beyond belief—but God's message of ultimate salvation gives strength to the righteous and is a candle of hope in the optional darkness of meaningless destruction.

So, Pope Vegemite the Last must speak truth to satanic worldly conflict but also change the fundamental structures of faith to give hope to the hopeful as well as to the hopeless.

The church must speak out more and more loudly with confidence and with consolation for the victims, the dispossessed, the marginalized, the faithful, the questing faithless, our intellectually honest opponents and for the last innocent, suffering child.

How many each day? No, each hour? And the meaning of that to every parent of a lost child?

Christ must renew the world.

A fine thought to console those parents, but who removes the everlasting shrapnel in the soul?

If only I knew.

Of course, I do. But in my heart of hearts and soul of souls, I…

Tuesday, January 20th

Worrying. Very. A weird but vivid dream of which I seem to have total recall. This has to be serious, medically and spiritually. What on earth can it mean? The onset of madness? Yes, I know God and the angels popped up in lots of Old Testament dreams, and that's easily explained away, but in the 21st century? And yet, somehow I felt I lived this curious experience. Best I tell nobody—you excepted, Dad—or within minutes, they'll have me locked up in the papal funny farm. And wouldn't they love that?

Yes, Mario, nice to know you haven't forgotten who I am. The <u>smiling</u> pope. Albino Luciani, John Paul I. Pope for thirty-three days back in 1978, and if you know your papal history (which I know you do) I'm equal tenth with Benedict V on the list of shortest papacies, though not in the race with Stephen II in 752, who, you recall, lasted just three days. I take my zucchetto off to him. After Paul VI—yes, the Vatican's very own Hamlet—the cardinals felt they needed a Dogberry—or did they think, 'dog's body'? Anyway, they wanted a pleasant simpleton who wouldn't rock the boat but steer the barque of Peter steady as she goes. So in record time they elected me: a labourer's son. First mistake. When you're brought up poor, you learn how to be careful with money. You quickly pick up how to read a family ledger or a bank statement. One week in the Vatican, and I realised a new broom was needed—and a heavy-duty one at that. I looked at the ledger, and none of it added up. I'm talking about The Vatican Bank: the mafia and Archbishop Marcinkus. In my first meeting with Marcinkus, I outlined my plan for a church of the poor. Marcinkus informed me that we couldn't run the Vatican on Hail Mary's. <u>He</u> certainly wasn't. When I found out exactly what he was running the Vatican Bank on, I realised we were in trouble. Big trouble. *Turbine mauris*. Latin. 'Shit storm', as we labourers' sons have been known to say. And Marcinkus soon knew I was on the case. I'd also decided to talk about 'God, our mother.' Seemed as obvious to me as I know it is to you. Four weeks into my papacy, few of the Curia were returning my smiles. A couple of days later, I died. Suddenly. Mysteriously. 'Heart attack', said the doctor they summoned. It was the first time he'd examined me. And the last. Only a few days before, my personal physician had given me a clean bill of health. No autopsy. Embalmed before you could say 'deliver us from evil' let alone 'Amen'. All nineteen rooms of the papal apartment were cleared in record time. Oh yes, the forever-stalling Curia can be ruthlessly efficient when they want to be. Like the mafia. I mean, look what tidal opposition happened to Francis in the end. And what was the result? You're living it. *Piu cambia*. The more things change and all that. Funny thing being pope—if you survive. *Dominus vobiscum*.

So is it God speaking through John Paul, or is it me talking to myself?

What did Hamlet say? 'The readiness is all. Let be.'

Please, God, make this a one-off.

That's a prayer.

And then, after all this, more INW.

And what am I meant to make of this? A source not to be named—heaven forbid it should be Cardinal Marcel Brulé of Paris currently visiting Rome—anyway, this morning, our un-named Gallic source mentioned in passing to Dario that three nights ago after dining with a friend at what he described as a modest but friendly trattoria on the outskirts of Rome… Mmm. Why on Rome's outskirts? And why not named? Some kind of ecclesiastical refuge? I'm always intrigued when certain clerics keep their companion unidentified. Anyway, while exiting from his modest but unusually outlying trattoria thirty minutes from Rome, His Eminence noticed leaving from the nearby gastronomically superior Benito al Bosco, Adrian Jellicoe and Bruno Westphalen hopping into a taxi for the long ride home.

What on earth can this mean?

And, indeed, who picked up that not inexpensive tab?

How to make sense of this?

For God's sake, Mario, stop being so paranoiac. Simply ask Adrian.

Which, of course, I will.

Occam's Razor.

Oh, and I almost forgot that today is the feast of Saint Sebastian, unusually muscular Roman soldier, convert, martyr, though not by the arrows depicted on the multiple paintings of this saint's sadistic punishment by his fellow soldiers.

He survived that hideous assassination attempt only to be eventually clubbed to death by a different mob of pagan warriors. When it comes to extreme cruelty, no one beats the Romans. Sebastian's arrow ordeal has made him more than any other saint the subject of scores of what seem to be erotic rather than spiritual studies. He is now universally acknowledged as an unintentional gay icon. I wonder in the peace and joy of his eternal reward what he thinks of this presumably unexpected adulation. When the time comes, I must ask him. His opinion might be… well, actually, I have no idea what it might be. As yet, he has not been formally declared the patron saint of gay men, though were a poll to be taken, I can't see who'd come in anywhere near second. Jesus? John? Possibly, though unlikely I'm afraid. Twenty-first century child that he is, Ennio has offered to be a model for any local contemporary artist interested in the subject. He decides the fee depending on how much he's required to disrobe and the intensity of the artist's request. The children of this world! I'm sure that as a result of the sitting, Mirella would be ravished by appropriately expensive jewellery. More to the point and for what it's worth, all the Sebastians I've met have been civilised and delightful. And fully clothed.

And contributing to my mellow mood was tonight's bounty: maccheroni alla chitarra with fresh tomato sauce, anchovies, ricotta and mint. *Chitarra's* Italian for guitar, and the pasta is apparently sliced through wires that resemble guitar strings, and as we all now know—and we would never dare google for mere electronic confirmation—anchovies and mint stimulate the brain.

I should consume kilos of them daily.

And yet… and yet throughout today, always at the back of my mind is that dinner between Adrian and Westphalen. I simply can't work it out. And then I think to myself, for God's sake stop being so paranoid. People—even cardinals—are allowed to have dinner together if they wish.

But why go that far out of Rome? Well, because they've heard that the food is excellent.

Yes, but… and, of course, the simple solution to my concern would be to say in passing to Adrian that informed Vatican sources—a joke we frequently share—told me he was dining the other night with Westphalen.

But given Westphalen's allegiance to Olivier, that surely would suggest that I was in some way suspicious of my kiwi friend. Which I'm not. Well, which I don't want to be. And the implied insult would be hurtful to him.

No, this whole business should be put aside. Dismissed. Forgotten.

There are much more pressing issues to be addressed.

And yet…

Wednesday, January 21st

Feast of a 13-year-old girl, Saint Agnes (c291–c304) virgin and martyr.

Patron Saint of young girls, rape victims, and chastity. I take notice. Painfully close to home. And I have doubts? What are my intellectual and theological meanderings compared to this amazing girl's faith? A sobering day in every sense. And no wacko dreams last night, thank God. And, if I may, thank you also, St Agnes, for putting me in my place.

The *ad limina apostolorum* (in reality, Rome checking up) visits of bishops are important, though their reports to HQ often seem to be written in fluent polystyrene, still the individual meetings can occasionally be enlightening.

The eight bishops of Accra in Ghana are a friendly lot, almost all optimistic in outlook despite the madness that can be Africa.

One in particular, Bishop Gyasi Owusu of Garural, is particularly engaging and positively bubbling over with ideas. He so impressed me that I arranged for a private meeting with him, and he had a thought bubble which struck me as either inspired or insane, and on reflection, I think the former.

He pointed to the obvious in Europe: empty and unused churches everywhere falling into disrepair and less than convincing advertisements for the vitality of the church. As he pointed out, even if the buildings are no longer functional, the land they're on can become missionary.

His brother is a successful developer with significant contacts in the Ghanaian government and throughout much of Africa. A given. And a possible worry. Perhaps very possible. But an African given. The children of this world.

Gyasi's idea is that every unused church, instead of being a sarcophagus for faith, should be linked to a city or town in Africa. When the silent and sometimes crumbling church is sold for land, the money is sent to the twinned African city or town to build the most modern of hospitals.

From death to life.

And, as he took delight in noting, apart from some mind-blowingly expensive new cathedral—my mind flies in fascinated horror to that Ozymandian monstrosity, *Notre Dame du Kitch*, a million miles from anywhere on the Ivory Coast—what more inspiring symbol could there be than a hospital?

Faith in action.
And a small chapel in each.
An idea to inspire and renew?
Time, I think, for a new and young African cardinal.
And an intelligent conclave vote.

Thursday, January 22nd

Feast of Saint Vincent of Saragossa (died 304) who must have been a talented and extraordinary man.

He was a deacon and during the unspeakable persecutions of Diocletian, he was imprisoned and horrendously tortured for his faith. He was stretched on the rack, and his flesh was torn with iron hooks. Then his wounds were rubbed with salt, and he was burned alive upon a red-hot gridiron. Finally, he was cast into prison and laid on a floor scattered with broken pottery, where he died. While in jail, he converted his jailer to Christianity—a miracle I rejoice in. I can hear the primitive taunts and evil laughs of his barbarian tormentors—today's aggressively infallible atheists echo that nasty satisfaction—but what a hero was Vincent suffering so abominably for his faith in Christ! And this pathetic excuse for a believer whines about curia bureaucrats delaying papal decisions! The all-inspiring St Vincent is now—amazingly and upliftingly—patron saint of vinegar makers, vintners, wine growers, wine makers, Portugal and World Youth Day in 2023. Extraordinary! With each new bottle, I'll pray to him. Deo gratias.

Miracle time again. Third strike and third time lucky!

God only knows how many phone calls come to the Vatican every hour from saints, sinners and nutters who say, 'This is urgent. Put me through to the pope immediately.'

Of course, they never get through, though they're offered the opportunity of speaking to a counsellor—and full marks to us for that—but understandably, they usually shout abuse then hang up.

Indeed, I fear I know all too well that intuitive response to papal bureaucracy.

But... this caller claimed to be the pope's brother—and there have been a few of them who've tried that on, all ratbags and/or mentally disturbed, alas, but such was my brother's background knowledge of my life that the operator rang me for advice.

And it was Tonio, ringing from Esperance, a town down the very bottom of Western Australia, next stop Antarctica.

I'm not superstitious—well, not very. Well, OK, somewhat, in a kind of post-Wollongong Italian Catholic upbringing background— but *esperance* means 'hope', and all I can say is that for the duration of the call and for the rest of the day, my heart and soul overflowed with hope, love and gratitude to God.

Tonio's now 69, clean, off the grog, and a fisherman in Esperance.

And I'm 78, on the grog and in the shoes of a fisherman in Rome. *Esperance en effet!*

And he's got a partner, a divorced lady from Perth, a bit younger than himself, and she's got a 35-year-old married daughter who's just had a baby girl. The mother wants to get her baptized, and Tonio asked her would she like the pope to be the kid's godfather.

When Tonio told her his brother was the pope, the mother naturally assumed Tonio was back on the turps, so he said, 'Hang on, I'll just ring him.'

And he did.

And I accepted.

And my heart sings.

> *God moves in a mysterious way*
> *His wonders to perform.*
> *He plants His footsteps in the sea*
> *And rides upon the storm.*
> *Deep in unsearchable mines*
> *Of never-failing skill,*
> *He treasures up His bright designs*
> *And works His sovereign will.*
>
> *And ye fearful saints, fresh courage take;*
> *The clouds you so much dread*
> *Are big with mercy and shall break*
> *In blessings, yes, in blessings*
> *And in blessings on your head.*

Judge not the Lord by feeble sense
But trust Him for His grace;
Behind a frowning providence
He hides a smiling face.
His purposes will ripen fast,
Unfolding every hour;
The bud may have a bitter taste,
But sweet will be the flower.

Blind unbelief is sure to err
And scan His work in vain,
For God is His own interpreter
And He will make it plain.
In His own time.
In His own way.

Thanks be to God.

Tonio, I love you.

Friday, January 23rd

Feast of Saint Marianne Cope (1838–1918) a quite amazing religious lady.

The oldest of ten children of German immigrants to America, at the age of 24, she entered the Franciscan order and quickly became a principal. Then she opened hospitals in New York caring for the sick, however destitute. In her 40s, she was elected Superior General of her order, and you might have thought that would have kept her busy and fulfilled for life. But no! At the age of 45, she upped and went to the Hawaiian island of Molokai to help the ailing Fr Damian de Veuster (now Saint Damian) and she founded a hospital for lepers and a home for the daughters of lepers. She worked on Molokai for thirty years! And I sometimes complain of being tired at the end of a day of meetings. Some saints help us to see our lives in true perspective. Now the patron saint of lepers, outcasts and those with HIV/AIDS, Saint Marianne Cope would surely have made a compassionate and inspiring pope.

I've now insisted that I must take one mad phone call each day—to keep me sane, and alternatively, either Dario or Angelica is to decide on which call will get through.

Their differing outlooks to some extent represent the church even in one phone call a day. And anyway, why in God's name can't one of the faithful talk to the pope about something that's bugging them?

Is God's apparent representative on earth too busy to deal with reality?

Dario does his diplomatic best to guide me and offers advice as to which callers might need the most immediate help.

Happily, Angelica says I'm the shepherd of the flock.

Try as I may, I can't disabuse her of the unfortunate overtones of that well-intentioned but dangerously dated metaphor.

But I absolutely value their instant advice in this new pastoral adventure for this ever-questing pope.

Oh, and when I occasionally mention this arguably dangerous initiative to Ennio—and he can be cheeky—Ennio says I need to be in contact with more sinners so I can be more Christ-like in forgiveness.

I think there may well be an element of shrewd self-interest in his amusing advice—and then I realise, he's of the generation which binned sin early in adolescence and as a result, are still in search of salvation even if they don't know it.

But that engaging smile of his suggests worldly wisdom.

So to today's mad call.

And stop there, Mario.

That dismissive label is arrogantly—disgustingly—insulting to God's people and must be immediately changed.

And let's face it, this receiver is almost surely more troubled than the caller, and I must provide the daily spiritual bounty to those in need of sustenance, so this exercise in charity will be that of the Grateful Samaritan.

And thinking more about this initiative, prudence as well as charity is required.

In the brief time I have with my unknown facetime friend, I mustn't assume that in a couple of minutes I have all the answers to the complexities of any individual's life. That would more than likely cause more harm than hope, and, indeed, I could well be responsible for all kinds of disasters.

No, what I must offer is general sensible spiritual advice which might just help my new parishioner to turn a corner.

First of all, I'll make it clear that our conversation is in no way confession. Rather, it's two people listening to each other, one of whom just happens to be the pope.

I'll therefore thank them for their time, sympathise with their trouble and offer two simple suggestions which may begin to bring consolation.

The first is to visit an empty church (pretty easy to find) during the day, sit down and for five minutes open themselves not to petitioning but to listening. I'll assure them that God will speak to and in their hearts.

If not, then then there is no God. My papal guarantee.

Then I'll ask them within the week to attend Mass, join in the responses, receive communion and afterwards, remain for five minutes after mass and, yes, listen with gratitude.

That's surely an act of faith and hope, one which our loving God would never ignore.

My one counsel to everyone will be that our all-loving God will never judge us by the worst act we are guilty of but rather by the best and noblest and most charitable thing we've done. So with faith, hope and love, let us all have confidence and dare to become our best selves day by day every day.

And I'll then explain that I have to go but that the pope will remember them tomorrow morning in his mass.

Such a five-minute act of charity might well be the most satisfactory achievement of my day.

Actually, I think I'll suggest it to every cardinal, hoping they might be able to find the time.

And, come to think of it, to every bishop.

Won't I be popular with the hierarchy!

That aside, I think Dario, Sister Angelica and even Ennio will approve of this initiative, and I have a shy hope that in this matter, Dad, you might have reason to feel that your son has done some small good work in his life.

INW.

Information I absolutely do not want. A close nun friend of Sister Angelica's told her that very late last night, she observed emerging from Westphalen's office that affable but no-nonsense administrator, Cardinal Thierry Etcheverry of Reims, Parisian Cardinal Patrick Brulé (The French Connection?) and my good friend Adrian Jellicoe. This is greatly disturbing. It's in every way a discordant quartet. Both Frenchmen are my supporters, Adrian is a valued—I want to say 'loyal'—friend, and Westphalen is an impressive, forceful Teutonic numbers man for Olivier. Do I hear chimes at midnight? If it's a changing alliance, should I confront Adrian or feign ignorance and remain vigilant for further defectors? I need to discuss this with Dario.

Saturday, January 24th

Feast of Saint Francis de Sales (1567–1622) who was as brilliant a theologian and doctor of the church as he was humble all his life as a bishop, so sadly, we don't have that much in common, but today is also the feast of Saint Macedonius Kritophagos (died around 430) whom, to my shame, I've once again never heard of.

Seems he was a hermit in Syria who refused to eat bread and lived on nothing but moistened barley for 40 years. He was also a healer who used prayer and holy water (though, oddly, not barley water) to work miracles. No loaves and fishes for picky old Macedonius. For some reason, I've never been tempted to be a hermit and now I'm beginning to discern the reason. Can't imagine Macedonius and Sister Angelica sitting down to a meal together, but then they wouldn't, since he was a hermit. Probably just as well. Some saints appear to us today to be a little odd. Or a lot odd in certain cases. Oh, and a few days ago I was expressing patronising cynicism about Blessed Christina Ciccarelli's ecstasies and now here I am meticulously remembering my own bizarre dreams or apparitions or whatever they are. Cynicism is clearly the eighth deadly sin—and the one which comes back and quite rightly bites us on the bum. My apologies, Blessed Christina. Psychology has explained away all mystical experience as mere sensory cortex confusion—not to put too fine a point on it, pious, self-activated delusion. Sorry about that Christina, but it's where we're at: increasingly scientifically enlightened and spiritually lost. Meanwhile, here's my latest visitation. Seems that for my sins, I'm destined to be subjected to what could be an endless papal pantomime. To sleep perchance to dream.

Yes, Mario, it's me, Pope Sixtus the Fourth 1471–1484. Very good, but then you always were a bit of know-all with boring dates. And yes, you're right: I built the Sistine Chapel, hence the title. Extravagance was my specialty. Beautiful, massive, glorious. My weakness. All the young cardinals I created had similar 'qualifications': beautiful, massive, glorious. I made them cardinals in return for their—shall we say 'loyalty.' Blond and muscular and loyal. Oh, and aristocratic, naturally. Which can't be said for some of my predecessors and successors, as I'm sure you'd agree. I mean, Julius the Second expired with a teenage altar boy up his arse. Athletic, understandably, but frankly—well, common. I'm sorry, but it's just not a good look for a pope. No, to rough trade. Still, we can all be redeemed. It's all in the timing. I recommend this consideration just before your last gasp. Still, let's face it, I suppose we all have our little weaknesses, and, of course, you know what I mean with your little—shall we say—Swiss dalliances. My other weakness? The arts. That's why your queues of tourists today pay fifty euros each to see my chapel. Nice little earner, eh? <u>And</u> I founded the Vatican library, gave Rome new sewers—and let's face it, as we both know, there's an awful lot of shit in the Holy City. And I brought water to the Trevi Fountain. But nobody seems to remember me for that these days. Still, all things considered, not a bad record I'd venture to suggest. Ah, those were the days! Mind you, good to know that there's life in the old institution. Funny thing being pope. I suggest you make the most of it while you can. As somebody once so observantly said, 'You know not the time nor the hour.' Bye bye, darlings. Oh, and I almost forgot: *dominus vobiscum.*

> How did those essays end?
> 'And then I woke to find it was all a dream.'
> Funny how it all comes back to you.
> Not.
> Pass me the barley water.
> On second thoughts, the Jamesons.
> What did Pope Sixtus warn? 'You know not the time nor the hour.'

A long and serious discussion with Dario in the corridors and well away from my Santa Marta apartment. His advice is that even here, in the home of conspiracy, it's prudent to beware of conspiracies which don't exist. As he said, to the guilty walking in the dark, shadows of branches can become shadows of bears. Trust in the light which illuminates the safe path beyond.

Been there, done that. Far too often. And that pathway always beckons. As it must.

As it must.

But… after our postulating various interpretations of that bizarre pre-midnight meeting—and so far out of Rome…

Dario's measured counsel was: wait and watch.

Wise.

Or?

Sunday, January 25th

Feast of the conversion of St Paul, well known horseman, Christian persecutor, convert, missionary, and letter writer.

His ferocious energy and faith transformed the church and all because he heard the voice of God. At least I have one thing in common with Paul: we both hear voices. It's a strange experience—out of body though obviously within it; a kind of internal drama with scripts written by God only knows whom? God, if we're to believe St Paul. Anyway, hearing voices seems to be all the rage right now, though I gather mental health professionals these days call hearing voices 'auditory hallucinations' and regard the experience as part of schizophrenia and other psychotic disorders. That's reassuring. As far as I can tell, changing the label doesn't make the experience any less real or impactful. If we changed the word 'pain' to 'momentary joy disruption', would that take away the agony? And while considering contemporary takes on traditional understanding, the excellent, indeed powerful Greek Australian novelist, Christos Tsiolkas, suggests that St Paul may well have been gay. I've noticed that lots of gay people think that just about everyone else on the planet is gay; it's just that they're too terrified to admit it. These enthusiastic advocates are either on to something or on something. Only God and gay people know. Or do they? And more to the point, does it matter? When God gave us the gift of sexuality: its passion, its needs and its ever-demanding fulfilment… may we assume that it wasn't some kind of cynical 'gotcha' revenge on people who hadn't yet been born? If so, strange God, thinks I. So why did God get it so wrong? Or could it be that Church teaching has failed to develop since effective contraception has made unwanted children no longer a sound social reason for condemning sexuality outside marriage? And is it possible for unmarried Christians to be sexually responsible while still being sexually active? And is all sexual activity between same sex couples a mortal sin that comes with a first-class express ticket to hell? Feel free to cite specific Gospel passages where Jesus leaves his followers in no doubt that all forms of non-marital consensual sex—not to mention same sex relationships—are unnatural, abominable and punishable for all eternity in the sight of our all loving God. Also feel free to perhaps offer suggestions likely to convince contemporary young people of the joy and wisdom of celibacy. Oh, and old people, too. Don't forget us! And good luck. And by the way, to whom am I speaking, I ask myself. And I know the answer.

Bounty of honey and red miso oven baked prawns. Looks as tempting as its taste is satisfying, and goodbye heart disease and cancer.

In Year 9, Sean O'Sullivan called me a raw prawn for not letting him pinch bits of my English essay on *Macbeth*. After leaving school, Sean joined the brothers but quickly left and became a dentist. I'm not sure which calling is sadder. Some in these corridors might argue that I haven't succeeded in shaking off Sean's slur.

Cracked record that I am, I simply don't subscribe to the endless bleatings of bishops about the crisis in vocations to the priesthood and to religious life, though I can no longer accept those offensive medieval hierarchies of religious status. We're all priests, and the sooner we rejoice in our baptismal ordination the better.

But perhaps that's for another rant.

Sorry about that, God, but I reckon that in this matter, you're on my side.

Anyway, yes, it's a crisis because the church is stubbornly deaf to those with manifestly obvious vocations: women. And women and men who eschew celibacy yet desperately want to become priests.

How much more loudly must God speak before we hear? Oh, and just remind me how many of the apostles were married.

I have every reason to welcome to the priesthood those who wish to embrace celibacy, but let's face it, they're necessarily a minority.

And a strange one.

This conversation must continue against all the opposition here in Rome.

Olivier is especially ferocious against the subject even being mentioned.

Methinks the cardinal doth protest too much.

And word of my Grateful Samaritan phone calls has got out, the current corridor buzz being that my lunacy is rapidly accelerating towards a major collision with rational judgment.

News flash: I'm the pope.

What must I do to bring sanity to a church refusing to listen to common sense?

An idea to inspire and renew?

A major advance?

Monday, January 26th

Australia Day, provided you're not one of the original Australians. Also India Day. What a curious and unconnected coincidence. Also the feast of first century Saints Timothy and Titus, bishops.

Young Timothy was a great friend of St Paul's so he must have been a very patient fellow. Timothy was also sickly, causing Saint Paul to tell him to stop drinking only water and have a little wine 'for thy stomach's sake and thine oft infirmities.' Advice to be scrupulously followed. Feral pagans bashed up Timothy, dragged him through the streets, and stoned him to death. Titus, too, was Paul's friend and was a Gentile, but Paul would not let him be forced to undergo circumcision at Jerusalem. Again, Paul was on the money. Titus died of old age. Both Timothy and Titus are now the patron saints of stomach disorders—probably Timothy for those requiring the odd heart start-er. I assume Titus must be the patron saint of uncircumcised male Christians, though I'm not entirely sure what they'd pray to him for.

I remember with pain what happened however many years ago in Islamic Aceh in Indonesia: two lads, 19 or 20, we caught (how? What disgusting measures were encouraged by the authorities?) having sexual relations. They were punished, each with 100 strokes of the cane in public, and a stadium was filled with (literally) blood thirsty voyeurs applauding the torture stroke by agonising stroke.

In God's eyes, who were the sinners, I ask myself.

Now it's happened again, and the same diabolical ritual is to be meted out on two similarly young males in that crazy Islamic state. All this in the name of God, the Prophet and some kind of perverted morality. It reminds me of our church's grievous sins of torture in the name of the same God, and often carried out with the perverted clergy observing.

And what harm to humanity or to the Almighty have these two Indonesian young men done?

I'll pray to St Edmund Campion at the precise time of these lads' extended agony that in some miraculous way, their suffering may be made somehow less unbearable. That would indeed be a miracle.

I only wish that I believed my prayers might have the slightest effect.

This horrible combination of despair and horror haunts my every moment.

St Edmund Campion and all the martyrs, give me strength. And faith. And grant all those victims of religious ignorance, prejudice and sheer fucking evil the perseverance and consolation of those of us who desperately pray with them as they endure their satanic torture.

In my despair, I hope. But in my hope, I despair. And if any ig-noremus ever again asks me to define original sin, I'll know where to look in all the fiction of all their creeds. The question they—we—can never answer is: what kind of God would offer that self-destructive option of free will to frail humanity?

Answer: how does the National Rifle Association of America in-variably respond to utterly meaningless, endlessly ongoing and cru-cifyingly dehumanising gun slaughter of the innocents?

'This is not the time for political points scoring. Thoughts and prayers.'

The NRA should put Judas up for canonisation. And they have the hide—and dollars—to do so.

Sleeping tonight would indeed be some kind miracle for me.

Though not for those poor two boys.

Tuesday, January 27th

Feast of Pope Saint Vitalian (died 672) with whom I feel papal empathy.

He was a complete nobody before his election. Check. Once elected, his pontificate was marked by endlessly constant conflict between bishops. Check. He settled the long-standing argument between the English and the Irish churches over the date of Easter. I, too, am expected to resolve such world-shattering theological wars of interest only to non-pastoral theologians who've never visited a prison or a home for alcoholics or a shelter for the homeless on the street— life's victims who didn't give a twopenny stuff about the date of Easter but might have appreciated a cup of tea, a ham sandwich and a passing glimpse of God's love. Check. Pope Saint Vitalian was in favour of organ music during church services. Check. He also made an enemy of a powerful Italian cleric (not a cardinal but an archbishop) who refused to obey him and declared unilateral independence. Both of them excommunicated each other. My version could be just around the corner. Stay tuned. Anyway, he's now a saint, so there's hope for us all.

INW.

Had a brief meeting this morning with Cardinal Thierry Etcheverry of Reims at his request.

At last. The explanation arrives.

Or the plot thickens.

Thierry told me he was concerned because slippery Honduras Cardinal Carlos Silva Gonzales asked him to lunch at Roscioli, a local haunt that cleverly combines delicatessen with restaurant. Over a bottle of Brunello di Montalcino 'Madonna delle Grazie' 2016—no doubt chosen by Carlos to infer that the Mother of All Graces sides with his ultra-conservative camp—Thierry told me that the Honduran Prefect of the Dicastery of Promoting Integral Human Development took to vigorously promoting Olivier's papal candidature. He knows how influential Thierry is in the French church and without even a suggestion of subtlety or diplomacy, asked him to rally *les cardinaux français* to vote in a bloc for the French speaking Cameroonian—as if being francophone somehow supposes stubbornly reactionary theological views.

Now, Carlos isn't the sharpest spike on the monstrance, but in the light of other recent unwasted information, given the vote trading festival this place is now undergoing, it's not impossible that he's tactically shrewder that I give him credit for.

Astutely, Thierry said that to the best of his knowledge, the papacy was currently occupied by a healthy Australian but that, yes, it was always prudent to consider the church's future and of course we must always keep an open mind, thus he'd be happy to speak with Olivier before returning to Reims on Friday.

The meeting is set for Thursday morning, after which Thierry will brief me on the prudence or otherwise of the Honduran's indelicate delicatessen sally.

Ultimate intelligence, as I now hope.

Or wheels within wheels.

What was Dario's advice? Wait and watch.

Yes, while agonising.

But when it comes to restaurants, I have a rather crazy little initiative of which I'm not unproud.

The secret truth is that, yes, when it comes to unlikely restaurant appearances, I have a papal confession to make about a minor failing of mine. Or a spiritual strength. The latter I'd like to think.

Once every four or five weeks—under secure papal undercover and discreet protection (Ennio)—I sneak away from the Vatican to a small trattoria a few minutes east of this city state to enjoy a plate of extravagant antipasto followed by *un piatto di spaghetti carbonara della casa*. Both are simple epicurean proofs of the existence of God.

The restaurant is run by one of Ennio's cousins—the Italian side—and is a small trattoria tucked away in a nondescript street on the wrong side of Trastevere. Sometimes, very occasionally and discreetly, I share a meal there with Ennio, but mostly, I dine alone while Ennio, disguised as a local yokel and not a Swiss Guard, keeps watch out front.

From the vantage point of my table, I observe. And think. And imagine. And dream. And try to understand the church of today—our increasingly rejected church of today—at the tables of these happy regulars—congregants?—at their joyful and convivial meal.

And I ask myself, how can we invite them to our even more simple yet life-sustaining eucharistic meal?

I try to learn.

I wear mufti and a *berretto* and am seated at a single, badly lit table in a small passage discreetly off the main restaurant area, a slim recess leading to the toilets and just next to the kitchen, the sliding door of which, as waiters hurry in and out with the elegance of ice skaters, is an amazing combination of apparent chaos and miraculous efficiency.

If only the Vatican were half as efficient.

From there, I observe with my half bottle of chianti—for popes, and thanks to Ennio, it's BYO... an Italian first! There's got to be a few perks for the successors of St Peter, and knowing of that fisherman first pope, I reckon he would have done more than the odd tax avoidance cash-in-the-hand deal with regular clients.

And so from my sly little passageway, what do I see?

By and large, happy families, smartly dressed gay (I assume) male couples and almost inevitably, a sad, ageing, solo, male eating alone and secretly watching the other diners.

And in that mirror moment, unseen I see myself: the misfit pope conflicted with love of the church and impatience with the institution I lead.

Actually, more than impatience. My worst (most honest?) self frequently borders on disdain for so much institutional self-interest, pettiness and cancerous clerical control-freakery.

Refracted shards of childhood and adolescent memories hit me from left field with the allegory of my ambitious father and second-rate me, and my paternal hope for the church and its frayed, defective, tawdry and superstitious institutions and teachings.

Try as we may, we can't be incognito to our true selves.

Wednesday, January 28th

Feast of St Thomas Aquinas (1225–1274), theologian extraordinaire of the timelessness and incomprehensibility and otherness of God who is being God's self and who, by God's very Godness, cannot not be.

I look forward to hearing Aquinas's conversation with Saint Richard Dawkins when the time comes. Might shut him up for a brief moment, though I have to admit that towards the end, he occasionally had the good manners to listen without sneering. To date, Aquinas is the Church's most distinguished theologian. I'm told that Mendoza can quote the entire Summa Theologica by heart, which might explain why he's not asked to dinner all that often. But St Thomas Aquinas is our convincing voice in the seminaries and universities. And also, just to give us all hope, today is also the feast of St Archebran who lived in Cornwall and about whom nothing else is known. Crazy. Get me to Cornwall.

And crazy it's been.

What am I on?

A sudden, unannounced visit by Melania Trump.

She wants to found an enclosed order of nuns in some castle in Slovenia.

As yet, she is unsure of the order's charism but is confident one will eventuate as she's commissioned three American cardinals, all Trump supporters, to come up with possible purposes for the proposed congregation.

And an Italian chef has already been chosen.

She brought with her eight lavish designs for the order's habit, each by a major French couturier, and asked me which one I thought the most stylish and appropriate to the community's as yet undiscerned rationale.

I think she's nuts.

Attractive, but totally bonkers.

And gloriously above all reality.

I suggested she call her convent Golgotha House.

She thanked me and said she loved the sound of the name and its branding possibilities. A perfume, perhaps?!

Talk about a fantasy gloriously above all reality!

Is she making a bid for the papacy?

And God knows, I'd be terrified to meet her postulants. I assume they come with hair dressers, maids and butlers in attendance. Their patron saint surely has to be St Jude, patron saint of lost causes and Australian popes.

Did I dream all this?

It's been one of those days.

The Irish ambassador to the Vatican, even barmier than half the Irish bishops, tells me that a devout drag queen he knows in Ballyshannon has had a vision of St Philomena who told him to build a basilica in her honour with a night club in the crypt.

I pointed out to him that St Philomena never existed. The ambassador said he'd relay the message to his friend who had high commercial hopes for the crypt.

You couldn't make this stuff up.

Unless I am.

The increasingly deaf Archbishop of Vientiane in Laos is on his *ad limina* visit. His English is totally indecipherable, and his understanding of the language, like the archbishop himself, is increasingly fragile.

At our meeting this morning, he asked me if I could lend him two thousand euros. I thought it odd but explained that since becoming pope, I never carry cash on me, but told him to ask my Secretary of State, who would see to it via my apostolic account.

The Archbishop winked at me. Not exactly papal protocol, but I guess, in the circumstances, best we remain on friendly terms despite his embarrassing indigence. Later, Cardinal Silvestrini told me the bishop said that in his diocese he intended to blend two Laotion bureaus, and that he thought I said 'alcoholic' account.

I think I'm cracking up.

Then I awoke.

Or did it all happen?

What is reality?

Indeed.

'Can today be any crazier?' I wondered, and if it did, would I notice?

It did.

I didn't.

I'm clearly not fit to be pope unless I make a difference.

Cornwall beckons.

Thursday, January 29th

Feast of Pope Saint Gelasius II (1058–1118).

Another pontiff I can relate to. He was the one-hundred-and-sixty-first pope, and his election was contested by some idiot called Cenzio Frangipani, a powerful wealthy Roman who spent his lifetime contesting popes. This pig-headed bully was no fragile frangipani. Anyway, after Frangipani imprisoned Gelasius, the Roman mob rescued him (always nice to hear a happy ending to papal imprisonment stories) but then Gelasius took on the Holy Roman Emperor who had by then appointed an anti-Pope. Result: Gelasius fled not to Cornwall but to France. Then he died and for some reason is now a saint. I seem to relate to all the weird ones.

Ah, what simple and simply glorious bounty! Pappa al pomodoro is how stale bread ascends into heaven in the company of tomatoes, olive oil, garlic (always), basil and the secret ingredient of Sister Angelica's prayers and love. And if I behave myself, I might just be given the left-over of the left-overs served chilled as a non-alcoholic aperitif in a shot glass for lunch tomorrow.

And as the Green Catechism will surely one day proclaim as an article of faith, basil wards off stress and depression.

Should be served on every papal plate.

INW.

Thierry Etcheverry's meeting with Olivier proved to be disturbingly predictable. The usual complaint about my liberalism accelerating the already disastrous fall away of the faithful and Olivier's guarantee that as the next pope, he'll bring back discipline, security, faith and a return of large congregations at mass. And, presumably, large second collections. Thierry asked Olivier when he imagined the next conclave would take place, and Olivier replied confidently, 'Much sooner than anyone expects, which is why we need to ensure the allegiance of our French traditionalist cardinal brothers.' Thierry told me there was a confidence in Olivier's prediction and that I needed to quickly outline my vision, assert my authority and demonstrate my leadership.

Wise advice.

In the end, wise advice aside, I simply couldn't not confront Adrian with the apparent French/German/Olivier conspiracy.

I did so over *diner à deux* which Sister Angelica ensured was pleasant while deftly signalling restraint: radishes with *demi-baguette*, butter and salt; spaghetti carbonara; gorgonzola and the rest of the *demi-baguette*. And that's yer lot!

Point made. And, I think, point taken.

I told Adrian of my knowledge of his meeting, and he replied that of course all three of them knew that their exit had been noted and expected this conversation to eventually take place, but that the conference was in every way loyal to our progressive cause, and they believed that time was on their side in their short—and long-term—soundings.

Soundings only.

He explained that where he and our French associates were currently at, potential vote counting once again suggested some kind of tie between Olivier and Mendoza, though this time for very different reasons, but that there was very much a significantly soft centre, not least, surprisingly, among certain African cardinals.

To complicate matters, the three of them had reservations about Mendoza's spiritual about-turn. They saw him as a failed candidate from the last conclave but still a wily and ambitious manipulator. Leopards and spots. They thought that it wouldn't be impossible for the newly progressive Mendoza to ride the currently progressive zeitgeist but then once elected, double back to his historically true disciplinary self.

I interrupted saying that in my opinion, Adrian's judgment of Mendoza was precisely the opposite of mine and that I believed God's grace via apparently terminal illness was a blessing and a clear encouragement to Mendoza to trust in the Lord.

He replied that with respect and loyally hoping for the best outcome, he and the French Connection maintained their unease, which is why they offered Westphalen a medium-term option likely to delay Olivier's immediate election though probably increase the likelihood of his eventual papacy.

Curiouser and curiouser.

Not totally, Adrian replied.

The arrangement would be for Olivier to back off any immediate conclave while holding the fort for the one after, as it were. The tactic would be that he'd magnanimously concede to bringing together the putative widely distributed concerned middle voters—more than a few Africans—and generously run with a *pro tem* neutral candidate.

Ah! Of course! Gallant little beige Luxembourg to the politically neutral rescue!

And yes, that was the plan. Then, the trio tried to convince Olivier via Westphalen that there would be time for 'consolidation'—though Adrian professed that while this ambiguity would be favourably interpreted by both sides, according to his numbers, ours would more likely benefit.

I asked him whether he realised how arithmetically optimistic Westphalen and Olivier were, to which he confidently replied that France and New Zealand had extensively explored African manoeuvring (slippery as water), had done their sums (the inevitably reversible pre-conclave fortune telling) and were as sure as anyone could be that delay was the only path to progress.

If only.

And their compromise candidate: Luxembourg's Jean-Franz Hoffman, of course, Mickey Mouse apparently being unavailable.

Where to look and whom to trust when Disneyland descends into the purview of the Holy Spirit?

And, of course, the inevitable daily crisis. Predictable brouhaha among the curia learning that in the UK, the Bishop of Lancaster, Richard Faulkner, has agreed to bless his 24-year-old youngest brother's wedding to his Ugandan refugee male partner and companion of seven years.

Bishop Faulkner (by all reports, sensible and reliable, though I've yet to meet him) told the press that as everyone is made in God's image and that after their trial period of living together affectionately, as these two young men wish now to vow lifelong love for and fidelity to each other, he saw in the integrity of their commitment and intention something noble and sacred deserving God's blessing.

And why not, indeed?

Respect for same sex relationships since the Old Testament time of David and Jonathan has become a tad more understood of late, and who can forget Francis's dramatic about-face, 'Who am I to judge'? It was a historic moment for the Church and gave the beginnings of hope to so many of our rejected brothers and sisters. All well and good, except...

...in his justification for his fraternal act, His Grace elected to cite the loyalty and affection between Jesus and His young apostle, John, and—OMG, to even utter the words—and the loyalty to and care for Pope Benedict by his strikingly handsome much younger secretary, Archbishop (rank conferred by Benedict) Ganswein, citing their relationship as one of chaste, admirable and enduring friendship, a relationship already looked on favourably by God.

Nuclear bomb!

The last thing we need is another papal scandal, though Ganswein has done his best to cause one with his book of complaints, pay-backs and tittle tattle. Though I must admit that in its innocence (I presume) that papal friendship wasn't in any way scandalous. It was natural and, I'd like to think, blessed.

I'll write to the Bishop of Lancaster commending him on his initiative and general good judgment, though not necessarily his diplomacy. And it might be interesting to hear Ennio's view on this state of affairs. As he delights in professing, he's not the last virgin in the brothel.

I'm wandering. All over the place. That Melania dream portends my impending lunacy.

I can only hope that Sister Angelica is in creative mode.

Dear God in heaven, assure your humble servant that while he may have a few kangaroos loose in the top paddock, he hasn't totally lost the farm.

Or the plot.

Ah, yes, the plot.

Friday, January 30th

Feast of Saint David Galvan-Bermudez (1881–1915), my kind of priest.

He entered the Guadalajara seminary in Mexico aged 14, a very bad move, in my opinion. Far too young and inexperienced in life. He proved to be a first-rate student (frankly concerning, given he'd never gone through a normal adolescence) then quit the seminary and hit the sex, drugs and whatever salacious melodies preceded the rock-n-roll scene. The waltz? From all reports, David more than made up for lost time. With that frenzied catch-up now behind him, he went back to the seminary and was ordained at the age of 28 with enough life experience to regard most penitents as clumsy amateurs. At the time of fierce Mexican persecution of the church, he ministered to rebels and was arrested for the crime of being a priest. He was condemned to death yet up until hours before his execution, he comforted fellow prisoners. A life indeed fully lived. I hope he can inspire more dissolute youths to become intrepid pastors. Meanwhile, in the parish of Nod just east of Eden, I encountered a pleasant surprise. Well, sort of. Well, not, actually. Instead of a papal visitation, I rose to the rank of receiving an angelic visitor. I assume that in the heavenly choir, he's the bass who sings out of tune but whom none of the other angels is game to call out. Here's why.

Archangel Michael here, and yes, you're dreaming and yes, I'm for real, and yes, you'd better believe it.

And as I expect you remember, this is not my first apparition. Fact. Monte Sant'Angelo, Castel Sant'Angelo, Mont St Michel—all me. Fact. And despite claims to the contrary, I'm the one and *only* archangel. I fight. I win. Fact. I was the one who cast Satan down to the inferno. Gabriel provided back-up, Raphael guarded the rear, but the one-on-one, hand-to-hand, blood and guts stuff—me and me alone. Fact. And you'd better believe it. And, yes, yes, I know we don't have bodies. It's a metaphor, for God's sake. Which settles that. And sceptics that you lot all too often are, think twice before you write off the supernatural. Like it or not, you'll all be weighed in the balance one day. And I hold the scales. If you haven't yet worked it out, the whole universe is all about good versus evil. Simple as that. Traditional and true. What conservatism's all about. God is great and God is good, but never underestimate Satan and all his pomps. Nonetheless, God runs the show, though every now and then He has to send you all-knowing doubters on earth the occasional plague to smarten yourselves up. Not that you ever learn. Anyway, that's why I'm here. Special mission. And mark my words: the church needs troops. The combat rages day in, day out. The good commander doesn't shilly-shally like certain watering-down Australians I could name. The good commander acts decisively. The African chappie gets it. You don't have to understand. Just take it on trust. Believe. Renounce Satan. And if that doesn't put the fear of God into you, don't say I didn't warn you. Carry on. *Dominus vobiscum.*

They get crazier and crazier.

Or more inspired?

It's out of control. Well, out of <u>my</u> control. I used to pray for sleep. Now I pray not perchance to dream.

Saturday, January 31st

Feast of St John Bosco (1815–1888).

According to a reputable Catholic website, today's saint was not a first-class thinker, eloquent writer, bloody martyr or path-breaking Church reformer, but his personality was so genuine that in his priestly work to help poor boys, the enterprise flourished because everyone he asked assistance from saw in him the genuine article. He'd been dirt poor himself and knew the territory. By the time of his death, his religious order had 250 houses the world over caring for 130,000 children, and they're still going strong. To paraphrase Milton in the argot of Wollongong, they also serve who stop whinging, get off their fat arses, roll up their sleeves and bloody well do something to make things better. I must try harder.

I've been negligent. And self-indulgent. And frightened.

Popes must decide on the nature of their papacy: fortress or lighthouse. The latter, surely: the way, the truth and the light; a church confident enough to listen, wise enough to learn, inspired enough to reform. John knew.

The Vatican is the problem.

This place is musty.
The solution?
Time to open these windows again.
Boldness be my friend.

Sunday, February 1st

Feast of Blessed Benedict Daswa (1946–1990) a married South African layman of the Lemba tribe associated with Jewish laws and traditions.

He converted to Catholicism at the age of 17 and became a dynamic teacher, principal and local leader. After his village suffered from violent storms in 1990, the local elders (old but ignorant, though I never said that, but it's true and needs to be said) demanded a tax be paid for magic (bullshit) to stop the inundation. Benedict wouldn't subscribe to such primitive superstition (though I never said that either, but it's true and needs to be said) and he was murdered by a local mob. To make such a stand would have required faith and courage I envy. And, yes, we Catholics, too, are guilty of ludicrous superstitions (don't get me started) and shouldn't be patronising about similar African idiocies. And I did say that. And it needs to be said. And why isn't Blessed Benedict Daswa better known and revered? So putting my money where my mouth is, I shall hasten his canonisation.

For some reason—and I know what it is—liberation after reflection—I'm feeling quite light-headed, not to mention extremely naughty today.

Time to wrong-foot the opposition.

A new candidate for the sainthood, to be cc'd to all Prefects of Dicasteries with request for evidence of holiness and miracles: Saint Christopher Hitchens.

Evidence: the elegance of his thesis that all religions are versions of the same untruth.

As he was a miracle of acidic conciseness, no further miracles are required.

Saint Christopher Hitchens. Patron saint of atheists.

Enough, Mario, but congratulations on an immature though not totally absurd playfulness!

Indeed, I dare to think that the newly canonised Saint Christopher Hitchens might join in the joke. We have more in common than, perhaps, we first thought.

I long for the day when atheists and theists can genuinely laugh in the communion of the intellectually honest.

Monday, February 2nd

Feast of the Presentation of Our Lord in the Temple, a religious duty of Jewish parents.

Clearly, Joseph and Mary were religiously observant, loving parents. Would that there were more. My parents did their best with what they had in money and children, though if you'd have told an Italian-Australian Wollongong couple that their mischievous though far from brilliant and then teenage all-over-the-place son would one day be the pope in Rome, I suspect you might have needed a course in colourful Italian dismissive pejoratives to appreciate what they would have regarded as raving insanity. Brother Edmund's response most certainly would have been an explosive earful. And they all just might have been right. Today is also the feast of Saint Apronian the Executioner (martyred 304) who witnessed the trial of Saint Sisinnius charged with the crime of being a Christian in the feral reign of that animal, Diocletian, and Sisinnius was therefore martyred. So moved was Apronian that he converted to Christianity and was beheaded soon after. No slacker he—I assume his disgusting profession required a hard heart not to mention any number of other revolting skills and dispositions, and that the volte-face must have been a mind-blowing about-turn for Apronian and his loathsome associates. I also assume—and fervently hope—that he's not the patron saint of executioners. And for good measure, there was also a Pope Sininnius who was pope for about three weeks in 708. Yikes! Understandably, not a popular name for a son for whom you wish a long, happy and successful life. I must check with my baptismal certificate. And, come to think of it, Sininnius is also a name likely to give rise to wounding nicknames in the playground and on the sports field.

OK, Francis's vision of synodality was—and remains—necessary and inspirational, but too much depends on the enthusiasm of the bishops—or their lack of same.

Accordingly, in the same spirit of inclusion, I shall call the Third Vatican Council.

The church must guard and treasure its heritage just as it must discern and define its faith for the future so that God's ongoing revelation may light the way to inspire future generations of believers.

All of our communicating faithful, lay and clerical, will be invited to submit subjects for discussion. In addition, all our Christian brothers and sisters of all persuasions will also be encouraged both to submit items for consideration and to offer their services as observers with the right of submitting reports. The same will apply to agnostics and atheists of good will.

As the pope, and with all the faith, hope and charity I can muster, I'm aware of how dangerous this concept is.

And of how stimulating and grace-giving it might well be.

Even though popes are human, the Holy Spirit guides us, but given that, I'd have to say that any pope worth his salt ought to offer theological rulings *pro tem* with the proviso that as knowledge advances, understanding deepens, philosophy refines itself and sociology reveals hitherto unknown fault lines in beliefs within humanity and therefore within the church. So then in the interest of truth, our church must always humbly and thoroughly re-examine and reconsider its doctrines.

We must have the faith of good faith and an openness to ongoing revelation; after all, name one intelligent contemporary theologian who believes that the earth was created in seven days. And if anyone can explain to me the precise meaning, method and necessity of Our Lady, body and soul, ascending into Heaven, I shall be grateful for the evidence.

And I'll require detail of how precisely this revelation is revealed and what assurances we have that such information is London-to-a-brick and dinky-di. I mean, let's face it, what passed for infallibility in 1896—the absolutely null and utterly void invalidity of Anglican orders—today surely sounds like the headmasterly blusterings and ravings of a slightly crazed CEO.

Why can't we just admit in all humility that 'because of circumstances' (power and prejudice) we got it wrong?

Oh, and for good measure, I repeat that I think we should have many more bells and much more incense in our masses. Their appeal to all the senses enriches the central message of the liturgy. God's gifts give delight and depth to our disposition to receive.

Cheers!

And with the guidance of the Holy Spirit, what could possibly go wrong?

Tuesday, February 3rd

Feast of Blessed Helinand of Pronleroy (died 1237) who was a court singer, a troubadour—in other words, a pop singer.

He became a Benedictine Cistercian monk in Froidmont, France. That's so lovely. I'm imaging Harry Styles as a Cistercian monk, and, surprisingly, it isn't hard. He'd enjoy the dressing up.

So, my clerical formation always excited me when my teachers rhapsodized on how Christianity was fundamentally a revolutionary religion; it turned the known world upside down because it proclaimed that the poorest of the poor—and, yes, even the slaves… or even more radically, women—were equal in God's sight and were entitled to the respect and dignity given to the highest of the high.

Love it.

Except what happened to the great Christian revolution?

Must have got lost in the comfort, wealth and security which popes, cardinals, bishops, abbots, abbesses, priests and the entrepreneurial laity found in evolving capitalism. They flourished while the evolving masses of the worldwide oppressed and the dispossessed increased exponentially.

What's the slogan I hear these days?

Our preferential option for the poor.

Then let the church opt and act.

To energise my resurrectional mission of salvation, I'll write an encyclical challenging all believers to join Our Saviour's revolution.

Starting at the core of the problem, all clergy, from the pope downwards—how tempted I am to say 'upwards'—in loving acceptance to Our Saviour's insistence on action rather than hollow exhortation, our entire church community, starting with this pope, must open every spare room in their quarters to refugee families, this to include bathrooms, none of which is to be reserved for sacred bodies or clerical bums. Every Vatican apartment, monastery, convent, presbytery and boarding house must respect this new rule. God's refugees are homeless, and God's church must give them shelter. And these guests must <u>never</u> be regarded or treated as servants. Just as in refugee camps where whole families must suffer the indignity of communal defecation and washing, so those of us who are truly Christ's servants must share all such facilities with our guests, there being no exception from the papal apartment to the poorest presbytery.

Certain western cardinals may consider storing their expensive soaps and fragrances in their wardrobes, though I would assume that like Christ, their first disposition would be to offer such sophisticated though totally unnecessary comforts to those who may not have experienced the luxury of toothpaste, shampoo, conditioner, moisturiser—God help us!—or even hot water since their birth.

We either live the faith or we delude ourselves that God's church must enjoy special comfort.

As the mere pope, I don't hear Christ crucified extolling luxury.

Affluence must rather be Christ's invitation to share, and if we don't radically lead the way, then surely our hypocrisy and selfishness must bring into question or even annul the rest of our beliefs.

Is there a more powerful parable in the bible than the example of the Good Samaritan?

There are excuses, and there's action.

Therefore, inspired by the enthusiastic justice of our clerical first responders, we invite all the faithful to open every spare room in their house to refugees and their families.

Yes, of course, from the comfortable the cry will go up that we have opened the floodgates.

Absolutely!

The alternative?

Close the floodgates and let the all the victims drown.

A worldwide problem must be solved by the whole wide world, and we must and will lead the way.

Should governments object to our Christlike care for His rejected—for example, dumping them on Pacific islands or in struggling African countries—then we must break such immoral laws and live with whatever penal consequences the unchristian oppressors apply.

Only by our revolution will God's revolution of the kingdom happen. And in the spirit of these papal declarations, I shall outline this next major structural advance in the reform of God's Kingdom sometime next week.

Meanwhile, let us joyfully and lovingly embrace this return to Our Saviour's clear demands with the blessings, confidence and assurance our faith grounds us in.

Dario to expedite.

Wednesday, February 4th

Feast of the 26 Jesuit martyrs of Japan who were crucified on this day in 1597, in Nagasaki.

There were four Jesuit priests and twenty-two of their companions. I'm trying to imagine the frightful scene and the agonising and extended suffering. I don't think I have the faith or the courage to even contemplate this for long. The church deserves a better pope.

Simultaneously with this first phase or returning to the spirit of the early church, I have now considered and approved (I keep reminding myself that I'm the pope) venues and conditions for the Third Vatican Council.

The council will take place in three nine-month sessions over three years in three different venues.

Recognising the ecumenical spirit of the times, this gathering of the faithful will also welcome inclusion as observers and occasional participants all our separated Christian brothers and sisters together with representatives of Jewish, Islamic, Buddhist, Hindu and other religious traditions offering to engage with us.

Included as well will be representatives of our atheist brothers and sisters who will be invited to bring their insights and beliefs—or questions and disbeliefs—to our open conversations.

I reckon the Holy Spirit is up to giving them a run for their money.

To ensure inclusion, balance and justice in all discussions, the council must comprise 46% males, 46% females and 8% transgender persons—proportions to be adjusted in the light of scientific measurement and agreement.

Recognising the biblical centrality of the desert in Christian discernment, with the permission and blessing of our Israeli and Palestinian friends, the council's first venue will be in the desert outside Be'er Sheva in Israel.

Tents and basic temporary facilities will be provided, and in the Lenten spirit of penance, food will be simple and sparse.

Clerical dress and all indications of church rank will be forbidden, and led by the pope, all will wear simple clothes appropriate to the climate.

The council agenda together with details of the dress code will be provided one year in advance.

Given that Africa will be the future centre of Christianity, the second venue will be on the outskirts of Kampala in Uganda, one of the poorest countries on that continent, and accommodation, facilities, food and dress will reflect the conditions of the poor of that nation.

The third venue will be in the Vatican, all council members sharing rooms and facilities with our resident refugee brothers and sisters.

Attendance of all invited clerics is compulsory under their vow of obedience to the Holy Father, exceptions being made only for those with serious medical conditions.

Beginning at the end of mass on the coming Easter Sunday, all subsequent masses before the Council's opening will conclude with the Prayer for God's Blessing on this momentous undertaking of the faithful.

A Latin translation of the prayer will be provided for those worshipping in the Tridentine rite.

Proposals for the agenda of the Council from all the faithful, clerical and lay, and from all our invited participants, will be appreciated by the newly appointed Chairman of the Council, Filipino Cardinal Carlos Caringal. He knows how to add up and subtract.

Everything.

And, Dad, this modest proposal is what your son would dare to call 'first-rate'.

I'm hoping that for once, you might agree.

Thursday, February 5th

Feast of the third century martyr, Saint Agatha.

She came from a well-off Sicilian family in Catania and because of her beauty, was wooed by a number of notable young suitors but she rejected them all and wished to live as a virgin dedicated to Christ. She was arrested, and appallingly tortured—she was stretched on a rack, torn with iron hooks, burned with torches, and whipped. Then her breasts were ripped off with pincers. She was then thrown into prison and left to die. The sheer horror and obscenity of this haunts me. I pray daily for women with breast cancer, of whom Saint Agatha is patron. The Romans really were unspeakably cruel. The evil human beings can rejoice in is dreadful proof of the power of Satan or however we now like to rethink that myth. Call it by whatever name we wish, the wretched fact remains and is one of the reasons why in my desolation and near despair, I fall to my knees and pray to God to reconcile me with His creation.

Oh dear!

A late night oversight.

These things happen.

After my yesterday's definitive decisions, in the current apparent crisis of papal authority and after a modest alcoholic *digestivo*—well, immodest, I suppose—and after a necessary late-night massage by Ennio following an overwhelmingly exhausting day of my Third Vatican Council proposals, I made a mistake.

I shared my ideas with Ennio, who was in every way supportive, but in my enthusiasm for this initiative and in the relief of my private conversation with Ennio, I neglected to take my customary security precautions against Vatican eavesdropping.

The result is that on waking up, I realized that I neglected to inform my Secretary of State of my instantaneously inspired action, and this morning I've received from my good friend, Dario, a note saying that he has no idea how, but that the entire Vatican is alive with gossip of the details of my intended Third Vatican Council, and that there's salacious gossip about my friendship with Ennio.

Truth to tell, they don't know the half of it, but these vicious corridors boil and bubble with envious backbiting, excited calumny and pornographic detraction.

Think the Sydney Mardi Gras but with swisher and much more expensive frocks.

Still, now I know for certain that I'm being bugged, though the immediate problem is how to extricate myself from my unfortunate oversight.

Though come to think of it, I'm unlikely to be given any more lectures about not having any vision for the church.

Actually, the real shit storm will rain down on all the local troglodytes and Neanderthals determined to keep the church locked in the middle ages.

If I play this shrewdly, all their shrieks and howls will cascade back on them like the excrement they are, and given the instant worldwide publicity, I'll be hailed as the church's visionary and saviour.

The papacy is ten tenths of the law, and not even a council can remove a pope.

Not the most charitable of dispositions, but in a crisis, needs must.

Time to draw round the wagons.

Friday, February 6th

Feast of Saints Paul Miki and Companions, martyrs (1562–1597).

Remembering and meditating on the heroic faith and suffering of our martyrs must reinforce our faith and hope, and so often it does. A pope should never think let alone commit to writing what I'm thinking and writing, but truth to tell, sometimes I find myself wilting with exhaustion and horror when reading the ghastly accounts of so many inspiring saints and their agony. And even more disconcerting is the fear that in some unintendedly perverse way, I'm intrigued by the descriptions of torture and may even be taking de-praved pleasure in the narration. This is unworthy of me, and yet some days I want to avert my mind from the endless cruelty and the sadistic delight wretchedly twisted children of God take in perpe-trating evil. Today is one of those days, yet face the frightful facts I must. Paul Miki was a Japanese Jesuit brother who evangelised his people in the new faith of Jesus. On the orders of the emperor, Miki and his companions were arrested, had their left ears cut off, were then marched hundreds of miles to Nagasaki where they were bound to crosses and pierced with lances until they died. And so, albeit often with strange ambivalence and ambiguity, we give thanks for the fortitude and valour of our martyrs.

Bounty of leeks vinaigrette with winter salad and mustard dressing. Mustard's role in preventing cancer is one of Sister Angelica's more exotic tenets, and as for promoting hair growth, as a contribution to world peace, I choose not to challenge her on that fantasy, but if, as she assures me, mustard soothes body aches, I'm a believer—even when it doesn't work. Fact is, I just like mustard.

I was right. Forty-eight hours later, The Vegemite has hit the Sao's, and the shit has hit my Vatican non-fans.

Outrage. Pandemonium. Chaos. Revolution.

'He's totally lost his marbles.'

'We have not just an Australian pope but a raving lunatic pon-tiff as well.'

'An eleven-year-old could tell him that to take every word or par-able of the gospel literally would result in total chaos and World War Whatever.'

'Scholarship and interpretation are the gifts of sanity applied to ancient texts. And besides, this latest inanity is decision without consultation.'

The cardinals are storming the barricades, and it ain't Gregorian chant they're singing.

This is the sound of angry men, and they're led by Olivier, our very own Enjolras, renewed with pontifical ambition and confidence.

I must remind him of Enjolras's fate.

The world press has Yours Infallibly on the front page, and a good half of the bishops are beating drums of war, but once again, I was right.

The only slight worry I have is that Mendoza seems to approve.

Could I be catastrophically wrong, and is his newfound progressive disposition some kind of trap?

There's no one more politically astute in these parts, and he's now survived three papacies. He says that renewal is the sanctifying life blood of the church and that while there may be some topics which may need 'extended conversation' (the inquisitorial rack?) with prayer and open-mindedness (not a concept I've ever associated with him) benevolent outcomes may be hoped for.

Guess I'll just have to navigate the waves of his ocean of hope.

That aside, almost all of the opposition to my council is from the hysterical clericals, but the groundswell of support from the pews is earth-shattering. And, of course, this means that almost every woman who attends Sunday mass is on side, as is the minority of males who get up early enough.

In other words, the punters are enthusiastic for radical reform.

And I'm the instant pin-up boy of the LGBTQI etc. warriors, not to mention the first pope in ages (ever?) to be top of the atheist pops.

Of course, a bit of predictable opposition from Africa—their theology is a century or three behind Europe's, though no one's allowed to say that aloud—mind you, buoyed by hosting the council, Uganda looks to revaluing the shilling and investing in cappuccino machines.

And faced with losing the economic boom which will come with the council, Uganda might just have to reconsider its evil approach to its gay citizens.

Nice one, Mario.

Other religions seem a bit slow to come on board—though forty-eight hours are just that—but there's been gentle applause from some non-radical imams (Abu Dhabi is a haven of Islamic moderation) and I certainly wouldn't be surprised if quite a few high-profile spokesmen and women from other traditions didn't accept the invitation to participate.

And it's reported that editors of most European Catholic journals have signalled support, and a few high-profile American ones are also enthusiastically on side, though of course, there'll be the usual backlash from the Southern and mid-Western Cro-Magnon cardinals, and I can certainly expect to be Wollongong's Person of the Year—the first pope in history to be given that coveted award.

How about that, Dad?

And on the subject of recognising the dignity (and naturalness) of same sex attraction, liberal (read logical) as I be on the matter, probably because of my age and upbringing (the Brother Edmund syndrome) while I'm happy to bless such unions, I can't bring myself to call them marriages and I wince at the mention of husband and husband/wife and wife.

I know these are only words, though I also know that in our struggle to discern meaning in this life, words matter greatly, but I simply can't bring myself to accept these obviously functional descriptors.

'Partners' I'm comfortable with. 'Lovers' strikes me as an unnecessary invasion of privacy. 'Paramours' sounds a tad grubby. 'Companions' is nice if a tad old-fashioned and prissy. *Innamorato/a* sits well enough with me though it still sounds… well, periphrastically precious. And 'significant other' suggests unthinly disguised disapproval.

Decisions. Decisions.

Who'd be a pope!

Don't reply, Mario.

Though suddenly, do reply, Mario.

'Spouse' does the job.

Deo gratias.

Saturday, February 7th

Feast of Saint Pope Pius IX.

While Pio Nono's timing during his papacy wasn't always spot on (to put it diplomatically) he doesn't miss an opportunity now he's elsewhere. Just in case I might miss his feast day, he thoughtfully popped by last night.

Of course you know who I am. Right! Pio Nono, Pius the Ninth, longest reigning pontiff in history—almost 32 years. You may remember I was known as Pope Popularity… until I painfully grew up and shed that wretched title. 1848 and all that. When I was a childish pope, I spake as a liberal, I understood as a liberal, I thought as a liberal: but when I became a prisoner of the Vatican, I put liberal treason behind me and opted for infallibility. Think about it—as well you might. The church is about discipline. Authority. Give every halfwit the right to proclaim the heretical nonsense they dream up, and you authorize theological anarchy. Worse. I should know. I lost the papal states. I started as pope and king. I finished up as history. But in all surety, truth is proclaimed by God. And so, necessarily, by the pope. Get it? No, I don't think you do. I stood not for opinion but for truth. We prosecute mountebank medical masqueraders, and rightly so. Why should we tolerate the ravings of ignorant theological quacks peddling their poison? Wrong prescription: damnation. Right prescription: salvation. Get back on track or you'll be cactus. I rest my case. Thank God for papal infallibility. It's the clean bomb to stop very dirty explosions. Over to you, Mario. And *dominus vobiscum.*

It's as if I'm talking to myself.
Because I am.

Sunday, February 8th

Feast of Saint Stephen of Muret (1046–1124), an intriguing and holy man I should like to have met.

He founded a Benedictine house in the Forest of Muret in France and was made abbot though he had never been formally made a monk, so when these days we hear the endless bleat of a drought of religious vocations, the example of Saint Stephen of Muret should cause us to reassess the nature of religious vocations. What is lay and what is religious? And in these times, what is needed? Imagination and courage required. Like, hello! And isn't it interesting that with female saints, we invariably describe them as virgins or otherwise. Why don't we do this for all male saints? Just asking. I can pray to Saint Stephen of Muret with a smile in my heart as well as on my face. Just think: he didn't obey the rules! What must God have thought? Thinks. Justifying that could keep an entire Vatican dicastery busy for months while thousands of African children die of starvation. Saint Stephen of Muret, pray for your brother in amused detachment from holy bureaucracy.

A virtual demand from Olivier for an urgent meeting re: the council.
He arrived fuming and exploded in volcanic anger at my arrogance in calling the council without consultation.

He said that in the history of the papacy, there was no greater insult to the church than my action.

I suggested the Inquisition, the Crusades, the selling of indulgences, our treatment of the Jews and rampant sexual abuse for starters, and why not throw in the simultaneous existence of three papal claimants, all as contenders on the insult front.

More nuclear outrage at my constant doubting of biblical truths and my insane plans for starting a revolution in the church.

I agreed that I have more than a few doubts and asked him whether he believed in the old testament price of women at thirty shekels, the stoning of female adulterers, royalty installed by God, the putting to death of homosexuals, torture, slavery, male heirs only, bastards unable to enter the priesthood. And come to think of it, castrating boy sopranos to improve the sound of our Vatican choir wasn't exactly respectful of the wretched victims.

I then agreed that I did indeed want to start a revolution. A revolution of the heart and soul of the faithful. A revolution of church government. A revolution of the place of women in the church. And a revolution of ecumenism.

More fury.

I then reminded him of his heretical views on sexuality (little does he know I'm in every way sympathetic to them, and why wouldn't I be?) especially his wild indifference to clerical celibacy just before ordination when we were friends.

He spluttered that I had no understanding of African culture and, in fact, no understanding of anything, and that the unanimous view of the Vatican cardinals is that I must resign, and the sooner the better.

When he began to criticize my private behaviour (such censure from <u>him</u>!) I thanked him for his frank and fearless advice and invited him to leave.

He said he would not go until he had finished what he came to say.

I replied that as he would not leave, I would, and immediately left the room, leaving him shouting like a madman in a vacuum.

What to do next?

A stiff whiskey, I think.

Or maybe two.

Monday, February 9th

Feast of Blessed Anne Catherine Emmerich (1774–1824) a religious lady I feel increasingly close to, and that may not be a compliment to either of us.

Anne was a pious child who received visions and prophesies. She thought she could see all the souls in purgatory, which is surely a worry in one so young. She claimed that she could also see a person's sins, which is a greater worry. Pre-internet porn. In 1802, she became a nun and was given to going into religious ecstasies in church, in her cell or while working. Concerning. Then she received the <u>stigmata</u> with wounds on her hands and feet, her head from the crown of thorns, and crosses on her chest. More concerning. Then, apparently, she was granted the gift of inedia: living off nothing but Holy Communion for the rest of her life. As a confessor, I'd want to seek wide and wise advice in the face of such a condition. Over the years, Anne's experiences were debated by clerical and lay experts of the time, but no agreement as to their validity seemed to be reached. Anne has been a source of consolation for many. In an age of faith, her experiences would have been assumed possible and deserving of investigation. Today, I fear that with all her apparitions and claims of Christ-like passion, she might well be written off as mentally unstable and, uncharitably, much more. Until recently, I would have inclined to subscribe to the latter diagnosis. Having now experienced voices and apparitions, however, I'm cautious in my dismissal of supernatural visitations. Religion and sanity deserve balanced investigation. Not that I'd diagnose myself as totally insane. Well, not totally. Yet… in the meantime, I want to give Blessed Anne Catherine Emmerich benefit of the doubt, especially as my distinguished predecessor, Paul VI, dismissed arguments against her sanctity. That said, and God forgive me, I think she was a nobly religious woman who was bonkers. And God knows, I should know.

By far the best and most graced and rewarding part of my day is early morning. As I may have mentioned, Dad, I meditate for an hour and then celebrate mass. Almost without exception, during this time

I am at peace with myself. I feel a loving connection with God and a confidence in God's mercy.

But once the day begins after breakfast, I'm afraid my weakness seems to increase with each hour.

I've never been more than adequate with administration (and that may well be hyperbole) and I tend to be quickly annoyed by bureaucrats and lawyers, especially the clerical variety.

I would describe myself as temperamentally and spiritually unfit to be pope, but by God—and with God's help—I'll now bloody well fight for my decision and rally the faithful to defeat the parking police opposition.

Yes, I understand that's hardly a charitable disposition and is distinctly unpapal in its selfishness, but I am who I am, and that's the way it's going to be.

And Olivier has asked for another appointment tomorrow.

I'll just remain silent, let him blow his top, thank him, then leave once more.

Actions can speak more louder than words.

Whoops! Sorry, Brother Edmund. 'More loudly'.

Two cuts of the strap.

It never leaves you.

Tuesday, February 10th

Feast of Saint Scholastica (died 547) twin sister of St Benedict, and foundress of a women's branch of the Benedictine order.

Her life of holiness inspired her sisters and, indeed, many others. But today is also the feast of an extraordinary boy canonised by Pope Francis: Saint Jose Sanchez del Rio (1913–1928). A pious and courageous lad, he was flag bearer for the Mexican Cristero army fighting to save Catholicism in that country. He was captured, imprisoned and abused. Unspeakable. He was made to watch the hanging of another Cristero, and then his torturers cut the bottom of his feet and obliged him to walk around the town towards the cemetery. Finally, he was hacked with machetes, stabbed with bayonets and shot. Appalled by his treatment and in humble envy of his faith and courage, I find myself… I really don't know where… lost in horror and frankly overwhelmed by this astonishing 15-year-old martyr. The necessity of heaven. The absolute necessity.

I have to hand it to Olivier; he's a shrewd adversary. He wrong-footed me from the start.

First, he apologized for his previous outburst, saying it was inappropriate behaviour in the presence of a pontiff (I noted the indefinite rather than the definite article) and he said that he should at all times be civil and respectful and that he hoped I would excuse 'the vehemence of his propositions'.

Dishonestly, I replied that I was not offended (I was) and that it was gracious of him to retract the statements he made, whereupon he civilly and not altogether disrespectfully replied that the many areas we disagree on remain and that in no way did he retract them. Rather, he now wished to re-express them with more clarity and less emotion.

Then off he went: here's Olivier's version of rational discussion.

'Most of the appointments made by Francis were modernist quislings—shallow, populist theological traitors, and I, as pope, needed to face divine facts and accept the destructive hurricane of my papacy to date.

I'm a superficial papal tabloid journalist forever catastrophising sensational headline moments which occur to me in whatever state I'm in…

… and he elaborated, though I remained guiltily yet furiously calm.

'… though never daring to submit my increasingly raving doubts to the curia with its centuries of scholarship and canonly legal expertise. The church is crying out for a period of stabilization—a return to order. The faithful need to recognize the facts of sin, eternal punishment but always the loving forgiveness of Christ. There is no salvation outside the church, full stop. And on the subject of alleged apparitions of the Blessed Virgin Mary, I had described them as beautiful imaginative illusions like Father Christmas: truths expressed in myth… some form of religious theatre.'

This, says, Olivier, is as false as it's disrespectful to the High Queen of Heaven.

Our Lady's apparitions are facts.

'My proposal for a council, as it stands, is a thought bubble (not untrue, but an epoch reforming thought bubble which terrifies him and all his clerical collaborators) and must immediately be sent for discussion and clarification…

… to a wilderness of committees who will, of course, emasculate it and eventually bury it.

'Likewise, my enquiry into the death of John Paul the First is to be immediately cancelled…

… though no reason was given—which may well suggest a dark reason.

'The church's traditional condemnation of homosexuality must be enforced, and the nonsense of even considering the ordination of women must once again become a strictly forbidden subject.'

Then to top it all off came this—pretty much verbatim peroration, as eloquent as it's deluded.

And my recall is meticulous:

'Our sacred mystery of our mass, your lot have turned into a vulgar discotheque. The Lord's supper is a sacrament, not a snack. And the rules and precepts of our faith are our map, our moral compass, not some smorgasbord of daily suggestions from whatever chef's on duty. The world is wrong, and we must hold on to the divine mystery of the truth. And so to achieve this, I must restore the old order of the Mass.'

Then finally, he said, 'May I ask you a simple question?'

Of course, I said, assuming a trap.

'Do you believe in God?'

Yes, I replied.

'God the Father?'

That is a metaphor, but I believe what it's trying to say.

'So God is a metaphor?'

All we have in our conjectures of meaning is mere language. Or the gift of language, as I understand that mystically endless spiral to the divine. If you're asking me to give you a comprehensive definition of God, you're asking me to <u>be</u> God, and surprising as it may sound, even though I'm the pope, I'm not God—perhaps one belief we both share. Like yourself, Olivier, I'm a pilgrim on the journey to...

'Where?' he snapped.

Good question. Perhaps I'll give you the answer you want to hear when we both get there.

And this time, <u>he</u> was the one who left the room.

Wednesday, February 11th

Feast of Our Lady of Lourdes. Also the feast of the intriguing Saint Caedmon (died 670). Legend and history—in whatever combination—have it that Caedmon, a layman cowherd working at a Whitby monastery in northern England, had a vision (I know! But then I know) commanding him to sing of God's glory. When Caedmon explained that his illiteracy prevented this (anything and everything is possible in dreams. God knows I know!) heaven gifted him with extraordinary poetic skills, and he consequently became the first known poet of vernacular English. This is recorded by St Bede (Would a saint lie?) and is a beautiful parable in which some lovely truth is hidden in the same way that diamonds come from coal which, scientifically, is also a beautiful myth though totally untrue yet somehow a necessary assurance for ongoing but totally ignorant conversation. We believe in what for so long we've said we believe in...which brings us back to Lourdes. Truth isn't simple. Far from it. Just as the Trinity can be true, in its magical way, then why not Lourdes? Though in its own complex way. Faith has heavenly power. As does poetry. Enter St Caedmon. QED.

The battle lines have been drawn: the foot soldiers versus the high command.

Thursday, February 12th

Feast of Blessed Jak Bushati (1890–1949) one of 40 Albanian martyrs viciously tortured and murdered by Albanian opponents of Catholicism.

The disgusting afflictions these sub-humans (to call them animals is to insult the entire animal kingdom) perpetrated on their victims, mostly priests, make me almost despair and drive me to prayer, listening desperately for God to make sense of such unimaginable evil. Christ's command that we must love our enemies is no soft option, and this pope is guilty of the sin of fierce hatred. There are days when I fear I become as sub-human as those I call down the wrath of God upon. For my mental health, I really must stop meditating on martyrs. I was surely not born to be pope. On which subject, a visit from another pestilential pontifex maximus. Why these raving revenants keep plaguing me I can't fathom.

Seems the right moment to make an appearance. Rodrigo de Borja. Yes, one of the Borgias, We're not unlike the Murdochs, though not nearly so gentle. You'll especially understand, mate. Or not. Yes, quite possibly not. And yes, you know me as Alexander VI, 1492–1503. From an early age, I believed in the natural law, and at that early age, lust came naturally to me. Very naturally. Beautifully. And often where you least expect it. Though why you shouldn't expect it beats me. Popes are people just like you and me. In every way—not that I have to remind <u>you</u>, especially when it comes to boiling with molten passion. And don't even think of disagreeing or you'll end up screaming in the Vatican torture chamber as your fundament is splayed on the Pear of Anguish. Or if I decide to show mercy, you'll simply be strangled and dumped at the bottom of the Tiber. Understood? Good. Popes must be efficient, and efficient I was. Just as in-efficient you are. Yes, we sewered in sin but we also floated on faith—and more importantly, survived in style. Popes and sex. Why not? Exactly. One of the perks of office. Personally, I'd be more concerned with the popes who never <u>had</u> sex than with those of us who did—and do. And I speak from experience. Ten children from a menu of mistresses surely suggests a commitment to the right to life. Plus, I was a pioneer in offering a variation on the paradigm of the nuclear family. My final lover, Giulia, lived with my daughter, Lucrezia—a tantalising cook, by the way—and they both lived happily together in the papal apartments. A trail blazer, that's what I was—and not just in buying votes in the papal conclave. People forget that I was also the pope who centralised control in the church. I ruled with a rod of iron. Faith is fine but faith's a gamble. And gaming's a business. And our business demands best practice. After all, God de-mands the best in every way. Which is why here in the Vatican, murder's the home industry. Best practice. What did Jesus say? 'I am the way, the truth and the light.' Translation: 'My way or the highway. To heaven.' Be-sides, paradox is at the heart of all religions. Thank God. Contradiction's the name of the game. Yes, like you, I was less than perfect, but frankly, just look at this ludicrous shambles your mess of a church is now in. For God's sake, get your act together. And *dominus vobiscum.*

He'll really need to be.

Oh, Brother Edmund, what spirits did you let loose?

Friday, February 13th

Feast of St Dyfnog, 7th century monk much venerated in Clwyd, Wales.

An anonymous Welsh poet of the period (The Welsh are a wildly poetic and imaginative people prone to glorious exaggeration of all things Welsh) described (imagined?) Dyfnog as a man who had renounced the world, wore a shirt of thick horse hair fastened with an iron belt, lived on bread and water and did penance by standing under the stream of cold water which is now known for its miraculous cures. Ice cold holy water. I'm surprised it hasn't been patented, bottled and sold in supermarkets. Or, more commercially and evangelically, in the local church. I haven't had a son, but among the baptismal names I'd choose for the putative fruit of my loins, Dyfnog doesn't feature in the top ten. But any Welsh saint is—indeed, all things Welsh are— to be marvelled at. Especially under the freezing shower. Madness. Heaven's revelations must surely include St Dyfnog's account of his penitential spiritual journey.

Bounty of winter vegetable pancakes: cavolo nero, Brussels sprouts, carrot, spring onions, chives, pepper, sour cream and asperges of lemon. Even Saint Dyfnog would surely have made a gastronomic exception for these slices of paradise—and he would, I'm sure, be the first to agree with Sister Angelica that chives contribute to peace of mind.

And why wouldn't they if that's what you seek?

And on the subject of sons, Dario Silvestrini's dirty little secret is the cleanest dirty little secret of fatherhood in the Vatican.

His sister, fifteen years younger, entered the convent, joining the Order of the Most Holy Annunciation, the blue nuns, at the age of 20 but left after a year. She had a wild affair with a handsome young man from the Ivory Coast and became pregnant. Handsome young man immediately left her. A son, Guido, was born, and Dario, then the recently ordained bishop of Gorizia—the youngest bishop in Italy and of the smallest diocese—became the boy's godfather.

With a modest inheritance and his episcopal salary, Dario bought his sister and his godson a small house in Segni, about an hour's drive south out of Rome. He visits his sister and godson for a weekend every month and sometimes more often, and with relish, plays the role of a loving father to Guido.

Dario has kept this relationship secret from the curia—an extraordinary achievement, God knows—and sees his guardianship of the lad as the greatest grace God has bestowed on him—a faithfully celibate cardinal with the fulfilling responsibility of being almost a parent or, as he likes to describe himself, 'This Father's an almost father.'

The filial affection of his godson and the ironic rewards of celibate fatherhood are gifts he treasures.

Guido, now a handsome 19-year-old black Italian—of whom there are now a few more than quite a few—left school last year, and Dario continues to support him as he studies medicine.

Everyone here knows that Dario visits his sister and looks after her, but no one here knows about Guido.

It's really the loveliest relationship imaginable, and I envy Dario his perfectly priestly double family life.

No wonder he's so sane.

Actually, in the circumstances, I'm a little surprised he isn't as warm to Ennio as I'd like him to be, but there's no law that says all our friends have to like each other.

I see in Ennio a contemporary, if secular Dario, though of course I'm aware of the difference between their sexual experiences, but both of them have a secret and beautiful integrity.

Saturday, February 14th

Feast of Saints Cyril and Methodius, brothers (827–869; 815–884) and holy missionary giants who transformed the Christian world.

It wouldn't be going too far to say that they established Christendom long before it became Europe. Cyril created a whole new alphabet (Cyrillic—more than most saints have done), and then he and Methodius translated Scripture, liturgical works and the Mass into written Slavonic. I gasp in wonder and gratitude at the achievements of these two sacred dynamos who made their world their parish. Little wonder Pope Saint John Paul II named Saints Cyril and Methodius co-patrons of Europe.

I woke up in the middle of the night asking myself for the n-th time if God is love and is omnipotent, then why the hell is the whole world unjust?

I know all the so-called answers—free will and all that—but isn't giving humanity free will akin to giving a three-year-old a fully-loaded machine gun?

The inevitable result is chaos and pain.

Since the beginning of humanity, there have been gazillions more slaves than there were masters, and over time, not all that much has changed except the increasingly emollient descriptors for the same 'employer-employee' relationship. Basically, with very few exceptions, the poor and the coloured are screwed from here to eternity, from cradle to grave.

Free will?

Tell that to all the pyramid builders and the children sacrificed to crazy Aztec gods, and the gladiators and the serfs and the urban poor and almost all the world's armies composed of life's helpless conscripted victims and then to their millions and millions of innocent, slaughtered victims, and don't forget the endless gazillions of non-whites corralled into service and... not to put too fine a point to it, almost every woman since time began.

Mary, Queen of heaven, fine in its pathetic and now offensive monarchism, but one woman out of how many?

As they say, God, you do the math.

Yes, yes, I know all the stock answers, the excuses, the justifications and the rest of the comfortable explanations and desperate apologetics posited by comfortable, safe and well-fed men. I've done the math—indeed, the maths—and right now at this terrifying time of night, it doesn't add up.

None of it makes sense, especially the overwhelmingly patronizing and insulting nonsense—yes, non-bloody-sense—dreamt up by the god-justifying and always comfortable non-victims.

And until recently, I always thought the pope was the guy with all the answers.

Silly me.

God's a mystery alright.

Teillhard de Chardin, come to my rescue.

Back to sleepless sleep.

Sunday, February 15th

Feast of Saint Dochow who moved from Wales to Cornwall where he founded a monastery and might have been a bishop, though, as they say, records are inconclusive.

What is it about Cornwall?

No dreams.

Woke up late in a waterfall of grace and solace.

Meditated for only half an hour and listened to God reassuring me that it all makes sense in the long run when every tear shall be wiped away and somehow divine justice and reward will make glorious sense and heavenly release of our struggle for meaning here, mourning and weeping in this valley of tears.

Monday, February 16th

No saints from Cornwall are listed today, and I need to avoid even considering the hideousness of the martyrdom of Saint Juliana of Nicomedia—google it, Dad, if you dare—but my heart and prayers celebrate her.

And they're racing in the Vatican Stakes, and first out of the starting gates, Cardinal Olivier Gabriel Foncha of Cameroon arrived this morning unannounced to make an announcement.

He was accompanied by Cardinal Desmond Wilenski from Colorado, think Donald Trump but with the ability to at least construct a simple sentence, and untrustworthy Chilean Cardinal Carlos Silva Gonzales: an unblessed trinity and a sure sign of disastrous judgment and major trouble ahead.

Both of my judgments proved to be the case in Olivier's first sentence.

'Holiness, we are here representing the vast majority of the cardinals, archbishops, bishops and clergy of the Vatican and of the traditionally loyal faithful to protest against your unpapal behaviour and the scandal and outrage you have caused the church in your frequent questioning of articles of faith, your irresponsible and unreasonable demands upon all clergy to accept immigrant families into their residences, and worst of all, your misguided and reckless summoning of a Third Vatican Council, an absurd whim, without any consultation with your brother clergy. The sad—no, tragic—fact is that you have the mind of a shallow journalist who thinks only in headlines and then delights in catastrophising every minor fault or unfortunate incident you find in God's holy church.

Silence, the best response?

Yes.

And so the charge list rolled on.

I could almost have joined in their quartet, singing in unharmonious descant, but I refrained, smiled, refused to say a word and let the two of them blather on until their predictably insolent peroration:

What have you to say to these charges?'

I replied, 'Thank you for coming. In the future, please have the courtesy to make an appointment should you have any further unsought advice to offer me. By the way, I'm the Pope and I can say and do what I like. And what I like at the moment, I'll say. You may leave.'

And then their heavy artillery.

'Holiness, as representatives of the entire church, we insist that you resign the papacy. Given the theological and almost certainly medical lunacy of your behaviour since ascending to the see of Peter, you have every reason to speak the truth in explaining that for health reasons, you have found the burden of office so crushing that after much prayer and reflection, you have come to the conclusion that your only option is to resign, which you freely do, and that you will spend your retirement in solitude and in prayer for the welfare of all the church.'

'All of which is a lie,' I replied, 'so get thee behind me, Satan, not least because I know that your gross impertinence reveals only one truth: that you believe you've lined up the votes for your proposed conclave victory and have no doubt already sent your personal measurements to Gammarelli Tailors for a comfortable set of papal cassocks to wear for your first balcony appearance.'

There was a guilty silence, and then,

'Should you refuse to act on the overwhelming advice of the church as represented by us, these private declarations of ours will be made public, the church will likely suffer shame and schism, and more to the point, your papacy will be seen as a terminal cancer requiring immediate surgery. And in the circumstances, the mortal danger of such surgery cannot be underestimated.'

'Thanks for suggestion,' I said, 'Now two papal commands. One, bring it on. Two, fuck off. No such instructions necessary for you, Olivier, though on second thoughts, perhaps a little more inventively, Olivier, three: go fuck <u>yourself</u>.'

On principle, I don't drink until supper time—well, I try not to. Actually, that's total nonsense. Every day I share a midday glass of wine with Ennio but I don't regard that as drinking. I must be under pressure. Anyway, that double whiskey at 10.30 in the morning left me confident and combative.

First, a prayer to St John Paul the First, 'Look after me, mate. Please.' And then a call to Dario asking him to join me.

The moment he entered, I immediately knew that the game was up.

Tuesday, February 17th

Feast of the Seven Holy Founders of the Servite Order which is devoted to the Seven Sorrows of Mary.

In the 13th century, they were guild members—trade unionists in today's terms. Could it happen today, or would they be dismissed as communists? Were the apostles members of the fishermen's trade union? Can't imagine St Peter keeping much order at a workplace meeting.

Of course, I knew he had to appear. The question was only when.

Pietro. Peter. The rock. Fisher of men. Wife abandoner. Confused simpleton. Denier. Thrice. At least I can count. But all this 'pope' carry-on—this basilica—dedicated, God help us, to <u>me</u>! This—*Vatican*. First, they missed the message, then they missed the boat. Or as we say, *the barque*. And as for all this *temple* bullshit: it's what <u>He</u> told us to chuck out. Crazy laws so there can be punishment for disobeying them. And all this *art*. I mean, how many carpenters or fisherman call the shots around here? I always reckoned Pontius Pilate's palace was over the top, but—this! It's a bloody long way from Golgotha. And I thought *I* denied Him. Some-one should tell these two papal contenders that fishers of men need to get back to their nets and the smell of fish. I mean, Jesus Christ! Which is exactly what I mean. Jesus Christ. *Dominus vobiscum.*

Wednesday, February 18th

Feast of the interesting—some might say strange—Saint Angil-bert of Centula (740–814).

Clearly a bright spark of noble birth, Angilbert was raised at the court of Charlemagne and became his friend and confidante. Personable young men do just that. I should know. Having studied under the brilliant English scholar, Alcuin, the charming Angilbert was nicknamed Homer because of his Latin poetry. Clearly, a courtier of some refinement. He married Charlemagne's daughter, Bertha—clearly, a shrewd and probably an ambitious career mover and shaker on the make. It seems that he prayed fervently for resistance to an attacking Danish fleet, and when a storm arose and dispersed the Danes, apparently Angilbert interpreted the event as God's answer to his prayers and asked his wife for permission to become a Benedictine monk, a licence which she gave. And then became a nun herself. Clearly unusual. Charlemagne then gave Angilbert the abbey of Saint Riquier (abbot, hermit but spoke English) in Centula—clearly a stroke of good fortune—and in the abbey, Angilbert introduced continuous chanting using 300 monks and 100 boys in relay. Glorious, probably heavenly, but, equally, a tad weird. And now he's a saint. Not as clear as… Actually, I find this all a bit bewildering.

So, is this what the morning after pill feels like?

Let's face it, Dad. You were right. I'm not even fit to be a second-rate pope—and God knows, there's plenty of opposition in that dishonourable litany of scum.

I don't often cry, but this morning, I cried.

No, I wept.

Tears of understanding who I am.

And I'm not sure I can face it any more.

And maybe, after all, yes, they're right.

Last night, having told myself all day that I'd knocked the curia out of the stadium to the cheers of the unclerical crowd, I had a sudden attack of doubt, despondency and what I can only describe as spiritual dizziness.

I had to literally lie down, close my eyes and pray.

Like crazy.

I thought I was going to die and wondered whether I'd been John Paul One-d in a surprise strike.

After I don't know how long, I got my breath back and felt a strange calm. The ever-increasing niggling had gone, and I felt a sensation of total relaxation I don't think I'd ever felt in my life. I felt embraced by benign nothingness, and from nowhere I had a need to recite the Apostles' Creed to myself in what I can only describe as floating conversation with myself. And I know this sounds crazy, but, Dad, the whole experience was just like what's supposed to happen to you just before you die—and that once happened to me in the surf at Wollongong when I was eighteen.

It was the whole caboodle, lock, stock and barrel, in a flash. Not line by line or thought by thought or moment by moment.

Swept away in the rift, I suddenly realised I was drowning.

And simultaneously choked by sin.

But not.

But yes.

And then, as if I'd been cleansed by tears, before me in a single frame was the abstract but real picture of everything in my life in a lucid explosion of clarity and response.

And forgiveness.

The best I can do is recall it, though as I say, it wasn't rolled out as it is here.

Rather, it was instantaneously, luminously, transparently and totally comprehensible.

You'd better believe it.

Or rather <u>I'd</u> better believe it, because it happened.

That was my experience.

And so to The Apostles' Creed.

This is now my experience.

I believe in one God,
the Father, the Almighty,
Maker of heaven and earth...

A creative and creating father without a mother? You'd have to be God to pull that one off, but with all respect to Whomever, go God!

Still, to my way of thinking, 'father' speaks to a male writer assuming that males run the joint. Which until recently they used to but now don't. Ask any articulate nun.

The whole gender thing seems to me Old Testament and old hat. Mind you, if you're God, then away we go, no questions asked... except God gave us the gift of enquiry, logic and intellectual honesty. Our understanding of our invention of God gives God the right and the power to do anything and everything.

And God made heaven?

Really?

God needed company?

God was all-powerful but stuck in the middle of nowhere with not much happening but just... well, being God.

...of all things visible...

God making the visible world... no problem... well, except for the odd earthquake or hurricane or hungry lion or great white shark or bushfire or flood or... all disturbingly visible, not to mention repetitive.

and invisible.

Guess I'll never know, though it's a poetic projection of lovely mystery.

I believe in one Lord Jesus Christ, the only-begotten Son of God,

All a bit male-centric. Still, at the time a motherless son.

born of the Father before all ages,

Time problem here, though again, God isn't restricted by human concepts or by mere logic. Or did some brilliant poet concoct this beautiful contradiction, in which case, I'm open to coming on board?

God from God, light from light,
true God from true God,

I love this. Don't understand it but am dazzled by the possibility of its meanings.

I mean, I know so many, many people... colleagues, friends amazing and serene people I've met; lay and religious, who for three minutes—and especially congregational leaders and their members, especially women—have been given the gift of simple and enduring faith in what has always seemed to me a mess of logical and spiritual contradictions.

These friends have surrendered themselves to God and in reply, they've received the assurance of comfort in the face of the challenges of life.

I profoundly envy their optimistic equanimity about heavenly reward for unflinchingly lifetime faith.

Yes, I know. The sacraments.

It always comes back to those amazing metaphorical mysteries.

But sadly, vestments and role-playing apart, in my mind and heart and soul, a spiritually scratching part of me is not of their congregation. Or tribe. Let's face it... no, let me face it. I'm a desperately believing sceptic and a sceptically questing believer.

So who's not?

Well, except, for whatever loopy reason, I'm the accidental pope.

God the glorious joker?

Popes shouldn't be thinking like this, but this pope is... well, running out of sympathy for my loving God. And that's not an encouraging sign for the rest of my papacy.

Oh, well, let's hope that on a good heavenly day with the choirs of angels singing in nine-part harmony, our God finds us strugglers especially intriguing, and—come on God—therefore worthy of grace and salvation.

Let's hope.

And thinking about religious orders and congregations, another anachronism (or what seems to me to be one) teases and, frankly, concerns me. It's the division between priests and brothers—not that there are many brothers left, and those that are will all have died by the end of the decade.

I think the whole concept of 'brothers' is medieval.

Yes, yes, I know, the idea was that educated and worthy males entered the seminary to study for the priesthood while those lower down the social scale and less well educated became the more menial 'brothers'.

Talk about class consciousness.

I appreciate that some good and holy men feel called to the vocation of teaching, but priests can become educators, and the fact is that both priests and brothers took vows of poverty, chastity and obedience, so on reflection and advice, why on earth would a person feeling called to the brotherhood not be guided to embrace the priesthood?

I can't imagine Jesus sifting the candidates into such social categories.

Anyway, over recent time, the brothers have voted with their feet. They've either not joined or quitted their religious orders, married and left their elderly superiors to sell their assets or employ lay teachers in schools.

Time and tide. And, hopefully, theological evolution.

Unintentional, accidental, but thunderingly resonant to the heavens.

Such is revelation.

Whoops! There I go catastrophising again. Sorry about that, Olivier.

Must be getting late.

Now where was I?

Oh, yes…

begotten, not made,

I think we've considered this.

consubstantial with the Father.

This, too.

Through him all things were made.

This, too.

For us and for our salvation
he came down from heaven:

'Down' is surely a problem. Why is heaven 'up'? Contemporary understanding of the time when this was written... ascension and all that? Does it matter or is it just another way to revel in godliness?

by the power of the Holy Spirit

First mention of this almighty dimension, but what a corker of an idea! I've always loved the Holy Spirit, the dove, the breeze, the creative instinct. And this same force guides papal conclaves, so I'm clearly the result of the Holy Spirit's inspired decision to gift the church with an Aussie CEO.

Beauty bottler! Except as I know myself pretty well, it would appear that not for the first time, the good old Holy Spirit landed the joint with a dud.

was incarnate of the Virgin Mary,

Happy enough to believe it as a mystery—though not exactly a compliment to human males, and to be honest, I've never understood why, if human procreation is such a glorious gift... but then God is the 'fatherless father', so... let's just say that if all that was OK by God, it had better be OK with God's human creation, so listen up and believe up, all you sad old questioners like me.

Stop trying to square the circle and just accept its simple, beautiful actuality.

Except, of course, unless humanity invented God and then had to come up with explanations for the whole box of tricks that came with the metaphor or whatever it was...

For our sake he was crucified under Pontius Pilate;
he suffered death and was buried,

This I believe. The whole wretched, Roman, sadistic agony of it gives me endless nightmares though it certainly makes sense of evil as a hideously destructive force inhabiting humans, and that brings me to why on earth—or in heaven—God created Satan when, by definition, God must have known that the whole set-up would eventually go belly-up in one almighty angelic nuclear war.

Is this necessary to justify the premise of the whole narrative?

and rose again on the third day
in accordance with the Scriptures.

Should these lines be reversed? Chicken and egg? Is the resurrection necessary <u>because</u> it was set up in the Old Testament and therefore had to be fulfilled to extend the legend?

I have no problem with Christ's 'rising from the dead' being a metaphor for the theology of Jesus having ever more power after the crucifixion.

Christ-God alive and ever revivified in bread and wine is to me the most glorious and psychologically and spiritually brilliant belief in the entire curriculum of Christianity.

No other religion has come up with such a sensational, inspirational, empowering and poetic reality.

And it works!

And that's why I'm a Christian.

The eucharist is beyond genius. Or ingenuity. Or... well, anything!

Humanity somehow shares in whatever God is.

Food for thought. Food for faith. Food for life.

And death?

And believe me, of late I've learnt a lot about the spirituality of food.

He ascended into heaven

'Up and down' again. And what is this 'ascension'? Vertical lift-off? Surely that's ridiculous. Or is it a metaphor? And if it's a metaphor, why isn't the rest of the package a metaphor?

and is seated at the right hand of the Father.

A metaphor, I presume. On thrones, no doubt.

He will come again in glory to judge the living and the dead,

Am still not sure whether this last judgment is what might be called a major universal event or whether it means we'll all have to give an account of ourselves one day—our last on earth.

and his kingdom will have no end.

Makes sense if the premise is true.

I believe in the Holy Spirit, the Lord, the giver of life,
who proceeds from the Father and the Son.

Onside all the way—with gratitude and consolation.

With the Father and the Son, he is adored and glorified.

Holy Spirit as a 'he' is surely a problem. Is no aspect of God feminine?

He has spoken through the Prophets.

Absolutely—provided, that is, we didn't invent the Holy Spirit.

I believe in one, holy, catholic and apostolic Church…

Yes, that's why I'm here, though 'one' should surely now include the other Christian traditions we're walking in pilgrimage with. After all, in retrospect, we did get quite a lot of matters what you might call 'wrong'. Purgatory and indulgences anyone? Fortunately, of late we've made the small but, in fact, vast advance to embrace rather than to exclude.

The communion of saints

All the way. Magnificent. Surely what keeps us going.

The forgiveness of sins

If not, let's face it: we're all totally fucked.

The resurrection of the body

I understand the concept but that said, I don't have the remotest understanding of the concept.

Seems to me a medieval dream wish projecting earth, which we understand, onto heaven, of which we can have no concept other than in the most abstract of nouns.

Besides, I'm not at all sure my gloriously resurrected body would be all that glorious, whatever that's meant to be.

In fact, knowing that body and its not inconsiderable adventures as well as I do, I'm not at all keen to re-inhabit it in whatever incarnation.

Haven't we outgrown this pathetic need?

And life everlasting

One of humanity's most beautiful and imaginative hopes. God willing and God giving.

Amen.

Wholeheartedly and whole-soul-ly.

And maybe I should pray to Saint Angilbert for guidance and hope that relays of cantors will soothe all my theological wrangling.

Thursday, February 19th

Feast of Saint Boniface of Lausanne (1183–1260).

A placid saint for those of us unlikely to have the heroic sancti-ty to endure martyrdom. Known for his scholarship, Boniface was clearly a linguist as well, fluent in Latin, French and German as he taught in universities in Paris, Cologne and Lausanne. He became a bishop, contributed to the First Council of Lyon and retired to his old monastery of Cambre where he spent his final years in prayer. Nice to know that a learned life well-lived can be crowned with sanctity. I would have loved to have had dinner with him. And in whatever dimension, still might, Hope so. And I know a heavenly cook. Much to discuss.

Funny how words can be barbs which wound.
   Catastrophising.
   Bullseye.
   And bloody hard to remove the arrow.
   Somehow, though, one day we must... we <u>will</u> become the welcoming and embracing pilgrim church of all religions, inviting them to join us in our newfound humility and our eternal hope on the journey to understanding our God who became one of us.
   I believe Teillhard de Chardin was prophetic: the universe is, in every way, large or small, evolving towards a maximum, concentrated state of perfection, an Omega point which will be Christ, and therefore, in the end, God.
   Teillhard posits a kind of evolution of revelation, and as it outraged the Congregation for the Doctrine of the Faith in 1962, it must surely have been on the right track.
   Teillhard even goes further than my hopes, arguing that by their shared faith in humanity (rather than the supernatural—I can see the Vatican inquisitors of old pooping their pants with a major dose of the screaming willies) Christians, Marxists, Darwinists and atheists will finally join forces in understanding that ultimate summit of evolution, the Omega Point which is Christ.
   I don't expect to be around when that happens, though I'd like to see the face of Christopher Hitchens at that magic and sacramental moment, but it's a gloriously reassuring and hopeful dream—and to me, that prophetic dream beautifully unites the sacred and the secular.
   That said—with no water added to Jamesons—in all honesty, the observation of *nature red in tooth and claw* I have no answer to and would appreciate enlightenment on that matter from on high.
   Or, indeed, from wherever.

Some things we just don't understand, or if we think we do, we get even more lost in the maze.

Well, I do.

So much for theology.

I'm tired… and more than a bit…

Friday, February 20th

Feast of St Cliff Penfold (1907?–1967?) Australian proof of the existence of God and the necessity of Heaven, and of all my dreams.

This is the one I most thank Brother Edmund for. I'm pretty sure he would be horrified by it, though now he's in Heaven (having asked forgiveness for all his beatings, especially those ambiguously dealt out to me) I assume his perspective is enhanced. I guess he might at least take credit for my imagination, if not my theology. And so to Father Cliff Penfold. My dream was in two parts. Talk about theatre of the sub-conscious. I'll explain later.

My Dream. Part 1

G'day. Cliff Penfold's the name. I was in Hellfire Pass during the war, so listen up. Sorry about the lingo but I come from west of Warren in north-west New South Wales where we tell it like it bloody well is. If there's a job to be done, we stop whingin' and get on with it. Fair dinkum about everything. So as I was sayin', Hellfire Pass. I swear to you as God's my witness, Hellfire Pass on the Burma Railway was hell's bloody torture chamber. We were starved and bashed and kicked and tortured day-in, day-out, until most of us died screamin' in bloody despair. Burma's a bloody long way from Rome. And the food wasn't as fancy. When you got any. All I could do was dole out—what do they call 'em?—'the last sacraments' to me mates dying in their puddle of bloody pulp.

'May the angels lead you to paradise…' I said. And believe you me, I knew, I <u>knew</u> those angels <u>would</u>. They must. They bloody well had to. Otherwise, nothin' in this… this crucifixion of a life… nothin' made any sense, and someone… someone… in the end, me… I had to be the bloody straight-shootin' priest from the outback for all of them. Me mates. In our endless bloody… yes, I'll call it… our crucifixion. The Japs' only rule was pain and then more pain and then mountains more. So what do you do? I'll tell ya. Ya just do what ya can. I was their only priest, so I did what I had to. My 'vocation'. The vocation Sister Dolorosa said I had in sixth class at St Joseph's Warren. Took a while to land. Anyway, I gave those poor bloody livin' corpses the last sacraments. Their passports to paradise. And God knows, I questioned 'Him' with every death. Every single, meaningless, excruciatin' endin'. But as each one of them left this life, at least I whispered *dominus vobiscum*. Whatever that's supposed to mean.

My Dream. Part 2

In World War Two, hundreds of Australians died on the Burma Railway. Among the slave labourers, there was one priest, Father Cliff Penfold, a rebel battler from the outback. Survivors speak of him as a bush saint. He nursed the sick. He prayed with the dying. He heard confessions. He gave absolution. He buried the dead. He secretly said a five-minute mass and gave communion to his faithful with crumbs of stale biscuits or anything that might remotely be considered bread, and I'm sure he extended that highly-refined boulangerie definition way beyond canon law.

Used grains of rice as well, I don't doubt.

He even shared his food ration with those poor wretches who were daily bashed to buggery by the even more brutal than the Japs (If possible. And it was) Korean guards.

A priest true to his vocation. Indeed, heroically so.

And after the war, one of the survivors—he'd become an Adelaide University Associate Professor of History—this chap decided Father Cliff Penfold's story needed to be told.

He set about his research only to find that Cliff Penfold wasn't ordained.

Father Cliff Penfold had never even been near a seminary.

He didn't even finish high school.

He was just an ordinary Catholic who simply saw the need for a priest in that jungle hell, so he took on the role.

And speaking as a mere Australian pope (though maybe not for much longer) in my view, Father Cliff Penfold was as magnificent a priest as any that's ever been ordained.

The necessity of heaven.

And the necessity for the existence of Father Cliff Penfold, if only in my imagination.

And I'm in full agreement with myself.

Saturday, February 21st

Feast of St Peter Damian (1007–1072) who against his will was made a cardinal and reformed the election of the pope from a sordid theological and political bunfight to the civilised theological and political bunfight we now call the conclave.

Dante places St Peter Damian in the highest rung of heaven.

A bad day.

Or is it good—in the sense of honest and liberating?

Am I the first pope to have had such dreams?

Certainly not the first pope to have gone to bed a few sheets to the wind.

Dad, as I've no doubt blathered on since whenever, I've always regarded the concept of the monarchy as total bloody nonsense and a tragically pathetic fairy floss invention appealing only to the desperate intellectually and religiously illiterate.

An addictive drug for the eternally dispossessed who grovel, yet absurdly revel in their own servile subservience.

Meanwhile these days, of course the so called 'royals'—for Christ's sake, they don't exist! They've invented themselves and brilliantly sold the lie!—anyway, they do their best with pledges of 'service'—and tax avoidance—to justify their historically military and their political supremacy, thus their consequent heaven-sanctioned wealth.

'Because I won, God was with me, and God therefore has decreed that all these lands are mine by divine right and are to be ruled over forever by the first of my male heirs.'

Really!

And I mean REALLY in bloody neon!

Like, how can… does… any sane and intellectually honest person believe this pathetic self-serving fantasy?

And, worse, coronations reinforce the blasphemy that God put the royals there.

But, yes, guiltily, I actually do understand how an institution can make its slaves grateful for their submission.

Ranks within the church?

As if!

And the difference?

Well, we did it brilliantly with women, making them embrace their chains: dress subserviently and always genuflect in every way to male priestly power.

Looking back, it makes me question the emotional intelligence of alleged celibates.

And their terror of equality.

Until recently, thank God.

But returning to monarchic history; self-serving thinking sure works with the first and second rung conquistadors of their bloodily triumphant king.

Those pathetic yet shrewdly self-serving grovelers buy the delusion because they receive the servile but financially profitable dukedoms, knighthoods and other such fictitious inventions which, with every absurd title, reinforce the raw power of the original murderous battle victor and his ever more comfortable arse-kissers.

Thank God that at least the papacy isn't premised in primogeniture.

Well, for the most part.

And thinking dangerously, but now, what the hell, if I believe all the above, then what am I to make of the similar nonsense that the poor bloody pope is put there by God and, in certain (crazy) circumstances declares himself infallible?

I mean, I should know.

And I do.

And I'm the proof that it's all a pack of cards.

The Holy Ghost guides and decides?

If anyone in the conclave, any honest believer who has been through Machiavellian preparations followed by however many closeted days and sometimes weeks of the theological, political, personal and frankly self-serving double somersaults with pike and tuck which result in a two-thirds majority... if even the odd one of them in his—always 'his'—heart believes that the result is the imprimatur of the Holy Ghost, then apart from adjusting their beliefs to the new pontificate and their ambitions to the next, they surely have to subscribe to the belief that The Holy Ghost put me there as the all-powerful monarch of the church… until…

I wonder how many popes before me have had similar reflections.

I quite like Pope Leo X who, on his election, said, 'Since God has given us the papacy, let us enjoy it.'

He almost makes me look like a saint.

So if a Holy Ghost ratified pope is the celestial goods, then what happens when that divinely appointed joker comes to the conclusion that he's… well, some kind of empyrean comedian?

Simple.

He knocks back a chaser, a full Aussie breakfast and then says quite a few prayers.

Not quite so sure that these morning diary entries are a prudent writing exercise.

Actually, I'm pretty sure they're not.

OK, yes, Dad, a Jamesons too many, too early.

And apologies, Dad, for the rant.

It's in the family.

And, Dario, cancel all this morning's appointments.

His Holiness is unwell.

Yes, like the church, this pope is pathetically human.

Sunday, February 22nd

Feast of the Chair of St Peter, of which enough said.

Also the feast of Saint Margaret of Cortona, a frankly sexy lass who lived an abandoned youth, was the mistress of a young Montepulciano nobleman for nine years, had a son by him, lost her lover when he was murdered, then with her son, took shelter with the local friars but because she was so attractive, found herself involved on and off with other randy young men, yet eventually she founded an order who looked after poor and sick women and as was the sometime custom of the day, was given to ecstasies during which she received messages from heaven. Whew! And I now have no problem with that. Apparently, Margaret spent a great deal of her later life railing against vice to anyone who would listen, and let's face it, she knew what she was talking about. She never managed to shake off her reputation as a show-me-what-you're-made-of young sexpot but she did prophesy the date of her own death. There's a great deal about Saint Margaret of Cortona that many of us can relate to, and I for one am delighted that she's a saint. Singing along in the celestial choir are some colourful customers with backstories to give us all hope of salvation. Not least, me.

Vegetarian bounty.

Whole roast carrots with lentils, goat's curd and lemon roast potatoes; lentils, of course, mentioned in the bible as an aide to meditation. Or not, as the case may be. Or more likely, perhaps, written on the flyleaf of somebody's discarded bible. Or, perhaps in a book of medieval recipes consulted by Sister Angelica. Or the hopeful exhortation of some pious monk. And looking back, for all his appeals to chastity as the path to salvation, Brother Edmund sure threw himself into acting out Marvell's *To His Coy Mistress.*

My vegetable love should grow.
Vaster than empires and more slow.

If only.

A world of endless injustice, or seeds of hope deep inside the pain and suffering?

There was a time when theologians fought to the logical death like gladiators to defend their beliefs against the so-called mistaken and heretical opposition.

Today, I find great solace and optimism in reading the insightful explorations of our Anglican brothers, Rowan Williams and Justin Welby.

They dare to explore our spiritual lives. And if people are frightened of honest conversation, deep down they're afraid that the foundations of their beliefs are shaky and precarious.

End of sermon to self, and a big thank you to Saint Margaret of Cortona for being such a sinner as well as a saint.

Monday, February 23rd

Feast of St Polycarp of Smyrna (69–155) who was converted by St John the Apostle (class) and proved to be a vigorous missionary. *He laboured in the field until the age of 86 (in today's old age, what's that?) and was condemned to be burnt alive for the entertainment of barbarians in Smyrna in modern Turkey. Tradition has it that the flames refused to kill him and that he was finally stabbed to death. The mind vomits in revulsion; the heart reverberates in exalted gratitude. Wherever we're at in our path to understanding God, our faith is drenched in blood and purified by pain. And that mystery of faith I try daily to understand and live. And to my shame, I still recoil and shudder, not least because in a broken world, such holocausts continue in their universal outrage. Saint Polycarp of Smyrna, in your extended agony, pray for this desperate pope.*

A pope without doubt is surely a fraud.
It's just that my doubts are...
...but they need to be suppressed.
And that's dishonest.
Vatican Catch 22.

Tuesday, February 24th

Feast of Saint Evetius of Nicomedia (died 303) whom I'd previously never heard spoken of, even by the most eccentric of archivists in this place.

And God knows, in that department, we have some fruitcakes. When a copy of that sub-human monster Diocletian's edict against Christianity was posted in public, Evetius vandalized it and was martyred. Vandalised it! How gruesomely magnificent! Our very own patron saint of graffiti artists! Only in Catholicism! Oh, how I wish I'd had the courage to be Pope Banksy the Second and scrawl my subversive 'installations', my similarly dismissive criticisms, across so many documents that have wasted my time since becoming pope. And for years and years before. But I would never have had the faith or the courage to die for my graffiti. All the more reason to celebrate the marvellously up-you-and-then-some Saint Evetius! He may well turn out to be my patron saint—not that I'd wish that on so holy an activist.

The more I think about it, the more I esteem acting as one of the noblest of the healing professions.

Dad, you always dismissed actors as shallow because, you presumed, they spend their lives pretending to be someone other than themselves.

But, Dad, what you don't understand and probably refused ever to, is that they're not pretending.

Dad, actors are brave enough to explore.

Yes, they dare to enter into the soul of another human being in order to tell that person's story and so allow audiences to appreciate the infinite variety of humanity.

Hopefully, to be transformed by the gift of ritual.

In a funny way—one you'd never be able to come to terms with—all those actors you so despised (though you loved the actresses... is there some kind of message here?) were, in their artistic ministry, priests for the moment.

They stood in place of someone and celebrated that person's precious existence in all its confusions, contradictions and... well, the humanity God gifted us with.

Discuss.

Anyway, those actors said the words, and their audiences received those phantom messages.

I see that as their privilege and the audience's grace.

And in any case, in a lesser way, surely we're all actors because we all role play. And 'play' links us with the truths professional actors try to embrace and reveal.

As a priest (because, let's face it, that's all we are. Walk-ons or stars. It's the same profession apart from the vestments/frocks)... so as a proud priest, I acknowledge my sacred performance.

With pride.

And why do I confess this?

Because, yes, I, too, am an actor, and a dangerous one.

I play Pope John XXIV, and my character and lines are (according to the programme) written by God and the church with, admittedly, a fair bit of editing by me, usually without too much consultation with the Director.

This may sound shallow or mad or hypocritical, but, Dad, every morning on waking, I put on my costume and take on the persona of the pope I'm playing.

And more often than not, I put aside the real person I am for the role I've been accidently graced with.

Dad, my audience is more than a billion—quite a house, though bums on pews have been dropping for half a century, and reviews of the script have been changing from mixed to more and more quite uncharitable pans.

Still, my role is to reassure the punters that their ticket to The Meaning of Life is worth what they continue to find meaning in and hope for.

As I do.

Fervently, as God's Vicar on Earth.

Just as those ancient Greeks invented theatre in their quest for an explanation of the mysteries of the universe, so, in our adaptation, we continue the exploration

A theatre is a church; a church is a theatre. A stage is an altar; an altar is a stage. And the performers act out a magical ceremony. They try to illuminate the plot of life, the momentary performance of which we're somehow represented by on that stage and altar.

And magic does exist when we authorise it and when we participate in it.

We know this to be true from our rich experience of theatre and ceremony.

Drawing a long bow?

I think not—and I perform daily.

It's powerful stuff and it works.

What do they say in the acting profession? 'The audience is never wrong.' Well, except when it is.

But audiences are now a worry for us with our increasingly diminishing houses.

Like, who's wronger?

Sorry about that, Brother Edmund, but the fact is, our audience is voting with their feet, and their feet are sprinting away from the box office.

But I'm tired. And also tired of dreaming.

Just at the moment, too much revelation is... far too much revelation.

Please, Lord, just for tonight: dark, warm, oblivious sleep.

And thank you in advance.

Wednesday, February 25th

We're told that in their way, all the souls in heaven (an ungraspable concept, but anyway...) are saints, so today for me is the feast of Blessed Mario Castaldi The First (1920–1976)—me being Blessed Mario Castaldi The Second.

As has become my experience, my visitations or ecstasies or whatever they are... these comprise one-way enlightenment: they speak, I listen and remember. With Blessed Mario, however, it's always been different, especially on his birthday/feast day. While I have to admit to not necessarily looking forward to this extended and tearful yearly conversation, I can't help myself. Dad is alive and living in two dimensions: my father, the patron saint of disappointment following my school and subsequent career with resigned chagrin; but he's also the man I speak to in heaven, apologising for not being the perfect son he hoped for and at the same time, increasingly understanding him and even sympathising with him for what was a tough, unhappy life he did his best in and failed in one important dimension: failing to be happy. We don't have much choice as to who we are when we're born, and Dad was born in Italy but in 1930 brought to Australia by his parents in search of a better life. At school, he was a wog with an accent, and worse, a working-class wog at that. The brothers gave him a religious education grounded in Irish Catholic guilt (which doesn't blend well with Italian sexual machismo) and they also gave him Wollongong ambition to move up the social ladder. In his awkward way, he combined a slice of Italian charm and confidence with a bucket of Aussie playground street smarts. He never went to university but worked as a builder's labourer and quickly became a successful builder himself. He married my mother, a beautiful Catholic girl from the region. Her par-

ents never approved, and she quickly learnt that within marriage, Latin charm becomes patriarchal demand. Dad built our splendid show-off house with a view of the ocean, and my little brother and I were expected to become the next generation school heroes and post-school Castaldi worldly successes. We both failed to be the adolescent gods Dad dreamt of and in our bumbling ways, we've failed to give him the next generation of all-conquering sons. I've often wondered how Dad would have responded to a granddaughter but then not dared to advance the thought beyond timid speculation. Of course, the grog didn't improve marital relations between Mum and Dad, and endless lectures about getting into top-school sporting teams and then studying medicine or law at university (a proper uni, not a bloody loser one like Wollongong) didn't exactly make for Fathers' Day embraces. And entering a seminary wasn't Dad's idea of career success. 'Running away from the world' he called it. 'You need a girlfriend. What's wrong with you?' In retrospect, he had a point: here I am now, the world's most professional bachelor with an artificial family of a friendly cardinal, a middle-aged nun and an athletic young man of the build and sexual prowess I was meant to have, though Ennio's disposition is more amused and worldly than Dad's limited concept of love. And all that said—and I say it to him frequently—in his dreadful way, he meant well. He wanted the best for his sons, but that best had to be the best he never achieved. No wonder Tonio and I kept our love lives a secret from Mum and Dad. And I keep asking him, 'Dad, isn't pope enough?' and, of course, I know the reply: 'Only if you're a first-rate one.' Mind you, given some of the dropkicks, fruitcakes, halfwits, sleazebags, raving loonies and frankly gob-smackingly criminal predecessors who haunt me, I doubt I'm destined for the ninth circle of hell or heaven. Anyway, that second-rate blister still stings twenty-four seven, and not even holy water blessed by me manages to sooth the mental pain. Happy feast day, Dad. I love you. And a prayer: one day, please can you manage to say that you love me? And yes, I know, proud of me might still be pushing it a bit. Christ all fucking mighty, one day all this… whatever it is… will be explained.

I despair.

Yet somehow I believe.

Bounty. How on earth did Sister Angelica come across the Gaelic recipe for baked potato farls? I'd never heard of the word. Apparently, it means a quarter of a round Irish soda flatbread which is always marked with a cross to let the devils out. Burn the bastards! And just for the record, the bread isn't baked but fried. Of course. The Irish! I expected Sister Angelica to tell me that consuming each farl brought a three hundred days' indulgence—that should have lifted the price of potatoes in ever-mocked County Fermanagh—but she merely mentioned that potatoes clear the head and encourage positive thinking. Must be in one of those bible passages I fell asleep over during seminary lectures. Anyway, I love spuds, so send in the farls!

In my oncoming darker night of the soul, I fully understand that praying to God to change my world is understandable but unintentionally offensive. If God knows everything, then acceptance is the right genuflection to the deity. Over time, humanity has far too slowly and far too painfully grasped at the straws of life, all of us in our ways hoping for salvation, whatever we want salvation to be. Maybe in some yet-to-be-understood way, this might have been God's seemingly crazy intention. But for Christ's sake—and absolutely for Christ's sake—I mean, what was He on? Over-volumed Angelic descant? Sorry, but it just doesn't make divine sense to me. I mean, why the aeons of unspeakable agony and fruitless waiting and hoping and working to alleviate that manifestly unjust suffering on the victims of His love?

It simply doesn't add up.

Maybe to theologians in their comfortable offices with well-stacked bookcases, but not to the gazillions of victims.

And their families.

And God knows, I know families.

Oh, yes, I know all the elegant theological justifications—as far as I can determine, deft sleight of hand… angels on pinheads—but in my heart, quite frankly… well, as a pope, almost quite frankly… how can I come to terms with this… What's the abstract noun for… nonsense?

Absurdity?

But desolation, consolation, life and death: theologians cleverer than I can tease this out.

My mind is and always has been a muddle, but in my heart I know one thing, and it's something I don't want to know: the only change I must pray for is change of myself.

God and truth: hard taskmasters.

And suddenly, in my bodily niggling—the peculiar fatigue and hot/cold flushes—the signal is now louder than even I can honestly dismiss. I realise that against all my lifetime rejection of confrontation in whatever expression, I must accept what gentle turbulence is now festering inside me. I don't want to admit to it, but where my Wollongong stubbornness denies, my now Roman body flags.

In this mortal world, medical expertise—and expertise outside these not always trustworthy medical Vatican walls as JP1 could attest to—has to be cautiously sought.

Fortunately, Canadian Cardinal Gino Amato's youngest sister married an Italian doctor who's now a professor of medicine at the Università degli Studi in Florence. I've met him on two Amato family occasions and liked him greatly.

I'm sure he can arrange a discreet visit to Rome.

At my age, something has to start going wrong. I must just hope that it's the result of stress.

Perhaps Sister Angelica has a medieval cure for the niggles.

But the professor's diagnosis first.

Thursday, February 26th

Feast of Blessed Martino Martini (died 1949 in Lisbon).

Now here's a saint-and-a-half. A convert, Martino joined the Franciscans though was never professed. He probably forgot. Barefooted and living on bread and water, he was happy to perform all the menial jobs in the monastery while simultaneously praying. Promoted to cook, he apparently got so carried away in prayer that one morning he forgot to cook breakfast for all the monks. When one famished friar popped into the kitchen to check on the bacon and eggs, whom did he find slaving over the stove? Of course: angels. What did I say? We desperately need more of them. As for saintly old Martino, OK, not so much saint-and-a-half as just the half, but how could anyone not love him? Except, maybe, at breakfast time? From now on, I'll pray to Blessed Martino Martini with each martini. And I must recommend his intercession to a certain holy angel of my kitchen whom I'd canonise if I could.

The Holloway dinner proved to be a blessing beyond my wildest hopes—richly rewarding on every front and utterly different from any expectation I'd toyed with.

We were four: Dario, Kiwi Cardinal Adrian Jellicoe and Alison Broderick who runs the Doctrinal Dicastery. Oh, and My Questionable Holiness.

Of course, Sister Angelica knew how important the event was for me, and gift of God that she is, she prepared what I can only describe as a modest feast.

Soup. Welcoming. Simple. Different. Engaging. Cauliflower and turmeric, with, dare I remember, salted croutons? Inviting. Sister Angelica understands the Latin prayers at the foot of the altar. *Introibo ad altare Dei. Ad Deum qui laetificat iuventutem meam.* I shall go unto the altar of God. To God who gives joy to my youth. And my appetite.

Next course brought surprise to supposed knowledge: rich coquilles Saint Jacques. Holloway admitted to that seafood being his favourite and politely asked Sister Angelica the provenance of such delicious molluscs. She asked him where he thought they originated. Normandy? 'Further south.' Of course, Brittany? 'Further south.' La Rochelle? 'Further south.' Bayonne? 'Further south.' I give up, but wherever they originated, your choice is indeed refined, Sister. So from Spain, presumably. 'Further south.' I give up. Tell me, please.

Sister Angelica smiled, turned to leave, turned back and replied, 'Australia', then departed.

Richard Holloway isn't exactly known for extended silences, but this may well have been his longest.

And the atmosphere around the table warmed even more.

The main course—also modest and all the more seductive for that—was lobster and pancetta tagliatelle accompanied by lemon pepper greens: Brussels sprouts, leeks, broccolini and silverbeet.

Finally, Italian cheeses: gorgonzola, taleggio, asiago and fontina served with Sister Angelica's home-baked bread not divided into farls.

Our wine—the gift of a case from the highly civilised archbishop of Agrigento—was Giovanni Rosso 2017 Bianco from Mount Etna vineyards. A reassurance or an eruption? We paused, however briefly, to consider.

But to the other meal: our conversation.

To begin, I invited Richard to say grace, and he asked us all to close our eyes and pray for each other.

After about a minute, he said, 'In the circumstances of my current beliefs, may I, as a compliment to my host, dare to recite a grace of my former and, I'm sure, your present spiritual state. Take, O Lord, and receive all my liberty, my memory, my understanding, and my entire will. Whatever I have or hold, You have given me; I restore it all to You and surrender it wholly to be governed by Your will. Give me only Your love and Your grace, and I am rich enough and ask for nothing more.'

And then he added. 'Nothing more, except the faith to believe in my prayer.'

And then smiling at Sister Angelica he said, 'And bless especially Sister Angelica whose faith and virtue, like Jesus turning water into wine, has, I'm told, imitated His miracles, turning produce into poetry.'

After that, we all knew that this was indeed to be a graced moment in our lives.

Which it quite unexpectedly was.

'Unexpectedly', because our expectation was that we four would listen with openness and fascination to the story of Richard's spiritual pilgrimage—which, indeed, we ultimately did—except that for the first half of our agape, in the gentlest yet most sincere way, Richard plied each of us with questions he said came from a questing soul.

Who planted our faith in us? Why had we chosen the priesthood? What is heaven? What must have it been like to be Jesus? Dare we separate myth from fact in the scriptures? Are the scriptures complete or always awaiting further discovery and interpretation? Is revelation from God or humanity or from God through humanity with all humanity's weaknesses and failings? What do we mean by 'the one true faith'? Is suffering redemptive? Is death, like birth, the universal sacrament? Is wine liquid prayer? (You had to be there!) What apparent insanity would Francis of Assisi embrace were he living today? Will God ever totally conquer the devil, and anyway, what does this question mean?

In the end, exhilarated, we asked if we could perhaps ask him questions! His smiling reply was that of late, answers have not been his forte but that he'd do his best.

And so our conversation deepened, each of his measured replies stimulating more questions.

Faith is meant to bring joy and hope, yet for you, Richard, it seems to have generated melancholy.

Why?

When you believed, what did you believe?

Are you a priest forever?

In religion, what is the relationship of ritual to the word?

Will religion ever die?

Why do we know that our gathering tonight is holy?

There's a divinity that shapes our ends, Rough-hew them how we will. Was Hamlet right?

To report our answers and his would require a book, and committed scribe that he is, he has already published his detailed reflections on just about everything under the sun, though fearlessly refining those judgments is his mintmark.

In our salvation game—a vulgar reduction, I know—yet to be overwhelmed by fearlessly informed honesty is a feast within a feast and a humbling seminar in God's invitation to daring discovery: the journey of open faith.

So much more than myself—and it's always been one of my few strengths—Richard seems to have a memory for every bloody text which has impacted on him! He's like some kind of Gospel Google; press Return, and he comes alive with poetry and prose which have stimulated, informed and given comfort and hope to him.

The whole embrace was curiously fortifying: inspirational doubt and open-minded reflection; and his phrases, quotations and cautious conclusions came across to us all as fanfares of rediscovered truths.

He is certainly strong on the poetic truth of myth and on the regrettability of centuries of theologians and teachers insisting on literal truths in the bible.

I wish we had recorded him, but I recall some gems. 'The sweet sorrow of melancholy. Poetry bears witness to what is happening on the battlefield of life. It's always the poor who pay the price for progress. To quieten our conscience for the destruction and injustice of progress, we plant daffodils amid the ruins we create. The untidiness of the universe. We're not entirely responsible for all we do yet we must nevertheless do our best.' (A sort of blend of predestination and free will. Having one's cake and eating it?). 'Forgiveness, as Christ insisted, must be central to the meaning of life.'

And I particularly liked his description of *gospelling atheists.*

He's a compendium of Hopkins's May mess, except his mess is autumnal and deeper for its tender melancholy, a state, by the way, that he doesn't dismiss as a defect; rather, he experiences it as a kind of sieve through which to cleanse his yearning for purpose and meaning.

Pessimist or prophet?

Or mirror?

...and miles to go before I sleep.

Richard is a priest of integrity, a pilgrim who counts each mile walked and each mile ahead as offering its optional and, dare he or I say, dark grace?

Dangerous yet crucial territory. Latin derivation: *crux-crucis*, the cross—instrument of the most cruel torture unto death.

My only surprise was that he didn't quote Tennyson: *There lives more faith in honest doubt, believe me, than in half the creeds.*

And this morning, Richard, Dario, Adrian and Alison attended my mass, and with grateful humility and overwhelming joy, Richard came to the altar for communion, and in controlled ecstasy, I placed the host in his hand, then passed the chalice to him. And at that sacred moment, I knew that in my fraught papacy, I had achieved at least one act which was indeed the proof that God can work through this most fragile and broken of human beings.

Friday, February 27th

Feast of St. Gregory of Narek, Abbot and Doctor (950–c.1003).

Not much is known about this delightful Armenian monk who wrote mystical poetry, hymns, and biblical commentaries, but they were 10th century bestsellers and the more off-the-planet they were, the more popular they became. Think Bob Dylan finding Jesus, though hopefully with a much better voice. Not all that hard. Gregory was never actually canonised; people just knew he was a saint. In point of fact, he wasn't even a Catholic, so watch out A.A. Grayling: God may get you yet! Some saints you gotta love, but right now I'm afraid, love isn't in the Vatican air.

Napoleon in Russia. The Duke of Wellington. Gallipoli. The Kokada Trail. The Vatican.

Dario says he stands by me but advises me to resign for the good of the church and for the consolation of my remaining days.

No sweet sorrow of melancholy for this pathetic mess of a human being: after the dark night of the soul, the loneliness of myself in a mirror and the despair of hell.

And then, the least expected glimpse of some kind of crazy victory in humiliating defeat.

Deus ex machina?

An urgent and surprising visit from Ernesto Mendoza looking healthy and years younger.

Was the whole event a drunken dream? A gleam of hope? If so, it may well prove what Galileo said: "Wine is sunlight held together by water."

Mendoza knew every detail of the coup—well, at the moment, the attempted coup—and seemed genuine is saying he could only imagine the pain I must be feeling. I replied that he must have a vivid imagination. He smiled and said, 'We now both understand the agony in the garden, and that's merely a prelude to the crucifixion.'

The man chooses his words with appropriate precision. He said that in the depths of despair, there is always hope and then he outlined a fiendishly constructed plan of Machiavellian insight.

Yes, Olivier largely understands the disposition of the curia and he has done his sums, but what he has not taken fully into account is the number of moderate to progressive cardinals Francis appointed, and while in conversation they may smile on Olivier as the new strongman the church arguably needs, they're not convinced that a return to doctrine, discipline and the banishing of all doubt is the way to invite the lost sheep back into the fold. Quite the reverse might well be the result. And for good measure, they knew that being the clever politician he is, Olivier would ensure that his curia would be like the gestapo in the Garden of Eden—permitted pleasure, fine; but step away from the party line, and grave consequences follow in this life and the next.

Not, as Mendoza said, the forgiveness which our Saviour offered in his invitation to salvation: 'Come to me, all you who are weary and burdened, and I will give you rest. Take my yoke upon you and learn from me, for I am gentle and humble of heart; and you will find rest. For my yoke is easy, and my burden is light.'

Then came his two-pronged proposition.

First, yes, for many sensitive reasons which he knew that in my heart I understood (he knows my heart better than I do? A sharp and effective stab) my resignation would bring me peace of mind, avoid scandal for the pope and for the church, allow me a gentle and dignified retirement, and most appealing of all, perhaps, would offer the church a new pope walking the middle road.

That pope being him.

His justification quickly followed before I could reply.

A summary. After death-threatening illness, his record in office remained one which reflected command of and confidence in church doctrine and tradition; his reassessment of the place of law in faith, his change of heart, his new openness to the spirit and thus his proof of spiritual progress and newfound humility... all these embraced both major factions in our divided church, and therefore if, in the next conclave, he were the candidate of healing and the dispenser of balm on the pilgrimage, in all likelihood he would be elected pope over Olivier and with God's grace in the time remaining to him, he would calm the storm and steady the barque of Peter.

No doubt he'd rehearsed his appeal well but he certainly spoke with the serenity, gentleness and, dare I say, hope of the man for the moment.

I almost softened and acquiesced, but then, just as I thought of my kitchen cabinet and my strange need for their approval, Mendoza caught me out and said, 'I think I know what you're thinking, and I think that on reflection, you'll realize that this decision must be yours and only yours. It may well be the most momentous and inspired act of your papacy, one which restores and saves the unity of the church and the salvation of souls. Holiness, let us both treasure the holiness of this moment and, in this pool of silence, pray for guidance and discernment.'

Was he God's blessed agent or the devil's devious henchman?

I obeyed, and after what must have been the longest unvoiced prayer of our lives, Mendoza embraced me and said, 'May the tranquility of the Father, the grace of the Son and the inspiration of the Holy Spirit descend upon you and remain with you now and forever. And now, Holiness, I ask for your blessing.'

Again, I obeyed.

He then took a document from his briefcase. It was on parchment, and the calligraphy was elegant.

In a daze of euphoric bewilderment and possibly sanctified terror, I skimmed through it, not remembering anything.

Mendoza handed me a fountain pen, 'Sign it but don't write any date. Your signature will be the assurance of your peace of mind henceforth. Our agreement will remain *in petto* (Latin for secret, Dad.) and your resignation will not come into effect until such time as you decide to date it, at which time I'll bring you the instrument for witnessing and dating. Until that time, of course you remain as pope, and our understanding is also best left between the two of us. The next few days will bring fulfilment of our hope and answers to our prayers. Leave everything to me,' he said. 'Everything.'

And he left.

I put my phone on silent and poured a martini.

I'm not sure what hell or what heaven I'm meant to be inhabiting.

For the time being, I suspect I'm treading holy water as two-thirds of four-fifths of fuck all.

Have I been I duchessed to death or am I the vessel of God's mercy and forgiveness?

What in the name of—frankly, I have no idea—made me sign that document?

And now, what's the strategy and what are the tactics?

And what possible difference can I now make to anything?

And suddenly I have this weird feeling that my whole life has been, well, some kind of a play, and a good play demands a plot with a surprise ending.

In which case, Mario, plot.

Meanwhile, I spoke to Gino's brother-in-law today, told him of my symptoms, and he has arranged for a haematologist friend here in Rome to privately take a blood sample.

Saturday, February 28th

Feast of Blessed Villana de' Botti (1332–1361) another very human saint the rest of us groping pleasure-seekers can grasp hope from.

We're told she was a pious child who, aged 13, ran away from home and tried to join a convent but was sent back to her family who quickly saw that she was appropriately married. As a result, she apparently became lazy, worldly and pleasure seeking—no need to read too closely between the pious lines—to the extent of having a sin-laden soul... as which of most of us did or do not?—repenting, she asked the Dominican fathers for help and became a Dominican tertiary, trying to be a good wife and reading scripture. At some stage, her family had to stop her begging from door to door and performing other penances. At mass, she believed she received religious ecstasies, though others dismissed her as crazy. She then received visions of Our Lady and the saints, and began to prophesy. Eventually, it would seem even her fiercest opponents recognised her as saintly. A disturbed, complex and very human lady. It seems to me right now that too much guilt is as unhelpful as too little.

So, time for some new characters to join the plot. I'll create half a dozen new cardinals, no less, and all of them progressive in outlook.

That should add spice to the conclave finale.

And I know just the actors.

From Hungary, the only bishop who isn't ferociously fascist in his theology is László Szabó in Szeged.

He studied in Germany and France, so his outlook on the world and the faith is post-medieval, unlike his fellow Magyar princes of the church.

Portuguese Osvaldo Almeida from Coimbra is also sophisticated and outward looking. And Osvaldo means *God's power*. I have it on good authority. Osvaldo's. God's power ought to throw a spanner into Olivier's works.

Indonesia's Cahya Hartono from Semarang in the middle of Java is a suave diplomat and a wonderful pastoral leader. He trained in Rome and Lyon, speaks any number of languages, passes as a moderate but always votes for the prophetic future, not the strangulated and strangling past. He'll bamboozle the dim American conservatives—surely a vital skill in any conclave. And as his first name means 'light in darkness', he's surely vital to any conclave.

Filipino Bayani Fabroa of Luzon has always stood up to his country's barbarian strongman leaders; just the ticket.

And gallant little Tasmania hasn't had a cardinal in all its brief Christian history, so for good measure I'll promote Oscar Kraegen in Hobart. He's almost certainly the only expert in ecclesiological hermeneutics on the island. Tasmanians will probably declare a public holiday in his honour.

And to stir up a little thunder Down Under, Michael Boland of Perth. Born and ordained for cardinal red.

Oh, and, of course, Ghana's Gyasi Owusu of Garural—a forward looking African who thinks outside the box. And the catechism. Just the man to hoist Olivier on his own petard.

Taken altogether, a positive parachute of prelates to spice up proceedings in the Sistine Chapel.

To work!

Dario is in for a busy few days.

Question. Is this the theological equivalent of branch stacking or political pork barrelling at election time?

Answer. Yes, but it's always done by all parties—and pontiffs.

Question. Does this make it right?

Answer. No.

Question. Why?

Answer. *The last temptation is the greatest treason:*
To do the right deed for the wrong reason.

Murder in the Cathedral. Or *In the Vatican.*

T.S Eliot was on the money.

And speaking as the victim, I agree with my decision.
Casting from heaven.

Sunday, February 29th

Not the best feast day to be awarded unless you're happy to be fêted only once every leap year. Of the four saints on my calendar, Sardinian Pope Hilary (died 29th February 468) seems something of a character.

He fought all kinds of heresies—they abounded like contemporary viruses—and exhorted bishops to curb their excesses. Sensible, if historically repetitive advice. He insisted that the pope and not the emperor should lay down the law in spiritual matters, which seems reasonable to me, though as yet, I've not been an emperor. He was involved in endless theological and ecclesiastical disputes—I sympathise with him—and apart from churches, convents and librar-ies, Pope Hilary erected two public baths. If we want to remember him more frequently than every four years, he has another feast day on November 17th. Two for the price of one-and-a-quarter. I shall think about him in the bath of which I suppose he must be the patron saint. Curious people, some popes. Clean, though. Well, some of us.

'My dear brothers in Christ,

Thank you for your recent unexpected visit.

While your advice might be judged by some as less than fraternal, as your holy father I naturally feel obliged to consider it.

Following the encouragement of St Ignatius of Loyola, I will not make any major decision while experiencing desolation, the senti-ment I assume you intended me to undergo.

Rather, over the next few days and weeks, I shall spend appropri-ate time in prayer and reflection while simultaneously attending to my normal administration of the worldwide church as, no doubt, you would wish and expect me to.

I'm sure that with civilised discussion, we can consider the ap-propriate feast to make appropriate announcements, and you may therefore confidently discuss this matter with my Secretary of State.

That agreed feast day might provide a suitable occasion for the four of us to concelebrate mass at the high altar in St Peter's.

You will recall that having dismissed Cardinal Becciu for financial mismanagement and potential criminality, as a gesture of good will, Francis invited him to concelebrate mass in the chapel of Santa Marta.

Our sharing of the sacrifice will send a strong message of Christian fellowship and amity to the faithful while also laying to rest any unfortunate rumours of power play or clerical ambition, neither of which any of us would wish to entertain or to be entertained by the ill-informed or the malicious.

In the meantime, as your good shepherd, may I recommend you read and meditate on a brief but insightful spiritual memoir I've found helpful. *The Heart of Things, An Anthology of Memory and Lament,* is by Richard Holloway, one-time Bishop of Edinburgh and Primus of the Scottish Episcopal Church.

I particularly urge you to ponder pages 134-7 in the chapter on forgiving.

The quotation from the British playwright, Simon Gray, will, I believe, provide help and comfort to you on your spiritual journey, and in your gratitude for his wisdom, I'm sure you will pardon Gray's use of the phrase 'the seminal fuck'.

In my experience, all of us at some time in our lives have used words which might have been more thoughtfully and charitably weighed before being spoken, and I am no exception.

Please feel free to make an appointment with my Secretary of State should you require any further reading or vocational advice, though I must alert you to the fact that the coming month is already heavily booked, and there may have to be some serious delay in my availability, for the which I crave your indulgence and apologise in advance.

With my blessing,

your loving and holy father,

John XXIV
Pontifex Maximus
et ut
Vegemite I'

Monday, March 1st

Feast of Pope St Felix III (died March 13, 483).

Great-grandfather of Pope Saint Gregory the Great. Married, father, and widower. Priest. Nothing else is known of his early life. Elected 48th pope and apparently did his best to unite the church. Hardly a wasted life.

Options
1. Continue as pope and tell the conspirators to go to hell.

Risks
They won't head hellwards and will increase pressure on me to resign.

The church will be seen to be divided, and both factions might well lose.

The conspirators' majority in the curia will ensure an even stronger go-slow policy on all my initiatives.

The conspirators will drip feed the media with salacious rumours about me.

Best Outcome
World synods will back the pope, and the conservatives will be seen as the nostalgic and retarded rump that they are.

Worst Outcome
I follow the fate of John Paul I.

2. Give way to Olivier and his traditionalist gang by resigning.

Risks
I admit my inadequacies to the church and the world.

The pilgrim church retreats to being the legalistic church triumphant. Mortal sin rides again.

Say goodbye to the young—well, to those who haven't already departed from the pews.

Africa and Italy will run the Vatican.

Best Outcome
With all its ongoing personal complications, what's left of my life will be slightly less scandalous.

Worst Outcome
A long and powerful papacy for Olivier.
3. Join Mendoza's conspiracy and ensure a moderate successor.

Risks
I become a co-conspirator, though the truth is, the whole conclave is a conspiracy anyhow.
Mendoza's health suddenly declines, and Olivier wins the next conclave.
Ongoing civil war in the curia.

Best Outcome
Mendoza becomes a shrewd middle-of-the-road pontiff and ensures that Olivier isn't simply waiting in the wings.

Worst Outcome
Olivier gets wind of Mendoza's moves and cuts him off at the pass.

Decision
Prayer
Delay
Miracle

Should God have thought things through a little more in God's plan for God's church, or has God's church simply stuffed it up from the start?
Or, dare I ask, is this almighty mess not really God's church at all?
Cloak and dagger discreet blood sample taken today.

Tuesday, March 2nd

Feast of Saint Eudocia of Heliopolis (beheaded in the 2nd century) who, in her youth, had been a courtesan—as which of us has not in our own desires, if not actions?

Very much a young lady for our times, I would have thought. Eudocia converted and spent the rest of her life repenting her riotous youth. She was beheaded under the depravities of the Emperor Trajan. How do we moderate and guide the young towards a richer and more fulfilling life than the understandable sexual abandon of freewheeling adolescence? Repentance is a process of liberation, not a lifelong prison sentence, and yet this strong-willed woman went to her death for her faith. I'm torn between total admiration of courage way beyond the character of this pope and yet a sadness that any human being should have to be an eternal victim of their past. And yet, God knows, we are. The more I reflect on the life of Saint Eudocia, I'd hope that any daughter of mine might not be forever trapped in whatever she or her past might have burdened her with. Rather, I hope that she might be liberated into a more tranquil and optimistic disposition allowing her to live for the present and, indeed, help others suffering under the demons which, with our loving God's help, she had conquered. As would any father.

As I've come to appreciate, when Sister Angelica wants to give me information she regards as important to the holy father, her comfortable method of bounty signalling the situation is to prepare a new dish, usually, though not always, as a starter, and then tell me its name and ingredients. This smooths the way to useful—and sometimes vital—information.

Medieval, yes.

Efficacious?

Tell me.

This evening, the first course she delivered was cavolfiore korma. It's as delicious as it's simple: cauliflower teamed with cashews and coconut in a creamy curry with just a suggestion of chilli.

Actually, more than a suggestion: an assault.

Her alerter.

Pain as pleasure as stand-by to process important intelligence.

Anyway, after the meal, she made sure no one else was around and then revealed to me the entire plot of Olivier and his henchmen.

How on earth she acquired such information I know not and will never know.

Sister Angelica's the perfect spy. She's ever-present but somehow invisible on the sidelines. At precisely the right time, she's always passing through wherever on the way to somewhere else. Apparently, she's never remotely suspected by the people she's surveilling. And she steadfastly refuses to explain her methods and will not implicate any accomplices—of whom, I suspect, she's so spectrally invisible as to require none. Maybe one day Hollywood will turn her into an unlikely espionage heroine.

My point being, that if Sister Angelica is in the know, that might mean that the papal putsch cancer may not be just a threat from a large traditional minority but may well have spread throughout the curia, which could mean that the cancelling wheels might already be furiously turning in triumphant annulment of everything I put forward.

But that aside, Sister Angelica is outraged and she insists that no matter what pressure I'm under, I must resist and never even consider resignation.

Yes, well, sadly, it ain't quite as simple as that, but in the circumstances, I must abide by the rules of...?

The rules of vicious ambition?

I'm beginning to think that there are no rules but the survival of the holiest... which, in the circumstances, isn't much help.

Sister Angelica tells me that she has 'confidential but damning information which can *annientare*—annihilate—any argument against me.' My problem being that if she has all the dirt on them, she must surely by now have the same dirt on me, and in the final round, that may not be totally reassuring, especially if she has to swear on the bible.

But for the moment, I need to consider my next move.

Over history, there must have been times when, in any dispute, the pope held all the aces.

All five, if necessary.

Now, has the pope's housekeeper got enough tricks up her sleeve?

Let's assume yes.

So what do I do?

Sister Angelica insists that I call their bluff and signal that I have detailed information as to their scandalously immoral personal behaviour over time. I then emphatically refuse to resign, otherwise, unless they unconditionally withdraw their challenge within twenty-four hours, the world will immediately learn of their total unfitness for papal office—unsuitability even greater than mine.

As I know, it's not quite as simple as that… in fact, it's considerably more complicated.

In fact, <u>very</u> much more complicated, but sufficient unto the day is the evil thereof, and in this crisis, not even Sister Angelica needs to be burdened with unnecessary information.

But what if they call <u>my</u> bluff?

What did Mendoza say?

'Leave everything to me.'

He doesn't know the half of it.

Wednesday, March 3nd

Feast of Blessed Charles the Good (1083–1127) who really was a good bloke.

I'm trying to imagine his life. Father, King Canute of Denmark, was murdered, and Charles was raised in court and fought in the Second Crusade, but let's not get involved with the shameful theology of that appalling misunderstanding of Christ's message. He became Count of Flanders, married well and spent his life defending the poor—presumably the vast majority of his realm—against both clerical and lay profiteers, and we may assume both mobs were merciless in their greed and disgusting justification of their self-serving oppression, all, no doubt, elegantly justified in God's name. So what's changed? He tried to make laws more fair—good luck with that against bishops, barons and bureaucrats—fed the hungry, walked barefoot as a sign of humility and was finally martyred (beheaded) in a church in Bruges as part of a conspiracy of the establishment threatened by Charles's sense of justice. May Charles the Good's perseverance bring on the dawn of social justice. And, tragically, it won't be without further martyrdoms. We must be on the side of the poor. If not, everything we profess is total hypocrisy, and we are nothing more than whitened sepulchres which indeed appear beautiful outwardly, but inside are full of dead men's bones and all uncleanness.

A phone call from Mendoza on my private mobile—or what I probably delude myself is private. For all I know, Sister Angelica and all of Olivier's lynch mob may well be listening. Anyway, Mendoza is now sure that the numbers are much closer than Olivier believes. He says that a lot of people are scared of Olivier and indicate support out of fear.

Mendoza is mining votes from three discrete factions, and they're not the conservative/progressive divide one might assume. Rather, he is sounding out the youngest of the cardinals (bravo me for those appointments!) then those from the poorest countries and finally, those who fear the accelerating rise of loopy, prosperity gospel con men (almost always men accepting all credit cards) with their transparently amateur and scripturally illiterate Hillsong bullshit.

I never said that, but anyone with half of one-tenth of a brain must surely see through that business plan... except the desperate and presumably ill-educated and bewildered punters who buy salvation as quickly as they buy the cretinous cd's of the oleaginous bands who sing the half-rhyming rubbish that passes for sacred music.

And I did say that.

Disney is suddenly looking bigger than Jesus.

And I did say that, too.

Just one more small nightcap, I think.

That off my chest, Mendoza thinks that all three groups are wary of Olivier because they think he sees himself as some kind of African pop star messiah, and his line of argument to all these cardinals is simple: if Olivier sees himself as representing the poorest of the poor, then how come he's personally so rich?

Isn't there some disturbing disconnect here? When it comes to poverty, chastity and obedience, though admittedly only religious orders take the poverty vow, simple living is lauded by the church as ideal, and Olivier's lifestyle is, to say the least, extremely comfortable. He's certainly very well known in all Rome's most expensive restaurants.

Mendoza's line is to wonder aloud how an African cardinal can want to live such a high life and then how he can afford it.

Doubt-sowing.

And chastity, Mendoza implies, is looked on differently by almost all African male clergy, the *difference* being their <u>in</u>difference to the concept and the rule.

And as for obedience, Mendoza's sales approach is that, yes, Olivier is gung-ho on this particular virtue, his understanding of obedience being submission by all the church to him as the next pope.

Mendoza believes that this approach is leeching votes away from Olivier, not least because Mendoza's medical and theological recovery are seen as signs of God's favour, which, I suppose, isn't totally silly though personally, I judge it as somewhere between simple and superstitious, but what would I know?

Anyway, Mendoza is confident and believes that in the time between the summoning of the conclave and its opening, the wind refreshing all the non-curia cardinals will be increasingly in his favour, in which case, I'll have an each-way bet on the Holy Spirit.

Thursday, March 4th

It was while I was feasting in the warmth of a bath that I had to admit to the naked and unlovely truth: this pope may well be agnostic. Not a good look for Christ's vicar on earth. I mean, what would the punters think if the boss of Qantas started flying American Airlines? Brand loyalty and all that. But stripped of my costume and reduced to poor naked humanity, the seeping truth is that I can't fend off the demon doubts. Try as I may to preach the good and the beauty and the solace and the strength of our faith and to banish the doubts and pain and puzzles and contradictions that encrust it, that splinter of 'Yes, but what if it's all just a brilliant humanly constructed spiritual crystal palace to cope with the finality and then the nothingness of death... a gorgeous chimera demanding acceptance rather than rational analysis on available evidence?' I'm wondering whether we have two modes of belief: clothed and naked. There are over one hundred saints worthy of memory today, and I need the intercession of every single one of them. That's if they're really in whatever heaven is. Dear Lord, I do believe; please help my unbelief.

I seriously considered whether or not to speak to Ennio about my current employment situation. My better judgment told me that this was a conversation in every way over and above his age, background, knowledge, education, professional function, responsibility and discretion.

My best judgment told me I was going to do it anyway.

So I did.

He rose to the conversation brilliantly and more so.

His indifference to theology is a refreshing cold shower for a pope. He couldn't care less about Vatican politics and he reckons if more popes were like me, more popes would be a bit more like all the people who aren't popes.

Can't see that recommendation getting through the curia, but on a universal church plebiscite, I reckon we might just come through with flying colours, probably on the back of rainbow enthusiasm.

But that happy decision is, at the moment, some papacies away in the scheme of things. And as, by the hour, I now come to terms with the term, *scheming…* that's what it's all about.

Despite Ennio's benevolent neutrality to religion (God is good, but God and sex shouldn't mix; if pleasure if God's gift, then we should glorify God at every opportunity) he told me that given the... *complications* of all the players, it only seemed to him reasonable that all those *complications* needed to be put on the table and considered.

His sly grin, which I'd become used to, now seemed to move from charming to strategic.

Significantly so.

Ennio told me that he plays soccer with a twenty-year-old good friend who's a junior gardener in the Vatican. The lad's name is Lucio, and Lucio's partner, Lucia, who is someone or other's daughter of one of Ennio's uncle's sons (it's either totally improbable or totally beautiful, and in Italian families, nothing is ever improbable)... anyway, Ennio's young soccer mate moonlights for payment far and away above his horticultural Vatican pursuits in a popular Rome gay sauna as a companion to a select few curia cardinals, and it just so happens that two of these cardinals are among Olivier's close associates.

And they say there isn't a God.

And why do sceptics disbelieve in miracles?

Adults can be so naïve.

Ennio and Lucio apparently see this arrangement as perfectly discreet untaxable income, and Lucio's Lucia couldn't care less and sees it as some kind of crazy bank which pays for endless revelling in Rome's finest restaurants and wildest nightclubs.

Never happened in Wollongong, but I suppose back then, none of those financial facilities let alone opportunities was offered to rising sportsmen or military cadets, but again, what would I know?

But thanks to Ennio, now I've got names and addresses. And this information is conclave gold.

If Mendoza doesn't already know my new dirt file, he'll be further in my debt.

Unless, of course...

No. Impossible. Utterly impossible. Mendoza couldn't possibly be involved in such... associations. That's totally beyond even the Vatican's wildest fantasies.

But the one thing I've learnt in my short time in this job is that beyond even the Vatican's wildest fantasies are... terrifying and destructive truths...

But no, not Mendoza. Not for a moment is that consideration even the remotest of remote possibilities.

He wouldn't have the... humanity.

But then, from left field, came the killer left field knockout, which, over seven or so months, had never even occurred to me.

What if, like Lucio's, Ennio's late-night alcoholic indiscretions had boasted that he, too, had a friendship with a high-ranking Vatican official.?

What if, in his cups, Ennio had...

No.

Not possible.

Impossible.

Totally.

I know Ennio and I know that our friendship is something which, in occasional encounters, is in every way innocent and normal.

For God's sake, we've both valued our accidental friendship.

And ongoing conversation.

Sacred and reassuring to both of us

He'd never dream of...

Never.

And on reflection, one of the many gifts of faith is surely that one can be agnostic and still believe in God.

Surely magical thinking is just that: magical.

And miracles happen in the mind <u>and</u> the soul.

Friendship, faith and… faith.

Friday, March 5th

Feast of Saint Adrian of Nicomedia, martyred in 304.

Oh my God! Talk about faith! I wish I could stop what strikes me as a disturbing fascination with human beings torturing other human beings to the most gruesome possible death, but Saint Adrian stands out as a beacon of faith and hope—not least to this tremulously agnostic pope. Adrian was a bodyguard at the imperial court of Nicomedia and was so moved by the strength and faith shown by persecuted Christians that he declared himself one of their number, though not having been baptised. No tepidly tremulous agnosticism for this amazing officer: he and his fellow Christian prisoners were immediately arrested and tortured. He was hurled to a lion which refused to touch him. His hands and feet were then chopped off, after which he was hacked to death with a sword. During all this depravity, he was tended to by his wife, Saint Natalia. My prayers are with and to both these beacons of faith. This heroic convert is now patron saint of epileptics, plague victims, arms dealers (God, those monsters need more than a dash of his spiritual valour), butchers, Flemish brewers, prison guards, soldiers and then throw in Flanders, Belgium, Germany and Metalica in Italy. They and we, every one of us, we all need such an inspirational saint. I shudder for his agony and for his… faith. I am a…

No. This is ridiculous. Worse, disgraceful. Worse, sinful. Blackmail. Unworthy even of a second-rate pope.

Use every man after his desert, and who shall 'scape whipping?

Thank you, Brother Edmund, even if none of us escaped whipping in the process of learning to answer Leaving Certificate questions on *Hamlet*.

Such grubby infighting is criminal and has no place in this place.

Well, it shouldn't, and if that's to be my legacy, then I'd rather stretch the truth a little, plead mental health issues and resign.

And I suppose in the ideal world, popes would not have nightly massages from young Swiss guards in the same way that they shouldn't permit espionage by their housekeepers.

I can't say I'm proud of what I've become though I'm not ashamed of it.

Not even embarrassed.

Why should I be?

It's just…

Well, on all the evidence, I'm…well… not cut out to be pope.

The truth is, I don't enjoy all this popery.

Secretly, when I was elected as Pope Stopgap the Useless, even though I knew the real reason for the promotion, I have to say that for a Wollongong moment or so, I did feel… well, ever so slightly, chuffed.

Like, how many times does your pathetically loser lottery ticket win the lottery?

Yes, I thought that might come as a surprise to you, Dad, but then once I had to start 'pope-ing'—as we say in this divine industry—the glamour quickly wore off, and this current crisis is… yes, is of my own making… is…

And while I doubt it, maybe… at a stretch… well, just maybe in his African way, Olivier will be inspired by the Holy Spirit and deliver the goods.

But, no.

Absolutely and papably, no.

The price of my resigning will absolutely have to be that Sister Angelica and Ennio remain in my new, diminished household.

And given his ambition, I'd say that Olivier would jump at such a bargain.

And now that I've made up my mind, I feel an inner peace I haven't felt for… well, ever.

The right decision.

And besides, Mendoza may well manoeuvre his way into the saddle. God knows, crazier things have happened inside these walls.

I'll inform Angelica and Ennio of my decision, and then Mendoza.

Thank God.

And a private call from Florence. Professor Morelli will come to Rome to discuss my health on Monday.

Hmmm.

Saturday, March 6th

Feast of Blessed Giovanna Irrizaldi, nun in Nalan, Asturia, Spain.

Known as a miracle worker who could travel across the sea by stretching a white veil over the water and riding it. Sorry, but no. Puzzles and contradictions encrusting rational belief. I wonder what the real story was. Magical thinking is more dangerous than reassuring. Except when I choose to believe it. The concept of miracle worker might today be medically described by a psychiatrist. Or just a sympathetic and desperately believing yet ongoing sceptical listener. And we're many. Maybe she should be the patron saint of Sydney Harbour Ferries. God knows, they need divine assistance of whatever white veil delivers efficient services from Circular Quay to Manly. She could be the saint Australian ferries have been waiting for. Or Qantas.

Done.

Must have been the right decision because each of the three people I told accepted it.

Mendoza accepted it generously and said by the time of the conclave, the votes would be in the bag—mind you, though the bag of what he didn't extrapolate on.

Ennio didn't mind, especially as I said that as his outgoing commander-in-chief, I'd arrange for him to be given a confidentially appropriate emolument for the transfer, enough to set him and Mirella up in a comfortable apartment in Lugarno (much cheaper than Geneva) and that he would still remain in service in my reduced household until such a time as he wished to return to Mirella and Switzerland.

His choice.

A little generosity never goes astray in resignation bounties.

Sister Angelica was obviously furious but smiled calmly—well, not so much smiled as glowered in a religiously resigned and obedient way—and agreed to her transfer, though I doubt that she'll be baking a Christmas cake for either Mendoza or Olivier.

All I have to do now is keep Olivier and his goons on tenterhooks for as long as possible and let Pope Vegemite the First and Last enjoy the doomsdays of his papacy.

Meanwhile, the church will cruise on automatic pilot unless…

Sunday, March 7th

Feast of Saint Baldred the Hermit (died 756) English hermit, priest, miracle worker.

Sounds good to me, especially the miracle working. Is there an instruction booklet?

… unless…and my prayers have been sanctified by more than few holy water fonts full of *unless-ing.*

These temptations are delicious.

Bounty like this evening's doesn't get much simpler than this and causes me to radically rethink.

What is obvious is obvious because no matter how much disguise can be thrown at what's staring you in the face, it's hard to escape from that simple, fundamental fact.

And so, bounty boiled potatoes with baked camembert. Less is more, but more is even more. Mind you, Sister Angelica did mention that this basic recipe also requires rosemary, cornichons and—not so secret ingredient—bloody pickled onions.

I knew the English would one day contribute something to world gastronomy.

Cornichons, as our cook reassures us, control blood pressure—if not in the bible, then footnoted somewhere in Sister Angelica's unique and secret gastronomic bible—and that control (as she shrewdly observes) is what is needed in the current critical papal circumstances.

Result?

Precisely the opposite.

Exhilarating.

Must be those pesky pommy pickled onions.

But I'm flying and so wickedly intoxicated—metaphorically, of course—that I can only hope that my thoughts are mortally sinful and then some.

And, gloriously, all in my mad power to accomplish.

So: instant papal approval for married priests, then immediately approval of women priests. Then license the third rite of internal confession as the norm for all mass attendees. Then invite all non-communicating Catholics, non-Catholics, adherents of other faiths, non-believers and all questors to participate in a series of our masses to experience our understanding of the divine and then invite them to join us in conversation about mutual understanding of the numinous.

And that's just for starters.

While there's time, use it!

In the What Would Jesus Do Department? my closing down sale just at the moment includes:

- selling off all the art stuffing up the corridors and rooms of this place, and with the money, building hospitals throughout Africa, a chapel attached to each one

- opening up the Vatican archives to all qualified scholars and letting the terrible truths we're so rightly ashamed of be known to the world so that in out acceptance, we might find forgiveness

- forbidding any Sunday sermon to be more than two minutes long—a gold-plated winner

- canonising Theillard de Chardin who is to theology what the moon landing was to space travel, except far more important

- creating fifty young female cardinals who must take part in the next conclave

No, even by my pathetically wacko standards, that's OTT…

… but …what if I removed the current *camerlengo* and replaced him with a female cardinal I have the power to create, thus ensuring that a woman runs the next conclave?

My word is law, and during the interregnum, the *camerlengo* runs the shop.

Could lead to some interesting conversations among the dressed-up dinosaurs.

Would I dare?

And now that I've looked over all I've written this evening, I realise that I am, indeed, something of a scatterbrained and cavalier dilettante who is definitely unfit to be pope.

Talk about a slow learner.

Time to grow up… if only I knew how.

But a female camerlengo…

Another nightcap, I think.

Monday, March 8th

No time for feasts today. And no feasting likely.

8 a.m.

Luca Morelli appointment at 2 p.m. today under the heading 'University of Florence Theology Department Matters'.

Everything is out of sync.

Alarm bell just when I least need one.

A missive this morning from American Cardinal Desmond Wilenski, unpleasant busybody and close associate of Olivier's, drawing my urgent attention to a potential curia scandal which he clearly is excited by and will, no doubt, announce at a time of his strategic choosing.

According to an unnamed source, Dario's Secretary of State account transferred five hundred and fifty thousand American dollars to Countess Allegra di Rossi, who lives in the countryside near Segni, as payment for her agency/professional services in the Vatican investing ninety million American dollars of the Secretary of State's Private Action Fund in a ten-apartment luxury Parisian *hôtel* in rue Danielle Casanova near the Place Vendôme.

It was meant to be a guilt-edged investment guaranteed to double in value over two years.

It transpires, however, that truth is stranger than fiction, and that the *hôtel* is valued under sixty million, and further, that the dodgy Parisian agent *immobilier* seems to have disappeared off the planet, which usually means living the life of Riley (whose feast day it probably is) under a false identity in Switzerland.

This all sounds like some improbable American movie starring Tom Cruise, except as recent history will attest, the Vatican has form—and then some—in this duplicitous area.

I immediately confronted Dario with the charge.

He vigorously denied any malfeasance while admitting that yes, he had overseen the transaction and on advice, enthusiastically confirmed it.

I asked him why he hadn't asked my permission, as was our clear arrangement from Day 1, and he explained that given the present and ongoing uncertainty in the papacy, the last thing he wanted was to burden me with mere business investments, those of which he'd taken responsibility for. I suggested that ninety million American dollars was hardly 'mere'. And furthermore, where had this huge amount of money come from? That was gigantically more than I had arranged for him to have.

Blushingly, he told me that with insider advice, he'd taken the liberty of making three or four small investments, all of which had proved almost miraculous in profits made, and that as he realised that I was overburdened with curia opposition and plotting, he thought it in my best interest not to add to my troubles, and would hold the good news until what he judged was 'the right moment'.

And the agency payment to Countess Allegra di Rossi?

Dario explained that the countess was a valued friend who lived near Segni where his nephew was raised and that she had been a wonderful support and benefactor to his sister and had acted as an unofficial godmother to Guido.

I asked him about the countess's real estate credentials, and he told me that she was known locally as a shrewd property investor (to her friends, no doubt) and that two previous small transactions she had recommended (of which I was also totally ignorant) had added seven million dollars to the trust.

And then the dreadfully inevitable question, the anguish of which devasted me to even formulate let alone pose.

Was there any… intimacy between Dario and the unofficial god-mother of his nephew?

Dario assured me that while over the years they had been close friends, such intimacy as they exchanged was affectionate rather than passionate.

But had there ever been physically amorous encounters within this ongoing affectionate association?

Dario said that we are all human and that our vulnerable humanity is what gives us hope in Christ's promise of redemption.

So, yes.

Up to our necks in it. *Serpenti e scale*. Snakes and ladders. *Quando verrà fuori tutto il casino*: when the whole bloody mess explodes. Or more precisely: *la merda colpisce il ventilatore;* in plain Wollongong terms, when the shit hits the fan.

We both understood.

I'm suddenly juggling whatever's Italian not for hot potatoes but incandescent cannon balls.

All I need.

And as my closest curia friend, Dario is the man I've confided in—not confessed to but opened my heart to, not infrequently over late-night whiskies—and told him all—well, almost all—about my messy youth.

Dario's the friend I've trusted with confidences I'd be frankly ashamed to share with anyone else.

And now this.

Of course, Olivier's faction know of our friendship and will seize on the situation whatever decision I make. If I cover up the disaster, I'm dishonest and dishonourable. If I fire Dario, it's proof of my appalling judgment and atrociously underhanded maladministration.

Damned if I do and damned if I don't.

Damn!

3 p.m.

As best I can remember, I thanked Luca for his discretion (deception) in coming to see me personally. I reassured him that popes, like paupers, were ever more God's paupers than popes. I then told him that I had no fear whatsoever of his diagnosis. Not altogether sure of that, but then in these crazy days, I'm not altogether sure about anything. To put his mind—and mine—to rest—I explained that I'd reflect on the medical details almost certainly without fully understanding them. I find the mental gymnastics of theology threatening enough, but anything about the human interior is information I instinctively recoil from. And then I asked him for his diagnosis and prognosis, preferably in the simplest possible English.

He was gently direct.

'Diagnosis: acute chronic myeloid leukemia.'

Doesn't sound encouraging.

A brief pause.

And prognosis? I'm the pope. Truth is meant to be my mint mark.

'Holiness, prognosis is always relative.'

So… in so many relative words… the best and worst prognoses, please?

Both come under the heading of *His Holiness died of a short illness.*

Thank you. And at best, how short?

'Perhaps eighteen months. A little longer, though not a lot. And to a large extent, we can control the pain.'

He then gave me a detailed outline of what was happening inside my body (an expert's lecture…invasive…lung…blood supply…stroke…haemorrhage… a sort of internal jigsaw puzzle that was apparently all over the place) and I nodded appropriately. Then he asked me whether I had any questions.

My reply was spontaneous, as if someone other than myself was answering.

No, Luca. Just gratitude for your explanation and for the strange feeling of relief surging through me. It's as though I've been somehow liberated. 'He died of a short illness.' I'll reflect on it and decide whom to tell and when. How soon will I need to go to hospital?

'Not for a while. Some months. I'll ensure that we'll track the disease's progress. You'll probably know before we do when to move to that stage.'

And the rest of the small talk I don't remember.
I know I'm in good hands: Luca's and God's.
And that I'll die of a short illness.
And the rest of my life is now mine to live as I will.

Tuesday, March 9th

There's no feast, only emotional famine.

The man I'd always turn to is the man I clearly must fire. My crazy Vatican family of four is now shattered, and it's certain that through her network, Sister Angelica knows of the scandal and there's no bounty even she could cook up which can uncook the Holy Father's books.

Mind you, as to another more modest investment transfer from the Holy Father's discretionary account closer to home… but sufficient to the day is the evil thereof.

The slimy Wilenski also included a vicious PS wondering whether I'm aware of whispers among some cardinals that my association with a young Swiss Guard might be considered *une amitié particulière*.

I was tempted to ask whether the concern was censure or envy, but I refrained.

When it comes to viciously distilled sinfulness, this place is in a league of its own—and all in the guise of outraged sanctity.

But I must face the facts: I'm ashamed of myself and my ludicrous life—or what's left of it.

There's now a fourth rite of confession invented by Yours Untruly: me confessing to myself but unable to forgive the sin.

No worst. There is none. O the mind, mind has mountains;
>> *cliffs of fall*
frightful, sheer, no-man-fathomed. Hold them cheap may
>> *who ne'er hung there.*
Comforter, where, where is your comforting?
All life death does end, but each day dies not with sleep.

Mea culpa. Mea culpa. Mea maxima culpa.

But wherefore cannot I pronounce 'Amen'? I have most need of blessing, and 'Amen' sticks in my throat.

I cast for comfort I can no more get
By groping round my comfortless, than blind
Eyes in their dark can day or thirst can find
Thirst's all-in-all in all a world of wet.

Consummatum est.

But this wallowing must stop.
Doing nothing—even hesitating—is the worst option.
Dario must go.
I must pope up before I pope off—in every sense.

Wednesday, March 10th

Feast of St Gregory of Nyssa (333–398) and how appropriate!

Married to Theosebeia, who may have been a deaconess, Gregory became a professor of rhetoric, but disillusioned with that profession, he became a priest and hermit, presumably leaving Theosebeia to get on with her now single life, though some say he continued living with her. Nice. He became Bishop of Nyssa then Archbishop of Sebaste and fought Arianism with mixed success. Then things got worse. Though meek, financially Gregory was something of a totally inept freewheeler and was taken to the cleaners by all and sundry in his archdiocese. The governor even accused him of stealing church property and irregularly ordaining bishops and so had him imprisoned. Gregory escaped but was then deposed by a synod of bishops in 376 though he was later restored. He was sent to Arabia to sort out which of two men claiming to be Bishop of Bostra was the real McCoy but failed. He then went to Jerusalem to resolve a similar matter but failed; indeed, he was accused of unorthodox views on the nature of Christ. Back in Nyssa, he got on badly with his metropolitan, Helladius. He had clear views about the unity of the Trinity. He also held that God is infinite and that his goodness and mercy are limitless. He was also totally against slavery as immoral. Lately, he has been considered an unconventional and a highly advanced, controversial thinker of his time. A mess or a saint? I can empathise with the former. He died after a long life.

Slept like a log, woke refreshed, and after prayer and mass, emerged to breakfast overflowing with acceptance and surely lunatic optimism. Maybe I've been wrong all along, and there's some truth in the argument that suffering is a redemptive gift. Or am I just one of those battered insomniacs who accidentally lands a single night's sleep and wakes up thinking they're the first person to have discovered gravity? But when in consolation, as St Ignatius urged, ride that wave into the shore! It may well be your last one, and in this case, it almost certainly is.

First thing was to summon Dario and tell him that I must dismiss him.

True friend that he is, he beat me to the gun and on entering, offered me his resignation, assuring me that he accepted full blame for his scandalous actions which were his and his alone. He would assure the world that he deliberately kept me in the dark, and while in retrospect his transgression was shocking, it was neither immoral nor illegal, not that that made it in any way excusable. He also asked me to exclude him from the next conclave (little does he know how soon that will be) which I agreed to, though I declined to take up his offer to resign from the college of cardinals as his behaviour was scandalous and financially reckless but avoided being felonious. He then asked my permission to retire to a monastery, a decision I acquiesced in.

We embraced.

So, now to tell Angelica and Ennio I'm resigning today, but that they're sworn to secrecy until midday. Then, close to midday, I'll ring Mendoza to give him a heads up. It's vital that I take the initiative on all fronts, otherwise Olivier will claim the high—though, in fact, low—moral ground.

We live in an imperfect world, and all motivation has a degree of self-interest and self-preservation.

After all that, Holy Spirit, it's over to you… and with due respect, I can only hope you'll get your act together better than your last disaster.

Me.

Besides, only you and I know where the bodies are buried… and thank God once I've dated that letter of resignation, that's no longer my problem.

Fasten your conclave seat belts; it's going to be a revelationary ride.

PS Just for the record, it was all very simple and there was no fuss. In fact, Mendoza brought in a new letter (same content) since the witnesses had to see me sign it. Devilish clever of him to have got me to sign the first letter as a kind of dress rehearsal to ensure my confidence and commitment. He doesn't miss a trick, old Mendoza. Anyway, I signed it in the presence of Mendoza, Dario (our friendship remains despite recent unhappy events) and to annoy just about everyone else in the Vatican, I got Sister Angelica to be the other witness. At last, a female was involved in a major papal decision. And if looks could kill, the hatred on Sister Angelica's face would have murdered a regiment of commandos.

Thursday, March 11th

Feast of Saint Blanchard about whom nothing is known but the existence of a fountain dedicated to him in 1878 and that is also known as the Saint-Alban fountain.

The faithful (superstitious?) locals believe the water flowing there is good for the kidneys, freshness of the complexion and to relieve rheumatism. And for chronic myeloid leukemia, I wonder? There's also a legend that every fertile woman who drinks this water will find herself pregnant and will give birth to a boy. Except when she doesn't, which is written off as God's will, I suppose, and is hardly a welcome to the world of the unwanted little girl. What degrading rubbish! And detective work has established that St Blanchard about whom we apparently know nothing is really the French version of St Alban since albus in Latin means white, and the feast of St Alban is June 22nd. We live in a time of confusion.

Deo gratias. I no longer exist and at last I can breathe.

Of all the world headlines, it's Wollongong's Illawarra *Mercury* which most delights me: Gong Pope Gonged.

Endless speculation about my successor, all from alleged 'informed Vatican sources.'

Most of these informants must have been roof tilers, traffic wardens or counter clerks at the Vatican post office for all the credibility their inside information carried.

Olivier seems to be the odds-on favourite, and not even the informed sources mention Mendoza.

It's probably part of his campaign to be invisible to the fourth estate. He's cunning as a fox not to mention discretion incarnate.

I'm tempted to add to my pension by tipping off *The New York Times* correspondent about The Bolter Pope, but on second thoughts, maybe a retired pontiff is no longer the informed Vatican source he once was—if, indeed, he ever was.

I've moved here to my convent, as they call it, and frankly can't be bothered worrying about all the boxes and files that I've accumulated; I'm just enjoying not being reverentially treated and fussed over as if I were some kind of pope.

Sister Angelica has totally rearranged the kitchen on heavenly angelic lines, and Ennio has been muscularly efficient in transferring basic furniture and all my boxes here. He's also once again set up my airport and added 'some back-up for the back-up' safety equipment, whatever that may mean. He calls it electronic insurance, so who am I to argue with the expert? He'll only bore and bamboozle me with technical jargon, and I'll feel even more maladroit and obsolete than I know I am.

That said, Ennio's guarding duties seem likely to involve little more than a daily sandwich and a glass of Frascati. I shall enjoy his uninterrupted company all the more, to facilitate which I'm thinking of hanging a sign on the door: *visitatores ingratus.* My translation: bugger off!

Meanwhile, rumours will abound, the Holy Spirit will do whatever the Holy Spirit does (visit expensive restaurants?) and time—though very much not alone—will tell.

Sunday, March 14th

Feast of the 5th century martyrs of Valeria: two unnamed monks martyred by Lombards in Valeria, Italy.

After they'd been hanged on a tree, their murderers could still hear them singing psalms. They died of a short hanging. Disturbing or beautiful? I'm confused.

Weird.

After keeping a diary for the first time in my life and over however many weeks, I now find myself gathering thoughts towards the end of the afternoon and almost needing to record them. Even after only a day or so of having de-poped myself, I want to keep thinking my thoughts through in this journal, and as I now have time on my hands—well, some—I'm thinking to myself, why not?

Why not take time to reflect on such strange questions as float into my mind and then commit my lucubrations to my own private posterity?

Good God! I've become a journal junkie!

Anyway, with the conclave still a fortnight away, time is no longer of the essence, so perhaps one of the rewards of resignation is the space to ponder, and first cab off the rank is the huge amount of time I now don't have to spend daily blessing dozens of rosary beads, prayer cards and miraculous medals to be sent round the world to well-meaning petitioners.

'Blessed by the pope.'

What's it supposed to mean?

A greater blessing than a cardinal's? Much more than a bishop's? And as for your common or garden-variety parish priest or curate, well, it's hardly worth bothering to ask them.

It's nothing more than condoning medieval superstition.

Saint Blanchard's fountain at work.

Shameful.

Yet we've been doing this same old everlasting life insurance policy for centuries, and anyone in that self-serving Vatican Bank of Eternal Salvation—eternally limited liability aside—with even a millionth of half-a-brain knew that this was bullshit from the start.

Though money-making.

OK. It caused little or no harm and may even have kicked along some granny's or auntie's piety, but the fact was and is that it's all meaningless, and we've been submissively collaborating in this hoax because as a miniscule yet clever part of so-called 'professional' clerical formation, it reinforced the medieval power structure of priestly exceptionalism.

Easy to admit now, but this ex-pope despairs, and, in the scheme of things, despair isn't quite our flag ship.

Therein lies our problem.

Because problem it is. And always has been to all the other intellectually honest questers whom we've dogmatically excluded from the conversation because of their… intellectually honest conversation.

Well, that's that sorted out, and I feel much better—though not much more useful to anybody.

Can a retired pope throw his triple tiara into the ring again, I wonder?

Now that <u>would</u> make for an interesting conclave!

And if re-elected, would I be Pope John the Twenty-Fourth or the Twenty-Fifth?

Gilbert and Sullivan join a canon lawyers' picnic. At least the new lyrics to the *Nightmare Song* would have the audience disbelieving their ears!

Maybe I should take up knitting.

This evening, Sister Angelica served an intriguing new dish: courgettes with gorgonzola sauce. I wonder what news she's picked up. No doubt she'll tell me tomorrow.

She assures me that courgettes are traditionally associated with chaos, though as usual, no evidence is supplied—well, no convincing evidence.

It might be argued that courgette and chaos both begin with a *c* although the Italian translation is zucchini and *z* being the last letter of the alphabet is only arrived at after the chaos of the previous 23.

Or possibly not.

Maybe I should take refuge in astrology.

Time will tell.

Monday, March 15th

Feast of St Bodian of Hanvec, a 6th century Welsh saint who may or may not have existed.

Like so many more Welsh saints. Also the feast of Blessed Lodovico de la Pena, a Spanish monk in Seville who was a miracle worker restoring sight to the blind, hearing to the deaf and raising the dead to life. He died during a vision of the Blessed Virgin Mary. As usual, I wonder what the real story was. Also the feast of Saint Menignus of Parium (died about 250) who was a cloth dyer and a married lay-man. During torture, he had his fingers hacked off for tearing down an edict of the Emperor Decius suppressing Christianity. He was be-headed, and witnesses say they saw his soul leave the mouth of his severed head in the form of a dove. Or not, as the case may be. Why does religion do such weird things to people? Like me. My head is in chaos. My soul, though, is curiously calm.

OMG! Late bounty! But then looking back, perhaps once or twice this referee was a bit behind the play, so casting no aspersions or asperges or asparagus on Sister Angelica, let's both of us get back to basics.

Blood orange and fennel salad. That's it. Take it or leave it. Or, as always in these parts, look more closely and read the meaning of diced shallots, oregano, black olives and whatever extra virgin olive oil is.

Am I an extra virgin? Can anyone be? I think that I hope not. I can't fathom what that 'extra' would be. Or how it might contribute to God's kingdom.

But shallots, oregano and black olives: what do the scriptures say? From she who knows because she invents them: optimism, strategy and victory.

And she's rarely wrong.

On my walk around the convent garden this morning, I saw Mendoza in the distance, hurrying towards the curia offices. He waved to me and smiled.

Angelica decoded that smile. Apparently, one of her sisters over-heard Olivier and two African cardinals discussing the whole con-cept of synods as beloved and proposed by Francis. Olivier argued that we have much to learn from the Anglicans. They have synods, and their worldwide community is totally split over women priests and homosexuality.

It's virtually mutual contempt and civil war.

Olivier also argues that synods are destructive as they enfranchise the ignorant. He repeated his argument pointing out that, for example, doctors spend six years of study and then a further many years of experience before taking up senior positions in hospitals. Likewise, the clergy undergo rigorous and scholarly formation and are experts in their fields. Imagine, he laughingly explained, if a few untrained or perhaps keen amateur first aid devotees rocked up to a major hospital and started telling the surgeons how to run the place.

Chaos, danger and destruction.

'Leave it to the experts' is Olivier's platform, and he has made it clear that if elected, he'll put the kibosh on synods.

His message is discipline, dogma and tradition: fortress Catholicism attacking from the commanding heights. And that's a clear rallying call to the African sub-continent and the rich American Trumpist cardinals.

So is Mendoza's smile that of a man who sees a majority coalescing if not exactly enthusiastic for synods, then certainly against the dead hand of traditional conservatives?

Given his record of defensive prosecution and now his born-again openness to change, Mendoza must more and more look like the safest bet for changing times.

Favourable wind.

No wonder he waved and smiled.

From chaos to hope to Pope.

Yes, miracles occur in the mind.

And I need to reconsider my scepticism.

Tuesday, March 16th

Feast of Saint Dentlin of Soignies (10th century) who must have been one of the most extraordinary children since Jesus.

It's almost unbelievable. He was the son of two saints, brother of three saints (two sisters and a brother) and nephew of another saint.

He was, unsurprisingly, an extraordinarily pious child and died at the age of 7. What on earth am I to make of this? When I was 7 in Wollongong... but that's best left unsaid and unremembered, especially down behind the back shed. Poor Dentlin never had a chance in hell or heaven—and I'm sure he must be in heaven, but for God's sake... a saint? Life experience? Anyway, he died after a short life.

As I may have said before, MI5 and ASIO have got nothing on Sister Angelica and Ennio.

Yesterday, Mendoza gave a sermon in St Paul Outside the Walls, and this morning over our daily sandwich and Frascati, Ennio gave me a recording!

James Bond, go to the back of the queue!

Mendoza was magnificent and to my mind, circled Olivier, outfoxed him and brought into the Mendoza circle the progressives, the waverers and even one or two of the Africans with his call to 'advance the representation and participation of our African brothers and sisters in the ongoing conversation of the church: a church which embraces the oppressed and the militant millions of faithful who are the new suffering disciples of the liberating Christ.'

And the odd few ambivalent red-hatted sheep rounded up there, I'd imagine.

In a close vote, emotion, nationalism and the hope of clerical advancement are not without their incentives to the cardinals of Africa's especially deprived dioceses, of which there are not a few—and then all the rest. And then some even more indigent and aspiring cardinals.

And Mendoza's eloquent mobilizing of the blood of the martyrs, loyalty to tradition, defence of the faith together with the contemporary embrace of scientific and scholarly understanding of revelation as God's ongoing invitation to the pilgrimage of faith... not too many participants excluded from that convivial conclave picnic.

In retrospect, maybe Wollongong wasn't that far from divinely inspired and deftly manoeuvred self-interest.

But it's too late now.

Je ne regrette rien. Sauf presque tout. Ignore that, Dad. Just Mario showing off his French.

These favourable voting winds continue, and the unspoken understanding between Angelica, Ennio and this papal pensioner make for mellow days ahead.

Deo gratias.

Wednesday, March 17th

Feast of Saint Patrick, the fifth-century English-born patron saint of Ireland.

His father was a deacon and his grandfather a married priest. We need more of them. But that's just the start. It gets better. Swashbuckling even. He was kidnapped by pirates at the age of sixteen and enslaved on the drenching coast of rural Ireland. This captivity turned a boy into an ardent Christian young man. After six years of tortured enslavement, Patrick escaped his captors and made the dangerous voyage back to his own nation, family, and language. Patrick heard voices—tell me!—urging him to return to the emerald isle, but he studied for years in France to prepare himself for his lifetime missionary adventure. He returned to pagan Ireland and converted the nation with his alleged supernatural powers such as turning an enemy into a fox, transforming his walking staff into a tree, conquering witches, wizards, and warlocks with the Holy Spirit and, rejoice rejoice, driving all the snakes out of Ireland. Maybe. And maybe not. Almost certainly not, or we'd still be performing such miracles today. Anyway, Ireland then converted much of the English-speaking world to Catholicism (and, eventually, Guinness), not least Australia, the result of which we will be forever grateful for and forever... but let's not go there other than to say that it's arguable that as many victims of bog Irish guilt propaganda ditched the faith as those who magnificently evangelised the protestant colonies. And I stand as testimony to...

Ever since his absurd and repulsive presence polluted the line-up of Republican candidates for the American presidency in 2016, I've tried and tried to articulate why my instant revulsion of Trump was so deep and visceral.

Love the sinner, hate the sin, we're told, but try as I might—and it wasn't very hard not to—I found the very thought let alone the sight of him disgusted me to the edge of vomiting.

Yes, he was fake; fake hair as ludicrous as his pathetically semi-literate sentence structure; fake tan which made him look like the comic monster I knew he was; fake personality weirdly captured in his soft hand-clapping, supposedly an obeisance to his dumb audience but in reality, a masturbatory applause to himself; fake smile that always seemed to be looking in a mirror; and that sad give-away of the amateur loser whose lack of talent still doesn't prevent him from somehow having an accidental lollipop hit and thus, when going on stage, points to someone—anyone—in the audience as if he knew them, smiles and from the generosity of his heart signals 'we're both overwhelmed at my being here.'

Ah, yes, the epitome of shallowness and the embodiment of emptiness.

But these minor personality defects aside, there was something much more sinister about this bloated invention, and yet I couldn't work out what it was.

Is.

And it's that ongoing is-ness of Trump that I've finally come to understand: the existence, the fascination and the power of evil to infect and destroy good. The metaphor of the devil made flesh: a human being gloatingly glorifying in the exhilaration of power, the delight in lying, the self-congratulation of fraud and the repetitive orgasm of being worshipped as a false god.

Moloch.

However many words it's taken me to stumble on describing the obvious, Hannah Arendt nailed it in four: the banality of evil.

Trump is and remains forever the Eichmann of politics, showbiz and superficiality.

He is to be feared because just as God is love, so the devil is evil.

But if my stumble through the maze of Trumpery makes some kind of flailing sense, then surely the devil is human at least inasmuch as a human being can be possessed by the devil—not in the squirming, screaming, writhing over the top amateur acting of Hollywood screen possession, but in a much more enticing way.

Well, enticing to the clueless.

Is it remotely possible that Trump is so brainless that he simply has no idea of the moral cancer he incarnates?

Not possible. He's so brilliant in his degeneracy.

A monster not even a mother could love.

And yet that must be false, or humanity makes no sense at all.

And so I must learn to love Trump while hating Trumpery.

And in my wallowing, my execration, my perverse joy in loathing the man, I have to ask myself whether my sin is as great or even greater than his?

St Paul on love trips off the tongue at weddings: *Love is patient, love is kind. It does not envy, it does not boast, it is not proud. It does not dishonour others, it is not self-seeking, it is not easily angered, it keeps no record of wrongs. Love does not delight in evil but rejoices with the truth. It always protects, always trusts, always hopes, always perseveres.*

Not so reassuring, though, when I'm supposed to be patient, not easily angered, keep no record of wrongs, delight not in evil and always hope for the best on the subject of Trump.

Then again, all this time to think may well be the devil's gift.

Thursday, March 18th

Feast of Saint Cyril of Jerusalem (315–386) who got Christ's message. 'Since He Himself has declared and said of the bread: This is My Body, who shall dare to doubt anymore?

He then asserts: 'This is My Blood, who shall ever hesitate and say it is not His Blood? Do not think it mere bread and wine, for it is the Body and Blood of Christ, according to the Lord's declaration.' In other words, faith brings miracles within, and all those glorious martyrs who have died for our faith had experienced miracles in their hearts and souls. For those millions upon millions upon trillions upon trillions upon infinite gazillions of daily miracles, I give God thanks, and, frankly, I doubt that we need all the other dazzling showpieces which an apparently insecure God needs to stage in order to both reinforce and, indeed, drum up adherence. The Eucharist must surely be God's greatest gift to humanity and to humanity's infinite imagination, and when all the historical theological and philosophical carry-on has been put aside (sorry about that, centuries of apologists) receiving Christ's Last Supper bread and wine in whatever denominational dispensation your head space is in, that moment, that thanksgiving, that exaltation, that confidence, those endlessly charitable consequences, that perennial miracle... all these are surely what we're about. Of course, I could be wrong because I'm no longer the pope (thank God) but when I strive to find a more poetic or more sustaining or more gloriously inspirational impetus to redeeming the unbearable injustice of the world, with the whole of Christianity and agnosticism and atheism I'll join benevolent forces, and together we'll give some kind of salvation to the next victim we're called upon to help. For Christ's sake, there are no barriers. When will we all learn? If only all our heartfelt and honest collaborators in the search for meaning could join with us in the mystery of bread and wine and infinite hope and the poetry of the imagination and refusal to submit to the forces of evil... Ah, but...

Bounty: tomato, watermelon and white onion salad with pickled fennel fronds. Fennel, as the world knows—well, anyway it has been divinely revealed to and promulgated by Sister Angelica—sharpens the intelligence.

INW.

And almost immediately, fresh intelligence. After dinner, Sister Angelica asked me whether I'd read the recent interview with Mendoza in *L'Osservatore Romano*. For a moment, I was bewildered and wondered whether my memory was finally giving up the ghost. An interview with Mendoza at this time would hardly be something I'd miss. Of course, I'd read—well, skimmed—the Vatican's *Pravda* over breakfast, but how on earth I missed the Mendoza piece had to be a worry.

No, a significant political and medical concern to be immediately addressed.

And addressed it was.

Angelica produced a downloaded copy headed "The New Listening Church."

How on earth did I skip over so flagrant a banner run up the conclave flagpole?

I didn't.

Angelica's sources discovered that the interview was suppressed by someone high up in the editorial hierarchy, and that unearthing it is what I'd call both a scoop and a major concern as its aim is clearly to silence a view which divides the cardinals. And merely fast-forwarding through the interview, I could immediately guess whose election campaign wanted to stymie Mendoza's born-again understanding of the value and structure of synods, and it is, of course, Olivier's.

Mendoza's basic argument is that Christ didn't harangue or boss his non-tertiary-educated apostles like a sergeant-major, platoon commander or, indeed, general or field marshal of his fortress church.

Rather, by parable and simple explanation, Christ patiently illustrated and drew conclusions which were all the more convincing for their gentleness and accurate landing. Accordingly, Mendoza wonders whether instead of bishops simply deciding on and enforcing issues relevant to the faith and the welfare of their dioceses, bishops should have a council of ten informed lay people, fifty percent male and female.

He points out that these days, it's more than likely that on any number of subjects, theological or social, the laity will be as or even better informed than the bishop, and Mendoza goes further in arguing that one of the main purposes of synods is to allow bishops to listen, not necessarily a virtue which instantly descends on episcopal ordinands.

I didn't believe I was reading this.

Furthermore, Mendoza proposes, to make significant decisions, the bishop would require a quorum of seven, three male and three female laity, with the bishop as chair. This would insure input by the laity and, in all likelihood, a degree of consensus. And if harmony eluded the quorum, a plenary session of twice that many representatives would take place as quickly as possible.

After this, the bishop would decide on what was to happen and how.

Mendoza argues that any sane bishop (good luck with that generalisation) would realise that frequent overruling of the council would quickly lead to a vote of no confidence in the chairman, and that vote would then be forwarded to the archbishop, the apostolic delegate or, if necessary, to Rome for judgment.

It's somewhat over-idealistic given the immediacy of day-to-day issues bishops have to wade through, but it's a not uncontroversial overview for the restructuring which is increasingly called for by the laity and any number of theologians—and, indeed, recent pontiffs. Well, two, at any rate. Especially in the face of ever-falling vocations to the priesthood as that calling has been understood and defined over centuries by the vicariously celibate clergy.

Not quite Olivier's return to pray, pay and stay away, but likely to appeal to moderates as well as progressives in the conclave.

And all this was censored!

We must hope that some sympathetic computer literate partisan doesn't download the interview online where it would be read by many times more than the boutique readership of *L'Osservatore Romano*.

Perish the thought.

A week is a long time in conclave preparation.

Friday, March 19th

Feast of Saint Joseph, husband of Mary and apparently foster father of Jesus.

Was he old, a widower or a teenager when he married Mary? Was he a carpenter? What sort of father was he? Did he have a sex life? Did he know that Jesus was the son of God? What on earth does that feel like? What was table conversation like at home? And bed banter? After all, they were presumably young and hot. Or not. Which is surely a worry. Anyway, as a father, I've thought about all this before, but we know almost nothing about Joseph. Was he a Joseph or a Joe? Up to Mary, I guess. I'd love to have met Joseph. So many questions to ask. We might have more in common than...

Small world. Billiard balls colliding.

At lunch today, Ennio had unlikely news—well, unlikely to me news.

His soccer playing and charitably companionable young friend, Lucio, was approached yesterday evening in the sauna where he moonlights, as it were, for what might be described as handsome emoluments from a middle-aged African with a view to ongoing 'conversation'.

Ever obliging, athletic Lucio took up the offer and in small talk on completion of his ministry, the lad discovered the congenial African to be none other than Mufaro Moya, Cardinal Archbishop of Harare in Zimbabwe and one of the youngest cardinals in the conclave. I should know as I raised him to the rank in the third month of my papacy having met him in Rome and heard great praise for his pastoral and diplomatic skills in that volatile country.

He is indeed engaging and very well educated, though in our meetings, the subject of his sexual preference didn't arise, and I simply assumed that like so many African clergy, he approached celibacy with a somewhat liberal, indeed optional outlook.

And as it would appear he does, though to the best of my knowledge, Africans loathe homosexuals and punish them with appallingly unchristian and uncivilised savagery.

But what the Adonis Lucio learnt in conversation during his occasional apostolate of comfort and relief was that not all African prelates are admirers of Olivier, whom many see as more ambitious than pious.

Extraordinary the conversations which are apparently struck up in the most bizarre circumstances between soccer-playing Vatican gardeners and visiting princes of the church.

Mufaro told Lucio that he knows many Africans, including not a few clerics, whose sexuality requires discreet expression both at home and abroad and who reject the western belief that the African church is universally fundamentalist and rabidly hierarchical.

He sees this judgment as ignorant, patronising and dangerous because of its refusal to take African discernment into account.

Wonderful what and how we can learn from the most unlikely sources, and this timely enlightenment is, as we say in the business, information never wasted.

Nor will it be.

I CONFESS

Saturday, March 20th

Feast of Saint John Nepomucene (1340–1393) famous Czech preacher and confessor in the royal household.

When he refused to disclose the Queen's confession to her jealous husband, the king had him burned then tied to a wheel and thrown off a bridge into the Moldau River. What a right royal bastard! Saint John must be a busy little Vegemite these days as he's currently the patron saint against calumnies, floods, indiscretions (I must pray to him) and slander, and is the patron saint of bridge builders, bridges, confessors (understandably and nobly), mariners, sailors, boatmen, watermen, running water, silence, Bohemia, the Czech Republic, Prague and Venice. I must find out which Vatican department allots these jobs and why running water and silence need a patron saint. What an intriguing and holy man! And on the patron saint front, I'm reminded that St Peregrine (1265–1345) is the patron saint of cancer sufferers. Except he was cured and died after a long cure.

The form guide for the Papal Cup in the Vatican Stakes largely comprises a small spectrum of predictable starters offered to journalists over long and free Trastevere lunches or dinners. Many of the candidates have underlings and associates (henchmen) who unsubtly propose and puff their patrons while offering uncharitable backgrounding of assumed opponents.

Frankly, the front runners could be nominated banquet-free by any nun cooking, cleaning or bed-making in the Domus Santa Marta.

These good and shrewd women hear the echoes, judge the characters and know all the kindnesses, foibles and stratagems of the ambitious, and I can attest to this as perhaps the most unambitious pope ever elected.

And 'unambitious with good reason' I hear reverberating throughout the venerable corridors across the road.

But heightened conclave gossip, clerical bitchery and journalistic fairy floss aside, with the possible exception of America's *National Catholic Reporter*, those of us in the know—and the un-know—know to trust the informed reporting of the English Catholic Weekly, *The Tablet*.

Since the days of the ultimate Vatican journalist insider, retired Jesuit, Peter Hebblethwaite (*The Year of the Three Popes.* Superb!) *The Tablet* correspondent has always been the one with the most informed local intelligence, which is why, this morning, this ex-pope was gobsmacked by *The Tablet's* report that as is always possible (and don't I know it!) with the shrewd intervention of the Holy Spirit, a complete outsider can sprint up the rails and win the stakes.

Except that candidate is the Cardinal Archbishop of Luxembourg, His Eminence Jean-Franz Hoffmann.

I mean, is this some kind of pre-pre-April Fool's Day joke?

Jean-Franz Hoffmann is without doubt the nicest cardinal living, and, yes, that's not, perhaps, a recommendation without qualification.

If you asked him how the weather was, his reply would be meteorologically detailed, accurate and appropriately qualified to the fourth or fifth predictive possibilities together with the most civilised and genuine invitation to join him for afternoon tea, but at the end of this warm and genuine reply, you wouldn't have the slightest idea of what the weather was like.

Jean-Franz is quite the loveliest of men and a refined scholar and antiquarian to boot. Were he to die tomorrow of excess politesse, he'd be immediately canonised as the patron saint of herbal afternoon tea.

No connoisseur knows of more esoteric herbal outliers than the Cardinal Archbishop of Luxembourg.

I think his secret vice may well be playing clavichord duets with retired mothers-superior, but as pope, the prospect for the church would be of universal loveliness, embracing niceness, abundant goodwill, radiant optimism, endless possibilities of sunny spiritual uplands and total theological and structural stasis followed by multi-continental revolutions owing to volcanic spiritual beige-ness.

I am to international wrestling as Jean-Franz is to the papacy.

For once, I'm stumped by *The Tablet.*

One of us is losing it, and in all humility, I'm fucked if on this issue it's me.

Dear God in heaven, save me from drowning in this bouillabaisse of conclave insanity.

I repeat my repetition: Jean-Franz remains, without doubt, the most amicable cardinal living, but as for piloting the barque of Peter in the time of spiritual nuclear warfare...

Sunday, March 21st

Feast of Blessed Mark Djani (1914–1947) another martyr to the barbarism of Albanian communism.

The strength of faith by the heroes of that plagued country must surely inspire us all. Blessed Mark was ordained in 1942 at the age of 28 and tortured to death by the Albanian communist government. These unspeakable servants of the people for a better and more just world repeatedly ordered him to curse Christ. Great for votes in Moscow, no doubt. Blessed Mark repeatedly answered, 'Long live Jesus Christ!' Clearly, that was a major threat to the universal humanitarianism of communism and its benevolent revolution. In 1947, Blessed Mark's body was dumped in a canal to be eaten by stray dogs. With all our religion's faults, I'm wondering whether the horrors we have perpetrated have even been surpassed in the 20th century, and whether or not we're all guilty of... I don't even want to name it, so shameful and sinful and animal and treacherous both histories have been to their inglorious statements of salvation. I must pray for the soul of Albania, if that nation still has the memory of a soul. The sadistic power of evil eats into every fibre of my faith—of my everything. Prayer is surely all that's left. And even then...

Over the last two days, in my newly discovered though still bewildered free time, I've read a 350-page book published in 2022.

The title is *The Escape Artist*, the author is *Guardian* journalist Jonathan Freedland, and the subject is the story of how a nineteen-year-old Jewish boy escaped from Auschwitz in 1942.

I'd heard of the book but for some reason it never appeared on my desk.

My belief is that this book should be read by every adult—OK, person over 18—on the planet.

It's as unputdownable as it's unbearable, and the world Freedland so chillingly describes is hell on earth: a barbed wire enclosed planet of depravity, evil, torture, starvation, murder on an industrial scale and human suffering beyond imagination.

Surely even the imagination of our all-loving God.

And it's also the story of human ingenuity and courage.

And yet so many millions died after extended agony, and this must lead readers to the recurring, bewildering, painful and oppressive theological question of how our loving God can permit such unspeakable atrocities.

Or does this loving God 'permit' it?

I keep coming back to the power of the devil or evil or whatever people want to call it, because name it humanity must. And a powerful imperative in my understanding tells me that if such blasphemy is the cost of the alleged gift of free will, then the cost of the gift isn't worth it—not if it's my three-year-old daughter being bashed in front of me by criminals, bitten by feral dogs and joining me in the gas chamber.

Contemplating this meaninglessness is beyond endurance, and yet every one of us must enter into this abomination of desolation in order to come to terms with the total injustice of the planet.

I can only open my heart and mind to the Lord and acknowledge my inability to thank the almighty for not myself being almighty.

I should never have entered the priesthood.

Lord, have mercy.

I need it.

Monday, March 22nd

Feast of Saint Nicholas Owen (tortured to death in Elizabethan England on this day in 1606).

I admire this saint more than... But to his heroic life. And if only my pathetic, muddled, exploratory, probably sinful possibly not (well, not always) comfortable pedestrian life could remotely aspire to this saint's extraordinary inspiration! If only. And Brother Nicholas Owen is in that league beyond even extraordinary saintliness. He should be the patron saint of Wollongong builders among a host of other trade callings. His father was a carpenter and faithful adherent to the old Catholic faith. Two of his brothers became priests, the third became a printer of underground Catholic books. Nicholas used his carpentry skills to build priest holes, hidden rooms and secret exits for priests in many Catholic family mansions in England. By day, he worked as a stonemason and carpenter to justify his presence on each property of his apostolate, and by night he dug tunnels and constructed escape passages. He became a Jesuit brother and continued his secretive work but finally gave himself up in November 1605 after four days hiding without food or water in one of his own constructions. In London, he was viciously tortured for information about his hiding places but refused to reveal any information. In March 1606, after unspeakable torments, he was suspended from a wall by his wrists, his ankles heavily weight down, then after much suffering, his stomach burst open spilling his intestines onto the chamber floor. Sometime later he died. Not of a short illness. This humble, gifted, brilliant, faithful, heartening, inspiriting heroic tradie gives me hope that faith will conquer suffering.

Challenging bounty: roast yellow squash (never heard of it) with anchovies and garlic.

Hot.

Something tells me that even without parsley and lemon, this is some kind of signal. Good or bad remains to be chewed over. Sister Angelica provides no commentary. A worry from one so herbally and heavenly infallible, but nonetheless, message received: prepare for uncertain news.

Given the inevitable electoral turbulence as the C-Day approaches, I'd have expected some unsurprising surprises right now, but the tactical silence doesn't quite make sense.

Reculer pour mieux advancer? Look it up, Dad. It doesn't add up herbally, heavenly or even strategically.

New revelation waiting for ideal moment of release?

Possibly, though with the exception of His Eminence Jean-Franz Hoffmann about whom no salacious disclosure seems remotely possible (OMG! He slightly prefers late fifteenth-century harpsichord music to the more raunchy early sixteenth century-bacchanalian variety?) any bombshell is possible—present company not excluded—but at this stage, the trick is to accelerate momentum rather than drip feed, and it's two days now since my domestic menu organiser has cooked up anything curiously piquant or even mildly spicy.

Either both parties are confident or they're desperately scrambling, and my hunch is that Mendoza is now nosing in front.

Come to think of it, what I haven't heard is Dario's overview.

Odd.

OK, he wasn't in the commentary box when Benedict resigned, but he's now well and truly behind the binoculars and knows the form better than anyone.

Of course, I must feign indifference, but surely old friends are entitled to meet for afternoon tea and a privileged slice of Sister Angelica's speciality, crostata cantarella, that mortally sinful Sicilian berry tart which she and only she makes the decision when to bake and to whom to offer it.

Yes, something important is up.

I must ask her.

Tuesday, March 23rd

Feast of St Benedict of Campagna (died c 550) a hermit, captured by the goths and thrown into the fire to die.

He remained in the flames until the next day when he miraculously emerged unharmed. He eventually died of natural causes. Once again, I wonder what the real story was.

The crostata cantarella did the trick.

Dario, currently in the process of packing to leave the Vatican, was all indiscretion.

Must be due to Sister Angelica's secret ingredient.

I've asked her any number of times what it is, but she smiles and says that if she tells me, she'll have to kill me, and as quite a few other religious are ahead of her in that queue, I've decided to remain towards the back of that condemned line.

Anyway, Dario's intelligence gatherers have discovered the most bizarre of movements among the cardinals.

Apparently, Jean-Franz Hoffmann's papal candidature isn't the joke I took it to be, and that change of attitude is in no small way due to my election, the result being that there's hope that un-lightning can strike twice.

Once again, there remain two major camps, Olivier's and Mendoza's, with what my philosophy professor in the seminary might have labelled 'the undistributed middle'.

I've always wondered if ever in life I'd find a situation to illustrate that academic concept, but then in two conclaves, I've observed quite a few wavering undistributed middle men, and it would appear that now they're apparently in the process of distributing themselves to Jean-Franz Hoffmann as the middle-of-the-road candidate.

Actually, he's much more the roundabout candidate, as when it comes to decision making, he'll be in perpetually friendly circular motion like some benevolently unstoppable merry-go-round.

The church will be dizzy from vacillation, hesitancy, tentativeness and endless buckets of charm, and I'll be remembered as the resolute and dogmatic successor to St John Paul II.

The age of miracles hasn't passed.

But the problem will be when different numbers from each camp move to the prevaricating centre.

If those voting blocs aren't equal, then which of the opposing camps' candidate will win?

Never a dull moment in the papacy board game.

Wednesday, March 24th

Feast of St Oscar Arnulfo Romero y Galdámez (1917–1980).

Saint Oscar Romero, the saint of the oppressed poor. Originally conservative and, indeed, anti-left, he eventually realised that the ruling class couldn't care less about the poor and, indeed, they manipulated the government to repress the demands of the oppressed. He was murdered while celebrating mass. Who will rid me of this troublesome priest? A brave martyr of our time. Even conservatives can listen to Christ's insistence on justice. Well, some. Saint Oscar Romero is a saint for all clergy... all clergy who will listen, that is.

I'm having nightmares from the details of grotesque torture and murder in Jonathan Freedland's *The Escape Artist.*

I'm trying to imagine those Auschwitz Germans accounting before God for their unspeakably… unimaginably monstrous delight in tormenting and killing millions of Jews.

And I can't.

I can only hear them explaining how much they exponentially enjoyed their atrocities and then I wonder how God can congratulate the godhead on the brilliant success of free will.

And whether the wretched victims are supposed to thank their God for their agony.

And if the all-just and all-loving God then condemns those monsters to the eternal fire of hell—as in my deepest self, I certainly would—how then is God all-loving, having fucked it up in the first place?

And God's supposed to be God.

And the reply that Jesus-God-made-man also suffered frankly doesn't assuage my pain and outrage.

And yes, again, I'm not God but, hey, I'm using my God-given mind as honestly as I can, and in any case, the usual God-get-out-of-jail card inevitably applies, meaning that it's not up to us to question God when it seems to me that if we don't, we close our minds, shut our hearts and deny our integrity in somehow acquiescing in divinely monstrous horror.

And just for the record, having a yearly memorial service or having the victims' names inscribed on some wall somewhere doesn't strike me as in any way approaching an explanation or a satisfactory atonement.

Far from it.

Impossibly far and excruciatingly unfathomable.

Guess we'll have to write it off as yet another mystery.

As I career to the grave, these mysteries multiply.

Not the most papal of thoughts.

Glad I'm not the pope, though I wouldn't mind relief from these nightly tribulations.

Thursday, March 25th

Feast of the Annunciation of the Lord. Date?

The angel of the Lord declared unto Mary, and she conceived of the Holy Ghost. The glorious poetry of salvation. So much theology is predicated on this mystery outside of all human experience. The more I ponder it...

Oh dear! One's worse fears have eventuated.
  Not!
  Mendoza's interview is now on the net and being reported, analysed and evaluated worldwide.
  And to think that if left uncensored on the *L'Osservatore Romano* vine, it might have withered unread except by rusted-on Latin Mass enthusiasts!
  Ah well, heigh ho!
  For the rain it raineth every day.
  Today, in beautiful buckets.
  A deluge from heaven.

Friday, March 26th

Feast of Saint Maxima (died 304) married to and martyred with Saint Montanus.

Both were drowned in the wretched persecutions of Diocletian whom I frequently hope is burning in hell. Yet I no longer believe in that theological fate as a place (or even a state) though God and Jesus must be in every way divine in their forgiveness. And in my angry bewilderment, I discuss this intensely with my Jewish friends. I think of the dreadful but holy death of this couple and see pain and love and faith and hope. And in my pain and... I desperately grasp at... ever diminishingly desperate hope. I hope they did not die alone in any sense.

Those niggles are occurring more frequently.

Despite Luca's detailed reports, I've decided I'd rather not understand what's happening inside me.

Sometimes, knowledge is not power, and ignorance, while hardly bliss, is at least a tepid blur.

INW.

Olivier has done an interview with a major Cameroon website, *Journal du Cameroun.* Huge circulation, no doubt—in Yaoundé.

Except now it's gone worldwide.

'Of late there has been loose talk in Rome about the rigidity of church discipline and its negative influence on young Catholics. But this is exactly what truth is not. We are the church militant. Fortress Catholicism. And every enlisted soldier of Christ must obey his lawful superior. Strength through authority and regulation. Subordination is liberation. Only through regulation and heartfelt submission can the forces of the devil be defeated. Let the flock trustingly obey their shepherd.'

Orwell would be proud.

War is peace. Slavery is freedom. Bullshit is wisdom.

And God resides only in the Vatican.

As did I!

End of argument.

Though the beginning of… the endless undermining of…

Dear God, I thought I was past despair yet now I'm the ongoing accomplice in… our universal conspiracy of ecclesiastical power.

What Olivier excludes from his disciplinary delights is what he writes off as his 'African male sexual needs.'

La condition humaine africaine.

Forgiveness in the confessional box by day. Playgrounds of delight by night.

Even a sinner like myself can see through this hypocrisy.

A clever move, though.

Trust Olivier to offer this bait to the cardinal waverers.

Reinforce the power of the clergy, those officers of the one true faith which controls salvation in holding the keys to the kingdom of heaven.

Fortunately, Mendoza is clever enough to expose Olivier's sleight of hand and will checkmate his devious adversary.

Game on.

Saturday, March 27th

Feast of Saint Augusta of Treviso (5th century), a fifth-century daughter of the Teutonic Duke of Friuli.

When she converted to Christianity, she was beheaded personally by her father. Some things in life are beyond my understanding. Thank God. The necessity for heaven.

Bounty of broccoli gratin.

Is it all as bloody simple as that?

Right again, Sister Angelica—as always. You are my recipe for salvation…which, needless to say, arrives—again, apparently, via Ennio.

I can't believe there's collaboration here.

By and large, they've both always kept a politely loyal but wary distance from each other (and thereby hangs a tale) but anyway, there's been a secondary advance by Olivier to bring the self-serving curia waverers into his triumphalist fold, yet Mendoza hasn't hit back.

INW

Ennio's ever accommodating sauna soccer friend apparently received an email from his African cardinal friend offering ongoing fraternal association.

On reading the request, Ennio followed up on the cardinal's email address, and with the assistance of a tech savvy soccer friend—ASIO ought to employ more young soccer players, as, indeed, might the curia—broke into the cardinal's computer and downloaded a proposed paragraph in a potential sermon from Olivier to his campaign manager, Chilean Cardinal Carlos Silva Gonzales, suggesting its publication in that universally scrutinized Cameroon daily, *Journal du Cameroun*. It read:

'Yes, within the church's faithful, there are always those extraordinary people of faith who can offer us new insights, though their helpful ranks are necessarily few, but synods are of their nature, subordinates offering their informed superiors well-meaning if usually enthusiastic rather than theologically refined advances for the faithful to accept their role in the mystery of salvation.

'Yes, we, the ordained, must listen, but also, yes, the flock, however agitated, must obey their shepherds, not least in an era of triumphalist paganism and mass media contempt for the absolute truths we hold to be evident and for the beliefs, since the time of Our Crucified and Resurrected Lord and afterwards drenched in the blood of our holy martyrs… those beliefs we affirm to be eternally true.'

Ennio felt that such information might be of interest to me.

He always knows the right buttons to press.

And between her housekeeping commitments and gastronomical explorations, apparently Sister Angelica received from some unknown source—nuns know everything. Of course, always from reliably undisclosed sources—anyway, these sources reveal Mendoza's notes for an impending sermon sent to, of all people, one of Olivier's more intelligent and balanced supporters, the Prefect of the Council of Cardinals, Cardinal Bruno Westphalen, for advice to include or delete.

Mendoza simply asks Westphalen whether he thinks that speaking of one's personal faith journey—even when it involves major rethinking and dramatic change of direction—whether this encourages the faithful questors or reinforces the uncertainty of the questioners and doubters.

He should have asked me!

Mendoza's text: 'Over centuries of time and failure—and here I add my personal errors, pain and, to my shame, sins of arrogance—over these millennia, we've learned that the church triumphant is not the message of the risen Christ. I've spent far too much of my life prosecuting heresy rather than discerning revelation, but my appointment with death has brought faith to my misguided certainty.

'I am a pilgrim, not a commander in some all-conquering almighty army of spiritual occupation.

'We must live our faith, and only by that example of the love and charity and understanding shown in our lives may we offer our understanding of God's hope for the world to those outside our current understanding.

'At my age, this is a difficult fact to accept, but that difficulty is now peacefully replaced by its acceptance.

'In my newfound faithful humility and in the glorious mystery of the eucharist—God dwelling within us and in all who open their hearts to Him—we can help our world to serve and not to rule.'

A bombshell here.

The annoying fact is that Westphalen, while being an Olivier man, is also rational and not unfair minded.

As well, he's a respected cleric of integrity, something which has always bamboozled me as he sides with Olivier.

But anyway, Westphalen was the recipient, and my fear is that sadly, loyalty will probably triumph over impartiality.

Why on earth would Mendoza declare his hand to a known Olivier lieutenant?

I can't make sense of it, unless Mendoza really believes that he can bring Westphalen across to our side—which in my heart I long for but in my gut I know is totally unlikely to happen.

I can't believe the pope is an hour-by-hour player in this sordid game, yet the fact is Mendoza's confession is an absolute game-changer for the waverers.

His new credo must receive universal coverage.

We must now be on the front foot.

Oh, and urgent memo to self: Mario, you're no longer the pope. Remember?

Sunday, March 28th

Feast of Blessed Dedë Maçaj (1920–1947).

The newly ordained Albanian, Dedë Maçaj, was called up on military service, refused, was imprisoned, tortured and executed as a Vatican spy. Probably because of the way that tragic country was hermetically sealed by its communist rulers with their fanatic hatred of the church. Surely behind it must have been a deep fear that Christian heaven in heaven would increasingly seem more likely than communist heaven on earth. More and more I fear those who proclaim that they have the ultimate truth. And I'm well aware of the irony.

Either Westphalen gave Mendoza the green light (I'd love to believe this but can't) or Mendoza decided to go ahead anyhow.

Still, a corker of an Olivier slap-down by Mendoza in a sermon today in St Peter's, the text of which artillery battering miraculously appeared in this week's *Tablet* not to mention all the London and Rome morning papers.

L'Osservatore Romano may have its Olivier-friendly censor, but Mendoza clearly has mates among the big press guns and he obviously knows when to call in a favour and how to hit the headlines:

PAPAL FAVOURITE SPEAKS OUT   *The Times*
A NEW LOOK CHURCH?   *The Guardian*
BY VATICAN INVITATION   *The Telegraph*
VATICANO VOLTAFACCIA   *Il Tempo*
UNA CHIESA GENTILE?   *La Stampa*
TRAFFIC CHAOS IN YAOUNDE   *Journal du Cameroun (!)*

...and a very, very sympathetic outline in *The Tablet's View From Rome.*

'Mendoza rejects the concept of a fortress and triumphalist church as a previous and limited understanding of Christ's message. While sympathizing with the power structures and world outlook of previous centuries, Mendoza argues that love cannot be imposed. Rather, the message of Jesus is an invitation to be considered and then to be either freely accepted or not. Gone are the days of eternal damnation for those who reject—or, it must be said, hadn't even heard of—Catholicism. For many years, Mendoza was known to theologians he was investigating for errors and heresy as The Grand Inquisitor, and his judgment was obeyed even by popes, but following a remarkable recovery from a death threatening cancer, the born-again cardinal is now the centre-left front runner for pope.

'The sub-text of his thinking seems to suggest the putting aside of the teaching that the pope is the all-knowing and rule-enforcing divine field marshal of Christ's army—the supreme commander of the *Gotcha God.* Missing Sunday mass is a mortal sin, mortal sin is highway to hell, confess, reform or down you'll go. The born-again Mendoza is now emphasising belief and hope in all-loving God.

'Mendoza's description of the new, gentle and friendly church is clearly a rebuke to his highly conservative African conclave opponent, Cardinal Olivier Gabriel Foncha. The African looks to a united, disciplined and missionary church well rid of the *cafeteria Catholics* (a term frequently used by deceased Australian Cardinal George Pell) who select the beliefs and rules they approve of but ignore teachings they see as outdated or simply wrong...in much the same way that Pell accepted Pope Francis's views if they coincided with the Australian's beliefs but strongly criticised them when they diverged from antipodean infallibility.

'Given a recent endorsement of church synods by Mendoza, this is another riposte to Foncha who will have none of *that conversation chamber waffle. Patients don't instruct surgeons in the intricacies of life-saving operations.*

'The stage is set for lively debate in the Sistine Chapel.

'It now remains to be seen whether one wing of the church will prevail or whether, for a second time, a compromise candidate will be the conclave's choice.

'As reported last week in *The Tablet*, the cardinal archbishop of Luxembourg, Cardinal Jean-Franz Hoffmann, is regarded as a safe, if indecisive moderate, but informed Vatican sources see the wavering centrist cardinals as likely to unenthusiastically vote for Mendoza given that the African is known to take no prisoners, meaning that curia power wielders will be totally loyal to him or quickly find themselves papal nuncios to disagreeable outposts of the Vatican diplomatic corps, ironically not a few of them in Africa.

'With only five days to the conclave, lunching and dining cardinals will be evaluating much more than their gnocchi, vitello, Barbera and Frascati, while scoop-hungry Vatican journalists will be doing the rounds of basilicas, sniffing out sermons or conversations pointing to which direction the wind of the Holy Spirit is blowing.'

From the horse's mouth, I'd say, and meanwhile, those 'informed Vatican sources' will be knocking back some fine vintages which editors will have to pick up the tab for.

Rome is at its most Roman during the conclave carnival.

Monday, March 29th

Feast of Welsh Saint Gladys (6th century) and surely there's a movie in her life.

Gladys was the daughter of a saint, Brychan of Brecknock. Another future saint, Saint Gwynllyn, asked Gladys's saintly father for his daughter's hand in marriage. Permission refused. So the two lovers then cleared out of town and lived an abandoned life on the run—a sort of pre-saintly but very sexy Bonnie and Clyde. Enter the mother of Saint Cadoc of Llancarvan or possibly Saint Cadoc, their son. Anyway, one of them gave the couple a good talking to, the result of which was Gladys crossing the border to become a nun in Monmouthshire and later a hermitess in rural Wales. Gwynllyn withdrew in every sense and lived a solitary life near a church he had built. He wore sackcloth, ate barley-bread strewn with ashes, and drank only water. To constant prayer and contemplation, he added the work of his hands. On his deathbed, Gwynllyn was visited by another saint, the unfortunately named Saint Dyfrig and then by Gwynllyn's own son, Cadoc, who provided him with the last rites of the Church. Talk about saints alive and all in the family. That's the Welsh for you. And every time I meet a Gladys, I suggest she checks out the saintly life of her 6th century namesake.

Our faith tells us that it is the guidance of the Holy Spirit which elects the new pope.

That pope can be any baptized male—he doesn't even have to be ordained a priest—though the likelihood of that happening in a locked room of 120 or so male cardinals, not a few of whom are ambitious clerics, is a million to one. It surely follows, therefore, that the Holy Spirit must be assumed to regard women as unsuitable to hold high office in the church, which suggests a divine misogynist, which to me suggests a crazy God.

The church, like Judaism, is a patriarchy, and power makes sure that power continues in as direct a line as possible. More and more I can't understand why, when we see 120 men in medieval frocks and funny hats claiming to somehow embody the will of God, we don't burst out laughing at the presumption and the absurdity of the absence of women who make up a little more than half of God's creatures.

But for the time being, them's the rules.

The ritual, ceremony, pomp, circumstance, majesty, holiness, politics and secrecy of the conclave make for fascinating watching and genuine excitement both within the walls of the Sistine Chapel and without.

I've only attended two conclaves, but what is rarely commented on—perhaps understandably—is the bodily functions of 120 late middled-aged to old men herded together and refused release until two-thirds of them vote for a new boss.

Thank the Lord and Pope Saint John Paul II, things are less olfactorially distressing these days after Domus Sanctae Marthae was built by that noble and supremely confident pontiff, now definitely in heaven. Make of that what you will, Mario. But, like my historically acclaimed predecessor, I subscribe to that uplifting act of poetic faith in my quest to understand the numinous.

Heaven's above?!

Basically, Domus Sanctae Marthae is a large motel to house visiting prelates reporting to the Vatican and, more importantly, cardinals during a papal conclave, and believe me, as divine get-togethers go, a conclave is as incrementally intense as they make them.

Unlike the Holy Spirit, ageing males are human—some of them alarmingly so—thus good taste and decorum demand that certain aspects of the conclave are not discussed outside the Sistine Chapel, but even now, with nightly oblutional respite in Domus Sanctae Marthae, for those of us thrown together in a confined space for heaven only knows how long, human needs and frailties suddenly become foregrounded.

Believe me, in the equally divine lottery for the next Dalai Lama, the Holy Spirit is not the only prevailing wind, and God only knows how suffocatingly the atmosphere must have been in the crowded Sistine Chapel.

Like the majority of non-clerics, especially male, cardinals fart, albeit holily, and some from countries which I'd best not name seem to regard such flatulence as an activity as normal as breathing, so without so much as an 'excuse me', they fire away at will.

Even to petitionary prayer, it can be distractingly nauseating.

I sometimes wonder how many votes potential popes lose on the F-scale.

Likewise on the aromatic front, American cardinals specialise in wearing oceans of expensive after-shave, each individual fragrance doubtless alluring, but the clashing of so many of which produces a sickening redolence which, in turn, blends with the previously mentioned emanations to distract even the most fervent prayer for discernment.

Simultaneously Divine Crucible and Pong Central.

And as middle-aged to old men have urinary and more immediately dramatic defecation needs which are exclusive to each individual, the regularity—or sadly—the irregularity of these demands results in constant processions to the limited toilet and washing facilities close to the Sistine Chapel.

For the elderly and infirm, however, it can be a challenging walk and wait. Think Sydney Town Hall Station in peak hour or similar crowding at 5 p.m. on London's Underground or in New York's Grand Central Terminal.

Thus the thrust of any pointed theological, pastoral or even political argument at that significant moment can distract potentially vital voters.

And as is the human condition in closed surroundings, other people offer their unique odours and fragrances.

My point being that for all its majesty and prayer and hallowed horse-trading, the conclave has distinct overtones of a run-down boarding school for young males pubescing all over the place.

As for the food, let's just say it's appropriately Lenten in celebration and unlikely to chalk up many Michelin stars. To date, no restaurant in the world has named itself Conclave, and for good reason.

Of course, all the above is tales out of school, though when you're praying through it, petitionary prayers may vary in their subject matter and intensity.

Look, I'm not bagging it out; rather telling the truth behind the costumed and reverent theatre selectively released on TV.

That said, full marks and a koala stamp to the Holy Spirit for overcoming so many human limitations and, in recent times, delivering the servant of the servants of God with comparative efficiency.

With the odd exception, that is.

Tuesday, March 30th

Feast of Saint Irene of Rome (died 288) who was married to Saint Castulus, martyred by the Emperor Diocletian for converting to Christianity.

Tradition has it that she healed the arrow wounds of Saint Sebastian the Beautiful though she failed to convince him to leave Rome. A pious lady.

And they're racing.

I confess that my alcohol intake isn't entirely altar wine but as I see the race through my post-papal binoculars, first out of the block has to be Mendoza because of his shrewd pre-conclave manoeuvring, and in these stakes, the older the nag, the better his chance of winning.

After John-Paul II, a long papacy isn't looked on as a blessing, though too short a one—vide J-P I—strikes me as a distinct un-blessing and one I'm still nervous about.

Of course, the first ballot on Day 1 will be black smoke, but if Mendoza establishes himself as the front runner, the pre-from guide suggests he can consolidate on both Day 2 votes and with luck (and, it goes without saying, the tail wind of the Holy Spirit) get to the two thirds finishing post by the third ballot on Day 3.

I wonder whether Rome has a TAB.

The Vatican doesn't, and, on reflection, it's crazy not to.

Let's face it: properly set up and disguised under some pious title (St Peter's Faith Investment) conclave gamblers would ensure we'd make millions to spend on good works, God's work and a few celebratory fireworks.

Also, it's only recently occurred to me—I'm a slow learner—that I may well have been bi-polar all my life. As COVID-19 cases still keep bouncing around, I find it a tad bewildering that a pope—me— should be so sceptical of so much that is central to the church which, the church teaches, God has entrusted me with.

Why on earth I can't simply accept and rejoice in every aspect and dimension of the faith is beyond me.

Some days—and nights, especially—I find myself amazed and grateful, but once I offer a prayer of thanks, the cloud… no, it's not a cloud… it's the fierce light of doubt which illuminates my mind, and this, together with my lifelong belief in the necessity of women to be equal in every tier of the church's hierarchy… this throws me into reverse gear, and a thousand injustices and illogicalities dance frenetically in my brain.

Pope requiring help beyond prayer is my somewhat late diagnosis.

As I look back on—released from?—the papacy, and have more than a little understanding of the burden of the weight of that office, I've come to the conclusion that I've been suffering from the sheer exhaustion caused by my faith and my struggles to believe in the face of endless difficulties.

And these are not difficulties that I invited, but difficulties which, against my desire for faith, descended on me uninvited and like an unwanted guest, refused to leave.

A second-rate mind, as somebody once observed.

As a younger priest, I actually enjoyed my faith most of the time and found easy answers to conventional objections; the seminary made us good debaters with mouthfuls and fistfuls of replies to frequently asked theological questions. It all made sense, and once you accepted the faith, it was something beautiful to be lived and to rejoice in.

It was only late in middle age that the uninvited guest of gnawing doubt plonked itself in the study of my mind and kept daring and outstaring me.

The guilt of what I believed was intellectual honesty infected my serenity and tortured so much of my day and my vocation.

You might say that I grew up.

What I discovered was—is—that so many different explanations of existence made a lot of sense to me... for a while. But then, my faith became porous, and while its structure remained, fluid doubts eddied and swirled around what was once a lake of relative tranquility. And then, of course, becoming pope brought tidal waves to my lake, and the barque of Peter was indeed tempest tossed.

Christ is our Light, but the church was my business.

In prophetic retrospect, maybe it still is.

Perhaps being un-poped is God's most blessed gift to me.

It's not that I've been living a lie—well, no more so than most of humanity—it's rather that so often, I've been treading water in a wild sea of deluging absence.

If that makes sense.

Which it doesn't.

But to me, it bloody well does.

Only bread and wine transform and fortify me.

God's mercy, as Francis ceaselessly proclaimed, rains down on me.

But the devil keeps whispering in my dreaming ear that life is no more than some turgid—if occasionally spectacular—confluence of ever-changing sensations. They explode and, in their piercing incandescence, offer glimpses of beautiful nothingness… thoughts… insights…pain… grace… and endless, endless wavering.

God's fool?

Makes sense.

None of us, not even popes, I suspect, ever confesses every one of our more, shall we say, exciting sins, not least those delicious sins of fleeting love or its seductive aberrations—those mortal moments of mere passion for which everyone gives themselves instant absolution.

But, hey, who cares now?

I'm rambling and don't know what I'm talking about.

Mind you, people in this neck of the woods have been telling me that for some time now.

Guess I've got to be first-rate at something.

Wednesday, March 31st

Feast of Blessed Natalia Tulasiewicz (1906–1945), a marvellously inspiring lay woman from Poznan in Poland.

A pillar of her parish, Natalia was arrested by Nazis, tortured, publicly taunted and ridiculed, deported, imprisoned and sentenced to forced labour in a number of inhuman camps. Fierce in her faith, she ministered to other prisoners in the days leading to her execution. She was martyred on Easter Sunday in the gas chambers of Ravensbruck. Heroic. The necessity of Heaven.

Bounty of Polenta Gnocchi Winter Green Pesto tasting of pecorino cheese, lemon zest, brie and hazelnuts and topped with purple basil leaves. Salvation on a dish. Sometimes I dare to think that the definition of a sacrament might be extended, but then I cancel that thought.

Slowly.

Mendoza's papacy will be so much easier than mine, lucky bugger.

To begin with, he knows every in and out of the Vatican, not to mention every monsignor, bishop, archbishop and cardinal.

Better still, he knows where all the bodies are buried and why they became bodies.

This makes for efficient administration. Mendoza knows better than any experienced delayer what momentum brakes to employ, and any head of a dicastery or congregation foolish enough to pull the lever against that pontiff won't reach cocktail hour in his preventative role.

Furthermore, because of his many international enquiries into progressive theologians—all, no doubt, about to become his new best mates—he's familiar with diocesan leaders worldwide, and they know that his instructions brook no 'interpretation'.

Literal will be the name of the game, and efficiency will be the password.

I wonder what name he'll take.

Pope Adolph the First?

Unworthy of you, Mario. Five decades of the rosary. The Sorrowful Mysteries.

That completed, I wonder which new high-ranking apostolate he'll entrust to Olivier.

Nuncio to Luxembourg, perhaps?

Thursday, April 1st

Feast of Saint Mary of Egypt (344–421).

Another movie here. Or even a musical. Some saints... well, surprise! Mary was the beautiful, spoiled, cynical, disenchanted, rich daughter who was the centre of her family's pride, and who repaid them by running away from home at the age of 12. I like her already. Her escapade took her to Alexandria where she worked as a dancer (stripper of its time, I assume) singer (note: accuracy optional) and prostitute (a sexy girl for others) carrying out her calling servicing religious pilgrims from Palestine and Jerusalem. I doubt she was the first to provide such services to tourists. On the feast of the Exaltation of the Cross, on the lookout for customers at church, Mary mingled, professionally, among the crowds. Now for the moment of metanoia. Mary decides to enter the church but finds herself repelled at the door. She is suddenly overcome with shame for her life of commercial pleasure and she repents. Good. Praying for guidance from Our Lady, Mary hears a voice telling her that to find counsel, she should cross the Jordan River. Obediently, she does, enters the desert and takes up the life of a hermit for 50 years. Now that's what I call quite a penance and a tribute to the faith and fortitude of this previously worldly and now holy woman. Pious but inevitably unreliable tradition assures us Mary lived on herbs, berries, and whatever came to hand. In the desert, probably little else did. Apparently, she met Saint Zosimus of Palestine (no son of mine will be christened Zosimus) whom at one stage she told to return exactly one year from that particular day. She'd clearly not totally lost her professional authority. He did, only to find that she'd died after a long and adventurous life. With the help of a lion (MGM?) Zosimus dug her grave and buried her. A lovely touch. Shrewdly, he wrote her biography—presumably with juicy details though just sufficiently airbrushed to stimulate—and to no one's surprise, it became something of a bestseller in the Middle Ages. And why wouldn't it? What an amazing life! Let's face it, Sweet Charity could take her correspondence course from St Mary of Egypt. This extraordinary woman must surely be named the patron saint of strippers and prostitutes. Before I check out, I'll approach the relevant dicastery for confirmation. Our church has patrons for every profession. Dear me, I fear I'm becoming quite light-headed. But, yes, there is, indeed, hope for all us sinners.

In the circumstances, fallow.

Friday, April 2nd

Feast of Saint Francis of Paola, Hermit (1416–1507).

Not by a long shot my favourite saint nor the cleric you'd choose to sit next to at dinner, but a holy man of ferocious faith and equally iron will power. Young Francis of Paola in Southern Italy was brought up *by his parents to be a very devout boy. At the age of twelve, he spent a year in a Franciscan (of Assisi, not Paola) monastery, something that strikes me as somewhat unhealthy for a pre-pubescent boy. Anyway, as a teenager, he demonstrated all forms of holiness and by twenty, he was living in a local cave where his ascetic lifestyle attracted similarly inclined men. Total self-abnegation was what they saw to be their calling and total it sure was. Naturally, they took the usual vows of poverty, chastity, and obedience, but some might observe that almost <u>un</u>naturally, they took a fourth vow all year long and all lifelong to abstain from meat, eggs, butter, cheese, milk, and all dairy products. I assume wine was never served with meals. Not a morning was to be welcomed with a hearty breakfast, nor an occasional feast day with modest feast or bounty. They went barefooted and slept on boards. This was mortification on a heroic scale: penance for the sins of the world. Their food was prayer. Discuss. In addition to prayer and fasting, Francis of Paola was also known as a miracle worker, though probably not in the kitchen. For his extraordinary sanctity (and, presumably, perseverance) he was canonised in 1519 twelve years after his death, and in 1562 in the name of God, French Calvinists desecrated his tomb. So excessively ascetic was he, Francis of Paola probably couldn't have cared less. As someone observed, he lived perpetual Lent. As I said, not a religious lifestyle I'd find appealing—surely joy and gratitude are equally God's gifts to be savoured—and I doubt Sister Angelica would be accepted into his feminine order, and I fear Ennio would find a number of the restrictions exceedingly restricting, but I guess if some earnest folk believe that a self-flagellating lifestyle is a path to heaven, then I suppose they should be left alone to what I judge to be their limited and limiting theology, but then I'm not the pope, so my view doesn't much matter these declining days. The question I can't avoid asking myself, and now clearly need reminding myself, is that if a life of excessive penance on earth is a path to the joys of heaven, wouldn't that transform heaven into hell? Some day in the increasingly near future I'll be able to question Saint Francis of Paola on this matter.*

The conclave opens tomorrow, and I think that Olivier has made a significant mistake in an interview published yesterday morning in *La Croix Internationale* and which, of course, he knew would go viral.

He said he believed that what the church now needs is an extended papacy of benevolent authority and ecclesiastical stability focusing on priestly vocations from Africa, a gift to the church from that grateful continent.

Not, I think, a vote winner in Europe.

Last night on RAI news, Mendoza neatly replied that every vocation to the priesthood is a gift from God. As a church, we are above nationalism. The God of love knows no boundaries and in His infinite wisdom transcends all man-made barriers.

There's a neon lit subtext in *man-made!*

Mendoza went on to say that we are all one in the Lord, and nationality dissolves in God's embrace.

Then, for good measure, he added that the time has come for the church to commit totally to synods of the people of God, to rethinking its attitude to sexuality, especially including the LGBTIQ+ faithful and to being realistic about welcoming women to the priesthood.

Touché.

Perfect timing, and quite the clincher, I'd say.

Every cardinal now knows what they'll get from either Olivier or Mendoza.

The choice couldn't be clearer, and momentum must be with Mendoza.

Now the praying begins, the trading heats up and the waiting drags on.

I'd give it three days.

Four max.

April 3rd

Feast of Blessed Drogo of Baume (10th century) who, perhaps following in the footsteps of Saint Mary of Egypt, led a young life of outrageous and dissolute pleasure.

As you do. Well, some of us. And following those years of erotic exertions, he became a Benedictine monk and was noted for his piety, not infrequently the other side of the youthfully promiscuous coin. We're told that sometime around 950, the now exhausted but holy Drogo (another one of those names I won't be bestowing on any of my male progeny) received a vision of St Benedict of Nursia endorsing Drogo's lifestyle conversion. He wasn't martyred. Except to pleasure.

Dear God,

I know You're expecting this prayer and I know that You know in advance what I'm going to ask. And I know that for You in Your omnipotence and me in my largely papal impotence, I've been a second-rate pontiff and more than a bit of a disappointment. But, Lord, please, <u>please</u> ensure that the right choice of the new pope is made.

And we both know whom I mean.

The good work of Francis must advance, and a return to the church militant over the pilgrim church together with fortress Vatican with an African twist is—as, of course, You know—bonkers.

Worse, it will ensure that the current haemorrhaging from the pews of middle-aged males, and worse, even more of the young will part company with their church, at least in Europe.

In Your mercy, God my hope and my desperation, guide Your cardinals in discernment and wisdom, and if at all possible, make them get a move on.

Sorry for the advice, but an early vote will be proof that Your church is definitely heading in the right direction.

Lord, bless Sister Angelica and thank You for Your grace which flows in her endlessly inventive recipes and her extraordinarily helpful eavesdroppings.

Bless the love of Ennio and Mirella and thank You for ensuring that Ennio is such a strong support and intimate confidant to this mess of a human being, though I've come to the conclusion that, You and the angels apart, just about everyone else on the planet is also weak and confused and a total mess as your humble servants. I've also discovered that those who are seemingly the strongest are, in reality, the weakest. They just put on a front. But then I don't need to tell You that, and come to think of it, I don't mean any criticism… I think I've finally come to accept that all humans are… well, human.

Sure, it's been staring me in the face for so long, You'd think I might have opened my eyes (and my heart) a little earlier.

Sorry it's taken so much time to see the obvious.
Still, while there's life, there's hope.

Hopefully.

Amen.

And cin cin!

Sunday, April 4th

Feast of Saint Plato—not the pre–Christian Greek one (Is he worthy of canonisation? Discuss.) but the Christian one in the 8th century (734–813).

A wealthy orphan at 13, Plato was raised by his financially astute uncle only to quickly surpass him in commercial shrewdness. But Plato was also a pious youth and aged 24, he put the court behind him, freed his slaves (imagine the current equivalent) sold up, gave the money to his sisters and the poor, and then moved into a monastery as a layman. Now that's humility and faith in buckets. He undertook menial labour, fasting and penance. He kept his financial hand in family matters, but when there were moves to make him a bishop, he headed back to the monastery. The rich family of one of his sisters also decided to commit to monasticism. He was imprisoned for not accepting the Emperor Constantine's divorce (always a touchy subject between clergy and monarchs) and was imprisoned until the death of the emperor. When the Saracens invaded, Plato and his monks moved, and he became a recluse in a small cell, living a life of perpetual prayer and manual labour with one foot fastened to the ground with a heavy iron chain, though he disguised this with a cloak when he was visited. I must say that with the recently weird exception of three or four frankly strange monks living in caravans in the windswept islands off the north east of Scotland, I can't see this way of life appealing to what remains of the religious youth of today, though I may be wrong. But God knows I'm not. Anyway, Plato then got into even deeper political and theological trouble and was persecuted, banished and finally returned to his monastic life of prayer and penance. If we are to believe tradition, when he felt death approaching, he dug his own grave, had himself carted to it and laid there for days praying and receiving guests, and then died after either a long or short lying in state. Extraordinary. I'm not sure though that Saint Plato is a role model for today, but religious fervency—and, arguably, religious madness—remain with the church, and our current anarchic state might well reassure St Plato in heaven that he lived a sane and relatively uneventful life. The way I feel now, I might not disagree with him. Who knows? Perhaps St Plato is now fervently praying for me. Go, St Plato!

How and where does she find these gifts of God? Tonight's bounty was grilled eggplant with garlic yoghurt sauce. Aubergines, Sister Angelica casually mentioned, are, as she supposed I knew, guides to wise decision making. We must hope that inside the conclave, aubergines are served for breakfast, lunch and dinner.

Black smoke as expected, but the gloves are off.

The people who matter now are the promoters of the two main candidates, and their focus is naturally on those wavering voters. The ballot is secret, but of course the conclave more or less knows the disposition of most of the electors, so from my limited experience, *discussions* tend to combine diplomatic generalities and practical church projections with gentle then firm arm twisting: think St Peter behind the message and Machiavelli behind the party machine.

The other person of potential interest is the poor sod who might finish up as the papal ham in the shit sandwich (a traditional Wollongong recipe) if neither main candidate can deliver enough votes.

In this case, it's Jean-Franz Hoffmann of Luxembourg, and if he's anything like me—a pleasant nonentity—I know how he feels, and it's a sick feeling in the pit of your stomach combined with a sudden insight that the Holy Spirit has headed south for a long weekend and left heaven's least competent angel to referee the sacred mud wrestling.

Boy, do you pray, and there's no false modesty in the cry, 'Lord, I am not worthy' because in your heart, you know you're not.

And if you've got half a brain, you immediately realise that should you land the job, you'll have two opposing teams match fit to chuck you out of the ring every time you try a new or old move in your papacy.

If that's what's in any way happening at the moment, poor old Jean-Franz will be thinking of gallant and boring little Luxembourg as the razzle-dazzle Paris of the north and be keen to hot foot it back to the false teeth capital of the world.

And he'll be right to do so.

Two votes tomorrow.

It would be wonderful were one of them white smoke. After all, our church teaches us to believe in miracles.

Prayer hands pressed, and fingers crossed.

Monday, April 5th

Feast of Saint Vincent Ferrer, Priest (c1350–1419).

What an almost divine accident! God must have a rich sense of humour. If ever a feast day verged on the appropriate, today has to be up there! This Spaniard was a good scholar and a brilliant Dominican preacher. He slept on the floor, fasted endlessly, performed miracles, and converted thousands. Of course. But he was also extremely broadminded for his time and studied Islam and Judaism, converting many of those traditions' believers to Christianity. Given the arguably (wrong) theology of the time, good so far, but then sinful humanity declares its foul hand. Welcome to the great western schism of 1378–1418: forty years of papal pandemonium with holy people genuinely divided on who the valid pope really was. Saint Vincent himself even changed sides to support the Avignon pontiff, Benedict XIII, but he was declared an anti-pope by the church and excommunicated. Backing losers isn't the best look for a popular preacher, still Saint Vincent continued to travel and preach, and his undoubted holiness triumphed over his ecclesiastically political clumsiness. The message seems to be to avoid papal squabbles at all costs. Physician, heal thyself. Ah! Healing. Not for everyone, it would seem. Well, we'll soon see.

Black smoke again this morning, but at this very moment as I write, white smoke is rejoicing out of the chimney.

Am writing this seconds after the first white puff triumphed through the pipe and rose prayerfully into a clear Roman sky.

I smile at Sister Angelica who smiles back, relieved.

I wink at Ennio who smiles, nods and gives me the thumbs up.

And how nice to be right for once: new pope elected on the fifth ballot—proof of strong backing, the result of careful campaigning and then polished performance within the conclave.

The huge crowd in front of St Peter's is wild with joy as we all wait for our new pope to appear on the balcony.

Once the candidate has accepted his papal election in the Room of Tears (aptly named, believe me), he'll put on one of the set of three white papal vestments (small, medium and large), receive the genuflected loyalty of each of the cardinals (how I'd love to see Olivier's face as he kneels to kiss the new pope's ring!) then the senior cardinal deacon will tell the world, *Habemus papam,* announce the name he has taken, at which point our new pontiff will appear on the balcony to the ecstasy of everyone present (except one disappointed Cameroonian cardinal) and of the Catholic world—and even beyond that.

And I'm the only living ex-pope watching this event with satisfaction and delight, and my successor will meet the world any minute now.

I haven't been so happy since… whenever.

My heart is high. My soul rejoices in the Lord.

Deo gratias.

And the name he takes will trumpet his agenda—instant shorthand for the duration of his papacy.

Francis the Second, perhaps, or John the Twenty-Fifth would be my each-way bets.

Any moment now!

No! No! No! **NO!**

It's not happening.

What an almighty clusterfuck!

Has the Holy Spirit totally lost his celestial marbles?

Has the church gone mad?

Olivier is Pope Pius the Thirteenth.

There is no God.

After the announcement, in this room there was the most painful silence I've ever not conversed in.

The three of us said nothing for I have no idea how long.

Frozen, bewildered, despairing in the depth of our disbelief, we just stared at the screen.

Forever.

Then, whenever, out of time, the Holy Spirit descended, slowly, gracefully.

In my heart, I said a prayer of acceptance.

In obedience, I genuflected in absentia to Pope Pius the Thirteenth, 267th servant of the servants of God.

Sister Angelica left the room in purposeful cuisine mode.

Ennio nodded to me—understanding? farewelling? Mirella?—and silently left.

I drowned in universal nothingness, seeing nothing, thinking nothing, being nothing.

I became the absence of myself, not the presence.

Impossibility following impossibility.

An out-of-faith experience.

The will of the Lord.

I shall lie down.

Later this mad day.

I feel I don't know what now—in space or at least in a bewildering space simultaneously weightless, yet oppressive.

Am I a shadow or a corpse?

Whichever, I must aspire to such dignity as I can fake.

After dinner.

Dinner was a Sister Angelica special, and she took pleasure in explaining that her smashed cucumber salad required repeatedly heavy bashing which she took great pleasure in delivering on the poor Lebanese cucumbers. Apparently, the more cuts a vegetable receives, the more the dressing can burrow into the flesh.

I got the strong impression she wished exquisitely transferred pain on the wretched *légume.*

The salad, however, was bitterly delicious.

Tuesday, April 6th

A day I'm unlikely to forget.

Every detail and every word are seared into my soul.

My daughter arrived unannounced only to immediately announce that she'd decided *on the necessary course to take in the circumstances.*

I said that in the circumstances, I couldn't disagree.

On her way out, she passed Olivier, now Pope Pius XIII, also arriving unannounced.

I thought he was unnecessarily brusque in dismissing Sister Angelica from the room, and his opening remark sounded like a medieval pope's declaration of excommunication.

'Holiness, let me be clear from the start. I don't intend to go down the friendship path of Francis and Benedict, such as it was. In our case, both parties to such a fiction would be hypocritical, so in order to avoid any misunderstanding, Holiness, you need to know that this will be our only conversation.'

No ambiguity there.

He continued confidently.

'You have everything here you need then?'

I replied that I lacked for nothing except that the company of Ennio seems to have disappeared.

'Halbadier Caspari's family underwent a crisis of some kind. It was imperative he return to Lugano. Naturally, I authorised his immediate release from the regiment.'

He never mentioned any domestic upheaval to me.

'Such is life. Now, in the light of your failed papacy and given the result of the recent conclave, there are four matters needing to be resolved this morning.'

Our meeting must have lasted for an hour and a half, but I'll leave aside such awkward pleasantries as there were and cut to the chase.

Before that, however, I should mention that with Olivier and Sister Angelica, it was dislike at first sight.

No, controlled hatred. And not all that controlled.

When she brought in coffee and her famed almond biscotti, Olivier said, 'I prefer tea. Black and strong, thank you.'

You could have sliced the ice in the air as she exited.

She did, however, immediately return, and in apparent conciliatory mode.

What followed that abrupt introduction, I'll recount as I remember our conversation.

Editor's note: although Pope John XXIV's memory is/was extraordinarily accurate, the reader may rest assured that what follows is not what Pope John claims to remember, but his verbatim conversation with Pope Pius XIII. This is verifiable as later events will authenticate with unrefutable evidence. It begins with the return of Sister Angelica.

Avanti.

SISTER ANGELICA

Pardon me for interrupting, Holiness.

What is it, Sorella?

SISTER ANGELICA

I wish to offer as a gift to His Holiness on his election: my crostata cantarella. I suddenly remembered that Guido Pasquale, cook to His Holiness Pope Innocent the Ninth, invented the recipe, and it was much spoken of at the time.

As it is now, Holiness. Unequalled in gastronomic delight. You will quite rightly celebrate your election with this unique desert.

'If I recall correctly, Innocent the Ninth died two months after his election.'

SISTER ANGELICA

It was just a fleeting thought, Holiness.

'As was the papacy of Innocent the Ninth.'

If I might offer Your Holiness just one and only one piece of advice for your papacy: Sister Angelica's crostata will lift your heart. And I can guarantee that there will be no left-overs.

'Very well then. Thank you, Sorella. I shall accept His Holiness's one and only once piece of advice. And now, His Holiness and I need to confer in private.

SISTER ANGELICA

Thank <u>you</u>, Holiness.

'So, to my first matter requiring resolution. Your subversive plan for an enquiry into the death of John Paul the First. You are never to mention it again, and I shall ensure the commission will be buried.'

Like him.

'The matter is settled.'

All except the facts.

'The facts are that it was a heart attack. There was no cover-up.'

If there was no cover-up, then there should be no fear of an investigation. It will close all legitimate concern.

'Conspiracy theorists like you wilfully ignore the simple fact that unexpected events happen all the time and they're in no way related. It's called life. Coincidence is not cause. Your lot search to find connection where there is none. The Agatha Christie syndrome. But that's fiction, not life. I'm visiting you today. Like anyone else on earth, I could drop dead tomorrow, but that wouldn't mean my visit here caused my demise. God calls us in His good time, and that's a mystery we have to accept, like it or not. It's entirely out of our hands. So grow up. Get over it. And be absolutely clear: there will be no investigation. The matter is closed. Besides, the pontificate of John Paul's saintly successor, Karol Wojtyla, was a twenty-seven-year blessing bestowed on the church.'

And his cover-up of sexual abuse among the clergy—sin and crime on what now seems like an industrial scale, even in the Vatican gardens—was that a blessing?

'Saint John Paul the second is in heaven. Such matters as he may have overlooked…'

Such matters as promoting the American Archbishop Mc-Carrick to cardinal when he had evidence of the man's serial seduction of young seminarians…

'In hindsight, Saint John Paul's judgment probably erred on the side of charity, but…'

Probably!

'Leave him to heaven. Let he who is without sin cast the first stone. On which subject, however, I've always wondered: what <u>was</u> the real reason for your removal from Australia?

Promotion.

'Whatever.'

It was a misunderstanding.

'That's usually code for…'

Misunderstanding.

'You'd rather not say.'

It's not unknown in these parts.

'The code?'

What is missed from the understanding. Humanity. Compassion. In other words, clerical politics.

'You seem to be its serial victim.'

The conclave giveth. The curia taketh away.

'They protect the pontiff.'

The Vatican's a grim place. Heavy on piety. Short on joy. The place has two gravities.

'Heaven and earth.'

No. Performance and control. And against little opposition, by far the most heavenly performance would have to be the cuisine of Sister Angelica.

'I must hope that woman's food is warmer than her personality.'

Sister Angelica is loyal, but she has been… wounded by life. She has been especially distressed by the circumstances of my resignation.

'I don't see what business that is of hers. And so, as I was saying, to my second and third matters.'

Being?

'Cancellations. Planning for the council will cease. I've already set the wheels in motion. The church's traditional condemnation of homosexuality will be enforced, and at the same time, the nonsense about ordaining women will, once again, be a strictly forbidden subject. On each of these matters, you will maintain obedient silence. *Entendu?* '

Understood. Though who understands it remains a moot point.

'Your characteristically Australian ambivalence. I believe it's called 'an each-way bet'.

Or intellectual honesty.

'No. Spiritual confusion.'

Our understanding of the world develops. There was a time when deformed—what we now call *disabled* children—were seen as God's punishment for their parents' sins.

'By superstitious parents, perhaps, but never in official church teaching.'

And with AIDS. And homosexuality?

'The rot set in with Francis. Ambivalence incarnate with his "Who am I to judge?"'

A Christlike question, surely?

'The answer to which was staring him in the face. Call it what it is. What is unnatural is unnatural.'

A characteristically unambiguous African mindset, might I say?

'A universal truth which, if you haven't looked further than permissive Europe, ninety per cent of the world believes.'

I'd question that. Just as Francis did.

'Francis was a different kind of pope: an anti-pope pope. And, happily, he has been called to his Maker. We live in the present. And so to the third matter. But just for the record, may I ask whether there's something… anything left in our sacred tradition that you actually <u>believe</u> in? I mean, might you, perhaps believe that the seal of the confessional may never be broken?'

Never.

'In any circumstances?'

Never ever.

'Assure me that 'never ever' means 'never ever in any circumstances whatsoever'.

Never ever <u>in any circumstances whatsoever</u>.

'Then the age of miracles has not passed. At least we share
one article of faith.'

Yes.

'Deo gratias.'

Holiness… Olivier…

'Holiness.'

Holiness… if we'd ever dreamt our friendship would come
to this…

'Yes, our friendship was special. At the time. In the strange
way friendships can be. Two priests trapped in a revolving
door. But friendships change… Mario.'

Thank you.

'We exit the door on opposite sides. Friendship's a need for
the moment. Dogma is truth for eternity. Growing up must
be spiritual as well as physical and emotional.'

All growing up's difficult for celibates.

'As you may have guessed at the time, I wasn't celibate.'

You were frank in our conversation back then, and you explained your justification for your conduct: male African physical and emotional need. Besides, a non-celibate candidate is hardly a papal first.

'In my case, it was the first of many... encounters.'

As a priest?

'As an African male. From the age of sixteen. And yes, as a priest.'

Holiness, the walls have ears. For all we know, the CIA could be eavesdropping on our every word.

'Or others.'

Meaning?

'Your papal apartment. Domus Santa Marta. This place. They were all bugged. Don't worry, they're clean now. First thing after my election, I had them all swept. Self-interest. But you need to know that what you deemed to be your private conversations have all been overheard. Indeed, intimate conversations, Holiness.'

I see.

'My carnal failings have at least been discreet. And more to the point, I have the courage to call them what they are and always have been. Sin.'

The need and its fulfilment are surely an argument for married priests. Besides, massage was the only way I could arrive at what little sleep was granted me.

'Celibacy's a challenge. The flesh is weak. Our faith is counter-cultural. We fight. We fall. We rise again.'

Why are you telling me all this?

'Full papal disclosure. After all, truth must always be our currency.'

I still can't work out why you're telling me all this?

'As I said, truth, honesty, prudence...'

And, perhaps, insurance?

'A pope must consider all options to protect the church above any personal limitations he may have. But, yes, I entertain the hope that someday your sanity will return. And then, perhaps, your faith. But also... in the dying embers of our friendship, perhaps we may have come to a kind of a confessional full stop. Pope to pope.'

My understanding of your initial full stop this morning was that it was just that: a first and last full stop.

'It's easy to be lax and laissez-faire. I'd rather be sinful but honest—the true path to salvation. And since I'm now in the business of proclaiming the truth to the world, to my predecessor I need to clean the slate by telling it.'

Am I hearing equivocation?

'If two pontiffs, no matter their differences... if they can't confess the truth to each other... if we can't, then the church has an even greater sacramental crisis than I thought.'

This isn't confession.

'It is now. And that's what I want it to be. In the circumstances, perhaps I should kneel. Bless me, Holiness, for I have sinned. For what I have confessed to you and for all my many other sins, I ask for God's forgiveness.'

Holiness, what you've told me just now was not signalled as sacramental confession.

'Then as I've just said, Holiness, let me signal that I wish it so to be.'

I'm not the confessor you should be seeking.

'But you're the confessor I seek. You've assured me your belief is that the wall of confession must never be porous. In any circumstances. I've spoken to you in confidence and wish that confidence to be my confession.'

This is irregular. This conversation should not be taking place.

'This conversion and this confession <u>have</u> taken place.'

And are you firmly resolved never to again commit what you believe to be sinful?

'Yes. Though as I said before, celibacy is always a challenge. But yes, I will try my best to… to discipline my weak humanity. This I swear to God. I will listen to His counsel and do all in my power never to sin again.' Now may I respectfully request absolution?'

Never to sin again?

'All in my power.'

Then I absolve you in the name of the Father, the Son and the Holy Ghost.

'And for my penance?'

For your penance, my brother, reflect on the fact that as well as black and white, God gave the world a rainbow. And now pray for me as I for thee. In the name of the Father, and of the Son and of the Holy Spirit, Amen.

'*Deo gratias,* Holiness.'

That was surely a graced moment.

'In every way. And you're now the guardian of information which can never be released. Under pain of excommunication and under sentence of hell fire.'

I will never break that seal.

'Then you, too, Mario, may now feel free to speak frankly. Do so. It's cleansing.'

What more have I to lose?

'Nothing. Now. Believe me.'

But outside the seal, I feel I must ask: might there be any possibility of the ancient papal need to nominate one's—what used to be called 'bastards'—as one's 'nephews'?

'Almost certainly not. My Roman theology instructed my African penis to choose the lesser of two evils. I always used condoms.'

And your… partners? What were… are… your relationships with them… now?

'*Nihil.* Nothing. All prostitutes.'

Professional sex workers.

'Prostitutes. They had no idea who I was.'

In the circumstances, that may well have been an act of considerable faith on your part.

'I was more careful than some who have risen to the papacy. But as we're speaking frankly—as, for the last time, we must—as I said, perhaps you might care to unburden yourself of <u>your</u> youthful wild oats.'

I confess—but in <u>no way</u> sacramentally… you <u>do</u> understand?

'Yes.'

You see, I have nothing further to hide.

'Then don't.'

My youthful follies were more erotic madeleines than wild oats.

'Yes, yes, yes. As with not a few of our predecessors, both of us have been there and done that. And we haven't got all day. So?'

Our old friendship.

'Yes.'

When I was sixteen at Christian Brothers' College Wollongong, I was on a Catholic leadership camp with our sister school, St Mary's. I met the most stunningly beautiful girl. Her name was Aileen. She gave me eight months and three weeks of Saturday night blow jobs.

'An experience I'm not unfamiliar with.'

Canon law refers to it as 'unnatural and disordered'.

'Therein lies the pleasure. Therein lies the sin.'

I found it totally natural and just what the doctor ordered.

'Of all people, I'd never have thought of you as…'

I thought about little else all thirty-five weeks and three days. Just as well I didn't keep a diary.

'Diaries are dangerous. And juvenile.'

Holiness, face the facts: the doorstep kiss of our grandparents' generation is now what today's youth expect as 'the Saturday night hoover'. Indeed, most sixteen-year-old males assume it as an entitlement.

'You're surprisingly *au fait* with contemporary slang.'

Young people confide in me.

'Young males, obviously.'

Anyway, it ended on Sunday, April 12th 1964. Passion Sunday.

'You finally repented.'

No. Aileen dumped me for the captain of the school swimming team. His name, ironically enough, was Xavier. Apparently, his 'athletic' skills were more… advanced than mine.

'A sad fact of fallen nature. Sport generates the need for post-game sexual release.'

Aileen was flirty but not what I'd call warm.

'You seem to attract such females. Sister Angelica seems in every way less than warm. Hardly a natural mother. Perhaps that's why she took the veil.'

Actually, she _is_ a natural mother. In her youth, she had a child out of wedlock.

'Fornication has its consequences. I'd be the last person to deny that.'

As does rape. Like its landscape, Sicily is tough country. Primitive and unforgiving. Like the cousin who raped her. Angelica's son was taken from her the moment he was born. She never saw the boy. Not once.

'Then I'm sorry for misjudging her. It was an offence against charity.'

She carries her cross daily. For Angelica, love is a wound, and hatred a prison. I think it's in service, especially cooking, that she finds some kind of maternal release. In a strange way, I think part of my vocation is to be God's companion to her.

'I will remember her in my prayers.'

And now, as we seem to have covered three of your concerns, and as I well remember how busy the early days of the papacy are, perhaps we can move to the final concerns.

'Indeed. The next is just one small technicality.'

Which is?

'I need your signature on this document.'

A tenant's agreement?

'In a way, yes. It's your solemn promise never again to express your perverse and inflammatory views on just about everything in any medium of communication whatsoever.'

My penance.

'Your liberation from error. Sign here.'

As you instruct, Holiness.

'And so to my final concern.'

Being?

'Halbadier Caspari and his… friendship.'

Ennio's taught me so much.

'Popes do not befriend young Swiss guards. At least, not since Julius III died in 1555.'

Ennio is a life force—a free spirit who makes love to life.

'As we've come to learn.'

… and like most healthy males of his age, he has a partner, Mirella.

'Among others. Why don't you just tell me the truth, Mario?'

I thought we'd…

'Mario Francis Xavier, before I dismissed Ennio, I interviewed him at length. He told me about your 'conversations.''

So?

'Everything about them. Much more, indeed, than even the ears Santa Marta's walls revealed. Popes do not receive massages from Swiss guards.'

As I explained to you, those massages helped me to sleep. But, yes, I was wrong to have arranged for Vatican money to be transferred to him. I wanted to help him buy his first apartment. So Ennio and Mirella would be happy. By the standards of most Vatican transactions, the amount was negligible. And from a private fund for the pontiff's good works. Into which, by the way, I always paid my papal salary. From time to time, you'll also find it useful. But yes, my actions were indiscreet.

'Indiscreet isn't the word. I said he told me <u>everything</u>. You're hardly the first resident of Vatican City to have succumbed to the charm of a twenty-one-year-old Swiss Guard.'

Yes, I've been lying.

'Your whole papacy was a lie.'

In one sense, perhaps, but…

'My brother, we know something's a sin when we go to so much trouble to hide it. And deny it.'

You're right. Of course. But I'm afraid the problem doesn't end there.

'Should I be concerned?'

I'm afraid I've also been less than totally truthful about my high school sexual experience. Experien<u>ces</u>.

'Go on.'

After the oral sex came…

'Love making. As it does.'

We didn't make love. We had sex. Through all thirty-five Saturdays.

'A kind of fidelity. Though I have to say I've never really thought of you as convincingly heterosexual.'

Deep down, neither did I. But at the time, I was determined to <u>be</u> one. 'Intrinsically disordered' wasn't going to be stamped on my passport to hell.

'Halbadier Caspari has come to an arrangement whereby for his continuing silence, he will receive an annual emolument to assist him in his post-military professional endeavours.'

A bribe.

'In these delicate matters, we can never be too careful. You may rest assured that any unhelpful publicity is now behind us.'

Not quite.

'Not quite'. In what way 'not quite'?'

You see, shortly after, I was replaced in the seductive Aileen's bed by the Captain of Swimming…

'Xavier.'

Yes. Aileen became pregnant. Xavier, the pool stud, was the father, and they had their daughter, Hayley, adopted. It was the way these things were done back then.

'So?'

Five years later, on a Kon Tiki tour of Europe, Xavier died of a drug overdose in an Amsterdam night club. Recently—and somewhat late in the piece, but who are we to be judgmental in these matters?—Hayley decided to meet her birth mother.

'Is this relevant?'

Very. The encounter was traumatic for both of them. It transpired that the good Catholic family Aileen had adopted Hayley out to sent her to the best Catholic convent in Wollongong.

'A blessing for the child.'

Except that in her final year, the convent's chaplain was apparently attracted to nubile young girls and made advances to her.

'I suppose that's marginally better than to boys.'

In the light of that remark, we must *certainly* both hope these walls have no ears.

'I was only…'

You said it nonetheless.

'Context is everything.'

As it proved for Hayley. When she reported the matter to the local bishop, unbelievably… totally unbelievably as it may sound—<u>impossible</u> as it sounds, but as we know, Holiness… Olivier… life invariably surpasses fiction when it comes to incredibility…

'Get to the point.'

The wretched point being that the same thing happened again. This time the bishop being the abuser.

'Dear God, if only it <u>was</u> unbelievable.'

If only. To prevent Hayley going to the press, His Grace came to a confidential financial arrangement with her. It was to last as long as her silence.

'Confidential.'

As long as her silence. There would appear to be a pattern here.

'Go on.'

But by then, Hayley was wounded—and shrewd enough—to ensure everything which had occurred was legally documented. Insurance.

'And returning to her meeting with her birth mother?'

At that meeting, Aileen told Hayley who her real father was.

'I see.'

Aileen then informed <u>me</u>.

'But why didn't Aileen get in touch with you years ago?'

I'd entered the seminary. As a father, I'd have been a somewhat distant relative. And Xavier's family were both good Catholic doctors. They believed what they were told and acquiesced in the adoption.

'And now?'

And now my daughter intends to sue the Vatican in the International Court of Justice. I'll almost certainly be called as a witness.

'Extradition from the Vatican isn't possible.'

Voluntary appearance on Zoom is.

'That would be… unhelpful.'

Unless, of course, I die first.

'As I said, each or both of us could die tomorrow. That's in the hands of the Lord.'

The fact is, Holiness, the faeces have hit the fan.

'Thank you for sharing that distinctly Australian insight. But my sins are now protected. Yours, it would seem, are about to be trumpeted to the world at large'.

Through no fault of my own.

'A moot point, though in the present circumstances, neither here nor there. Fortunately, should the worse come to the worst, your vow of silence must prevail.'

Qui tacet consentire. Silence means consent.

'Your signed vow protects you.'

Protects the church. Well, arguably. Though as you must surely realise, only canon lawyers would buy that flimsy defence. And once my daughter begins her legal proceedings, to the best of my knowledge, canon lawyers don't write newspaper, TV or radio headlines. And as for social media…

'There may be a need for correspondence in this matter.'

I understand. *(knock on door)* Avanti.

SISTER ANGELICA

Your crostata Santità. Forester's tart made from wild raspberries and blackberries marinated in strega and dusted with the finest *zucchero a velo*. I had made it this morning for His Holiness, but I'm sure he would wish you to enjoy it.

Which I do. As I said, it's Sister Angelica's *pièce de résistance,* Holiness. The nearest a pope can get to gastronomic mortal sin while remaining in the state of grace.

'Holiness, by now all dimensions of this theological debate are best left behind us. Grazie, Suor Angelica. I shall enjoy it tonight with my supper.'

SISTER ANGELICA
Grazie ancora Santità, e buon appetito.

'You may leave. His Holiness will see me out.'

SISTER ANGELICA
Grazie, Sancticà .

'So may I ask? That woman on the staircase… she wasn't… surely…?'

Yes. My daughter, Hayley.

'I see. Don't get up. I'll see myself out. Oh, I almost forgot. There's one other small matter we must address before I leave.'

'Small' is to be welcomed.

'What we know as 'informed Vatican sources'…'

Our lavender cardinals.

'… such sources make mention of an… unfortunate photo of a recent German pontiff and his handsome Teutonic archbishop secretary… a photo which in the wrong hands might possibly be deemed to be… compromising.'

It was, I'm sure, an innocently fraternal embrace. The sort of greeting or farewell the majority of liberated males now engage in without embarrassment.

'Of course. Nonetheless, in the wrong hands, a fraternal moment perhaps open to misinterpretation should it ever find its way into the secular media.'

 Which is why...

'... which is why with fraternal authority, Holiness, I order you to immediately hand over the original to me. Now. In holy obedience.'

Holiness, when I became pope, almost the first Italian word the curia taught me was *ricatto.*

'I will not...'

Ricatto. Blackmail.

'You will not...'

Sadly, a hallowed Vatican tradition.

'This pope will not be blackmailed.'

Of course not. But in the circumstances...

'What 'circumstances'?'

Ours. Trust me, I shall guard that particular photo to protect those involved. And also to protect myself from any... any 'unfortunate accident' which might befall me. Self-interest. Insurance. In these delicate matters, we can never be too careful.

'You seem to have come to politics late in the day.'

Very late. Though by now, well taught.

'Power is given to us. God given. Rest assured, we shall use that power.'

Your blessing before you depart.

'Such blessings as we might be to each other henceforth are indeed hidden in the mystery of faith. Goodbye, Holiness. *Dominus vobiscum.*'

Et cum spiritu tuo.

PIUS exits.

Door knock.

Avanti. Yes, Sorella?

SISTER ANGELICA
Santità, will you be so kind as to hear my confession?

Perhaps it can wait till later, Sorella?

SISTER ANGELICA
If Your Holiness can spare me the time, I would like to unburden my soul.

Sorella, already this day's burden has been heavy. I'm sure the sacrament will be even more efficacious tomorrow.

SISTER ANGELICA
I fear not, Santità.

Have no fear, Sorella. "Trust in the Lord with all your heart, and do not lean too heavily on your own understanding. In all your ways acknowledge Him, and He will make straight your paths."

SISTER ANGELICA
But if I do lean on my own understanding?

He will make straight your path. Trust to His way. God's will is God's will, not ours. We can only do our best and accept what the Lord allows.

SISTER ANGELICA

I hope so, santità.

Be strong and let your heart take courage.

SISTER ANGELICA

He will make straight my path.

More than I always do, Sorella, I'll pray for you especially in my mass tomorrow. And so, good night and God bless.

SISTER ANGELICA

Thank you, Santità.

Editor's note. Here, Pope John's diary entries remain true to his every addition, but the authenticity of conversations inside his convent also remains verifiable and will soon be validated.

Wednesday, April 7th

My mobile—still can't bring myself to say 'cell phone—rang at 6.07 this morning: an uncharacteristically disturbed Dario telling me that he'd just been informed that Pope Pius XIII was found dead in his bedroom this morning.

I heard the information but at the same time couldn't grasp the reality.
It suddenly becomes unreal.
No, surreal.
John-Paul I all over again?
Only yesterday, Olivier had lectured me on unexpected events, coincidence not being cause… I remember his words 'I could drop dead tomorrow, but that wouldn't mean my visit here caused my demise.'
He talked about God calling us in His good time and our need for acceptance of His will.
Sermons are one thing; events something other. Like John-Paul I, Olivier was surely in good health for a man of his age.

What on earth will the world make of this, and how will the Vatican handle such an implausible… unimaginable… what's the word?

Scandal?

Too tepid by miles.

Coincidence beyond all credibility?

Way beyond.

God moving in a mysterious way His wonders to perform?

An impossible sales pitch when it's almost a carbon copy of a previously unprecedented papal passing.

I said I'd delay my morning mass and asked Dario to come straight over here with such details as he could quickly gather. I'm assuming there's nothing melodramatic about the circumstances—struggle, murder weapon… what Olivier referred to as my Agatha Christie syndrome. And, of course, the post mortem will be carried out by a Vatican doctor, so…

Exactly.

Once again, the Vatican investigating itself.

Nothing to see here.

My mind is a blur, yet in that fog I see with instant clarity that all the world's conclave cardinals are still in Rome. That despite its unthinkableness, a new conclave is the only possible course of events. That the two likely candidates must surely be Mendoza and Luxembourg's John-Franz Hoffman.

In the midst of tragedy, calculation.

But is it tragedy?

Am I kidding myself?

Yes, I feel shock but not grief. Not pain. Not loss. Far from it. I'm just trapped in a moment of history. Life as theatre. Theatre as life. Whatever. And I should feel the immediate need for prayer, yet that response seems buried.

In desperation for meaning, I'd put my trust in the Holy Spirit, but…

Stand back, Mario. Let this aberrant reality play out.

Such meaning as there may be… I don't know what.

Later today.

Sister Angelica brought in my coffee and gave the impression of being somewhat shocked but nevertheless accepting of God's plan.

Her faith is firm but uncomplicated. If only mine were as simple and as strong.

While she's aware of the drama of this event, she's certainly free from anything approaching sympathy for Olivier, unlike her ongoing suspicion of the similarly early death of John Paul I whom, when she was a younger Vatican nun, she knew and revered.

This time, however, she sees the hand of God pointing to the election of a less unsympathetic pontiff, and I must also take into account that she makes no apology for her antipathy to Olivier's campaign for my resignation.

As with her cuisine, her outlook is bold, confident… indeed, not to be confronted, or if so, only on her own infallible terms.

I know the feeling although I…

But that's said and done and past.

Sister Angelica's faith combines her inflexible understanding of God's will with her unique interpretation of the precise virtues of heaven-sent ingredients. Sentimentality abandoned her in her youthful affliction, and that I totally empathise with. Wise woman that she is, here where the world will triumphantly leap to see conspiracy, Sister Angelica sees providence.

And what does Philosophy 101 advise?

Occam's Razer.

The simplest explanation is usually the best one.

We can only hope so.

In any event, the official coronial report is likely to be quick.

I once again apologized to Sister Angelica for not hearing her confession yesterday, but she was gracious and said that my decision was the right one and that she, too, had much on her mind at the time and shouldn't have bothered me. I offered my services later today, but she said all was now well and that she needed to get on with her humble tasks. I replied that God resists the proud but gives grace to the humble, and to my surprise, she quoted Second Corinthians: 'My grace is sufficient for thee, for my strength is made perfect in weakness.'

Touché.

And at this point, Dario arrived.

Later.

The Vatican's leading forensic pathologist, Professor Guido Leoni—daily communicant, but within these walls, universally regarded as independent—has been immediately commissioned to find the cause of death, and with Vatican approval, he has insisted on the expert opinion of two external and totally independent Italian specialists, neither of whom is Catholic or in any way associated with the Vatican.

The first is Professor Lorenzo Costanzo from Sapienza, the University of Rome. The second is Professor Valentino Gallintari from University of Rome Tor Vergata. Professor Valentino also writes on the history of medicine and pharmacy.

It's expected that all three will report within five days or so.

That is certainly a prudent initiative clearly undertaken to deflect the inevitable criticism of foul play. I doubt it will prevent the tsunami of international clamour, but the fact is that after last time, the Vatican has no other options.

Meanwhile, the papal apartment Olivier moved into only yesterday is now undergoing a thorough clearing out. Apparently, files are being packed into boxes at a rate of knots. We certainly won't be seeing them again in the near future.

Amazing how, in a once-in-a-whatever crisis, this medieval establishment can jump to it and demonstrate intergalactic efficiency.

Amazing. And, dare I say, not unconcerning.

Dario tells me that Olivier's campaigning was relentless and that the word is that he's been not ungenerous with unholy spiritous self-support. Not that I'd criticise him too harshly for that. But that despite his fine figure—for his age, he's not without, shall we say, a certain athletic African *bella figura* swagger... which, in its way, makes sensual sense—he's known, late in the night, to consume surprising amounts of self-medication.

We all have our failings.

My mind jumps from conspiracy to confusion to fantasy to...

But such options are unworthy and must be dismissed.

So... the sudden death of a new pontiff aside, the resurrection of a new conclave contest is already well and truly up and running, albeit with less than convincing crocodile tears for the recently deceased.

Mendoza must surely be the favoured candidate, with Luxembourg a long way behind second. That said, balances change, and younger cardinals look to the future, especially when the next candidate is unlikely to enjoy a long pontificate.

So in the few frantic days ahead, who is the ideal compromise?

They'll surely chose a venerable but terminal seat warmer, and it has to be miraculous Mendoza, but his putative pontificate must surely be measured in months... well, surely a year or two or three at most.

Even miraculous cures end in in heavenly release—not least in these parts. And just now, I see our challenged but less than universally united church poised between two totally divisive paths, either one of them not offering harmony on almost every front.

The so-called Reformation—for which I'm not without sympathy on many issues—was nothing compared with today's impending train wreck schism.

It'll be gloves off, dirt files at the ready and for the next three weeks or so, gourmet Roman restaurants will be offering private dining rooms at exorbitant prices.

But Mendoza's our candidate, and short of some dramatic and unlikely fall from electoral grace, he must surely win on the first or second ballot.

An extended conclave would reveal a church approaching suicidal division.

In my confected mourning, I'm confident that this time, the Holy Spirit will get it right.

Thursday, April 8th

Feast of no saint I find drawn to. Mea maxima culpa, but saints are meant to inspire, and right now I need inspiration not pedestrian piety.

I'm not superstitious and I don't want to tempt fate—did I, as once a pope, say that?—but everything I'm hearing adds up to Mendoza being elected, even by his adversaries, as Pope Whoever For The Shortest Time Being until the church comes to its senses and runs with the future... or whatever's left of it as our younger Catholics depart in their millions after the finest of western Catholic religious education.

If any pontiff can, perhaps only Mendoza will be able to theologically square the agnostic circle.

The assumed stop gap John XXIII transformed the church, and the stop gap and repentant Mendoza has the credentials to join the divergent exit roads into a freeway with a direction.

Friday, April 9th

Feast of St Acacius of Amida (died 421 of natural causes. Bewildering mystery, that get-out concept, 'nature'.)

Acacius helped Persian prisoners of war. To pay their ransom, he melted down the altar pieces and sacred vessels of his church. This guy was on the money. Literally. Imagine if he'd done that today. Or if I had.

Although oddly distant, indeed—uncharacteristically—almost on edge, Sister Angelica has been understandably upset by recent events. She would not unnaturally feel, perhaps, slight guilt—no, perhaps, uncharitable discomfort—about her... unwarmness to my predecessor.

Her suddenly urgent need for confession may well have prompted that disposition, but a day of such overwhelming events occurs only once in a lifetime, and there are historic moments when distance, however brief, necessarily adds perspective to the impactful drama of that historic moment.

But probably against her better judgment, she did have second thoughts. And remembering the moment, at least, with cold grace, she gave a small gastronomic peace offering to the new pope who, deep in her heart, she blamed for my removal.

As to when bounty will be about to be received, I'll just have to wait.

And more positive news. In a well-reported sermon in *Corriere della Sera*—a masterclass in purple prose, international grief and wildly international papal speculation—John-Franz of Luxembourg has discussed at length the current state of the church. He says that God has clearly spoken and that the time for conversation has passed. Now is the moment for leadership of experience and renewal in strength and clarity. The church must look for the signs of the times and respond with resolution and faith. The faithful must rejoice in their faith and practice it. Our duty is to trust to the Holy Ghost's wisdom and unite behind a new pope of vision and decision.

Decision at last!

Not too many conclave withdrawals could be louder. Or more apt.

Hoffman would be pleasantly but ditheringly hopeless. He has made straight the ways of the Lord's conclave, and everything now points to Mendoza as the man.

Of course, the losing faction will scramble for a few desperate but unlikely alternatives, but the numbers will never add up.

Thank God, it's too late.

Not even the Holy Ghost on a bad day can get this one wrong.

Saturday, April 10th

Feast of I can't be bothered looking up. Right now, the Vatican is in crisis mode, and we must all just hope that the Holy Spirit is in divinely prophetic mode or we're… but that's not my call.

No bounty as yet.

Word has reached this far that the post mortem has been concluded and the results will be announced first thing tomorrow.

Sister Angelica delivered me a note this morning from the young Vatican gardener who is Ennio's soccer playing friend and occasional sauna companion. The young man asked that no one else should know about the communication. It was in Ennio's handwriting and read: 'Mario, admit nothing. We part as friends. Mirella and I owe you much. Throughout your life, you know you can trust me. E.'

The end of an unlikely chapter of my life.

Prefect of the Council of Cardinals, German Cardinal Bruno Westphalen, has taken over the promotion of Olivier's conclave faction. Westphalen enjoys respect across the board and has few if any skeletons in his closet, but the German church is divided, and the candidate this faction is putting forward is frankly crazy:

Colorado's Cardinal Desmond Wilenski, a parody of wealthy American clerical conservatism.

There's no way the universal church could possibly accept a Pope Trump. In fact, the proposition is so ludicrous, I'm striving to find a strategy of genius behind the absurdity.

Is it a brilliant ploy to make the die-hards and the waverers suddenly look to an unlikely compromise?

Ghana's Gyasi Owusu?

Nonsense. Yes, he's African, and I suppose some would claim to see divine guidance in two African popes in succession, but he's the youngest cardinal voting, and after John Paul II's seemingly endless pontificate, no one in the curia wants to undergo that penance again. And Owusu's highly intelligent and theologically liberal but he's not the ambitious prelate who'd switch sides to snatch the papacy.

It's becoming beyond all possibility, even for the Holy Spirit.

So why this opaque contradiction?

There has to be another candidate who suddenly and miraculously appears from the centre and hopes to sweep up the votes, but for the life of me, I can't see who this embryonic messiah could be.

And what hurts is that now when it comes to conclave, my first thought is conspiracy not grace. And while I'm totally bewildered by whatever Westphalen's convoluted intrigue might be, I think he's well and truly lost in his own maze.

Too clever by two-and-a-half.

Mendoza's the nearest to a papal certainty that God and man have somehow contrived to deliver.

And not before time.

Sunday, April 11

Feast of Saint Stanislaus (1030–1079) Bishop and Martyr.

When Stanislaus excommunicated Poland's King Bolesław II over a war and the king's moral failings, Bolesław sent in his henchman to kill Stanislaus while he was saying mass. They were too scared to obey orders, so Bolesław himself murdered the bishop who is now the patron saint of Poland. There are ways and ways of removing troublesome prelates.

I've made it abundantly clear that no visitors are welcome to my convent.

I'm not the leader of the opposition in exile, I don't do interviews, and unannounced journalists, clerics, Australian tourists or prospective biographers are politely but firmly turned away by Sister Angelica.

Today, however, she surprised me.

Why should I not ever be surprised by Sister Angelica?

Well, she surprised me when she re-appeared just after breakfast to say that Professor Alison Broderick, formerly Professor of Catholic Theology at Durham University and whom I'd appointed as Prefect of the Dicastery of Doctrine of the Faith… without prior notice and with profound apologies, was downstairs and asked to see me on a matter of some urgency.

Sister Angelica said she knew of my generous response and would provide Sicilian almond biscotti and coffee.

Such enticements enticing—bounty still scarce—and against my better judgment… though Sister Angelica's better judgment becomes almost invariably my own… well, almost.

After reflection.

Anyway, I asked for a minute or so to consider breaking the inflexible rule I'd emphatically laid down.

Sister Angelica immediately headed to the door saying she would show Professor Broderick up.

'I thought I was the pope,' I replied as firmly as I could.

'So did I,' she replied with ever firmer authority and disappeared, returning immediately to usher Alison into my living room. Well, my other room of lounges, boxes and post-papal bric-a-brac.

How did I feel?

Devoid of power yet strangely joyful to welcome Alison.

I also felt in sudden need of almond biscotti and coffee.

Alison smiled and began, 'I know what you're thinking, Holiness, and with your blessing, I'd like to try and change that.'

I replied that I was glad somebody knew what I was thinking, although that somebody wasn't always me.

'Mendoza is not the answer to our prayers. Sudden conversion is a grace for the convert, but not necessarily for the institution. Mendoza has experience, but I doubt that he has the energy or the longevity to steer the church safely through the current storm.'

You discern a better candidate for the times?

'Yes.'

Let me guess. Not Hoffman, surely.

'As I said, a seat warmer's the last thing the church needs. Strength and vision need to come from the sure and balanced centre. Our deceased pope would have divided the church into black and white, literally and metaphorically. He wasn't a man to reach out. He was a ruler who valued obedience above the living and complex and individual experience of faith. Our next pontiff needs to actually be the embodiment of the pilgrim church: a man of strong intellect, calm confidence and gentle encouragement. This time round, the next pope's mintmark mustn't be gentle charisma. That's too superficial and dangerous in these times. No, that has to be the strong charisma of trust.'

I know not the man.

'But you do.'

Tell me.

'Carlos Caringal. He has all the qualities: super bright, Jesuit education in England, lawyer, financially literate, multi-lingual, calm in a crisis and by happy accident of birth, Asian. The perfect blend.'

Carlos has all those qualities and more. I think he's also holy in his modest way. But the power brokers in the curia will never vote for him. Too independent. A threat to their ambition. And by papal standards, he's far too young. Fifteen years in the job—even longer. No, the curia want a pope they can control. They took a risk with Francis, and that was far too bumpy a ride. After Mendoza, Carlos maybe yes, depending on Mendoza's significant appointments, but no. Carlos's moment isn't now.

'I pray that you're mistaken.'

In the light of my papacy, such a prayer has every chance of success.

'You wouldn't consider perhaps… well, what's the word? *Floating* the idea to the *camerlengo?* Or even just to some appropriate cardinal elector?'

It would be the kiss of death. A living ex-pope is bad enough. A failed living ex-pope even worse. And a failed living ex-pope campaigning is the stuff of dreadful Hollywood blockbusters starring yesterday's left-over and rapidly declining heart throbs from the 70s.

Retirement means closing the door behind you.

Then locking it.

'But that doesn't mean you mightn't just happen to mention it in passing to our *camerlengo?* After all, he is… what shall I say?… well, one of us.'

Gino Amato is Canadian and therefore saner than anyone from the southern hemisphere. He's also shrewd enough to realise that once he's known to support one cardinal, that candidate's on a hiding to nothing. No, Gino will be impeccably impartial. Though off the record and just between us, you can be sure that in his impeccable impartiality, he'll vote for Mendoza.

'I never heard that.'

Because I never said it.

I repeat, I have no advice to offer anyone other than to thank you for taking the trouble to visit me. It means a lot. And the future of the church lies with people of balanced judgment. I think the technical term is 'women'.

And on cue, look! Sister Angelica, coffee and biscotti.

Monday, April 12th

Feast of Saint Artemón of Caesarea.

Interesting chap. This elderly man was ordered to sacrifice to Roman gods. When Artemón refused, he was dragged to the temple of Asclepius and again ordered to sacrifice. When they released him, he attacked the statues and destroyed several before being captured, tortured and martyred. Such energy. I must ask him to intercede that such reserves of strength may yet be found in this elderly, though dying man.

Olivier's postmortem has been completed in under two days.

Slightly surprising, but… unanimity.

Well, almost unanimous unanimity.

In a much shorter time frame than was expected, three distinguished forensic pathologists have independently agreed that Pope Pius XIII died in the night of Wednesday, April 7th of cardiac arrest and that after individual and rigorously supervised and recorded autopsies—sparing here the paragraphs of meticulously compiled medical detail (which, no doubt, will now be argued from here to kingdom come)—they find no evidence of malpractice of any kind… although in an unguarded, off-camera aside (meant to be dismissive throwaway, which henceforth it never, ever will be) pharmaceutical historian, Professor Alessandro Gallintari, a distinguished historian of pharmacy, said that unless five hundred years of rigorous scientific progress have failed to discover some hitherto undetected and fantastical herb of magical extermination power, then, in the present state of scientific knowledge, further speculation is the stuff of third-rate fiction.

Then, realizing that he was still being recorded, he asked that his exhausted and ironic *obiter dicta* be immediately deleted.

Speaking as a not infrequently misquoted pope, I'd say good luck with that one.

Still conspiracy theories thrive on unlikeliness: the more fanciful, the more appealing to adventurous imaginations.

Alas, like it or not, we're back in John Paul I territory, though surely no two early papal deaths necessarily share similar suspicion.

And in my hearts of hearts and soul of souls, I'm praying that lethal medieval recipes are a fiction of the past.

Further thought is unworthy of reflection.

Saint Saint Artemón of Caesarea, please pray for me. Energetically.

Tuesday, April 13th

Feast of Saint Martin I (c. 590–655) Pope and Martyr.

Pope Martin had strong views on the two wills of Christ: theological speculation about divine and human will. I suspect salvation is just possible without a complete understanding of these abstruse conjectural alternatives. WTF are all these theological calisthenics about? Does everyone have to have a doctorate in putative pre-an-

gelology to get to heaven, even on cattle class? God knows, I bloody well hope not, otherwise the damned will include every intellectually honest questor together with every genuinely thoughtful if less-than-articulate doubter, and believe me, that's a bloody universal parish. And growing by the week. Surely a bad look for our all-loving Creator. Sorry, God. Just trying to think all this through. Anyway, Byzantine Emperor Constans II didn't agree with St Martin. The usual church-state power struggle. Constans had Martin abducted from Rome to Constantinople and proceeded to have him ritually humiliated. Martin was imprisoned, publicly flogged, constantly roughed up, condemned for treason and exiled from Constantinople to the Crimean Peninsula on the Black Sea where he died naked, starving, forgotten, and alone. Popes who rock the barque don't always make it to the shore. So what changes?

It had to happen and it will. The universal church needs the pope whose faith journey has been a saga so that his range of experience has brought him empathy and compassion.

From prosecutor to pilgrim: humanity finally understood.

Cometh the hour, cometh the pope.

There's only one answer.

Mendoza.

May he not meet the fate of St Martin I.

Wednesday, April 14th

Feast of Saint Ardalion the Actor (circa 300).

Ardalion apparently specialized in mocking Christianity on stage and was a big hit with pagan audiences. One day during a performance in Asia Minor, he suddenly announced that he had converted to Christianity. His last act was martyrdom. He died after a long season and a short finale. If I had a son, I'd consider Ardalion as a Christian name. Adventure.

Informed Vatican sources—and much more reliably, Sister Angelica—tell me that all soundings agree on the likelihood of Mendoza being elected on the first or second vote.

In the current circumstances, the church is crying out for unity and security.

And tolerance.

Also in the current circumstances and surprisingly, although, of course, I miss him, I… well… I find that I don't miss Ennio as much as I feared I would.

Normality has been reinstated.

Life has its unlikely chapters as well as its predictable ones.

I have a strong sense of calm and confidence.

Wednesday, April 14th

Feast of Saint Benezet the Bridge Builder (1163–1184).

Benezet was a shepherd. During an eclipse (bewildered?) he received a vision telling him to build a bridge over the Rhone at Avignon. The word was that angels would watch his flocks while he was gone. When, understandably, even in those supernaturally adventurous times, the church and civil officials refused to help him, he lifted a huge stone into place, and announced it would be the start of the foundation. In quick succession, eighteen miracles occurred. The officials recanted. Wouldn't we, after eighteen miracles? I would after one—if I believed in it. Anyway Le Pont d'Avignon was built. Benezet is now patron saint of bridge builders. And, for some reason, bachelors. What on earth do bachelors beseech him for? An end to the misery he patronises? A bridge to… what? Beats me. But right now, the church is in critical need of a bridge-building bachelor. And angelic assistance.

A call on my private mobile—still can't quite bring myself to be comfortable with *cellulare*. Wollongong has mobiles.

Tonio.

God of surprises, but Satan of sewage.

Some wretchedly, still living ancient journo from Wollongong's *Illawarra Mercury* had a memory of Tonio's undistinguished ten months at the paper however many years ago, and in the current circumstances, this *passé* provincial relic managed to trace Tonio to Esperance in Western Australia.

The grub then contacted this ex-pope's little brother and seduced him, for a shitload of money—the label is, for once, apt—and has funded him to fly to Rome to investigate then write *Thief in the Night: Papal Highway to Heaven*—Tonio's offensive long-form investigation into the sudden deaths of John Paul I and Pius XIII.

This is not helpful to any outcome, and I made myself ex-pontifically clear to Tonio.

He says that those who have nothing to fear have nothing to fear.

A Vatican subject Tonio has supreme ignorance of.

Add to that, his extraordinary question of whether I might put him up in what he describes as my retreat house!

I mean, family's family, but I as explained to him—not uncrisply—ex-popes don't do home stay or bed and breakfast.

He also said that what he described as informed South Western Australian sources—some prissy Perth cleric, no doubt—suggested that Tonio's story might include a community human interest interview with Sister Angelica who is somehow known down under as a Vatican historian of papal recipes from the middle ages.

That won't happen.

I'm painfully conflicted.

Of course I want to see my long-lost brother, but his acceptance of this squalid undertaking is… to say the least, hurtful.

And it's as clear as daylight that our relationship will almost certainly become the story bigger than the story.

Hazard ahead.

Approach with extreme caution.

Blast!

Thursday, April 15th

Feast of 20 saints not one of whom appealed to me.

Their fault or mine?

Dario tells me Mendoza's prospects look better by the day.

And only two days to go.

Tonio has found a pensione in Trastevere.

For some reason, Sister Angelica is withholding bounty.

It's not a subject I care to raise with her as I assume that like me, she's on tenterhooks about the conclave.

Days without papal meetings are surely the divine fanfare for heaven.

Friday, April 16th

OK. Yes, over time (short) I've had a surfeit of feast days. Maybe I'll celebrate when the conclave delivers.

And so the conclave begins. Since whenever, has there ever been...?

Dear Lord, I firmly believe that some prayers are answered, and today, I believe my fervent prayer will be one of those.

Dear Lord, Your will, not mine, but, dear Lord... if I dare... please...

Later

This recording is word for word, the original kept in Lugano and available for authentication despite the Vatican's continual denial of its existence. Editors.

Perhaps turn up the volume a little more, Sorella.

'Si, Santità.'

RADIO ANNOUNCER
SFX: Soundscape: St Peter's Square.
V/O (enthusiastically over triumphant bell ringing)
... and amazingly, after the first ballot, white smoke is rising from the Sistine Chapel which means that the next pope has been elected.

SISTER ANGELICA

Per favore, Dio.

JOHN

Three conclaves in eighteen months. More than any pope
should have to live through.

RADIO ANNOUNCER

SFX: Soundscape: St Peter's Square.

And the door to the papal balcony is opening. We're about
to see the new pope. The senior Cardinal, Cardinal Luciano
Moretti of Catania, who will announce the new pontiff, has
moved to the microphone.

VOICE OF OLD CARDINAL

SFX: Soundscape: St Peter's Square

Habemus papam.

RADIO ANNOUNCER

SFX: Soundscape: St Peter's Square

That's odd. Most unusual. The tradition is that the senior
cardinal announces the name the new pope has taken. Maybe we're in for a surprise. Anyway here he comes. And, yes…
yes, it's the favourite candidate, the formerly conservative
but recently progressive Cardinal Ernesto Mendoza who is
the next pope.

SISTER ANGELICA

Deo gratias.

JOHN

The age of miracles is not past.

RADIO ANNOUNCER

SFX: cheers from St Peter's Square

And the new pope is holding up his hands, asking crowd to
be silent.

SFX: cheering stops.

MENDOZA
(soundscape: Pope speaking from Vatican balcony)
I miei fratelli e sorelle in Cristo. My brothers and sisters in Christ, it is with profound humility yet confident acceptance that I, Ernesto Mendoza, take on the heavenly burden of becoming the two hundred and seventieth successor of *San Pietro:* St Peter.

JOHN
You're right, Sorella. *Deo gratias.*

MENDOZA
(soundscape: Pope speaking from Vatican balcony)
As we all know, over recent turbulent times, our world has travelled through challenging nightmares of doubt, confusion and plague. But through the intervention of the Holy Spirit, our heavenly father has imposed on me, his unworthy servant, Ernesto Mendoza, the task of restoring the church to its divine authority and to its benevolent yoke of obedience.

(soundscape: papal apartment)

SISTER ANGELICA
What is he…?

JOHN
Sssh! Sssh! Listen.

MENDOZA
(soundscape: Pope speaking from Vatican balcony)
At the moment of my election, I felt myself… liberated… yes, liberated onto a sea of <u>faith</u>. The certainty of faith. The absolute certainty of faith. The reassurance of doctrine. The strength of discipline. The divine protection of our fortress of faith. The infallibility of truth.

SISTER ANGELICA
Mendoza???

MENDOZA

(soundscape: Pope speaking from Vatican balcony)
Therefore, in loving memory of my holy predecessor, *Pio il Tredicesimo*, Pius the Thirteenth, I have taken the name of *Pio il Quattordicesimo:* Pius the Fourteenth.

SFX: cheers from St Peter's Square.

JOHN

Holy fuck!

SFX: Wild cheering for a few seconds, after which the noise suddenly stops. Gasps. Screams.

RADIO ANNOUNCER

Oh, my god! It can't be true! This isn't happening! Just as he's begun to bless the crowd, the new pope has clutched his heart. He's gasping. The new pope is gasping. Pope Pius the Fourteenth has collapsed on the papal balcony. The new pope has collapsed. The two cardinals attending him are now kneeling. They seem to be trying to carry out CPR. And they don't appear to be all that competent. One cardinal is now signalling inside for help. And now both cardinals are looking at each other in horror. A man—I'm not sure who he is—a man has hurried onto the balcony. He's applying cardiac arrest massage. <u>He</u> certainly knows what he's doing. Surely a doctor. The first cardinal has now gone inside. And now two men are bringing out a stretcher. In the square, everyone's faces are grim. There's a strange silence. This must surely be one of the most amazing, the most dramatic moments, perhaps even the <u>most</u> tragic ever in papal history. Pope for less than an hour. Pope Pius the Fourteenth is now being lifted onto the stretcher. He seems totally inert. By the looks on the faces of the papal entourage, they don't seem to be holding much hope.

JOHN

There is a god.
Deus ex machina.
Pentecost.
Deo gratias.

The pope's mobile phone rings.

My brother. He'll have to wait.

'Is now the time for confession, Santità?'

I think the question, Sorella, is rather who must confess.
And to whom.

Editor's note.

The diary of Pope Emeritus John XXIV ends here.

He died after a short illness on May 14th, 2025, the feast of Saint John I, pope and martyr (Late Fifth Century–526).

Pope John I was impossibly wedged in a tense and highly complicated political and religious battle between empire and church.

Despite heroic efforts, he failed to resolve the situation.

He was imprisoned and died in Ravenna, either of shock or mistreatment.

With the assistance of Pope John XXIV and further clandestine financial help from a Vatican account, my partner Mirella and I bought an apartment in the appropriately named suburb of Paradiso, 3K south of Lugano.

The Vatican denies all knowledge of this written and, now by me, live recorded diary despite our offer of access to the original, also installed by me and copied and kept by me.

And then the Vatican original wiped by me, Ennio Donato.

To date, we have not received any response from the current pope Leo XV, (the first pope to come from Luxembourg) or from any Vatican office.

Our offer remains.

GLOSSARY

AUSTRALIAN TERMS

antipodean – a person from Australia or New Zealand

beauty bottler – something or someone exciting admiration

bogan – uncouth, unsophisticated

BYO – Bring your own (wine) which many Australian restaurants allow and only charge a small fee for. Or, alas, a large one.

charabang – a sightseeing bus, sometimes open-topped

cock-up – a total mess

cooee – a vocal call over distances that translates to "come here"

fair dinkum – a phrase used to emphasise

Illawarra – a coastal region of New South Wales, Australia

Jameson – a brand of blended Irish whiskey

KC – King's Counsel, or lawyer

koala stamp – the inked image of a koala bear stamped by a teacher on the wrists of kindergarten students who have done well

muggins – a fool

North Beach – Wollongong's busiest beach, known for swimming and surfing

wog – slang for a non-white person

Wollongong – a coastal city in Australia, south of Sydney

FRENCH TERMS

à deux visages – two-faced

collaborateur - collaborator

de trop – too much

diner à deux – dinner for two

en effet – in effect

en passant – by the way

entendu – understood

esperance – hope

esperance en effet – hope actually, hope indeed

Je ne regrette rien. Sauf presque tout. – I don't regret anything.
                              Except almost everything.

le mot juste – the right word

merde – shit

Notre Dame du Kitch – Invented slang! Our Lady of Vulgarity – a
                ludicrously absurd cathedral built by President
                for Life Félix Houphouët-boigny in the middle of
                nowhere on the Ivory Coast

patois – uneducated or provincial speech

reculer pour mieux advancer – to draw back in order to make a better
                              jump, to make a strategic withdrawal

soi-disant – supposedly, so-called

touché - you win

un instantané – a snapshot

LATIN & ITALIAN PHRASES

ad limina – to the threshold; i.e. The Vatican and the Pope

ad limina apostolorum – to the threshold of the apostles

bella figura – good impression; fine appearance

berretto – cap

camerlengo – chamberlain

Che Tempo Che Fa – What the weather's like or what the times are like; Italian TV talk show

Christus natus est – Christ is born

Corriere della Sera - Italy's *Evening Post* newspaper

Deo gratias – thanks be to God

Dominus vobiscum – the Lord be with you

et cum spiritu tuo – and with your spirit

et ut – otherwise known as

finocchio – Fennel; slang for gay

habemus papam – we have a Pope

in absentia – not present at the event being referred to

innamorato/a – sweetheart

L'Osservatore Romano – The Roman Observer, Vatican daily newspaper

Laudato Si - *Praised Be* by Pope Francis, the most comprehensive
Vatican document to date on environmentalism, ethics
and Christian faith

mea maxima culpa. – my most grievous fault

melius esse honestus quam auto-fallax – better to be honest than
self-deceiving

mens sana in corpore sano – a sound mind in a sound body

per favore – please

per favore, Dio – Dear Lord, please

piu cambia – the more it changes

Pontifex Maximus - supreme pontiff

pro tem – for the time being

qui audet adipiscitur – she who dares wins

reductio ad absurdum – reduction to the absurd

ricatto – blackmail

sparse ed esitanti – scattered and hesitant

stigmata - bodily marks, scars, or pains corresponding to those of
the crucified Jesus Christ

turbine mauris – 'shit storm'

un casino totale – a total mess

un piatto di spaghetti carbonara della casa – a plate of house spaghetti
carbonara

urbi et orbi – to the city (of Rome) and to the world

MELVYN MORROW

Melvyn Morrow's first revue scripts were for Australia's biggest TV satirical hit, ***The Mavis Branston Show.*** Melvyn's musicals (books & lyrics) include: ***Postcards From Provence, Offenbach In The Underworld*** and seven Christmas at the Opera House pantomimes including the nationally popular ***Santa Meets The Bushrangers***. His musical ***A Song To Sing, O,*** the story of Gilbert and Sullivan and George Grossmith, was produced by Dame Bridget D'Oyly Carte at London's Savoy Theatre and directed by the author. It then toured Australia. He has adapted book and lyrics for Opera Australia's G&S productions. He received the Australian Writers' Guild Award for Best Libretto for his musical, ***Shakespearean Idol.*** He is the co-writer of the Australian musical hits, ***SHOUT!*** and ***Dusty-The Original Pop Diva***. He wrote book and lyrics for and directed the musical ***Dorian Gray Naked***. Melvyn is an international member of the Dramatists Guild of America.

He co-wrote the musicals ***Peter Dawson-Off The Record*** and ***Here Comes Showtime*** and the lyrics for the song *Lest I Forget* (***Rebel*** the movie starring Matt Dillon). Melvyn's plays include ***Beating A Retreat, A Touch Of Paradise, Vice, Acts of Faith*** and ***Pope2Pope.*** His Victoriana vaudeville, ***Dickens Down Under***, premiered at Sydney's Genesian Theatre. He devised and directed the cabarets ***Broadway Bard, Tae Kwon Shakespeare,*** and ***mozart and ME***. In 1996, Melvyn was nominated for a Mo Award for Outstanding Contribution to Australian Musical Theatre.

He was producer, writer and director of *Cabaret in the Day* at Mosman Art Gallery where seasons have included: ***Glorious Mud!*** (Flanders & Swann), ***Our Glad*** (Gladys Moncrieff), ***Gilbert & Sullivan Forever!*** (starring Andrew O'Keefe), ***Of Bing I Sing*** (Bing Crosby) and ***Poisoning Pigeons in the Park*** (Tom Lehrer). With composer Dion Condack, he wrote and directed the musical ***Dorian Gray Naked***, starring Blake Appelqvist. The musical received rave reviews and was the only original Australian musical nominated for the 2019 Glugs of Gosh 2019 Sydney Theatre Awards.

CHECK OUT OTHER GREAT READS FROM

HENRY GRAY PUBLISHING

THE MAN FROM BELIZE by Steven Kobrin

Life-saving heart surgeon Dr. Kent Stirling lives in paradise, dividing his time between two medical practices in the exotic Yucatan. Deeply in love with the woman of his dreams, he has everything a man could desire... until enemies from his secret past as a government hitman convene to eliminate him, including a death-dealing assassin known as the Viper.

THE LAST STAGE by Bruce Scivally

Dying in his small Los Angeles bungalow, with his Jewish wife, Josephine, whom he calls Sadie, at his side, famed lawman Wyatt Earp imagines an ending more befitting a man of his reputation: returning to his mining claims in a small desert town, tying up loose ends with Sadie, and – after he strikes gold – confronting a quartet of robbers in a showdown.

VEIL OF SEDUCTION by Emily Dinova

1922. Lorelei Alba, a fiercely independent and ambitious woman, is determined to break into the male-dominated world of investigative journalism by doing the unimaginable – infiltrating Morning Falls Asylum, the gothic hospital to which "troublesome" women are dispatched, never to be seen again. Once there, she meets the darkly handsome and enigmatic Doctor Roman Dreugue, who claims to have found the cure for insanity. But Lorelei's instincts tell her something is terribly wrong, even as her curiosity pulls her deeper into Roman's intimate and isolated world of intrigue.

THE UNDERSTUDY by Charlie Peters

"Tell your boss that I have one of his employees." With those words a kidnapping plot begins in the middle of a high-stakes corporate merger. But the kidnappers' plans don't unfold—they unravel.

"If you're thinking of committing the perfect crime, read Charlie Peters' elegant new thriller first. Find out just how many ways perfection can go wrong." – Dan Hearn, author of *Bad August*

For more info visit HenryGrayPublishing.com

...AND ENJOY OUR NEW RELEASES!

THE DEVIL IN THE DIAMOND by Gregory Cioffi

World War II is coming to a violent close. As the Battle of Okinawa rages on, American soldiers seize Shuri Castle and find a single survivor: Yuujin Miyano. The U.S. private put in charge of watching the prisoner is Eugene Durante.

Although enemies, the two men find they have a common multi-generational bond: baseball. Their grandfathers – one in Japan, one in America – bore witness to the magical birth of the game and helped shape it in the 1800s.

When the war ends, the two men return to their homes to face a postwar world neither expected. Then both receive unexpected messages that will change their lives forever: once more, the veterans will face off in a final dramatic clash.

SHELBY'S VACATION by Nancy Beverly

Fantasy. Sex. Despair. (Hey, what are vacations for?)

Shelby sets out from L.A. on a much-needed vacation to mend her heart from her latest unrequited crush. By happenstance, she ends up at a rustic mountain resort where she meets the manager, Carol, who has her own memories of the past inhibiting her ability to create a real relationship in the present. Their casual vacation encounter turns into something more profound than either of them bargained for, as each learns what holds them back from living and loving.

"This is an uplifting and romantic novel about the power of love to heal hearts and minds."
   - Elizabeth Sims, author of the award-winning
     Lillian Byrd crime series

TOO MUCH IN THE SON by Charlie Peters

In Martinique, Leo Malone meets Taylor Hoffman, a young man who could be his identical twin. Whey they run afoul of a local gangster, Taylor is murdered and Leo assumes his identity to sneak safely out of the country and back to Los Angeles. But when Taylor's estranged parents meet Leo at the airport, mistaking him for their son, Leo's best-laid plans spiral out of control.

Full of surprising twists and turns, **Too Much in the Son** is part Agatha Christie, part Elmore Leonard, with a dash of David Mamet and served with a Larry David chaser, examining the lies, intrigue and violence that make an unexpected family.